I0761883

CROWNING ESSENCE

CROWNING ESSENCE

SAHIRA JAVAID

To receive special offers, bonus content,
and info on new releases
sign up to the author's newsletter
https://sahirajavaid.com

ISBN 978-1-7772690-3-6 (hardcover)

Cover art by Fahmi Fauzi.

Map by the author Sahira Javaid.

To my baba.

"Sadke jawan."

When darkness wraps his wings around me,

I don't want your 'get well soons' or your

'reach out to mes'.'

Don't tell me how you would breathe

as you watch me drown

Don't coat me in your blood and tears

as you watch me bleed out

I need your warm gaze,

I need your kindness and presence

and 'let's go do this'

I need your patience

Make me laugh to melt the ice on my teeth

Make me smile, to warm my soul

So when his thinning wings reveal my bleeding heart,

scarred lips and bruised skin,

your kindness and gentleness can be a salve

I don't need you to cure me,

I need to know you'd search for me

Wounds do not need advice

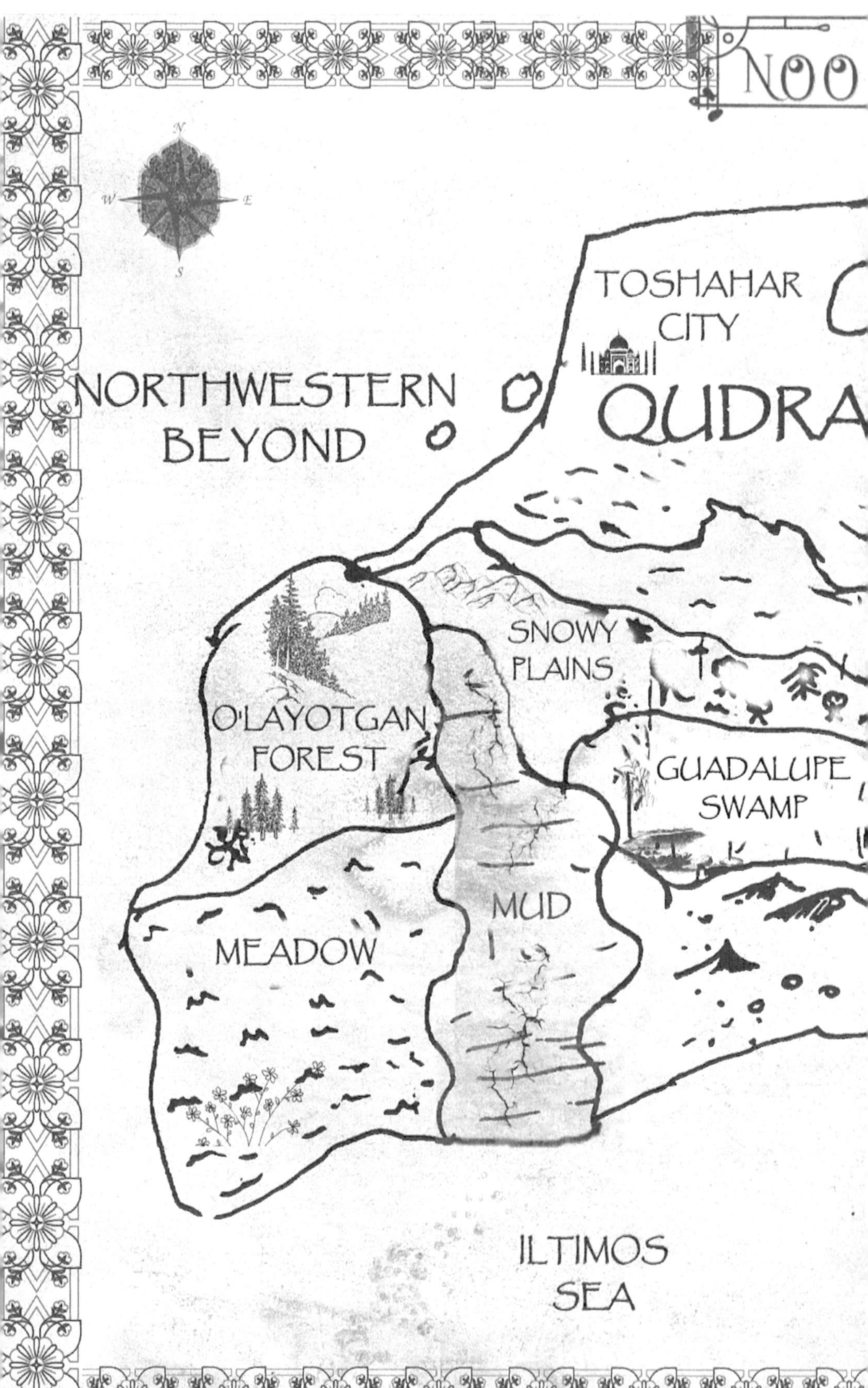
NOO
N
W
E
S
TOSHAHAR
CITY
QUDRA
NORTHWESTERN
BEYOND
SNOWY
PLAINS
O'LAYOTGAN
FOREST
GUADALUPE
SWAMP
MUD
MEADOW
ILTIMOS
SEA

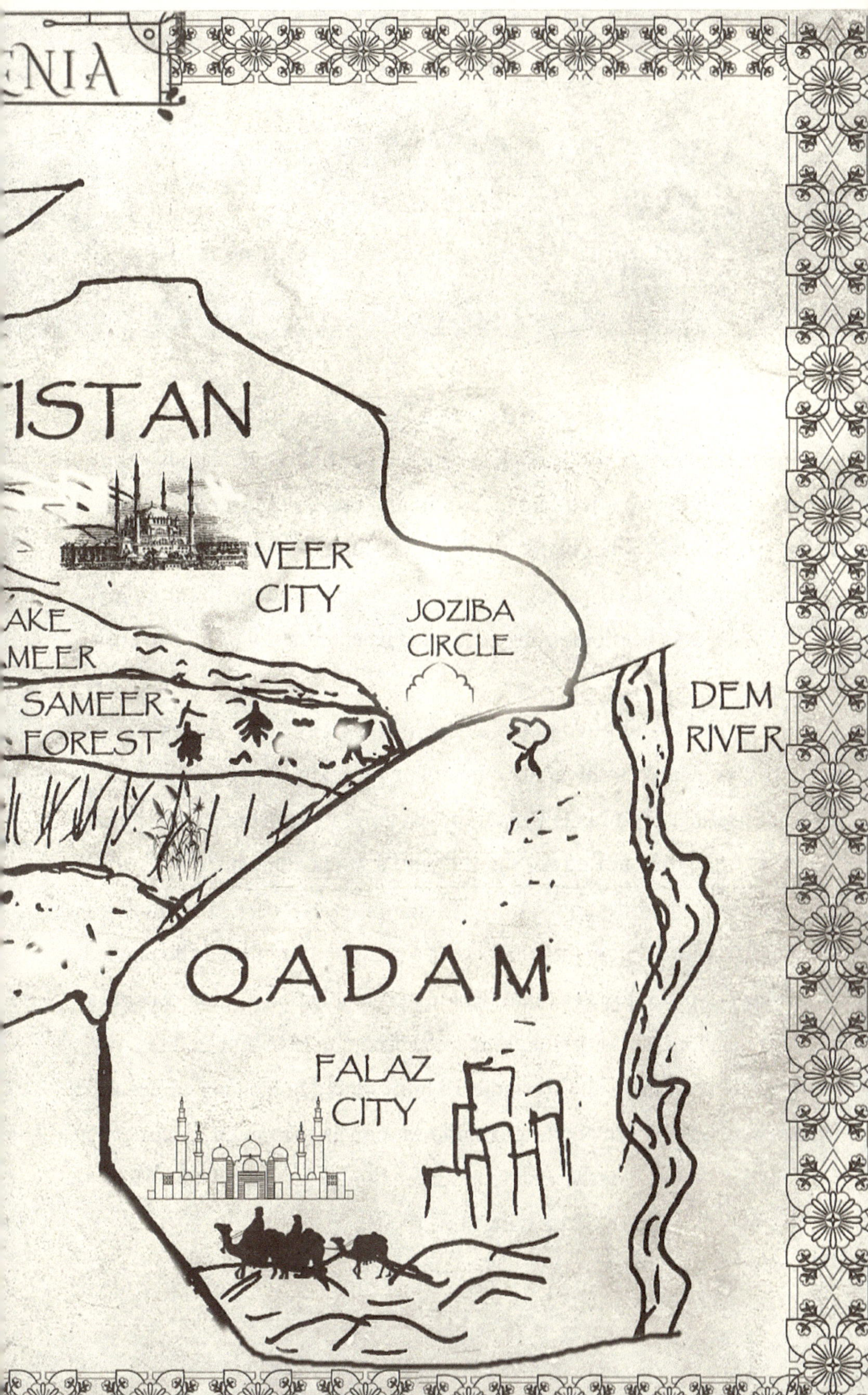
ENIA
ISTAN
VEER
CITY
JOZIBA
CIRCLE
AKE
MEER
SAMEER
FOREST
DEM
RIVER
QADAM
FALAZ
CITY

Chapter 1 Butterfly

It was on these butterfly wings that Amaya felt free.

On the way to the pool, she tucked her fingers beneath her cap, adjusting it for what felt like the millionth time.

Hours of schoolwork cramping her fingers, lectures that made her mind buzz, the sleepless nights studying, it all sucked the life from her. The water was her home and she needed its endless sky of blue to soar through.

Her gaze shifted to the large crowd as they cheered for their teams. Togenkyo's university banner hung proudly above them on the wall, reading: 'Tominaga University. Culture. Leadership.'

She tried to find her family, until a glint caught her eye. A small fox charm, dangling from a little girl's bracelet. It loosened memories she couldn't afford digging into her heart. Papa's smiling face as he jangled his keys, a metal fox keychain winking back at her on a sunny weekend. Papa thanking her for giving him a new friend to help him find his way home. On one night she'd overheard him coming home late, circles under his eyes, but a warm and bright smile as soon as she ran up to him and he took her to her favourite restaurant. Even though he should have been sleeping early. Then, Papa lying still.

Her heart boomed in her chest. She had to count her breath and calm her mind. One, and she was closer to the edge of the pool. Two, three, Amaya lined up beside the other girls. Four.

The buzzer sounded and she leapt into the water.

The crown of her head led her body through the blue as she propelled herself forward. Water drops glimmered as her arms extended above her head. Her thumbs led her hands into the water. These were her wings.

Life demanded she carry burdens and they weighed heavily in her chest. When she rose her head up to breathe, all of it fell away. Freeing, powerful, the energy rushed through her body whenever she performed the butterfly, the most difficult swimming move.

Amaya Koizumi was taking part in the relay semi finals. It had been her dream to become a competitive swimmer since her first swimming lesson, aged just six. In the swimming club Amaya had won seven medals. She'd been in second place for four of them, but it never quashed her determination.

Just as life needed water, water was life to her. Amaya craved its cool caress. The way it soaked through her skin, merging with her soul. It wasn't just swimming to her. It was a chance to get away from responsibility. With the water lulling against her, she was on the wings of calm and ease.

"Amaya-chan!" her teammates called out.

They were two teams of four. This time Amaya and her friends were swimming against four other members of the swimming club. Now, it wasn't calm settling in her heart. It was anxiety leaping in her chest. She needed to reach the wall as fast as she could.

Papa's smiling face floated into her mind. Each push of her arm, each kick of her legs, her muscles burned. Her thoughts blurred. Swim. She needed to swim. Her legs felt light. She couldn't feel them anymore. Was she even moving? The water wasn't gliding by her, it was as if she were floating. A butterfly hovering until it was not in the sky anymore, it was in a spiderweb. It was just a wave of emotion she tried to tell herself. It would pass. But this wave was taking her under.

Her breath was the loudest thing after her thoughts. She glanced at the girl beside her, and she passed Amaya.

With a gasp, her head surfaced one last time as she reached the end and touched the wall. Breathing deeply, she pulled her goggles off. Claps echoed as people cheered. In the sea of chanting, she could make out the faint call of her name.

"Amaya-chan!" Many called out.

She could only pray she didn't let down her team. A part of her didn't want to come in second. A small part of her heart wanted to win.

After the teams totalled the combined times, they called out the winners.

"Yui-chan!" The winner's name crashed most into Amaya's mind. She'd come second. Again.

"Good job, blue butterfly." One of her friends Saki, patted her back as she rested her arm on the ropes.

"Thanks." Amaya smiled as she pulled herself out of the water and grabbed the towel Saki handed her and dried herself. Her other three friends joined in to congratulate her. The twinge in her arm, and the sinking feeling in her chest didn't make her feel like she'd accomplished anything. She pulled her yellow cap off and let her auburn locks fall to her shoulders once more.

***

The sun had set when Amaya left the university and headed to catch the train. Togenkyo was one of Japan's most scenic cities. With mountains in the east, and peach trees with their bright fruit and the bluest ocean to the west.

Amaya chatted with Saki and three of her other friends as they made their way to the station, where they took the most vibrant transportation in her city. The turquoise train was embellished in silver, whimsical with the sakura trees bowing over it and the pink blossoms caressing the train as it rumbled off on the tracks.

She'd come second place. She didn't mind being second. It was comfortable. If she'd been in first, then there would be too much attention on her. Too much to have to live up to. She knew, because the girl who was always in first smiled bright, but she'd seen the dark hollows under her eyes and how she tried covering them with concealer. Drained, high expectations, she could never live like that. Second was good, second was high enough. Butterflies didn't need to be in the mountains. The flower-filled meadows were sweet, the treetops were high enough.

Amaya slid out of her seat, Saki and the three girls were up with her as they hopped out of the train. More sakura flowers painted the tracks and drifted over Amaya's head.

Saki nudged her as they made their way to the sidewalk. "Hey, we should go to karaoke next weekend."

"Yeah, we should." Amaya toyed with her ponytail in contemplation. It hung over her left shoulder. She wasn't sure if she could take her up on the offer.

"I have to head this way. Say hi to Inoue kun for me. See you later!" Saki threw up a peace sign and waved to her as she turned a corner with the girls. Her house was just two blocks from here.

Amaya waved to the group and turned to the street. *Tama said he'd meet me here.* Amaya searched for him. Most of the time he'd be standing at the corner to meet her after school. So how come he wasn't here?

After a few minutes she clutched her cell phone in her hands, fingers ready to dial his number if he took longer.

"Am I late?" A voice called from behind her.

"Tama..." Amaya walked up to him. The boy was Tamaki Inoue, her fiancé.

"Gomen." *Sorry*. He shrugged and an apologetic smile pulled up his lips. "I had to get something on the way." The edges of his pointed eyes crinkled, making them softer.

"I forgive you this time." How could she be mad at him when his bright smile made her heart flutter? Amaya walked with him, her red sweater billowing around her waist as she wrapped an arm around his. Her long black skirt rippled from the breeze. Amaya was always soft spoken, but with those close to her, her voice had the vibrancy of a windchime.

Tamaki mussed his golden-brown hair. His wavy bangs bounced over his eyebrows. "Oh, this is why I was late. I got you something!" Tamaki loosened his arm from hers and pulled out a small brown paper bag and held it up in the air with both hands. "It's Dango."

"You're so sweet." She grinned and poked his shoulder, accepting the treats.

Tamaki stuffed his hands into his pockets as they walked down the street. "So how was your relay?"

"Good. We came in second place." The grin that lit Amaya's face was genuine.

"Congratulations. I'm proud of you, Amaya." They held each other's gaze as they crossed an intersection, a warmth in her chest.

They continued to laugh and chat as they ascended the stairs to Amaya's apartment building. They were at the final step when Tamaki's finger grazed hers.

Amaya brought her sleeve to her lips for a moment, then gently hooked her pinky with his as he led her up the final step to the apartment's front door. *Don't go.* She wanted to stay with him longer.

"Are we doing anything tomorrow?" Tamaki asked as they stood at the door while Amaya turned the key into the lock.

"Mmm I'm going over to Okaasan's?" Amaya suggested.

Tamaki smiled. "Sounds good!"

She stepped inside as Tamaki held the door.

"Thank you for the dango." Amaya smiled sweetly.

"Anything for you Maya!" Tamaki stood closer to her, his voice down to a whisper. "So cute." His lips were parted and so close to her cheek. He paused and then added, "I love stuffing your face with sweets!"

Amaya chuckled and clapped him on the shoulder.

"Tama…"

"Oyasumi."

"Good night, my dango," she said.

Tamaki waved to her before turning and walking down the stairs.

Amaya's shoulders slouched as she made her way up to the silver elevator. Lately, whenever he left, her chest tightened and she couldn't breathe. She stepped inside and pressed the button for the ninth floor and the elevator's doors closed.

She kicked her shoes off at the entrance and slipped into a pair of pink slippers. "Salaam. Tadai— ma." *I'm back— home.* Her voice trailed off as she stepped into her apartment with her bag of dango in hand. That's right. She wasn't living with okaasan anymore. Why hadn't she gotten used to it yet?

She had recently moved out. After turning eighteen, she'd taken up various jobs. Okaasan had told her to make sure she always had money on hand. She wanted her daughter to have more than she had when she'd been younger. Amaya had made sure then. It took five, maybe six years to save up for her own place. Okaasan insisted on giving her money to support her. Maybe, she'd been so insistent because of papa. After being a single mom, Okaasan never let her feel like she couldn't stand up on her own two feet. When Amaya lost a job, it was Okaasan who helped her find another and send out resumes. It was her who stood by her side with joyful tears when she found the cozy apartment, she now lived in. "I want you to stand tall. Never have to bend to the weight of loss," Is what she'd told her once Amaya had settled into her home.

She blew a breath. Despite it being a one-bedroom apartment, with no other person by her side, the walls seemed to stretch, making the silence invite a loneliness that made her crave for someone's company. She slumped over the kitchen table, leaving the bag and her keys on the counter. She lifted a sweet dango from the bag Tamaki gave her. "Bismillah," she mumbled and took a bite. The sweet ones were her go-to snack.

Amaya crossed the living room, passing by her cream counter, and futon. The walls were painted taupe. Okaasan had gifted her the futon and armoire in the corner. Just a sofa and coffee table were what she needed, with various cushions embroidered with inspirational quotes and one with a curtain of ocean waves meeting the shore. Her papa had painted the scene, and her okaasan had turned it into a threaded cushion. No matter what, she'd never throw it out.

She pulled back the curtains and looked out at the sprawling cityscape. The view from the ninth floor was expansive, the skyscrapers rose into the sky like beams of light. The billboards flickered with bold signs, casting neon colors across the city streets. People rushed to and fro on the sidewalk below, and cars scuttled between the buildings like bugs. It was always busy.

It had been a long day. She finished her dango and glanced at the clock. She was relieved she arrived home on time tonight. It was lonely sometimes, living on her own in her apartment. She had Tamaki, but they lived separately. Her okaasan followed her Japanese heritage, even if she allowed her to be around Tamaki alone. It would give her mother a heart attack if he ever moved in. Besides, they were going to get married in a few months.

Amaya lowered herself to her futon and traced a wave on the cushion. Seeing Okaasan tomorrow would do her some good. It had been a week since she'd seen her. Amaya stood up and glided over to her bathroom to do wudu and pray before heading to bed. She'd have to sleep early to see her tomorrow. She'd head there right after university.

"Okaasan." Amaya addressed her mother, slipping out of her flats, and into a pair of slippers kept at the front door. "Konnichiwa."

"How are you?" Amaya's mother Haruka Koizumi smothered her in an embrace, before pulling back and poking Amaya in the side, her round face scrunching up.

"Hmm?" Amaya squeaked and pulled back, clapping a hand over the ticklish spot.

"You look so thin. Don't you eat? You need to eat. Come in, come in and let's eat." Her mother smiled and turned to the kitchen.

"Neechan!" Her younger sister ran up to her, her small arms flinging up and around Amaya's waist. She was in an orange blouse. Her short black hair was styled into twin buns.

"Are you trying to impress someone Rin?" Amaya lowered to her sister's face and pinched her cheek.

"Mmm-hmm. Tamaki-kun needs to know someone in the family makes sure we dress nicely."

Amaya pinched both of Rin's cheeks this time. "Are you saying I'm a slob?"

Rin stuck her tongue out. "Mama! Neechan's being mean to me." Amaya pushed her in the direction of the dining table with an amused smile.

Their mother only laughed and then clapped Amaya on the head with one hand, the other holding a pan.

"Neechan is going to help me cook as punishment, right?"

"Right." Amaya nodded, her face heating up.

"When's Tamaki kun coming?" Rin asked as she drummed her fingers on the dinner table and puffed up her cheeks.

Amaya chuckled. "He said he'll be here soon. He has a surprise for you." She tapped on her smartphone, reading Tamaki's message. He'd said he was on his way and would be there soon.

"Did you do anything fun while I was aw—" Okaasan turned Amaya's chin to her and poked a spoon at her face. She allowed her to feed her the seasoned rice.

"Yeah. Mama bought me a new doll."

"I'm glad," Amaya said and then gave Okaasan a nod. "It's so good!"

"Of course." Okaasan said, a smug smile on her lips.

The doorbell rang in Amaya's ears. That must have been Tamaki.

It was him, bowing at the door carrying bags.

"Salaam, everyone. Hope you didn't eat without me."

"You're lucky Rin didn't make a hole in the table," Okaasan said to him.

They greeted each other and Rin ran up to him.

"Hello little flower." Tamaki kun winked and handed her a bag.

"It's for me, right?" Rin said.

Tamaki shrugged with mock disappointment. "Yes. I guess your neechan won't get anything today."

"Is that so? Well," Amaya said, facing her Okaasan. "I guess we won't be sending Tamaki home with his favorite food tonight. Too bad."

Tamaki pressed a bag into Amaya's hand. "Oh look. I guess I was wrong."

Amaya met his gaze and smiled. She hadn't teased him in a while. Studying, swimming, it had taken over her life the past few weeks. Being around the ones she loved was a balm to her soul.

"Wow, I've missed your cooking! It's been so long since I've had a decent meal!" The table was laden with a veritable feast. Alongside the huge plate of teriyaki salmon, there was a bowl of rice, two side dishes of steamed and fermented vegetables and miso soup.

Rin spoke up after she slurped her soup. "Neechan, are you going to stay here?"

Amaya smiled. "I won't be here for too long."

Rin's eyes were cast down as she prodded a fermented carrot.

"But, we do get to catch up," Amaya whispered and Rin's small face lit up.

Amaya and Rin were in the living room after they sent Tamaki home with bags of food. Rin was playing with her dolls. One had a middle school uniform with a blue bow. Her hair was made into two buns. One on each side of her head. Maybe she was a magical schoolgirl. It was a recent style she'd seen all over Togenkyo, especially since an anime was said to be getting a reboot and the heroine had twin buns.

Along the mantelpiece were pictures of Amaya's papa. She pressed a thumb against one of the frames. It had been eight years since her father had passed away. Rin was born nine months later. But, Amaya still remembered him. The times they went to the festivals, how he'd pick her up onto his shoulders so she could see the fireworks. He'd tell her to never choose the easy path. The toughest path always bore the most beautiful flowers. His words, his smiles and his kindness stuck with her as she grew. She passed the same wisdom onto Rin as she grew up. Rin knew they had a father. Okaasan would tell her they'd see him again one day. That he'd have his own throne and be treated like a king. But Rin only had that ethereal notion and his pictures to cling to.

"Amaya." Her mother's touch on her shoulder lifted her out of her reverie.

Amaya ran her finger over the picture frame once more before setting it back down onto the dresser.

"Okaasan, how is everything? Are you and Rin doing well?" Amaya asked as her mama patted her shoulder.

"Amaya, you always put us first. Sometimes, you need to take care of yourself." She stood and glanced outside.

"I just want to make sure you're both well." Amaya followed her gaze.

"We are good. You study hard and work hard. With that I am happy." Mrs. Koizumi gazed out at the setting sun, the golden glow stretching out like fingers through the blinds.

Amaya smiled in thought. "Hmm." But working hard had been keeping her away from them. She didn't want to sound like she was complaining, so she stayed quiet. Even though she wanted to tell her she felt like there was a hole in her heart that she couldn't fill. That her wings were getting heavy.

"Neechan…" Rin said as she pulled on Amaya's teal sweater.

"Yes?"

Rin studied Amaya's face, her head tilted. She reached her hands up and Amaya bent down to her eye level. Her eyebrows lifted. A film of tears started to blur Amaya's vision. Rin had noticed. Her small hand wiped at her older sister's eyes. Amaya embraced her, her hold tight, her heart turbulent.

She didn't want to leave them again. She needed to be around Rin's pretty smile, to eat together with okaasan, and be in their company. She felt that loneliness dig into her heart. She'd wanted to move out. But as more time passed, she wasn't sure anymore. But she had to be closer to the university and finish her studies.

Amaya wanted to be with her family. She'd always wanted them to be happy. But, ever since her papa passed away, she'd been left feeling like she had to grow up quicker. She worked part time at the Smoky Grill Restaurant. It wasn't her dream job, but it was something which could keep her busy. Her mom had her own small business selling pastries in their own bakery and it was going well. She never noticed anything wrong when she visited. There was food in the fridge, health glowing on their faces and the house was clean and well taken care of. It wasn't enough, she knew. So, Amaya would hand money to them every month. She was the eldest, and as a daughter, she'd been told to be responsible and take care of her family. They relied on her. She had to have the cadence of a calm koi pond, not the unpredictable waves of a sea.

"I'll visit when I can, Rin. We'll go to the festival together," Amaya said and kissed her little sister on her forehead.

"We'll all go together." Rin smiled back.

Amaya's okaasan turned her daughter's face toward her, searching her eyes. That warm concerned look made Amaya's chest tighten. She never wanted to see tears in her eyes, never wanted to see frown lines around her beautiful smile. To bring her comfort, she'd sacrifice her own. Just for her and Rin.

Okaasan kissed her head. “It’s getting late. Head home and we’ll see you again my darling.”

Amaya smiled and kissed her okaasan’s cheek. “I’ll see you later.”

Chapter 2 Ripples

She lifted the white brim of her sun hat. Her eyes met the clear blue of the ocean, its surface glittering in the sunlight. Amaya walked along the sand, grains clinging to her feet and meeting between her toes. Her blouse fluttered in the soothing breeze that whipped up across the ocean's surface. She'd been thinking of spending time alone this weekend. Last weekend she had fun doing karaoke with Tamaki and her friends.

Gulls squawked overhead, weaving in and out over the beach.

She tugged at one strap of her bag, finally finding a place to sit and relax.

She swung her bag to the sand and unpacked a blanket. The cloth rippled like waves over the grains of sand. After sitting and sticking an umbrella with red hearts into the sand, Amaya took a swig of water from her bottle and rummaged through her bag. She wasn't planning on doing any physical activities— other than swimming of course, so she brought a book with her.

Finally, she got to finish where she had left off. The book Amaya had been so excited to finish reading was the fifth volume of a manga. *I was on chapter forty. Oh, my goodness, his hair!*

After finishing her book, it was time for a swim. She headed toward the frothing waves, to where the sand beneath her feet grew firm, and bent down. She drew a heart. A moment later, the waves foamed and bubbled toward her feet, enveloping the heart, wiping the slate clean. She took another step, the waves filling in the spaces her footsteps left.

Her earrings were glowing, a blue light reflected off the water. Amaya's smile slipped off her face as the current yanked at her legs, knocking her down. She kicked at the water, but it was somehow snaking around her legs and dragging her into its maw of bubbles. Her nails dug into the sand, but she couldn't crawl away. There was no one close to her. No one to see her being ripped away from the shore and into the sea.

Bubbles spiraled around her body as she was submerged within the water. The force that pulled her down now pushed her up, and she was floating. She tried to catch her breath. To grab onto something. Her powerful swimming muscles were no match for the invisible grip holding her locked into place.

Just then, the pressure lifted, and she felt like she was falling. But she wasn't falling. The feeling was a deception. Actually, she was flying up like a butterfly through the water. She recalled her swimming competition, the thought a mere flicker as her head surfaced.

Her breath came in stammers. Her shaking hands scrambled for purchase as she pulled herself out of the water and onto grassy land. It was night. The shadows clung to their surroundings.

Amaya scrambled to her feet, and once her head had finally settled enough for her to take in her surroundings, she stood there in frozen silence. She was not on the beach anymore. Instead, she'd just stepped out from a river, the towering trees of a forest stood proud around her, and she was completely dry.

Amaya coiled her arms around her chest. A rush of panic filled her body. It was a dream. An illusion. A lapse in her sanity, maybe. But the creaking of the trees said otherwise, and the crispness of the leaves beneath her feet begged her belief.

Something in her compelled her to walk. To go onward and not look back.

Where was she? She was all alone. Okasaan, Tamaki… Rin. No one was here. Creator. She was just alone. She needed to find help. Help with what? She didn't even know.

Amaya continued to walk until she heard rustling from one of the nearby bushes. A crack of sticks and the patter of feet. She peered behind her. There was nothing there. The sound came from in front of her, this time accompanied by a low growl. Amaya's head snapped back round and her eyes met with a fox.

The animal stood silent for a few moments; its head held high. Everything was darkness all around her—the fox looked like a red stain painted in the brush. His eyes flashed white as they caught the light of the moon. Amaya was frozen still, a curious sheep in the headlights of the animal's reflecting eyes.

The fox's ears swiveled to her, then it began walking toward her, each footfall hesitant and slow.

Amaya whistled and held out a timid hand. "I won't hurt you. You're a good fox, aren't you? I'm just lost." She wasn't sure if talking to it would do her any good, but the silence shot her anxiety up. Amaya's steps forward were more assured as human and animal made their ways into the brightness of the moonlight. The fox slunk forward with beguiling grace, its head tilted and its eyes forming discerning slits.

Amaya's earrings caught the light and flickered.

The fox halted and tipped its head forward, raised its hackles and growled.

"No…no." Amaya backed up as the fox sprung at her. "No!" She sprang clear of the fox's trajectory and made a break for it into the forest. Her hands scraped against bark and branches as she zigzagged through the trees.

The fox's cry was a guttural scream as its body streamed through the thick foliage, buoyant and fluid.

The river was running by on her left, the flow of the water a mirror of the tears that ran down her cheeks.

It can't be. I'm all alone. There's no one to help me. Please Creator, help me. I don't know where to go!

Her foot lodged in a root and Amaya hit the ground. Cold ran down her spine, though her cheeks were heated from the blood that desperately coursed through her body.

As soon as Amaya raised her head and scrambled to lift herself, the fox launched into the air. His rumbling growl reverberated around the woods. Then, a series of events happened in succession: She curled herself into a ball. She raised a hand in front of her face, shielding it from the fury of teeth and claws flying through the air towards her. Then water. Everywhere. Gushing from her palm and her fingers, rippling and bubbling around her, bursting forth with such a force that it knocked her backwards, pushing her into the rough ground below and tearing a scream from her lungs.

A blurred image of red rose in front of her. The fox whined and Amaya heard the faint footsteps of the animal carrying off into the night.

As silence settled back in and Amaya's panting slowly receded, a prickle crawled down her neck, and heat mingled with sharp pain. The throbbing pushed deep into her bones.

Amaya's head burned and black dots scattered across her vision, until finally everything went dark.

***

Blood drenched her parted lips. Her tongue emerged to sweep up the liquid. The woman's fingers splayed over her face, one of them pressed over her mouth. She leaned over Amaya.

"Why is she so quiet?" It looked like a shadow cast over the woman's face as she crept closer.

"Don't let her excite you, Rana. She's not your prey." The man stood next to Amaya and pushed a handkerchief into Rana's hand. She stared at Rana and then back at him once more.

"W-who are you?" Amaya's voice was weak, but her expression was alive as her eyes raced between the man and Rana. Amaya's gaze landed on Rana's blood-soaked lips for a few seconds before she dropped it back down to her bed.

"Mmm, I admire how you keep your instincts at bay." The other woman whispered, and then made her way to the man. "How's our guest?" The woman's voice was awfully cheery.

Amaya turned to her. The memory of the red figure appeared in her mind's eye. "It was you. You saved me from the fox?"

The woman introduced herself and the others. Lexa pushed Zul aside. “Don’t crowd her, Sire. The poor thing just woke up.” Lexa smiled. “I was just in time. You were about to be his meal.”

“What…where am I?” Amaya’s eyes flickered around the room. The walls were stark white and the pillows and the throw were brightly coloured in shades of purple and red. The three people in front of her were dressed in dark coloured clothing. Besides Lexa’s fiery red hair, they looked so out of place. As if they were shadows haunting the mansion. Fear shot through her. What would they do to her? She wanted to run, but to where?

“Noorenia. A dread—odd name, but this is where you are. Do you like our mansion?” Lexa giggled and hooked her arm around Zul’s. He scowled at her and shrugged out of her grasp.

“Noor...enia?” Amaya pressed shaking fingers to her mouth. The way they looked at her sent shivers running over her skin. Especially the one with the red hair. A hunger welled up in the woman’s eyes like blood.

Lexa’s eyebrow shot up. “You don’t need to fear us. We know you’re not from here.” Lexa held out a glass of water to Amaya.

She took the glass and cupped her shaking hands around it. *Wait, there was water. Did I do that?* As a swimmer, Amaya knew how it felt to manipulate water with the power of her body, but what happened there... it was more like she'd manipulated it with her mind. She must have hallucinated. She did hit her head pretty hard.

“I…” Amaya’s voice trailed off as she stared down at the water.

“Don’t worry. We didn’t poison it.” Zul Sharr smirked.

Amaya set the glass on the table, her shaking hands almost dropping it.

"Great, Sire. Now she's terrified of us," Lexa said and back-handed his shoulder. She took a step closer to Amaya. "What's your name? We can help you find your way back home."

"Amaya. You can?" She thought of her mother and sister and her fiancé, their memories entering her mind in waves.

Lexa tilted her head. "Amaya, do you know who you are?"

Amaya started thinking. "Who I am? What are you talking about?"

Lexa smiled without mirth. "The water, my girl. You could form it. You're a water elemental. A water jawhar. Although it's not magic," Lexa made a face, as if she had a bad taste in her mouth, and then continued. "It's through the Creator's will that you can twist the water to your own will. Didn't you know?" Lexa bit her lip.

Amaya's head ached, a surge of hot and cold rippling through her body.

Lexa continued; her voice sultry. "You are so fortunate. You should rest, sweetheart."

Amaya's eyes drooped and she started swaying to one side until her head hit the bed and she'd fallen asleep again.

***

Zul Sharr stood over the bed, staring at the sleeping girl. "Lexa…how'd you do that?"

"The girl is in a fragile state, Sire. Since she's a water elemental, she'll be even easier to influence. We'll bring out her inner turmoil. The pain, the guilt and horror will turn her icy. She will help us cripple those wretched angels and humans. It'll be so much fun, seeing their faces!" A toothy smile crept wide over her face.

"Terrifying." Zul Sharr's hand glided over the front of his maroon tunic, fiddling with the buttons. He'd become used to Lexa and her creepy glee, but the way she smiled with strange delight that licked out of her aura, was something he'd yet to come to terms with. She was a shadow jinni, and he knew there were such evils even he didn't want to know she'd committed.

"Now, watch how truly delectable my shadow magic is." Lexa knelt on the bed where Amaya lay. She raised her hands and the shadows around her slinked up and around her arms before they slipped like a silk cloth over Amaya's body. "Wake up."

Amaya's eyes snapped open and she bolted upright, a dull haze hindering the sheen of her gray eyes.

"That fox was your enemy Amaya. He's actually a fox jinni who attacked you long ago. It wasn't the first time. And, we can help you find the answers you need."

"How? Will I find out why he did it? Why I'm here all alone?" Amaya's voice was flat and lifeless.

"Yes. You wanted to be a professional swimmer, right? It's sad that you can't do what you want. I know how much you love your family. It's heartbreaking. Your mother, your sister, all alone and your fiancé… Tamaki must be so worried about you. You have no one here…except us." Her lips curled in a devilish grin.

"How can I trust you?"

"The foolish hand out trust like charity, but you know it has to be earned." Lexa procured a dagger from the holster at her thigh. "You want to know where the fox is and we want something in return. If we fail to tell you the whereabouts of the fox and harm you, you may attack us with this."

"If I am a water elemental, I don't need a blade," Amaya said coolly. She lifted her hand and water droplets flowed in her palm, rocking back and forth.

"Good. First, agree to my task or my shadows will suffocate you." Lexa said, her face twisting with the hint of a snarl. "You will find the fox, Amaya. Allow your anger, your pain and loneliness to guide you. You are such a kind girl. You deserve to get answers."

The way Lexa spoke to the girl made Zul's neck prickle. It was that same trance-like voice she'd spoken to him with long ago. When she had made the deal with him. When she had cursed him with magic.

Amaya met eyes with Lexa. "I'll do it."

"That's delightful!" Lexa trilled as the shadows trembled around Amaya. They pulsed as they wrapped around her body, twisting into a long curling black dress. "You're afraid of being alone, but you don't need to be now. That fox tried to kill you. He will surely regret it. You want to kill him, don't you? It's his fault that you are all alone. His fault that you lost your father."

Amaya raised her head. Lexa had hit a nerve.

A slight smile tugged at Amaya's lips, and then with bitter scorn, she spoke. "I'll never be alone again. He doesn't deserve the escape of death. He will suffer. Now, tell me what you need done."

"Rest for now, until we have everything prepared."

Amaya stumbled to her feet.

"How long? I want to find him. I need to know what happened." Amaya's eyes burned with hatred as she leaned against the bedframe.

"It'll be tonight, don't you worry. Now, rest." Lexa waved at her and Amaya lay back down, closing her eyes as her head sank into the pillow.

***

Zul Sharr leaned into Lexa as they left the room. "Is that all true what you just said?"

"That jinni didn't kill her father, but it will feel like he did, to her. Scream one truth and no one listens. Whisper enough lies and everyone does." Lexa walked on, leaving Zul behind.

Zul Sharr glanced back at the door before following her to the main room.

"Are you planning on killing her?" The way Lexa entered her prey's mind was frightening. Knowing someone's inner demons, their wants and regrets. Fracturing thoughts led to dangerous acts. He knew that too well. The thought of his mother convincing him his memories were wrong jabbed at his mind. He inhaled sharply, and focused on Lexa's gaze.

"Of course I'm not, Sire!" Lexa was back to her sprightly self. Her lips in a smug smile, and a bounce in her step. "Why would I kill her, when she can be used to our advantage? The jawhars and angels can't simply die. That's too easy for them. I want them to suffer, Sire. They may have the Angel of Mercy's complete soul, but they can't return it to him, if they don't even know where he is. And after what I've done, they don't have a chance of finding him."

"Good. I knew I could rely on you." Zul Sharr paused a second. "Lexa, I don't know how to revive Sanari. I've tried all the magical incantations you gave me. Still nothing."

"Hmm." Lexa tapped a finger to her cheek in thought. "Well, we'll keep trying and I'll look for more incantations. Shouldn't we break the jawhars' hopes in the meantime? The water elemental will be keeping them distracted."

"But, I can't just do nothing, Lexa! What if it's not magic that'll help her? Maybe it's me."

Lexa regarded him. "Sire, maybe it's time for you to strengthen your iron manipulation. Learn to move the iron within a body."

"You mean, moving their blood?"

"Yes, blood manipulation. Practice it, but trust me Sire, right now, we must not let them try and take this girl as a companion. She must break their spirits."

Chapter 3 Black Ice

Below the moon, someone with hooves stood upon a bed of autumn leaves. Oranges and browns contrasted against the black of his skin. The feathers sprouting from his shoulder bones spread wide into the expansive night. He was awaiting Lexa's command. She'd told him earlier that something was going to begin tonight. He didn't need to wait any longer. He would be needed. He was unsure how long he had been standing here, the mansion behind him looming above like an obelisk.

He gazed at the sky. What was he waiting for? A hollow sensation settled above his heart. An emptiness for someone he needed to see. He turned again, both ears and horn catching a glimpse of moonlight. The snow started to fall and speckled his body like stars. The black karkadann's eyes met with Lexa's.

"Obsidian, are you done staring into the sky? We're going."

"We're ready?" The wind played with Obsidian's mane as it circled his head like the leaves at his hooves.

"I have someone you need to meet first." Lexa headed back to the mansion.

As Obsidian trotted down the hill after her, somewhere within his being, he knew whoever it was, it was not the one his heart had been longing to see.

***

Obsidian folded his wings as he followed Lexa through the door. The entrance opened up to a luxurious villa. The hall led to the living room, where Zul Sharr sat on one of the black sofas. He was hunched over, his fingers steepled and his forearms resting on his knees. Rana was folded in the maroon loveseat with a notebook and pen in hand. She turned her head as Lexa spoke.

"How is our little swimmer doing?"

"She's been asleep in the room since you've been gone," Zul Sharr said. He stood and walked toward Obsidian.

"Well, I'll tell her to come down and meet her partner." Lexa headed to the kitchen. "But first, I need a treat!"

Obsidian's hooves clopped against the brown glossed floor.

"So, what's it like to finally be in on the plans?" Zul Sharr wrapped on arm over Obsidian's neck.

"Useful." Obsidian replied and shook his head. The melted snow had run a passage through his mane.

"I can imagine. You've been waiting a long time too." Zul Sharr breathed in through his nose and folded his arms across his chest. "Have you been up to anything while you've been here?" Zul Sharr had been craving conversation with another man. And if that man was a male unicorn with wings, he'd take whatever he could get.

"Just gathering information, and training," Obsidian said as he and Zul stood in the middle of the living room.

"I can't wait to learn about blood manipulation. Although it sounds rather scary," Zul said and widened his eyes at the thought.

Obsidian glanced at Zul and then at the stairs. "Have you been trying to awaken the princess?"

Zul pressed his lips into a straight line. After a moment's pause, he spoke. "Yeah. I've tried Lexa's magic. Nothing's been working. I've decided it's time for me to do something different. I just need to learn how to manipulate iron when it's in someone's body. It'll get easier to do it when someone's encased in it." Speaking with Obsidian almost brought back the easygoing nature of his past life.

His shoulders softened and jaw unclenched. He hadn't had many male friends to speak to. When he was living as a prince, he had a few people, but most didn't know him too well. His humorous, empathetic and helpful side. But, no one knew about his mother's abuse, or the numbness he felt, the anger that chewed him from the inside.

"Sometimes the truth starts as an empty feeling inside us. It's waiting for the other part of the truth that has real shape. Like a puzzle piece," Obsidian stated, his voice softer.

"Whoa. Maybe you're right," Zul Sharr said just as Lexa entered the living room.

"Tonight, Amaya will be our catalyst. There has to be sacrifice in order to cause discord."

Zul Sharr cringed at her words. "I want minimal bloodshed, Lexa."

Lexa had a red lollipop in hand. "Oh, Sire. How else will we catch attention? It's like we're waving a treat at them." She waved the lollipop in front of his face.

Zul blinked at her and pushed his head back.

"Temptation will lure them in and then when they think they'll get what they desire ..." She licked the candy and popped it into her mouth. Lexa's lips slithered into a smile and, with venom in her voice, she said, "They're trapped."

***

Amaya opened her eyes. She sat up, her auburn hair falling over her shoulder like a curtain. She wasn't sure when her braid had come undone. Amaya groaned as she heaved herself from the bed and made for the door of the bedroom.

It's time Amaya. Come downstairs and meet your partner. Lexa's voice echoed in her mind among the distant thoughts of her okaasan, Rin and Tama. She could hardly grasp the memories. The smell of sea water and the dark quiet forest muddled her mind.

I don't need a partner. Finding the fox is my business. Tell me what you want, first. So that your plans are met. Amaya replied. She opened the door. It made a small clunk.

How wise. You and your partner will be playing with the water tonight. The swamp will be your playground.

Be specific. Amaya said, her voice sounded grating in her mind. She walked toward the white marbled stairs. Her fingers clawed at the railing. Sharp anger twisted in her chest. She didn't want to sit back and wonder what to do next. The fox flashed in her mind. She wanted to hunt him down.

You're no fun. Lexa's voice said back to her. Amaya could imagine her pouting at her. *Come downstairs and I'll reveal our plan.* Lexa's voice faded from her mind.

The thought of her friends entered Amaya's mind next. Four girls whose names she couldn't remember. Only their smiling faces, their warm voices. Her family, okasaan... Rin… Tama. Their voices and faces were an echo, falling silent the further she tried to remember them. Fortunately, she had a week off of school since it was the fall. But family and friends would contact her sometime, and she needed to find a way home. At least after finding the fox.

That fervent need to find him and seek answers about her papa was like a second pulse in her heart. That was all she could think of. Her mother didn't mind if she visited too often, since she knew Amaya was busy. But, what of Tamaki? He would definitely call her. She fiddled with the ring around her finger on her left hand. She didn't have anything with her. She'd left everything at the beach.

The beach. Papa used to bring her hishi mochi from the old women's cart at the beach every year. The jasmine flowers topped on the pink layer of the mochi. Eating the diamond-shaped treat with papa and okasaan displaying the hina dolls in the house, the warmth, the smiles, the delicious food made her feel so full at the memory. They would pray for her long life and happiness. She longed for that warmth to fill her heart, that was submerged in the cold waters of emptiness. Just as panic gained purchase in her chest, images of the fox and his murderous eyes rose in her vision, battering down any rising thoughts of home. He was her purpose now. He had to die.

***

The ocean waves licked at the sand. The coast guard stood before a small blue bag, abandoned in the middle of a blanket, sinking slowly into the hungry sand. The umbrella had toppled over and was drifting its way down towards the waves.

***

Amaya's mother was in the kitchen laying out dinner.

"Finish your salmon and then you can have some strawberries." Mrs. Koizumi poked Rin's cheek and laid a plate of gyoza for herself.

Just as she went to lift her chopsticks, the phone rang. Leaving Rin, who was happily spooning soup into her mouth. She stood, brushed herself down, and answered the call.

It was the coast guard.

"Evening Ma'am. Sorry to disturb you tonight. Are you Mrs. Koizumi?"

"Y-yes. Did something happen?"

"Ma'am, we found your daughter's bag, towel and an umbrella on the beach. We have a witness who says she may have disappeared. Has she returned home?"

Mrs. Koizumi's chest tightened. She battled to keep her composure. "Disappeared? She— She lives in her own apartment," She said, her voice quaking as disbelief rattled her mind.

"I do hope you find her well. Please take care."

"Thank you." Mrs. Koizumi could hardly speak.

"Have a good night, Ma'am and stay safe."

Mrs. Koizumi ended the call.

"Mama? Did something happen?" Rin asked as she stood at the kitchen's entrance.

"Don't worry my little one. Have you finished dinner?" She asked and smiled faintly at her.

"Yeah, most of it, mama." Rin beamed at her and skipped back to her chair.

After dinner, and after Mrs. Koizumi had tucked Rin into bed, she phoned her mother.

"Mama? Could you come over tonight to take care of Rin? I need to go somewhere."

"Is something wrong, dear?"

"It's nothing, mama."

"I'll be there. Don't worry about Rin."

"Thank you. I'll see you when I get home." Mrs. Koizumi breathed out.

It was nine at night when Mrs. Koizumi reached the door of Amaya's apartment. Amaya had given her mother the keys so it was easy for her to visit when she wanted to.

Her heart slammed against her ribcage and her eyes burned as she turned the key and turned the knob.

"Amaya?" She called out. No answer. But it was late; she was probably in bed. Mrs. Koizumi rushed to the bedroom and barged in. There was nothing. Amaya wasn't here. The bed was empty, and as she searched with teary eyes, she found the whole apartment devoid of her daughter.

“Amaya!” Only silence, only her heartbeat responded to her shaky voice. Where was she? She couldn’t really be gone.

She fell to the couch, swiping at her tears with trembling hands. She couldn’t even reach Amaya by phone. She’d tried three times. Since her belongings had been on the beach, that meant her phone was in her bag too. Mrs. Koizumi continued crying.

When Mrs. Koizumi got home, she explained to her mother what happened with Amaya, who told her she would stay by her side. She insisted to stay a week, since Rin had school holidays.

Mrs. Koizumi couldn’t sleep, tossing and turning when she had tried to. Her chest ached; her legs wobbly when she tried to stand. A crazy idea popped into her mind.

She peeked into the next room, seeing her mother asleep. She pulled out the drawer of her side table and turned a key to a brown box and unlocked it. Inside was a pair of blue tear-drop earrings. They had been given to her by her grandmother. Her pulse sounded in her ears and throbbed in her fingertips as she gripped the box. With careful movements, she closed the door and lifted the earrings from the box and pushed them through her lobes.

She thought of Amaya. The way her soft voice sent calm to her heart, when they would watch dramas together. Amaya was a warm girl who was her reason to live.

“Amaya?” She spoke in a whisper. The earrings began to light up. The jewellery was imbued with the living pulse of Noorenia itself. They would act as their connection, since Amaya owned the sister pair.

“Amaya? Can you hear me?

***

Amaya was just about to descend the stairs when the voice entered her mind. This time it wasn't Lexa's.

"Okaasan?" She said, echoing her mother's whisper.

"Can you hear me?" Her mother said.

"Yes. Yes, I can hear you." Amaya said. Her breathing deepened. It couldn't be okaasan. But, it sounded like her.

"Oh, Amaya. Where are you?"

"I'm in…another place. Mama… I'm in Noorenia. I'm all alone, mama. I'm scared." Amaya's voice trembled. Most of Lexa's hold on her faltered.

"Amaya, my sweetheart. Are you okay? You're not hurt?"

"No. No, I'm not hurt." Amaya backed up into the wall. She didn't want Lexa or the others to hear her.

"Listen. Find Kagami. She's your aunt. Find her. She lives in Toshahar City. Remember that. She will help you."

"Mama… I will— wait, no. I can finally get answers! I need to find the fox. Did you know? He's the one who attacked me when I was younger. I need to know," Amaya said.

"Amaya. Please. I know your confused, but find Kagami."

"I need answers. I need them," Amaya said her voice deepening in her desperation.

"I will respect your decision, Amaya. But, please, promise me you will find her. Kagami will keep you safe until you can find a way back to Togenkyo."

“I promise. I need to find him first.”

“Amaya... I still don’t understand—”

“It’s his fault that papa is gone!” Amaya’s arms throbbed, the cold sensation travelling up to her chest.

“Your papa—" Her mother’s voice cut in and out.

“Okaasan! You’re breaking up. I’ll find my way home again!”

“I love you, my sweet girl.” Her Okaasan’s voice shook with emotion.

“I love you too Okaasan. Take care of Rin! Take care of yourself.” Amaya’s chest rose and fell rapidly as her gaze kept returning to the stairs.

“Take care!”

Her mother’s voice faded and Amaya slumped against the wall. She wiped the tears away. That’s when she felt that strange coldness and heat grating over her skin again. The hold of Lexa’s shadows gripped her like frostbite.

“The fox… I must find him. And then that woman, Kagami.” Amaya’s words bit the air, harsh and cold as the icy shadows that held her mind. She made her way down the stairs.

Amaya’s steps were as fluid as the black dress of shadows that clung to her body. Each step rippled the fabric which seemed to lick at her legs.

***

“Here’s our water jawhar,” Zul Sharr said. Obsidian turned his head to her. He took a few steps toward Amaya, but halted when Lexa joined them.

"Amaya, this is Obsidian. Your partner." Lexa raised her eyebrows and gestured toward the unicorn.

"He's a unicorn," Amaya said, her eyebrows shot up. "He has wings?"

"Yes. He's an angel too." Lexa placed a hand on Obsidian's shoulder. "Though I don't much like that form," Lexa muttered.

Obsidian nodded his head in greeting. She crossed the room towards him, her steps were slow and silent, drifting more like a shadow than a human.

"Who are you exactly?" Obsidian asked Amaya as she ran a gentle hand over his nose and cupped his cheek with the other.

"A wayfarer seeking answers, and a water elemental who's tired of the current taking her to lonely depths."

"She's a poet too then, huh?" Zul Sharr said and grinned as Rana side glanced at Amaya and frowned.

"I miss the fear in her eyes." Rana's husky voice made Obsidian's neck shiver.

"Well, you two have a lot of time to get to know each other, so let's not waste precious time," Lexa said as she flicked her red locks.

"I agree. Lexa, how should we begin?" Amaya asked. Her hands were still touching Obsidian. He was unsure of her at first. Now, something, very deep inside his heart, a small voice which was muffled, said she was not a foe. She was a calm soul, just here at the wrong time, in the wrong place.

Lexa's sinister smile crept up her face and her features darkened. "You will be going to Guadalupe Swamp. There, raise the tides and stain the waters with blood. That will be enough for now. Then our plan will begin."

Amaya nodded her head and her fingers finally left Obsidian's mane. She had been petting his velveteen nose and his silky hair.

"What will I be doing?" Asked Obsidian as his eyes fixed onto Amaya's dress. The thing seemed to be alive and breathing.

"Your time will come. This is just the beginning. Now, make haste."

Amaya leaned in towards Obsidian. His ears twitched when she spoke, wishing it was another's voice. "Shall we go?"

Obsidian nodded.

Amaya climbed onto the unicorn's back and sat tall. She twined her fingers in his mane and guided him to the right. His hooves clicked against the floor as they headed for the door.

"Wait for us at the swamp," Zul Sharr said, opening the door. "Then, we'll let you know what's next."

Amaya nodded as she patted the side of Obsidian's front leg. "Lead me to the swamp, Obsidian."

"You will have to keep a tight grip on me, Amaya the wayfarer," Obsidian said, as he galloped off into the night, both becoming a part of the darkness.

Chapter 4 An Old flame

It was Eid today and she was ending her prayer. Nezha turned her head to the left and whispered, “As Salaamu alaykum wa Rahmatullah.” *May peace and mercy be with you.* She found the greatest serenity in congregation at the masjid. Nezha prayed for her family. She prayed for health, happiness and love and for help for the siblings. *Oh Most High, oh The Loving One, The Most Merciful, please help Sapphire and Thunderbolt free their family from the iron.*

As Nezha stood to leave and find her father at the men’s entrance, she thought of Tasa. *I should give her a call sometime today to say EID Mubarak.*

On EID the day would start with prayer and a feast with family and friends. Nezha was glad they’d donated the week before EID, since today they had to give charity—Zakat Al Fitr—for those who were less fortunate, so they could enjoy the celebrations too.

When Nezha and her parents arrived home, the first thing she did was head for the kitchen. “Need help making anything ma?”

“You mean, eating anything, hain na?” Her mother Najwa teased, placing her dupatta back on its hook and following Nezha to the kitchen.

“Yeah, that too.” Nezha took a sugar cookie from a decorated plate. There were turquoise masjids, blue minarets, orange crescents and purple stars. Each was dotted in white icing.

“Hey, Nezha, leave some for me. I decorated some too,” Wasi said as he entered the kitchen.

“I can’t make any promises.” Nezha nibbled her cookie and flopped on the blue futon.

Comet wove between Nezha’s legs, marking her with her scent. She looked up at Nezha and meowed in greeting.

“Hey, Comet. EID Mubarak.” Nezha chuckled and scratched the cat behind her soft ears and her chin.

“Want to put mehndi on, after?” Najwa said.

Wasi placed a taupe cloth over the table and then helped his wife lay out the food.

“Yeah. Are we meeting everyone after that?”

“Yes.”

Nezha joined her parents at the table. They had Krachel—sweet rolls infused with orange floral water and sprinkled with sesame and anise seeds. Closer to Nezha was a plate of dates, omelettes with vegetables and a platter of parathas. Butter glistened over the crispy tops. To her right was Meloui. Nezha always ate the pancakes with a sweet syrup of melted butter and honey.

After they finished their breakfast, Wasi eyed the sugar cookies.

“I think I should cover these up and put them away for later,” Najwa said as she looked at her husband and swiped them from the table.

“She always lets you have one.” Wasi complained, looking at Nezha.

"You have to be quick, baba," Nezha said with a grin, tucking one into his hand before helping her mother put the dishes away.

***

"Come here." Her mother gestured for her to sit before her.

Nezha complied as her mother took hold of her hair. "Wait, ma, are you braiding it?" She turned back, but her mother swiftly made her face forward again.

"Oi, who knows when I'll get the chance again. So, sit still and let me braid your hair." Her mother's fingers wove through her hair, and then she playfully nudged her head. Her mother laughed. And that laugh made Nezha's heart warm.

It had been a while since she'd heard her mother's laugh. It was a beautiful song like chudiyan chiming on her wrists, or a fragrance as delicate and yet as heavy as the guava fruits that grew in her mother's home back in Pakistan. She'd longed to have moments like this with her ma. When she'd first stepped into Noorenia, she didn't know if she would ever get to see Ma, or her family ever again. She'd felt so alone, so lost.

There was pain in her mother's laugh. A pain she knew held such a debt, Nezha could never lighten it. A mother carried her child and burdened her body. To them it wasn't a burden, but a blessing. Nezha could only make dua that her mother would never have a reason to carry anything until it became a burden. But, this laugh, this laugh sounded like a hefty one.

"Ma… did your ammi braid your hair everyday?" Nezha just wanted to talk to her. She wanted to be with her as long as she could.

Before Noorenia would take her away. Until it called out to her as if she were a bride starting her own family.

"Haan," her mother agreed. "She'd have her hand full of oil rubbed into my scalp, and her chatter buzzing at my ears…" Nezha heard the smile in her voice. At least, she hoped it was a pleasant smile. Not a melancholic one. "…that was the only hairstyle I had. Braids. When I would practice doing mehndi on our hands, she'd get mad when I stained her dupattas. I was too impatient for it to dry. But, when she would cool down, she'd say it was the most beautiful dupatta she owned. She'd drape it over her shoulders and laugh."

Anxiety twisted in her chest. Nezha didn't want her ma to cry. Maybe, this would bring her to tears. "Sounds like naani was quite the character."

Her mother's fingers pulled her hair a little too tight as she continued to braid Nezha's hair.

"You're like her, meri Nezho."

Nezho. Ma hadn't called her that, what felt like another lifetime. When Nezha was a little girl, all her ma said was meri jaan, her Nezho. Back then when her ma said it, Nezho was filled with innocence and a child's laugh. It made Nezha think back to the times before her ma had found out Nezha could manipulate flames. Before the fear. Now, it didn't sound like she was talking to a baby. It felt like she was talking to her with acceptance. Her pride. Her Nezho. Her daughter.

"Ma, you're gonna pull my hair out."

"Sorry jaanu. I'm done now." Her ma's finger grazed her back, as she coiled an elastic on the end of Nezha's braid.

Nezha walked over to the mirror on the wall. "Wow, it looks just like yours."

"It'll make it easier to keep your hair inside your hijab and out of your eyes." Her mother looked at her through the mirror and smiled. Nezha searched her eyes and then threw her arms around her.

"Ki o ya?" *What's wrong*? Her mother raised her eyebrows at her and returned the embrace with a wide smile.

Nezha shook her head. "Nothing. Can't I show you I appreciate your hard work?" She wanted to stay longer.

Nezha couldn't be sure if Noorenia would even allow her to return again. That's why she wanted to savour the moments here. She knew as long as she had the angel's soul with her, that world was safe. The jinn there couldn't do anything. But, the angel still needed its soul returned. And that meant Nezha would need to return again too. She wasn't sure if she'd ever be back on Earth with her parents ever again.

Nezha and her ma sat in front of the window. Najwa had brought a golden cone filled with henna. She snipped a bit of the tip so she could squeeze out the green paste.

Nezha placed her hand, palm up into Najwa's hand. She went to work, some strokes quick, others fluid and repetitive. The cone was a brush in her fingertips. With precision and accuracy, she decorated Nezha's skin with a floral design.

"It's interesting how the longer you wait, the deeper the colour becomes."

Nezha relaxed into the hypnotic sensation of the cool henna tickling the skin of her palm and allowed her attention to drift out the window. The leaves of the orange blossom tree had turned rich with maroon and umber; the same colours as her henna. Outside, the natural world was falling asleep.

Nezha's mind drifted again, and she thought of Noorenia. She hadn't heard from Sapphire for over a week. She hoped all was well. They must be. Surely, Sapphire would have contacted her if not. But still, Nezha couldn't stop the seed of worry that planted itself in her chest. Hopefully everything was going well in Noorenia. Even the angel hadn't tried to say anything to her. Not once. Maybe it's because the angel followed divine will.

Her mother drew her out from her reverie.

"All done. What do you think?"

"It's great ma!" Nezha smiled at her.

Nezha's mother stood and returned to the kitchen. Once alone, Nezha considered drying the henna with her fire powers, but she didn't want to risk destroying the beautiful designs… or anything in the house, for that matter.

Nezha didn't take the henna off until noon, by which time it had become cracked and flaky. Nezha rubbed her palms together watching the dark green clumps crumble away, then used a cloth to remove the last stubborn specks. The colour beneath was a deep red.

***

"Nez!" Jessenia Kareem was waving her hands, her whole face bright as she ran up to Nezha and pulled her into a quick embrace.

“Salaam! Eid Mubarak!” She held Nezha’s shoulders and looked her up and down. “Ooh, you look utterly stunning!"

“Wa alaykum as Salaam. Khayr Mubarak, Jess! Of course! You can expect nothing less from either of us!”

They’d all received new clothes for Eid. Nezha’s ensemble was a royal blue kaftan with mustard yellow silk underneath, and the same colour in details. The cuffs were striped in blue and white and she wore a dark brown shawl that had one long curl of fabric that fell over one shoulder.

“Why, thank you!” Jessenia’s brown curly hair bounced about her shoulders as she did a small twirl. Her wrists and ears dripped in gold jewellery. Her turquoise blouse fanned out like a spinning top.

“Eid Mubarak.” Aisha Imtayaz was next to hug Nezha. Aisha had a purple khimar wrapped around her head which flowed to her elbows. In her right hand was a black hand bag, now pressed against her long silver kaftan.

“Khayr Mubarak Aisha." Nezha said as Jessenia greeted her and pressed her cheek to hers and kissed the air.

Aisha simply smiled.

Nezha gestured to the food table. “Anyone hungry?”

“Yes! How did you know?” Jessenia pulled Nezha’s arm and dragged her to the table with Aisha following behind.

“No need to be so aggressive Jessenia,” Aisha scolded.

“I can’t help it, I'm so hungry right now.” Jessenia pouted.

“I hope we’re not interrupting,” Najwa said, her and Wasi joining the three girls and greeting them.

"Mr and Mrs. Zaman, how are you?" Aisha smiled as Najwa turned to her and kissed her cheek.

"Alhamdulillah. I'm good. How are you, darling?" said Najwa.

"Very good," said Wasi with a smile.

"With good health, by the Most Merciful." A hesitant smile curled Aisha's lips as she saw Jessenia with a cupcake in her hand and stuffing her face.

"Mrs. Zam-um." Jessenia's mouth was stuffed and her lips were glossed with icing.

"Jessenia dear, you are as lively as ever." Najwa grinned.

"By all means, enjoy more treats," Wasi said with a chuckle.

Jessenia's cheeks flushed as she wiped her face with a napkin. Najwa gave her a kiss on her cake-crumbed cheek.

Aisha handed Jessenia a pocket mirror to clean herself up.

"Oh, come on, I'm not a baby."

"Oh? well, stop eating like one, then!" Aisha said with a tease.

Najwa smiled at the girls. "Nezha, let me know when you're all ready for dinner."

"I will," Nezha said.

Wasi gave Nezha's head a gentle touch. "Nezha, if there's any food you want us to bring back, let me know." His warm smile paired with the concern in his eyes made Nezha want to stay longer by her parents' sides.

Her baba hadn't smiled in so long. After Lamis's passing, Nezha hadn't been sure if she could ever find a reason to smile either.

She nodded, and with a laugh she said, "Are you sure we'll have enough room in our car?"

Wasi's smile deepened. "Of course! I made sure to bring crates as back up."

Nezha laughed. She wasn't surprised. He'd once brought home a box of chocolate chip muffins and asked her if she'd liked them. She'd told him they were good, and the next day, he'd brought two crates full. They'd had muffins for breakfast for weeks.

Nezha waved at her parents and then turned to her friends. Seeing them again after so long made her heart full. It was bright, and so warm.

"Have I ever told you, you guys are awesome?"

"Flattery with me," Jessenia clucked her tongue. "…will get you anything your heart desires."

Aisha raised an eyebrow. "What is that supposed to mean? Are you a queen?"

"Your royal highness." Nezha spun her hand and gave a bow.

"I am worthy of being a queen, aren't I?" Jessenia winked. Then her attention drifted to Nezha's hands. "Did your ummi do that? It looks gorgeous!"

"Yeah! She's so talented, right?" Nezha said as she lifted her palms to her friends.

"It looks beautiful. I had mine done too." Aisha's henna was on her palms too, and so was Jessenia's.

"I'm not surprised at your vanity."

Nezha turned to the voice, finding a boy beside her. A familiar one who liked to tease.

"Vafa!" Jessenia said and nudged Nezha.

"Nezha!" Vafa's lips turned into a wide smile.

“Still trying to be cool and forgetting to say Salaam, Vafa?” Nezha gave him a pointed look.

“Of course not. Why would I deprive myself of your blessings?”

Then they both burst into laughter. She could always joke around with him.

Vafa grinned. He combed his fingers through his dark brown hair. “As Salaamu alaykum, Nezy.” He was wearing a black coat over his collared long white tunic.

“Wa alaykum as Salaam. Be- Vafa,” Nezha laughed.

Vafa feigned hurt. “Bewafa? I’m as loyal as it gets. Sorry for being busy.”

“It feels like it’s been half a year!” His presence always brought a smile to her face. It had been too long since they’d talked.

He hadn’t changed much from when they were children. His skin was much browner now. A dark golden shade. His short hair was still that mess of waves over his forehead. He had only lost that innocence that lent itself to his once chubby cheeks. Now he had a more oval face with a prominent jaw line. He was much older than her now. In his twenties.

Jessenia raised an eyebrow. “Aww, aren’t you sweet, Vafa?” And then laughed when he made a silly face at her.

“I only came over to greet you. Besides, I don’t mix with non-mahrams,” Vafa told Jessenia with a smirk, before returning his attention to Nezha. “Eid Mubarak to you, ladies. I’ll see you later. Don’t be a stranger!” He pulled a cigarette from the pocket of his white pants and tucked it between his lips. He turned his back and waved as he walked away.

“See ya, Vafa!” Nezha called out.

“I can always smell the smoke off of him, mixed with cologne,” Jessenia said and sighed. “I wonder why he started so young.”

Nezha watched his back as he walked away. The smoke never really bothered her. She supposed it was because of her affinity with flames.

Nezha’s phone rang. “Oh.”

“Don’t worry, Nez, we’ll wait for you. Just don’t take long, or you’ll be late for dinner!”

“Don’t mind her. Take your time,” Aisha said.

“Thanks.” When Nezha saw who the caller was, a wide smile tugged at her lips. She tried to ignore the worry now taking root in her gut.

Chapter 5 Blood in the Water

His steps were quick as Zul ran through the forest, his boots imprinting the wet ground. The sky grew churlish as clouds sent forth a torrent of rain, pelting the ground in a surge of moisture. The downpour pulled the scent out of the soil and the trees, heightening each earthy and rich note. He felt so free as he ran. He always imagined just running in a field, where there were no boundaries. Where he could simply keep running with the wind through his hair, the rain refreshing him as it pecked his skin.

He looked back. A black wolf was right at his heels. The creature barked and lunged at him, its incisors bared as its lips pulled back. Zul laughed, and lifted his arm, throwing the dog backward. The beast fell to its side. He continued his run, not waiting to catch his breath.

Trees scratched at his hands, nicking him and drawing blood. He swatted at the branches which came his way. Finally, he had made it to a clear path in the forest.

A murder of crows swooped down at his head. He could make out their forms as their clawed feet grabbed at him, the flaps of their wings drowned by the rain. Zul waved his arms and formed a scythe out of the iron he kept in his pocket. He twirled the weapon, swiping and slashing at the flocking birds. The crows gave out rumbling caws and flapped away into the darkness of the trees, disappearing as if they too were shadows. With deep breaths Zul continued his run, until he missed his footing and slipped on a wet bit of earth and tumbled down the steep side of a hill. He emitted a grunt as he rolled down and onto his back. He lay there breathing deeply, trying to compose himself before struggling to his feet. The cry of the wolf echoed around him. Zul Sharr peered left and right. The animal was nowhere to be seen. He once again continued his run.

Moments later, the wolf appeared behind him, its barks pounding within Zul's eardrums. His speed increased as he shot spikes of iron at the beast. It zigged and zagged through the onslaught of metal, until finally it darted to his left, disappearing again. Zul stood in the middle of a clearing, his heart drumming against his rib cage. He drew a deep breath and cringed at the pain in his hands. His head whipped to the side. A single crow perched on top of a tree stump crooned at him. The wolf jumped at him from behind, tackling him to the ground.

"Lexa. Damn it, you got me."

The wolf transformed into the demonic, red-haired Lexa.

Her jade eyes fastened onto his orange ones. "Sire, you really shouldn't let your guard down. Now, get up, before I eat you up."

"My liege, you have improved," Rana spoke as she too transformed from a crow into her human form.

Lexa licked her red lips. "Sire, do you believe they are ready?"

Zul stood to his feet. "Of course they are." He was calm but he clenched his jaw.

“Have a few moments to think, Sire. We’ll be over here before we begin. Obsidian and Amaya haven’t even arrived yet,” Lexa said, jabbing her chin to the tree nearby.

“Are you sure I can’t drain the water jawhar of some of her energy? She’s wasting it.” Rana’s lips turned into a menacing grin.

“No way, Rana,” Lexa chided, as their voices drifted off and they walked into the swamp.

It was after midnight, and the darkness was suffocating him. The nicks on his hands had begun stitching up, thanks to the jinni aura running through his veins. An alien inside his human body. It marked him as a half-jinni. But a fake one. At least that’s what he told himself.

This had been the last day of fasting.

He had broken his fast when the sun had set. All he could pray for was for the iron that encased Sanari to be broken. And because the month was one of mercy, he even caught himself hoping that the valley, too, would be freed from its prison of metal, that he could patch things up with Thunderbolt again and that the world would forgive him. No one would hate him.

Ramadan was a month where jinn—beings made of smokeless flame—were shackled, and that was indeed what had happened. Even the day before, Lexa told him she had felt weaker and that she’d lose her strength and not be able to speak to him for the whole month.

In a way, Zul Sharr welcomed it. The day before Ramadan was very strange. Lexa had been unusually filled with malice, insisting he attack the angels while Nezha was gone. His mind had filled with the same kind of thoughts. As Ramadan began and he woke up at dawn, it was as if his head had cleared. The storm had ceased, and it was serenity which embraced him in its solitude. His jinni energy was subdued after all. To the point where he could not hear its scratchy voice, or feel its whims to harm him and cause mischief.

Silence. The silence was a luxury he never could afford. Not when his mother would scream at him to die, and say she wished he hadn't been born.

The moments in dimmed light, he made himself breakfast —or suhoor—the meal for which he would fast on, he almost felt like a content person. He wasn't thinking of the ways to keep the angel from taking back its soul. He just thought of doing good things and wanting peace. He had wanted to think of God. His tongue would be weighed with words of gratefulness and sweetened with the hope, albeit specks of hope—feeling he had inside. He didn't hang onto or let it grow too much. Unlike how he used to be, before his mother beat him, before she began arguing over the smallest matters into the night. A living hell.

As the rain fell, he welcomed that silence again. Lexa and Rana stood at a distance beside the swamp, chatting.

Zul dearly missed it. A part of his soul yearned for the month to return. What would he do now? Were all those good deeds and prayers just a lie? He'd done all the good he thought he could. Giving charity in every way possible. Trying his best to mentally scrub away all the darkness. But, truth was, the darkness, Lexa and the numbing pain, were a sick comfort. He didn't want to endure more struggles, but he knew that if he wanted Sanari to wake up, he had to do something.

Tonight, he didn't want to do anything that would hurt his soul. Even though the jinni aura coursed through him and the pulse of energy beckoned him to fight, to break and deliver his sorrows to the world, he would do his best to hold back. At least for tomorrow. After tomorrow, when the sun set, he could go back to fighting. He just wanted to enjoy the peace a little while longer.

***

Rain pelted down around Amaya, soaking her hair and clothes, but she barely noticed, the sound of Obsidian's hooves gnashing at the ground like teeth drowned out everything else around her. The need to fulfill Lexa's orders and find the fox was all that embraced her.

"Are we close?" Amaya yelled as Obsidian sped through a forest. She clenched harder at her fistful of his mane.

"We're here." Obsidian slowed to a trot and stopped in front of the large swamp.

Amaya slipped down his back, the bottom of her dress trailing in the murky water. The moon was full tonight. The glow caught the curl of her hair, and the cloth at her back as Amaya walked to the waters. "Obsidian… Lexa said I need to do something to the tides? To stain the water red, with blood…" Amaya's voice was a whisper, speaking more to herself.

Obsidian joined her side, his steps hesitant as he lowered his head to her and spoke. He folded his wings close to his body. "You are a water jawhar. Don't you know how?"

Amaya didn't reply. She simply stared at the water, and at the group of fireflies who widened like a maw of glistening teeth.

Amaya turned to meet his gaze.

Obsidian stared back, but calm was what she found in his eyes. Or perhaps it was boredom.

"It's not only the water that will rise tonight," she said with a closed lipped smile. She raised her hands. The water whipped up, and her hands swirled with droplets and trembling waves. Soon the swamp shook, the plant life obeying the movement.

The murky water swirled as it rose, lapping at Amaya's legs, thirsty for the life she was feeding it.

Obsidian stepped back as the swamp continued to rise, stopping just under Amaya's knees.

She lowered her hands and allowed her body to relax. The shadows from her dress snaked around her leg. A pointed tendril pierced her skin. Blood welled and, like smoke, it flowed into the water soon tainting the whole swamp a deep red.

The red moon dilated like a pupil. A drop of blood in the pitch dark.

Obsidian whinnied.

The wolves howled. Their chorus echoed from the distance in the forest.

Amaya's cool fingers ran over Obsidian's neck. She patted him and shushed him, her voice soothing. "Our job is done. Thank you for the ride here."

Obsidian's nostrils flared and he stretched his wings. "We… we need to meet with the others. They must be here somewhere in the swamp."

"No need." Lexa said, morphing from within the shadows, Zul Sharr and Rana alongside her. "You did it!" Lexa stared into the bloody swamp.

The wolves continued to howl, their voices peeling through the night.

Rana bolted upright. "Lexa, why are we calling the wolves? You're not planning to sacrifice them, are you? You know how close they are to me."

"Rana…Rana, you don't think I'd do that to you, do you? We're not shedding their blood." Lexa turned to Zul Sharr, who was staring up at the moon. "Sire, remember our little talk about blood manipulation? I think now would be the perfect time. It should be easy to cause some chaos in the night."

Zul Sharr narrowed his eyes at the bloodied swamp. "Carry out your plan, Lexa."

The howls faded. Amaya stood at Lexa's side.

"Amaya, you and Obsidian lead the wolves around the city. No bloodshed yet. Sire's keen on keeping it clean." Lexa threw a look back at Zul Sharr.

"All right," Amaya replied. She sat upon Obsidian's back, the dress of shadows trembling around her.

Obsidian galloped in the red water, the droplets like blood splattered around them as Amaya stretched her hand out, a pulse at her fingertips. The water stirred at her command, churning around Obsidian's hooves.

The wolves sang once more. Their voices carrying out into the darkness.

With the rhythm of obsidian's hooves in the sodden ground and the water swirling at her side, Amaya felt lighter than she ever had before. It was as if, all this time, she had been a pool of stagnant water, her fears and responsibilities keeping her from moving and allowing the full freedom of life to flow through her.

Somewhere in the recesses of her mind was the thought of her mother and sister back home, worried and alone. She tried to reach out to it, but it was buried behind the shadow of the fox. She needed that fox. When she found him, she wanted him to beg for forgiveness and submit to her demand.

The dress of shadows reached out around her neck, its cold kiss marring her thoughts. Darkness pooled around the thoughts of Okaasan and Rin, choking them. Amaya's fingers stiffened around the dark locks of Obsidian's mane.

The shadows squeezed her waist, their coldness seeping into her bones.

Amaya stretched out her right arm and concentrated on the water as it poured and grew at her command. Gone were the thoughts of yesterday or tomorrow. All that now clung to her mind was the water, the wolves and the chaos.

Slinking creatures of silvers, whites, blacks and greys poured in around them. Wolves, drunk from the swollen moon. Their mouths formed O's as if they intended to drink the water Amaya was stirring and manipulating.

Amaya felt the muscles around Obsidian's abdomen coil and tense.

"Don't worry, Obsidian. They're not here to make a meal out of you. They're here for the dance."

Amaya felt her own wolfish grin spread across her face as they slipped into the forest. The water gushed through trees and thick roots like blood through a graveyard of bones.

Amaya's heart pounded so hard she could feel it in her mouth. The once-dormant forest was alive with the thrumming cacophony. Her heart, the storming waters, and the cries of the wolves; everything was in sync, ripping through the darkness of the night like a battle cry.

In her mind, she was being chased by the fox all over again. She saw the deep orange of his form slinking through the trees. The glow of his eyes as they latched onto hers. She gripped Obsidian's mane tighter, riding him faster through the bloody forest. She could hear his breath and taste the saltiness of sweat and the scent of cyprus which the water pulled from the trees. Above them, the moon seemed to glow redder and brighter.

The wolves slowed and spread out as they neared the city, their howls quieting to a soft murmur.

Amaya and her army of wolves spilled over a small hill and into the city just as the sky began to lighten, hinting at the oncoming dawn.

The beasts split and surrounded the city, quiet and stealthy.

The clamor of the wolves had now turned deathly quiet, and there was an eerie and expectant silence, like a gasp, or like the still before a storm.

The wolves began to howl again, their heads turned up to the bleeding moon.

The city screamed. Doors began to shudder and slam closed. Cars shrieked as they spun to flee.

A blue vehicle approached them, reaching the edge of the city, where a large lake separated it from the forest. It was the very lake where Amaya had struggled onto land. How different her fate would've been if she'd surfaced on the other side and discovered the city first. The red waters cascaded into the city, causing even more pandemonium.

Amaya strained her eyes to see the vehicle had two red lights, circling and flashing as it pulled up by a dock and a man stepped out of it.

Amaya slapped a hand to obsidian's back to urge him forward.

"I can understand you…" He muttered as the two of them emerged out of the shadows. When she reached the edge of the bank, she stopped. The man stared up at her.

The wolves ended their chorus and sat, waiting for their next command.

The man remained where he stood. Amaya could see his lips move but was too far away to hear him.

Amaya said nothing. Her appearance alone served as a warning. Her icy gaze and bloody form held the message. Slowly, she turned Obsidian and walked away, and the wolves dispersed, fleeing back into the woods.

As the dawn broke and the sunlight started to wash away the red from the sky, Amaya and Obsidian made their way back. She smiled, but her satisfaction was only on the surface. As soon as she saw Lexa, she would demand she tell her where the fox was.

Chapter 6 Familia

Zul had been up since daybreak. He had stepped outside for prayer in congregation. It had felt like it was years since he had prayed with anyone, since he'd always prayed alone in his room.

When he returned to the hide out, he stood in the main room. The wide rectangular windows shone as the light poured through. He walked toward the glass and pushed it open, feeling the cool wind play with his hair. Birds began their symphony, diving through the skies. The light through trees and branches cast shadows like lace over the ground.

Zul Sharr remembered what Lexa told him last night after he returned to the mansion with her and Rana.

"Sire, I know what day it is tomorrow. Even though I don't like it, no one can force you, so… enjoy yourself. No one will get in your way." She had rolled her eyes, her voice not her usual cheerful tone.

"How did you know I was still celebrating?"

"I found your gifts under the bed. That's not a good hiding place when you have a jinni around. Thank you for the pendant. Red was a good choice, Sire." Lexa grinned, toying with the gold chain and the ruby star-shaped gem around her neck that Zul hadn't even noticed until that moment.

Despite the flush creeping up his cheeks, he couldn't help but smile. After all, he'd put a lot of thought into the presents. He'd bought Obsidian new shoes and Rana another notebook. He wasn't sure what Amaya wanted and had even asked her. In the end, he'd bought her a hat.

Zul Sharr himself was dressed in a new set of clothes. He'd bought them last month when he was at the bazaar: a silver embroidered kaftan and a blue and black inner shirt.

Even though he was meant to be the prince of Qadam, it was alongside Sanari that Zul Sharr would make his first appearance. Not many knew how the prince looked. Save for a few friends and close family, he could go virtually undetected in the busy streets outside the country of Qadam.

Princess Sanari however was well known and was rarely seen without her crown of flowers sitting atop her mass of curly hair.

Zul Sharr took off through the forest and, for the first time, the chill in the air didn't match his heart. He actually felt giddy to be celebrating, instead of fighting and planning to keep the angel's soul contained. He'd heard from one of Lexa's companions that Nezha wasn't in Noorenia. He knew she was probably celebrating in her dimension as well.

He pulled the hood of his coat that was keeping his new clothes from the effects of the weather. There wasn't supposed to be snow today, but it was always best to be safe.

Zul Sharr made his way into the city, his head lowered. When he reached the outside of Veer. He headed toward the winding road which led to Falaz City.

The journey was still another three miles. He'd have to take transport.

The driver left Zul as close to the Iron Kingdom as he could get. Zul Sharr walked through the streets, the lamps looming over him. What was he thinking, coming back here? He craved the ignorance of bliss when he would celebrate Eid with his family when he was younger.

Zul Sharr walked up to the silver gate of the palace where he was met by the guards. The two young men were both dressed in the purple and silver garb of the kingdom.

"State your purpose," one said.

Zul Sharr had his hood drawn low over his head, his gaze avoiding the guards'. He gulped. His mouth had gone dry. After so long, his own name had become a shell he'd shed himself of. A name which linked him with the kingdom. A kingdom he had wished he could find safety and peace in. A kingdom he wished he could call a home. He brushed aside his hood and titled his head up, meeting the gaze of the guards.

"I am Eisen ibn Hariz." His jaw clenched and his eyes seemed to shudder as he spoke the name he had banished to his nightmares.

"Prince?" The guard's eyes widened and he beamed at him.

"Welcome, Prince Eisen," The other guard said and pressed a hand to his forehead in greeting. "Please forgive us. It's been too long dear brother!"

"No worries, Shohaib," Zul said. The young man before him had always been so quiet before he'd met him. Zul noticed that whenever they spoke, Shohaib would smile and talk as much as he wanted to. It had made

Zul happy knowing that the young man had someone he could talk to. Someone that could be a friend.

"Was I expected?" Zul forced himself to speak. He hated how weak he sounded. He wanted to look away. His heart hammered, and his mind wanted him to turn and run.

"Oh, the King and Queen would be delighted at your visit," said the other guard. But, Zul saw the look in Shohaib's eyes. A look of pity as he glanced at the palace.

"Welcome home, Habibi," The guards both said in unison, and pulled open the gates.

Zul Sharr walked towards the mansion with heavy and forced steps. It was Eid, and he was going to be the bigger person. It had been so long since he'd last seen his family, and they hadn't even tried to get in contact with him. Though, he supposed, maybe they were justified in that. But still, he wasn't going to turn back. He needed this. This was for him. Not them.

The guard, Shohaib followed behind Zul Sharr until they reached the door. "Be safe, Eisen. Remember, la Hawla wa la quwatta illah billah." *There's no might or power except with God.*

Zul pressed a hand to his heart. "May the Divine smile upon you, brother. I'm glad to see you."

"Me too," said Shohaib, a small sad smile appearing over his lips. Zul hated to see it. Even more so, when he noticed the scar across the guard's forehead.

The guard knocked and then unlocked the door.

Zul Sharr's heart thundered, and his fingers tightened around the bag he carried. He heard his father's voice inside. "Who has graced us with a visit this blessed day?"

"Respected young prince Eisen has arrived. May the Most Merciful smile upon you. May you make the respected Queen and King honoured. Have a blessed day today on this joyous day of Eid." The guard nodded his head and Zul Sharr nodded back.

They both gave each other a look. And Zul could tell the guard was putting on a mask. The very same mask most wore around the prince. Addressing him with the utmost respect, especially in public, or around the king and queen. Speaking to him as if they were nothing but beneath him. His eyes spoke, as if Shohaib was saying to be careful, but to also not worry. The man walked back to his post. The only one here who seemed to see him for who he truly was.

His father was first to appear. As he approached, Zul saw his brows furrow. Before he could speak, Zul Sharr's mother, Queen Laiqa, glided to her husband's side.

"Eisen? Oh, he decided to return! See Hariz? The silly boy's senses returned. My poor son. I told you he's not the monster you always say he is." Her voice lilted with a sort of sickly delight that made Zul feel nauseous.

"I never said that, Laiqa…"

"Come in! You brought gifts? Oh… we've prepared such a feast! And this time I cooked it, so you know how great it'll be." She pulled Zul Sharr inside.

Zul's arm trembled. He abhorred her touch. His own skin held the memory. Her touch equated pain and fear. The times she'd beaten him.

The time she'd pulled his limbs so strongly, he thought she would snap his bones to the marrow.

"Look at you. You've dressed so nicely. Just like a handsome prince. You are my handsome young man." She grinned at him and looked him up and down. She left to the living room.

He knew what she was doing. She was buttering him up, softening his mind until it was weak and pliable, just the way she liked it.

"What name would you prefer I call you?" King Harriz spoke tersely.

Zul's lips turned into a lopsided smirk. "If you can manage calling me son. That would be great," Zul Sharr said and before he could walk to the living room, his father spoke again.

"Today is Eid, so for that reason, I will forgive you for what you did. The last time you came here."

"You know the Iron Grip is with Ansam, so why mention that?" Zul said as they walked into the main living room.

It wasn't the same as he'd remembered it. The deep blue hardwood flooring, the iron ceiling lamps and gray walls. It made him think of dusk. When he could hear the faint quarrelling of his parents before he woke. The gold couches were familiar. He pressed a finger to a nook in the wall, where he had marked how tall he was getting. His name was still engraved there.

"You still took it. It is an act of treason."

Zul regarded his father. "I'm not here to fight, father. It's Eid today and I wanted to celebrate. We have a right to uphold ties of kinship. And I expect to enjoy this. However much mother might try otherwise. How do you still live with her?"

Hariz didn't meet Zul's gaze when he spoke. "I keep quiet. That's how."

Queen Laiqa entered the room, Zul's two sisters following behind her.

"Eisen? Oh my God! It's you!" His youngest sister, aged twelve ran up to him. She grabbed his arm and giggled as he messed with her hair.

"Looks like you've gotten stronger, Fariza," Zul said and smiled. He sat up straight and kissed the top of her head. A slim braid was coiled around her head while locks of loose hair brushed the top of her red and gold blouse.

"You're here? It's been so long, Eisen!" Twenty-year old Aliya rushed to him, beaming.

"Have you been annoying your aunt like usual?" Zul Sharr said, clasping her hands warmly with his own.

A mischievous grin crept up Aliya's face. "Yeah… but I've been good." She pulled him toward the kitchen. "Come on, can we see what you brought?"

"Ah, Eisen. You've become such a handsome man." His aunt sat on one of the black loveseats.

Zul walked up to her with a smile and she passed a hand over his head. He leaned in and she kissed the top of his head. "Are you doing well?"

"The Divine be praised. Your sisters are little angels."

Then Aliya and Fariza pulled him toward the kitchen.

Zul Sharr enjoyed the presence of his sisters. With all the darkness from his mother, his sisters were a light. They were a reminder to him, that somewhere deep inside him was still a person who wanted to smile, to care for others, to nurture and protect and to live. To love.

"Your aunt and uncle have been spoiling you two. Have they been taking care of you?" Queen Laiqa whispered as she tugged on Fariza's arm and inspected her face and hands.

"Yeah, I'm fine." Fariza squirmed out of her hold and nearly smacked Laiqa in the face, as she ran to Zul Sharr's side.

"See, your sister has taken my daughters from me," Queen Laiqa said to her husband, the familiar bite in her voice now rising to the surface. The tension in her voice now coming to life.

"Oh no... she's starting to lose it," Aliya whispered to Zul and chuckled. "How have you been?"

Zul's smile fell, his heart beating loud, and he pulled out the boxes from his bag and lay them on the dining table. "Oh, I've been good. I've been busy."

His mother walked in. "Yeah, too busy defying us. Probably living with that jinni."

"Mom!" Zul Sharr said, his voice biting. "Don't say that around them. Besides, she doesn't live with us anymore. More like pops out of nowhere." His voice a whisper as he tilted toward her.

"It's true. Who knows what shameless things you do." Queen Laiqa shrugged.

The heat rose in Zul's face. Anger was bubbling on the surface and he was afraid she'd make him lose his cool. Always jabbing at his heart. Why did she have to think the worst of him?

“That’s enough, Laiqa,” Hariz said as he walked past her and to the table. “We’re going to have breakfast soon. Our… son came here. The least you can do is be nicer to him today.”

“Thank you, father. At least you know how to think,” Zul said with a sigh and cringed at his own words. He shouldn’t say anything to anger her. It didn’t matter. She’d always find a way to hurt him.

“Fine. Let’s eat. Before I lose my appetite,” Queen Laiqa said and sat at the end of the table.

The food soon arrived, and the Queen became surprisingly mellow as they ate. She spoke, but Zul tried not to pay any attention; he had learned to block out her voice for so long, it had become an art form.

After they had their meal of spiced rice with lamb and eggs, his sisters opened their gifts. For Aliya, he’d bought a gorgeous silk dress. She held it up against her.

“It’s gorgeous, Eisen! And it’s blue and not too girly either. You know me so well, thank you.”

For Fariza he found a necklace with a tear-dropped blue lapis lazuli gem and a new blouse. He’d also brought beignets for them to share.

Fariza played with the gem, slipping it over in her fingertips. “I love it, Eisy. Thank you!” When she was little she couldn’t pronounce his name, so Eisy had become his nickname.

He could still remember little Fariza, her small face bereft of colour, her eyes wide as she stilled. She had clung to him as his mother’s voice grew loud, spreading poison through the house, suffocating everyone. He’d been there to comfort his sisters. When his mother yelled at them, he was their shield, taking the blows. And of course, his interference only earned him further beatings. But he would always reemerge smiling at his sisters. He would hide the pain, always for their sake.

"You're welcome, sweet Fariza." He pushed back a lock of her hair and smiled at her. "Now, come on, eat up the beignets, before I take yours too."

"No, Eisy, we have to share!"

"Hey, I'm not the one who doesn't know how to share," Zul Sharr said with a teasing wink and grabbed the treat from Fariza's sticky fingers.

His mother tutted from the other end of the table. "Why are you always keeping them away from me?"

"What?" Zul Sharr said. "We're just eating the desserts. You should have one."

"No, I made them for my children. What happened to you, Eisen? I loved you more than them. Why did you have to hurt us like you did?"

"You shouldn't love one child more than the other…" Zul Sharr stopped himself. If he said more, she'd use his emotions against him. It was still hard to stay quiet though.

"Oh? Well your father has always loved you more than he loves me! Hariz! Tell him. Tell us the truth, once and for all. Tell him that, even though he betrayed us, and even though I've stood by your side, running this family as well as this kingdom, you would still choose him over me."

"Laiqa…" Hariz's voice was tense.

"See? You can't even answer me. He's the reason for all my problems. My daughters don't love me. He took them away from me. I should have never given birth to him! He should have died. He's the reason this family's so broken!"

Zul pressed his hands against his ears, but he could still hear the noise.

His aunt was with his sisters. She'd always keep them away from their mother when she became loud.

Fariza turned to their mother. "Shut up!"

Their aunt pulled Fariza away, turning her to the living room. "It's so pretty on you." Her voice was composed as she held up the blouse to Fariza's body.

"When will you stop? Today is Eid, for Divine's sake. We're not supposed to be fighting." Zul finally spoke out.

"I'm so sick of you yelling at us. Eisen came to visit! He's finally here and you're messing it up!" Aliya said.

Zul met his sister's gaze. The circles under her eyes and the way her face was pinched showed just how much she'd been through. He wanted to pull her into a hug.

"Laiqa. It's Eid, we need to enjoy, not fight and become angry."

"Angry?" Laiqa turned to Zul. "You are my heart Eisen. I loved you so much. And now you want to leave us. I haven't said anything to hurt you," she said, her voice softening.

Zul's chest tightened and his breath was heavy. "You just said I should have died," he said sharply.

"I never said that! I would never!" Laiqa breathed.

"You just said that a few minutes ago. I can't believe this…" Zul turned his back to her and his sister had walked into the living room.

"Eisy, you want to see the latest facts I learned?" Fariza called out to him.

“I… yeah.” Zul sighed and before he left, he gave his mother a cold stare.

Zul pushed away from the table, taking Aliya with him, but his mother’s voice continued to trail after him.

“See how spoilt he’s become?” Laiqa said to Hariz. “He doesn’t even respect his own mother anymore. It’s your fault. If only he would listen and do what he’s told.”

His mother’s words simmered within him. Spoiled, was he? When he had lived here, everyday she’d scream at him. Everyday she’d beat him. Everyday she’d blame him. Every single damn day she’d remind him that she owned him like a toy. To play with. Never appreciating that she had a family who wanted to love her. He was a prisoner in his own kingdom. But he’d escaped now, and he’d be damned if he was ever going to return to the life he had fought so hard to be free of.

In the guest bedroom, Fariza was showing off her dress to their aunt.

“Don’t worry, son.” His aunt passed her hand over his head. “You are not alone. If you ever need anything, I am here. My door is always open to you.”

His aunt had already done so much by taking in his sisters. “Thank you...” He couldn’t burden her.

“You could come live with us,” Aliya said.

That pleading look in her eyes made his heart ache. He wished he could. He’d never planned to leave his sisters alone with their mother. Before he had gone over to Sanari’s palace, he had replayed the scenario over and over in his head days before: Go to Sanari’s palace, talk to her parents about wanting to marry Sanari. Have Sanari talk to him in their living room and spend hours talking. Take weeks, even if it took months to get to know her better and eventually, he hoped to marry her. Then, take Aliya and Fariza with him. But, he'd never thought it would go: Get beaten by his mother, go over to Sanari's palace, and have his iron lose control and have his beloved and her family go into a cursed sleep. Become drowned in despair and his blood cursed by jinni magic.

He smiled. "Don't worry about me. I'm just glad you're both okay."

Zul and his aunt decided it was enough by the time it was the afternoon.

"We're leaving," Zul Sharr said as he slipped his arms into his coat.

"Already?" Fariza said.

"Yeah. But, I'll try to visit you with our aunt, okay?"

"Take care and don't listen to her, Eisen." His aunt held his shoulder. "You are a great young man and it's not your fault." She kissed the top of his head.

If only he could believe her.

"Eisen… take care of yourself, okay? Don't forget to visit us," Aliya said and stood at the door in a coat and hat.

"You've shamed me enough. Telling me that I wronged you? A mother never wrongs her children!" Her voice softened, but he could only hear desperation. "Even my rebukes are only sweetness in disguise," Laiqa said as she stood in front of the door.

Zul was out of the door, before she had a chance to stand too close to him.

“Eid Mubarak,” He said, his face emotionless when he looked at his mother and father.

Zul could see something of both regret and pity in his father’s eyes.

Zul Sharr waved to his sisters and aunt and smiled at them widely. The best fake smile he could muster and walked on ahead.

He walked through the gate, hardly noticing the guards. The gate was the cage he had just been released from once again. But even as the gates of his personal prison faded into the distance, he knew he was far from free.

Chapter 7 Taste of life

Now back in Veer City, Zul Sharr rushed up the stairs. His heart was pounding as he opened the door to one room. His face reddened and with slow steps he walked in.

Sanari was in one of the beds, her mother and father beside her. Slick metal still encapsulated their bodies. They were painted in silver.

Zul Sharr walked up to her bed. "Eid Mubarak, Sanari. I'm sorry you couldn't even see Ramadan or Eid this year." He smiled faintly at the memories of her. When he saw her enter the Eid festivals which were one of the largest celebrations in Noorenia. When she'd press her lips together when she felt surprised. She used to illuminate his life and the lives of others with her kindness and determination. Now, she was laying still.

"I promise you, Sanari. I will find a way to break this curse." Zul's voice wavered as he sank to his knees. He looked over at the Fire Kingdom King and Queen. "I never meant for this to happen. I didn't do it on purpose. Please—"

Tears rolled down his cheek. "I hope you forgive me. I'm sorry. I'll wake up all of you one day."

***

The energy which had flowed through her like her own blood had opened Amaya to another feeling of control. She'd felt like things in her world were all becoming mundane. No flow like the water that rushed through the swamp last night.

She'd been too exhausted to say anything to Lexa when she had returned. She'd been asleep till the afternoon. The sun's thin strands of light peeked from the curtains as Amaya entered the kitchen, finding Lexa. Zul Sharr joined them shortly after.

"Oh, hello there, Zul Sharr," Amaya said and smiled faintly.

"Looks like you're well rested. You hungry for lunch?" Zul Sharr asked as he headed to the table.

Amaya walked up to the table as they both took a seat.

Someone new stared at her, making her flinch.

Then she noticed his black wings, which were flattened to his sides. The sadness that always remained in his light green eyes also gave him away. The pale brown of his human-looking skin was a shocking contrast to the rich pelt Amaya had become used to associating him with. His lips were pouty, and he had high cheekbones. This was Obsidian.

"Hello, Obsidian. You aren't a unicorn?" Amaya said and sat in front of him. She noticed the red collar gleaming around his neck. She thought she saw it ripple.

Obsidian's intense gaze landed on Amaya for a couple of seconds.

Amaya's lips twitched. "I'm sorry." She felt like his eyes were prying into her soul.

Lexa appeared at the entrance of the kitchen. "Hello my darling water elemental. You did a great job last night." She grinned at her.

Amaya sat with her back pressed to the chair, unable to relax her posture. *It's strange interacting with them… I hardly know them.*

Lexa tilted her head at her and smirked. She had a strange hunger in her eyes. "I was thinking of going out to get ice cream as a dessert."

"You eat human food?" Amaya blurted and stared at the plate of what Zul Sharr had called chicken bastilla, which he placed in the middle of the table. Beside it was a bowl of salad with various vegetables and salad dressing.

"Yes, actually, we eat too! Just because I'm a jinni, doesn't mean we don't have lives," Lexa said and looked at Amaya in a disapproving manner.

Amaya shook her head. "I didn't know."

"Ice cream huh? Bring mint chocolate ripple. It's my favourite!" Zul Sharr said as he plated out portions of the bastilla for everyone.

"I was thinking of fudge ice cream with brownie pieces and caramel sauce."

"Even your treats are indulgent," Zul Sharr said with sarcasm and started eating.

"Hmmpf. What about you, Amaya? What's your favorite?" Lexa asked.

"Well… mango ice cream… or vanilla."

"They fit your personality," Zul said after a gulp of water.

"What do you mean by that?" Amaya asked.

Zul Sharr placed the glass down. "Both seem simple, but mango carries a tang, while vanilla is a base that's popular, it can compliment other flavours."

"Are you trying to get along with me?" Amaya asked.

Zul Sharr smiled. "Well, yeah."

"What about you, Obsidian? You've been away since morning," Lexa said.

"It took a while to wash off that blood from last night." Obsidian grunted in disgust. "Peanut butter ice cream for me."

"Oh." Zul Sharr drawled and then smirked at Lexa. "Are you sure you don't want anyone with you?"

"What for, Sire?"

"For damage control."

Rana snickered from the living room.

"No need. Can't you trust me?" Lexa said with a grin.

"Not when you're alone." Zul Sharr grinned.

***

Lexa walked the cobblestone walkway through the main market square in downtown Veer City. To her right, was the produce stands.

"Ugh, I'm so bored…ever since Sire's been saying he wants to celebrate today, I haven't had a chance to taunt anyone," Lexa mumbled.

People started filling the area as she walked deeper into the markets and crossed a street. She had checked online about ice cream shops, but wasn't sure which to choose and would be best. Reviews didn't help. Both parlours were around the same area too.

Decayed leaves swirled over her head as she passed an alleyway. *I'll have to make my own fun.* Lexa walked into the darkness and took the form of a grey cat, her eyes the same stunning green. She walked back out and sat, her tongue lapping at her fur. She purred and kept glancing at the people who would pass.

Finally, a woman with a half-eaten ice cream cone walked by. All alone, with no one by her side. Perfect.

"Aww, you're so cute!" The woman said as Lexa weaved in and around her legs and meowed up at her. She walked a few steps toward the alley and stared back at the woman. The shadows crept by Lexa's feet and pulled the woman, ever so gently, fooling her into believing it was her own heart who led her toward the seemingly sweet-natured feline.

"Hehe, I guess I can pet you a little more." The woman bent down to pet Lexa's back. In return Lexa pushed her head into the woman's palm and then walked closer toward the alley, until they were right in front of it.

The woman finished her ice cream and wiped her fingers on a napkin. "Hmm, where's the garbage can? Oh, there's a bin in the alley. I guess I can throw this in there."

Perfect.

As the woman threw her garbage in the bin, the shadows around Lexa pulled the woman and pinned her to the wall.

A man walked into the alley and she did not expect that would happen.

"What?" The woman breathed out and gasped. "Let go!"

This was not what Lexa had in mind. She'd simply wanted to toy with the human. Besides, she enjoyed torturing. Killing was only when she was in a very bad mood.

The man grabbed the woman by the waist as she thrashed. "Shut up, or else!" The man shouted.

Lexa jumped up to her and became her human form.

The woman tried to scream, but the shadows muffled her voice.

Several dark fingers clasped around the man who had his hands around the woman and threw him into the bins.

The shadows held the woman before she had a chance to run. "Don't tell anyone what happened here," Lexa said to her in a sharp voice as the woman nodded. "By the way, where did you get that ice cream from?" Lexa asked sweetly.

"I…the Dulce Parlor…Thank you…" the woman sniffled and rushed out into the street.

Lexa turned her attention to the man who groaned and elbowed off a bag from his chest.

"Wanting to fulfill your greed in broad daylight? How despicable. For a mere coin. You humans can be truly disgusting creatures." Lexa walked over to him and with her shadows she lifted him out of the bin and pinned him to the floor of the alley.

"What?" The man looked around. He was still dazed from his fall.

"Trying to find the other woman?" Lexa said as she stood in front of him.

He tried to grab her, but the shadows crawled over his hand and broke his wrist. He yelped.

"You made me lose my prey. You think I'm a fragile human woman? You men folk think a slip of skin is an invitation. Women owe you nothing. I could taste your desires off you like a confection. It was delectable. And your suffering will be even more decadent." Her eyes swam with malice as she sat beside him.

"W—what? A jinni… no…stay away!"

Lexa's lips curled. She summoned her daggers of shadow and held three to his neck. "I'll peel you bit by bit, and savour the flavour of agony." Her eyes shot to him and she licked her lips. "Let's have fun!"

The man's muffled screams were heard by no one.

"Mm, so Dulce Parlor huh?" Lexa smiled as she saw the sign before her. Outside, the shop was built with terra cotta stone. After she'd killed and disposed of the man, she had found the ice cream shop.

"Oh, how I spoil myself."

They were well known for their cold treats for being thick and creamy.

"Hello miss! Welcome. What flavour can I get you?" A woman spoke at the counter, a cheery smile glowing over her face.

Lexa nearly had a laughing fit as she covered her mouth. *I've already tasted an addictive flavour.* After she composed herself, she spoke. "I'll buy four of your tubs of ice cream."

***

"Where's Lexa?" Rana asked as she sat on the sofa.

"Oh, she went to get ice cream," said Zul Sharr

"And, no one asked me?" Rana said and glanced at Zul.

"I wasn't sure. I thought you only ate meat…"

"Ah, I see." Rana's gaze drifted off into the distance.

"Where's your mind at? Are you all right?" Zul Sharr asked.

"Sire, I just need to speak to Lexa."

Rana had spent last night with the wolves.

In the form of a crow, she'd fled into the forest. The night air held the scent of a deer long dead. Four wolves sat on their bellies, filled with their recent prey. Rana landed beside them and shifted into her jinni form. Rana stretched her arms out, her black hair falling into veins over her shoulder. Her hand met the soft fur of her comrade.

One of the wolves pressed their muzzle against her neck, her wet nose and soft fur comforting Rana. She'd been with this pack for years. Following them for every meal, gathering with them during the night to sleep under the canopy of stars. When they howled at the moon calling each other, she would heed the call. When they had taken her in on the night she'd lost her parents, she'd become family.

"Nina…I was worried when you told me about the other wolves." Rana slouched and then moved to lie beside the grey wolf. The mother of this pack.

"You have been too careless Rana." Nina licked Rana's forehead. "I do not understand why you take the company of that shadow jinni. They are known to be ruthless, wicked, and secretive creatures."

Rana played with the lighter cream fur sticking out from Nina's belly. "She is a beloved friend… She is ruthless no doubt, but so are we." A small delicate smile cracked from her lips.

Nina gave a small huff of approval.

Lexa never stayed too long in the presence of the wolves, saying she preferred the other shadow jinn and shapeshifters. When Lexa was with Rana, they always found time to simply sit and chat. A luxury Rana never believed she could afford.

Rana had always thrived on staying moving. Taking a breath, keeping one location to rest was not in her nature, but with Lexa she had taken those risks. They had shared their meals and, reluctantly, Lexa had once even spent a short period with the wolves after one of their hunts.

Rana would not forget the times other jinn had tried to kill them in the middle of the night and how gracefully Lexa had defended her. Even when Rana had spent the nights crying in the days after losing her family, Lexa had been there beside her. More than a shadow. She'd been a comfort, a hope, and the ever-present hunger for chaos in her eyes was somehow exciting. Rana would be her confidante to her last breath.

She looked up toward the open mouth of their den. The stars winked back at her and she felt Nina's breathing slow. She'd fallen asleep. Rana shifted onto her side. Tonight, she would rest at ease. For tonight her heart was not filled with doubts, but with the salve of opportunities. Reminding her of the bonds she'd forged and wished to keep.

***

Lexa materialized into the kitchen, startling Amaya and nearly causing her to drop the glass she'd been filling with water.

"Get your ice cream, here! Cold and creamy!" Lexa announced.

"Damn it, Lexa! Use the door!" Zul said and jumped in his seat.

"Lexa!" Rana crowed.

Lexa placed the tubs on the dinner table and laughed.

Obsidian rushed into the kitchen. "What's going on here?"

He was still tying the strings that dangled from the waist of his tunic, its chainmail shoulders rattling.

"I brought ice cream and nearly gave everyone a heart attack," Lexa said with a smirk.

"Come on, let's try to enjoy ourselves. We probably won't get another chance too for a while." Zul Sharr helped Lexa place sundae glasses and cones on the table.

Rana poked Lexa's shoulder. "Lexa, I need a word with you."

"At a time like thi—oh. Okay." Lexa noticed the murderous look in Rana's eyes.

Lexa led Rana to the farthest end of the living room.

"I know that water jawhar was manipulating the wolves. They told me what transpired last night," Rana said and played with her hands.

"I didn't hurt them, Rana. You remember I told you there would be no bloodshed, except for Amaya. It pricked her. There was no wolf blood, I assure you."

"Lexa, I don't want them to be involved," Rana said sharply. "They became my family when my parents were slaughtered in front of me. You know that!"

When she was sixteen, Rana's parents had been slaughtered by another, larger jinni who was defending his territory. She had seen for herself the last blow, just as two wolves tried to protect them. She had run off into the woods. That's where a pack of wolves found her. The clan took her in and told her they could be family. They would never abandon their own.

Lexa's eyes softened. "I know your bond with the creatures. From here on out, I won't use them."

Rana heaved a sigh. "Good."

“Oh, Rana. Why do you stick with me? I can’t imagine how you put up with me.” Lexa chuckled, but Rana answered her in a serious tone.

“You gave me your friendship in my time of need. Companionship when I was alone. I owe you that with my love and loyalty, Lexa.”

Lexa turned to her, a wistful look in her eyes that disappeared as soon as it flashed on her face. She embraced her. “Come on, my voluptuous gal, are you sure you don’t want ice cream? Mine has caramel sauce. Maybe you’ll enjoy that?”

Rana gave her a closed lipped smile. “You’ll let me lick off all the caramel?”

“That’s gross. No. You get your own glass.” Lexa said and chuckled as they walked back into the kitchen.

***

At the table, Amaya stared at Lexa. “Why haven’t you told me who the fox is yet? I demand you tell me!” Amaya said.

“She’s determined. I respect someone who doesn’t keep silent when something needs to be done,” Obsidian said as he spooned some of the peanut butter ice cream into his mouth.

“That was only the first phase of my plan. You haven’t even met the angels or the humans who journey with them. As soon as you can battle them, I’ll tell you where the fox is. Remember the deal Amaya.” Lexa’s eyes flashed as she licked her spoon.

Amaya looked down at her vanilla ice cream, stirring it with her spoon. “After I’m done with your plan, you’ll tell me,” Amaya said, her voice quiet.

“I will. I told you I will. Now, enjoy your dessert, because soon we need to get serious,” Lexa said and sucked off the caramel that enrobed her finger.

Chapter 8 Veer City

Nezha answered the call as she stood outside the centre where they were celebrating. “Hey! How are you?”

“I’m fine, Nezha. How are you?” Sapphire spoke on the other end of the call.

“I’m good. I didn’t hear from you in a while. Is everything okay, or has Zul Sharr been up to something?”

“I’m not sure if it’s him. Something did come up. I cannot explain on the phone.”

“Does that mean I should return to Noorenia?” Nezha was smiling.

“Yes. I’m sorry, I know you’re on holiday.”

“This is an emergency, isn’t it?”

“I wanted to keep you updated. It’s not necessarily something we can’t handle. But you needed to know.”

“Are you sure you can’t be any more specific about it?” Nezha’s chest tightened. She really hoped that nothing bad had happened.

There was a pause from Sapphire before she spoke. “Veer City was threatened. The mayor notified the Iron Kingdom and they want us to go and see what happened. They believe it had something to do with elementals.”

“Oh. Well, that does sound like an emergency…”

"Nezha dear. Don't leave your family on our account. This was just to keep you updated."

"Nezha! Come on, it's time for dinner!" Her mother called her from the door. "Who's on the line?"

"One moment, Sapphire," Nezha said and cupped her hand over her cell.

"It's Sapphire from Noorenia, ma. She was calling to update me."

"Oh. Wonderful. Can you tell her to give my regards to Tasa and Sanari?"

Nezha smiled faintly. The mention of Sanari reminded her of the orb, and how important it was that the Angel of Mercy receive his soul. The natural flow of Noorenia, also called the beating heart of the land, was deteriorating. They had no idea where the body even was. Nezha didn't want Noorenia to die. That world had become a home to her. A place she felt she belonged. Losing it would mean losing a part of herself. She couldn't let that happen.

"I will mom," Nezha said softly.

"Okay. When you're done, please come in to eat. We have Milk bastilla and chum chum," Najwa sang as she left.

Nezha spoke into the phone once more. "My mother wants you to give her regards to Tasa and, Sapphire, I'll be there tonight."

"No rush. We will see you later!" Sapphire said.

"See you later, bye!" Nezha disconnected the call.

She turned to see the smoky sky. The greys were brushstrokes against the white of the clouds. Above the setting sun, the sky became a wavy line of lava.

Nezha yearned to go back to Noorenia. She knew her time there had just begun. She couldn't keep the soul forever. Even if it was whole, there would still be those who would want her dead.

***

Zul Sharr had managed to persuade Lexa and the others to leave him to his own devices.

He walked down the street and headed downtown. Veer was a big city. It had several communities scattered within it. It was known as the most modern in both economy and thinking. The swamp and forest were the only greenery in it, besides the field which separated it from his country, Qadam which neighboured it.

Zul passed countless malls, cafes, and a small flower shop. He made it to a bus station. The walls of the station were made of slick and polished purple stone which was so pale it almost looked grey in the shadows.

He stuffed his hands into his pockets. He hadn't yet had a chance to change out of his Eid clothes.

"Eisen? Salaam, bud!" It was his friend Shayan.

Zul Sharr nodded at him. "Wa alaykum as Salaam, Shay." Hearing his old name made him shiver even more than the cold did.

"I'm glad you decided to go to the festival with me. I haven't seen you in so long! Give me a hug brother!" Shayan flashed him a smile and wrapped an arm around Zul's shoulders. His teeth shone white as if they were pearls in the sand. He wore a burnt orange knee-length coat that seemed two-tone. A purple scarf was wrapped around his neck and tucked into his top. It was chilly at this time of the day. His black hair was wavy and reminded Zul of a lion's mane.

"Yeah, life's been really chaotic." Zul shrugged and chuckled as he returned the embrace.

"Well, the Divine's given you a chance to relax a little and have some fun, prince." Shayan nudged Zul's arm. "Don't you think?"

"Yeah. You're right." Zul smiled. After so long, he was truly smiling, his eyes mirroring the joy. Right now, he felt free. He felt like an individual who could make his own decisions. When the bus arrived, they boarded it to the festival.

***

Nezha returned home at nightfall and was standing by the pond. Comet was in front of her, kicking at and chewing her toy mouse filled with catnip. Nezha sighed and stared at the pond. It had been a long and fun day for her. She'd already packed up and kissed and hugged her parents.

"Let's go, Comet! Our return to Noorenia!" Nezha said as she tugged at the straps of her bag and then grabbed Comet with one arm. She jumped into the pond as she thought of her intention to return.

It was the afternoon in Noorenia as Nezha emerged from the pond and the instant she did, it was Thunderbolt who helped her out of the water, his hand meeting hers.

"She's back!" He smiled at her and turned to Sapphire and Kayan who stood a foot behind him.

"Nezha!" Sapphire embraced her. "Welcome back." She kissed the top of her head.

"It's good to be back, everyone!"

"Hey, Nezha!" Kayan smiled widely at her. When he got closer, his jaw dropped.

Nezha looked at him in confusion. Then she realized she didn't change from her Eid clothing. Although she had her hijab on, she still looked more like she was going to a party. Perhaps even dressed as a royal.

"Uh…" Kayan's face reddened, and he averted his gaze. He started to rapidly breathe in and out and mumbled. "Don't ever stare…just breathe."

Nezha tilted her head. "Um, hey, is he hyperventilating?"

"Oh, he'll be fine! You're a jaw dropper." Thunderbolt slapped Kayan's back. "She is beautiful as always."

"Did you miss me?" Nezha asked Thunderbolt and poked his head.

"Miss you? Why? You weren't gone too long," he said, averting his gaze and ruffling his hair.

Nezha raised an eyebrow. "I was gone for three months."

"Okay… fine! I did miss you! Welcome home!" He pulled her in by the shoulders, letting her go as quickly.

"I knew it, you big softie." Nezha rearranged her hijab. "By the way, I brought gifts!"

"Right. For Eid." Kayan smiled bashfully as he regained his composure.

"Yeah! You didn't think I'd forget to get you all something, did you?" Nezha walked with them to Tasa's house.

Nezha nearly fell back as Tasa hugged her at the door. “Nezha! Oh, I’m so happy to see you again! How are you? Did you eat well? You probably ate a ton of sweets!”

Comet nuzzled Sapphire who carried her back to the house.

“Nezha smiled at her. “I’m good. Oh, you know me… of course I ate sweets!”

Kayan held up a purple tunic. “You bought us clothes too? You spoil us, Nezha.”

“Now, we should all discuss about what the mayor of Veer wants us to investigate,” Sapphire said as she slipped on a silver bangle which Nezha had brought for her. “It may involve another jawhar and possibly linked to Zul Sharr or the jinni Lexa.”

At the mention of Lexa, Nezha’s mind wandered to the memory of Savan, the jinni who had killed her aunt. He’d mentioned a lady. A jinni who had been behind it all. Who was the jinni that orchestrated Lamis’s death and just what was she after?

“No way. You’re all going to relax at least for tonight,” Tasa said before Nezha had a chance to say anything. “You know cous’, since you’ve been gone, they’ve been busy running around. Kayan spent time with his family, Sapphire and Thunderbolt went around the different cities including Veer City this morning. They all deserve rest.”

“I’m glad you’ve been keeping busy,” Nezha said as she pet Comet on her head.

“For the record, I didn’t agree to this,” Sapphire said.

“Sis, remember you once told me rest is good,” Thunderbolt said.

Sapphire folded her arms against her chest. “One night.”

Nezha smiled. “Hey, are there others celebrating Eid here today?”

“There is,” Thunderbolt said and stretched. “I saw posters downtown. They’re in every city.”

“I have an idea! Why not we go to the festivities, *and* we go and see the mayor! That way we get our break and do something productive,” Kayan said and smiled as Sapphire’s eyes lit up.

“I can agree with that,” Sapphire said.

“Hmm. I guess that sounds good. But, you all need to have fun too and relax a little,” Tasa said and shot Sapphire a look.

“We will, *mom*,” Thunderbolt said.

“Why does everyone think I act like a mom?”

“Because you do!” They all said in unison.

Tasa placed her hands on her hips.

Nezha leaned in to Tasa. “But we need another authority figure, so Thunderbolt doesn’t needlessly pummel someone.”

Tasa smiled. “Well, I don’t mind taking care of you, *kids*.”

“Hey, I am not a bully! I’m a guardian angel, so I can pummel an evil doer if I want to.” Thunderbolt rolled his eyes.

“I’ll take care of Comet, so you won’t need to worry about her,” Tasa said.

“See? She’s our pet sitter too.” Thunderbolt nudged Sapphire as Kayan and Nezha walked to the door with them.

“And unwilling babysitter.” Tasa flashed him a cheeky smile.

Thunderbolt chuckled.

***

Shayan and Zul walked out of the centre where the Eid festival was held.

"Praying and seeing everyone enjoy themselves at the festival was refreshing to see!" Zul said, a smile lit across his face.

"Yeah, I bought more treats for my kids too," Shayan said as he held a gold paper bag stuffed with boxes of zalabia coated in honey and cinnamon and a bag of various toys.

"Why didn't the rest of your family join you?"

"We came here in the morning. I stayed back to help out, since I was volunteering," Shayan said.

"Oh, well you haven't changed," Zul Sharr said.

Shayan regarded him. "Something about you has changed though."

Zul was taken aback. "Yeah? Like what?" He laughed.

"I'm not exactly sure… you seemed sadder before. It's like you're a little brighter."

Zul widened his eyes.

"Or, maybe all that royal duty and responsibility isn't as hard as before, respected Iron Prince." Shayan smiled.

"Yeah, maybe so." Zul couldn't hide who he was from his friend. They'd spilled their hearts to each other for many years. Still, guilt buried into his heart when he realized how it felt like he'd lost a part of his self. The part of him that used to want friends and keep them. Now, it was enemies he had to keep close, so no one could hurt him again.

***

After flying across the field, Nezha and the group landed in Veer City. There, they walked through downtown. Nezha stared up at the tall buildings, and teal accented architecture, the glass winking in the sunlight. The white marble and sand-brown monuments merged with the metal structure of the business centre. In the distance a masjid in the same colour theme of teal, stood over a courtyard.

"I love when it's kind of cold," Kayan said with a grin.

"I prefer the warmth of summer," Nezha said unzipping her coat. The chill in the afternoon air was a mere tickle on her skin.

"No surprise there. You're a fire jawhar. This probably doesn't even bother you."

"Yeah. I don't feel it as much."

"Let's head to the bus station to get to the festival," Sapphire said.

Nezha's gaze shifted to the bus pulling in. People of different skin tones poured out. She noticed women in hijabs, some wrapped shawls around their heads and woolen hats. There were people who wore metal bracelets, and one person even had a robotic arm, tattooed like her henna adorned hands.

Two conversing men walked toward them. The one with a head cover was smiling and had a familiar face.

"Hey, isn't that…" Kayan said.

When the pair grew closer, the young man in a black coat looked up and met her gaze.

"Zul Sharr?" Nezha said and the two men stopped walking.

Sapphire and Thunderbolt soon noticed too and stood on either side of Nezha.

"Hey, Eisen, do you know them?" Shayan asked as they faced the group.

Nezha noticed the silver kaftan peeking from his coat and the bags which had the words Eid written on them.

"Eid Mubarak Nezha. How are you?" Zul Sharr smiled.

"Did he hit his head?" Thunderbolt whispered to Kayan.

"Maybe it's his doppelganger…" Kayan said and stared.

"Khayr Mubarak… Eisen." Nezha said after a pause. She kept her face composed. Without that solemn expression or exposed scorpion mark on his neck, he seemed like any normal young man.

"Oh, so you do know them," Shayan said and smiled, his shoulders easing.

"I'll be with you in a moment. I need to catch up with them," Zul said.

"Oh, okay. I'll see you soon. Eid Mubarak!" Shayan waved as he walked into the bus shelter.

"Interesting seeing you here," Thunderbolt said.

"Hey, it's Eid today. I'm not plotting anything so don't think this is some kind of trap," Zul said, the side of his lips upturned. "I won't consider you an enemy today. We are of the same faith."

"I never considered you an enemy, Zul Sharr. Only misguided," Nezha said.

He regarded her for a moment until speaking. "Well, then. I just came back from the festival. Did you know it was going on?" He asked, a bit hesitantly.

"Yeah, we know. We're headed there," Nezha replied.

"So… you had fun?" Thunderbolt asked. "When I see you next, I'll fight to destroy that evil inside you."

"Y-yeah. It was fun. They have sweets and the company is great," He quietly said back, "Looking forward to it." Zul's lips tugged into a slight smile.

Sapphire stared into his eyes. "May you have a blessed day. Eid Mubarak."

Zul's eyes widened and then he averted his gaze. "Thanks, Eid Mubarak."

"Well, we'll be on our way," Nezha said.

"Zul. Did you hear anything about Veer City? Something about a jawhar that gave them a scare," Thunderbolt said.

Nezha elbowed him. "What are you doing?"

"I can't say I have," Zul said as Thunderbolt stared at him with suspicion.

"Anyways, we'll be going," Nezha said.

"Enjoy the festivities everyone," Zul joined his friend.

"Well, that was kind of awkward, wasn't it?" Kayan said.

"Hmm. He and that jinni are probably behind that mess," Thunderbolt said, and formed fists.

"Well, maybe, but we're supposed to be enjoying the festival before we do anything else," Nezha said as they walked to the farther side of the station.

After the festival, they had taken one of the buses toward the mayor's office. The sun was beginning to set, and the sky bloomed with orange and pink clouds.

"Why didn't we just fly there?" Kayan asked. He was sitting beside Thunderbolt, with Nezha and Sapphire seated in front of them.

"The rules here a bit different in Veer City. It's not as open to elementals or even other creatures. They wouldn't appreciate us flying," Sapphire said.

The siblings' wings were tucked into their coats. "Seven hells, if I sprain my wings..." Thunderbolt grit his teeth and squirmed in his seat.

Nezha stared out of the window. Zul seemed happy. Without Lexa hovering around him, and without seeing the mark on his neck, he seemed like he was being himself. A part of her felt warmth knowing there was a glow to his face when he smiled.

"Nezha? We're here," Sapphire said.

They arrived in front of a tall, black-stoned building topped with a teal dome and frosted windows. The windowpanes were patterned in various shapes all in shades of blue, orange and green.

A man opened the door to greet them after they wrung the bell.

"Greetings! As Salaamu alaykum. I am Mayor Rustam. Welcome to Qudratistan! Veer City welcomes you in open arms." He smiled and held his hands out in a grand manner. He wore a quadrangular iroki scullcap on his head which was dark blue and embroidered in white. He had stubble over his oval face, and his hair was shaven on the sides, with short silvery-black hair on his head. He looked to be in his forties.

Rustam looked at his watch. "Come in, my guests."

"Thank you. We were concerned when you told us what happened recently," Sapphire said as they walked in.

"Please take a seat while we discuss," The mayor said.

Light blue walls contrasted the mayor’s terracotta skin, the orange-brown tone like the sun at midday. The short sleeves left his muscles bare.

As they seated, a man came in to place glasses of tea and plates of manti, glistening dumplings filled with lamb and served with yogurt for dipping. With freshly baked bread on the side and a large platter of halva and toasted apricot seeds, Nezha’s mouth was watering.

“Please eat as much as you like,” Rustam said. “You must be

Nezha Zaman of the Fire Kingdom family.”

“Yes, sir.” Nezha said.

“Call me uncle Rustam, child.” Rustam’s lips tautened before he spoke. “My city had an ominous intruder at dawn. Our swamp looked like it was bleeding, the moon just as red. A woman appeared in Sameer Forest. I still remember her eyes icy with hatred. She sat on a black karkadann with wings, and both were bathed in blood.”

Chapter 9 Acquisition

The curtain billowed as the stormy wind tumbled through the open window.

"Looks like I forgot to close it," Zul Sharr muttered. The storm had begun just a few minutes ago. Rain scattered around him as he stood, silhouetted by the setting sun. The horizon glowed in pinks and purples.

There was something red on the tree before his window. One white dove sat on a branch. Beside it rested another, its wing covered in blood.

Zul Sharr stared as the curtain whipped his face and lightning cleaved the sky.

"It's hurt." Zul turned to his bedroom door and locked it. He walked back to the window and opened his hand. His scythe flew to his palms, and he firmly grasped it. It melted into a ball of iron in his palm. He peeked his head out and regarded the wall. The rain pecked at his skin, sending cool bursts over his face and arms.

He pushed the iron and it sunk to the side of the window.

He wanted to save them. Something in him unhinged his fear of heights. He hesitated as he pulled the metal and formed a rope that coiled around a thick branch just above the two birds. The one that wasn't injured flapped its wings in protest at the metal's appearance.

Zul inhaled sharply and tugged at the rope. It didn't budge. It was at an incline, once he'd hang on it, he was sure he could slide to them. He formed a layer of iron over his palms. The last things he wanted were blisters.

He didn't dare look down. Lightning flashed again in the sky and thunder roared in response. He stood out on the ledge and as soon as his feet met the edge, he swung himself and grabbed the metal rope with both hands.

He slid to the tree. His heart was thumping in his throat, fear spilling over his chest, but he pressed the meaty parts of his fingers tightly around the rope as hard as he could. His mind screamed at him to grip his hands around the metal and stop his ride, but he couldn't, not when he'd gone this far. "Almost there…" he whispered.

He nearly slipped as he wove his legs around a branch and grasped the iron rope tightly to stop his movement. He breathed in heavily and reached out to the metal. It slipped and bent to his palms. Like putty, it obeyed him as he formed a slide under the branch where the doves remained perched. The one that bled let out a whimpering peep as the metal snaked down and into the gaping window. "Don't die… Don't let go…" Zul Sharr said between his teeth as he formed a metal ladder to the birds.

He was playing a deadly game with the storm. Too long out here and the lightning could strike him. Killing both him and possibly the other two lives in the tree.

"Shh. I won't hurt you," he said gently and placed a finger near the livelier bird. It crooned and peeped at him. He cupped his hands over the two birds, being careful with the wounded one's wing. He enveloped them in his shirt. "Shh. You're going to be okay," he purred to them, trying his best to calm them as he sat on the makeshift slide and slid.

Fortunately, by the time he reached the window, he dug in his heels and stopped. He looked down at the two birds. The wounded one looked up at him in quiet regard. "See? I told you you'd be okay." He smiled and placed them on his bed.

Zul Sharr sighed loudly. *What am I doing? But I couldn't leave them there. I know how it feels to be in pain, bleeding on the inside, with no one knowing. No one there to help me.*

He rummaged through his clothes and found a blue sweater. He formed the best nest he could and carefully sat the pair in the middle of it. "This'll keep you warm." Turning to the window, he pulled back the metal and formed his scythe, sending his weapon to the corner, and then shut the window.

"I'll have to clean your wing. Let's see how it looks." Zul sat on the bed and inspected the dove's wing. Its eyes were wide and it clearly was still afraid as the other one dug its head under its mate's chest. "I won't hurt you, I promise. I'll even find some food and water for you." He placed a finger on the bird's wing and the blood stopped. He couldn't heal it, but he could aid the healing. The best he could do was stop the bleeding and form a layer of dried blood over the open wound. "There. Doesn't that feel a little better?" Zul stood up.

The other bird cooed and the injured one fluffed its feathers. It squirmed a bit in his sweater, still rather tense, but appearing more relaxed than before.

"Now… I need to find food and water." He stared at the birds.

“Sire?” A knock sounded at the door. Lexa stood behind it. “You keep saying you want privacy and to knock, and what not…so, I’m knocking.”

“Lexa? Wait a second.” Zul glanced at his table. How was he supposed to hide them?

He then formed a square out of iron and tried making it look like a cage with bars. He cocked his head. “Close enough.”

Zul Sharr picked up their nest, placed them on the table and placed the cage over them. “Sorry… I’m not much of an architect.” He threw a shirt over them and then opened the door to Lexa.

“Sire? I was thinking of...” Lexa looked at his face and then glanced around the room. “Why are you red? What have you been doing in here?” she asked, a lilt in her voice.

“Nothing, just working out,” Zul lied, and stretched. “Why’d you say it like that?”

“I’m not sorry, Sire. You just seemed so out of breath.”

“Lexa…”

Lexa chuckled. “Okay, Okay... I’m sorry,” she drawled. “Better? Anyways, Sire, I was thinking, if you’re not busy anymore, you could try that blood manipulation. Amaya is up for helping you. Even if she resists, I can make her.” Lexa’s grin grew and the shadows around her arms deepened, coiling up to her neck.

Zul Sharr raised a brow. “No need for force, when she’ll do it in order to get answers.” Zul’s voice regained a malicious tone. “Actually, let’s do that.” He was reminded of his true motivation. Sanari. Although, he glanced at the corner belonging to the covered birds. *Later. I’ll get to them later. They’ll be fine.* Lexa and Zul left the room.

***

Numbness wrapped Amaya's skin again. The cold sunk into her bones like teeth. She'd felt it whenever a thought about her family, or the fox crept in. She felt as if the dress of shadows had entered her bloodstream and had taken her hostage. She had to please Lexa and the others' plans. She had to indulge her desire to wield water in battle and fight the angels and jawhars she kept being told about. She couldn't be herself. The swimmer, the daughter, the sister, the individual who hated loneliness. Loneliness felt like water becoming stagnant. She wanted the rush of love and joy. To be a current.

"Nezha and the angels are your enemies, Amaya. They are *our* enemies. I don't want you to kill them. Death would deprive me of inflicting my wrath upon them. No one but I will get to be Death's apprentice. As Death greets everyone, it does not warn you when it will take you, or how." Lexa spoke as Zul Sharr stood by her side.

Amaya nodded. "What is your request?"

"Darling, you must taunt them." Lexa bit her lip.

Zul Sharr whispered, "Lexa… Hello, the blood manipulation."

"Yes, I'm getting to that," Lexa said and grabbed Amaya's hand, tugging her toward Zul.

"Blood manipulation?" Amaya asked.

"Yes, it would help you with your elemental powers in return. Sire needs to refine his forte." Lexa's eyes glittered.

"Amaya, there's a storm out, so there's a lot of water. It's ideal conditions for it, don't you think?" Zul Sharr asked.

"Yes. I'll agree…but… the answers… The fox…" Amaya struggled to say.

"Lexa… I think you'll break her if you pressure her too much," Zul Sharr warned, noticing the way Amaya trembled.

"You're right, Sire. I think I'm overdoing it. We need her… I can't break her. Not yet," Lexa said under her breath and licked her lips. "Forgive me, Amaya. Now, yes, we will. You are just so determined, I forget that I might be treating you too harshly," she spoke in a saccharine tone.

The bitter cold eased from her skin. Amaya adjusted her braid and threw it over her shoulder. "Zul…if you're going to manipulate blood, remember, it's fluid like water. Treat it like a prisoner and it escapes." Amaya raised her hand and showcased the water gushing through the gaps of her fingers. "But, if you show it a path, you will be its leader." Her fingers danced as if she were playing a piano. The water was her orchestra as it slipped and threaded around Zul's arms like a net.

"I have to let it flow?" Zul guessed.

"Yes." Amaya did as she had been instructed by Lexa as they stood outside, across from the small hill. She concentrated on a swirl of water and it formed ice. She directed it to her ankle. It pricked her skin and stained the water with her blood. A globule of water hovered over her palms.

"Blood has iron…so all I need to do is concentrate on moving the iron. I mean, it shouldn't be too hard," Zul mused.

He stared at the water as it sloshed back and forth. He wanted to pull the blood upward.

Nothing budged.

He raised his hands.

Still no movement.

Zul Sharr continued for ten minutes until he gave up. "It won't move…but why? It's iron!"

"Maybe it's the water too," Amaya said and let the water splash to the ground.

"No. I've moved iron from water before. Just never iron in blood. This is making me nauseous anyways. I think we're done for tonight," Zul Sharr said sharply and then turned back to Amaya. "Wait, there's something I wanted your help with. Can you heal with water?"

"Heal? I'm not sure…"

"Oh…right. You recently learned about your powers," he said as they walked back to the mansion.

"Why do you ask?"

"It's for a friend. More like two."

"Sire, what are you doing with these creatures?" Lexa said. Lexa and Amaya stood in his room before the two doves. Obsidian and Rana had decided to go to bed. They were early risers.

"They were hurt. I understand pain, so I couldn't just leave them."

"Sire, this is a great opportunity for you to manipulate the blood in their bodies and do what you will with them," Lexa said, a sneer pulling at her lips.

"No. No way am I doing that! I might kill them, Lexa." Zul Sharr looked at the two birds with softness in his eyes. "Look, I just want you to find food for them. You know, seeds and fruit, just until that one recovers."

"Why take care of them? They're just birds."

Zul shook his head. "They're two lives. Whenever I would be in physical pain, I used to stay quiet. No screaming or crying. Unless it was severe. When my mom beat me and yelled at me for crying out when she hurt me, I stopped showing others I was hurt. I'm like this bird that's injured. I'll pretend I'm fine and happy, so the hawks don't pluck me."

Lexa searched his eyes with strange softness. "I understand. Will do, Sire." Lexa gave a slight bow. "By the way, Amaya, I need you to do something for me before you head to bed tonight."

In the corner of Zul's bedroom, Lexa had brought food for the two doves, water and even a branch as a perch. With Rana's help, they'd even created a bigger cage for them. Zul could see the two birds snuggled up to each other and asleep. He felt an ache flash through his heart. They had each other. One day, he'd have Sanari smiling by *his* side.

He turned his gaze away, turning onto his side and pulling his comforter up to his chest. He always kept his leg out since he wanted to be covered but felt too warm if he didn't keep it out. The fan hummed and he no longer wanted to think. Just drift to sleep.

***

He stood before a fountain fashioned from white marble. Water spouted from the top and gurgled around the base. Lotus flowers danced and skittered across it.

"Welcome. Peace, Eisen." A man stood before him. Zul couldn't see his face. It was hazy by the sunlight, or as if all he could see was his smiling mouth.

Zul didn't mind being called by his real name.

Serenity and warmth enveloped him as he walked over to the joyful and kind man. He couldn't smell any flowers, or the scent of trees. The only senses he could experience were feelings. They filled his heart and mind. Kindness, goodness and mercy.

The man smiled at him and gestured for him to sit beside the fountain on a small wooden bench.

Feelings continued to flood through him. No words were spoken by the man or by himself. The man wanted to help him. With what? Zul wasn't sure.

"Divine love is the truest form. The purest form, the one not everyone attains, but needs. Eisen… The divine loves you." The man held his hand out.

The same image. He thought the perspective would change, but it didn't. He could see the man's whole body, but only the smile and his skin seemed white like milk. For a few moments he thought the scent of musk had wrapped around them. So sweet, warm, and so familiar. He couldn't understand why it felt so true. He just knew there was something important and special about this person. If it even was a person. Or, maybe an angel in disguise?

"Truest form…" Zul reached for the man's hand. It turned black.

He stood over two people who lay on the ground. He wasn't sure who they were. Only that it was a girl and a boy. His lips recited something under his breath, his hand hovering over their chests. There was water rushing over him. He had to do it quickly. The water surged past him and morphed into glass, shattering at his feet. They'd be okay. They had to be. Satisfied they'd be all right, he hid behind a wall and peeked out at them. They'd both woken up. Praise the Creator, they were okay. He took a step and a slow breath, and then his eyes opened as if he had blinked.

***

Zul woke up, only to see his comforter over him and the darkness of his room. Those dreams were both odd. First a strange gentleman, and then, who were the two people?

Chapter 10 Essence

"Black karkadann?" Nezha asked, glancing at Thunderbolt and Sapphire.

Unicorn Valley was the only place in all of Noorenia where karkadann or unicorns lived. Even though her mind debated with her heart about the black unicorn, Sapphire didn't want to believe her mind when she thought it may have been just a horse or one of the jinn unicorns. Not someone who was close to her.

"Yes, Nezha. I saw it in the light. It had wings," Rustam said.

As Rustam began to speak about them staying here to keep an eye out and find more information about the elemental and her unicorn, Sapphire's mind fogged.

"Sapphire?" Nezha asked as the mayor left to the kitchen. "Do you know about that unicorn?"

Thunderbolt looked at Sapphire in concern. "Nezha… it's not something we should talk about right now…"

Nezha searched Thunderbolt eyes, probably concerned about the way he said her name. Usually when he did that, he was serious.

"Sapphire, we're here for each other. When you do want to talk about it, I'll listen," Nezha said and rubbed Sapphire's shoulder.

Sapphire turned to her. "Thank you, Nezha. I'm more concerned about the safety of Noorenia. While you were away, the jinn did not have any reason to attack. The pulse is weakening, but it was kept at a standstill. If another jawhar has joined a dark force, then all this negativity will only deteriorate Noorenia's pulse. And with your return, Noorenia will become more desperate to strengthen its heartbeat." She had to push the thoughts of the black unicorn away. Even if her heart was loud in her ears. Even if pain cut through her chest at the memory of his warm eyes.

"The pulse…you mean the balance?" Kayan asked.

"Yes. The heartbeat of the land," said Sapphire.

"Did I hear, heartbeat of the land?" Rustam had returned with a plate of fries with glistening chocolate and almond butter sauce. Topped off with pomegranate arils, whipped cream and chopped cashews and nuts. It was flecked with gold.

Sapphire sat straighter in her seat. "Yes. I am concerned about Noorenia's balance. Since there is a jawhar on the side of the jinn, Noorenia will be more desperate to have the angel return."

The mayor placed the plate and sat down. "That is why I wanted you all here. You have become well-known ever since the Angel of Mercy's soul shattered. Now that Nezha has returned, jinni activity has risen."

"Is it because it's not within the angel?" Nezha asked.

Rustam pushed the plate to them. "Please eat while we discuss. You are human, child. Noorenia needs the Angel of Mercy. He was our connection with Noorenia's heartbeat. Jinni magic is sinister and since the angel is not here, jinn have managed to taint the world with their darkness."

“What should we do about that jawhar?” Nezha’s jaw tightened.

“Her appearance was a warning, that I am sure of. She will return and when she does, you will all be here for it.” The mayor sighed. “Will you consider staying here for at least another night?”

“Rustam, my brother and I are guardians. It is our duty to protect Noorenia and its inhabitants,” Sapphire said and took a sip of water.

“Exactly. We’re not going to abandon you. Besides, this is probably Zul Sharr and Lexa’s doing. They know if they cause more havoc, it’ll hurt Noorenia. Even if it isn’t, I’m not the type t’ back out of a fight,” Thunderbolt said.

“I’m up for it. Protecting others and going on adventures is our thing, after all,” Kayan chimed in with a smile.

Nezha regarded the others. “Looks like you’ve got your answer.”

“Splendid! Don’t worry about your accommodation. There is a cozy and luxurious hotel just down this street. Fit for a princess.” The mayor handed Nezha a card with the address and details.

“Anything nice is enough,” Nezha said as she looked down at the card.

“Oh, no, I insist, Nezha. It’s not often that Angels and royalty are in our presence. We *were* expecting the famous poetess Ishya in our city.”

“Ishya?” Nezha asked.

“She goes by many names: Warrior Poet, the Healer of Ruhaan, Ruqya of Noorenia and Ishya the Many Talents. She had planned to visit our city to promote her latest book, but she cancelled last minute,” Rustam explained.

Sapphire had heard of the renowned warrior poetess. She was famous for being both strong with her words and sword. “She is a warrior and poet from the South. Ishya became famous for her talents in swordplay, healing with her words and with recitations. Once her book became a bestseller, she became known worldwide," said Sapphire.

"She sounds amazing," Nezha said in awe.

"Perhaps you will meet her one day. For now, I hope you all rest for the night." Rustam smiled.

***

"Hey, looks like we're on another adventure. This makes me really excited," Kayan said with a grin as he walked alongside Nezha and the others.

"You're excited? I'm just hoping we get t' beat up some jinn." Sparks netted between Thunderbolt's fingers.

"Yeah, you two really want that action-adventure combo, huh?" Nezha chuckled. Joining in their high energy, she hoped it would rub off a little on Sapphire. She seemed more quiet than usual. Her eyes were unfocused and in thought. Nezha wasn't sure what exactly to say, but she spoke. "Sapphire, maybe you'll get to learn more about Veer City?"

Sapphire lifted her head. The cold grew as the night air hung over them. It felt dense due to the snow falling around them. "Yes, I would like to learn about their technology," She spoke absentmindedly.

A crow swooped over them, cawing loudly, and landed on a lamp post. It flitted its wings and burst into flight, gliding into the night.

"A crow? But it's night," Nezha said.

"I've seen them roost in trees at night. Odd behaviour to us, but it may be a ritual we don't understand." Sapphire's eyes carried a look of doubt.

Kayan inhaled sharply. The wind spun around him. He stumbled from the sudden movement into Thunderbolt.

"Hey, Kayan, what's wrong?" Thunderbolt raised a brow at him.

Nezha's heart thrummed. Flames escaped her palms. The tendrils grew, the heat bright and warm against her skin. It was that sensation again. A familiarity. Identical to when she had first met Kayan. The flames pulled her toward someone. She almost stumbled. She glanced at Kayan and met his gaze. Maybe they were both going through the same thing. They walked in long strides as the siblings followed behind them.

"Nezha? What is going on?" Sapphire called out.

"I think…we're being drawn to someone." Panic edged Nezha's voice.

They made their way through the crowd and stopped near a lamp. The light bathed a girl. The black fabric fell over her body like a shadow. Her gaze met Nezha's. A red-tinged braid swept over the girl's shoulder.

Water rippled and sloshed at the young woman's legs. It formed spheres of liquid—beaded drops like planets being pulled into orbit around her hands.

The girl stared at them.

"A water jawhar…just like the mayor said." Kayan stood beside Nezha. "Nezha…we're connected." Kayan breathed.

"Yeah." Nezha took a step closer.

The girl's gaze lowered to the water pooling around her and then up at Nezha and the flames coiling around her arm. She fled.

"Wait!" Nezha ran after her, with Kayan right behind her. The siblings jolted into action and followed in step with them. Along the sidewalk, they had a view of her back as water continued to sway and flow around her body. She moved as elegantly as the waves that lapped at her waist. Goosebumps pebbled their skin and the cool air rushed through their mouths, numbing their throats with bitter cold. The only sounds Nezha could hear were their breaths, her heartbeat and a steady hum as their shoes hit the pavement.

A crowd swelled outside a building with pulsing neon lights. A bouncer stood at the mouth of the entryway. Techno music blared at the line. The line was long and they soon lost the girl as Kayan pushed and jostled bodies. Nezha stopped right in front of the people who nodded their heads and tapped their feet.

Kayan soon emerged out of the crowd and shook his head.

"I lost her." The wind no longer tugged at his shirt or played with his hair.

"You two felt it, didn't you?" Thunderbolt said.

"Yeah. I even contemplated using the wind to stop her, but it didn't let me," Kayan said.

"Like the first time I met Kayan, our elements reacted to her. She's the water jawhar the mayor was talking about. I don't get it. If she's on our side, then…" Nezha didn't know if this girl was a bad person or not.

"Ah, zaan… I don't think she is," Thunderbolt groaned.

"But she must be!" Nezha insisted.

Sapphire narrowed her eyes at the sky and spoke. “I sensed something from her, Nezha. The same sensation that Lexa carries. That miasma of darkness.”

Nezha gaped at her and ran a hand over her feather bracelet. “Well, this is something I wasn’t expecting.”

After finding their way, they made it to the hotel. The lobby was expansive and pristine. The floor was carpeted in red. The receptionist's desk sported a gold fountain which emitted a pleasant gurgle. A gilded elevator spanned the front wall. Once they told the receptionist who they were, she smiled and informed them she was instructed to await their arrival.

Their suite was large, boasting four king-sized beds.

When Nezha sunk into one mattress she had half expected Comet to jump into her lap. She missed her, especially right now, when the mysterious water jawhar had decided to show up and creep into Nezha’s mind. They were in over their heads.

“The beds are so comfy.” Kayan squeezed the side as he sat cross-legged.

“Yeah…” Nezha was sitting on the other bed.

There was a partition which they could pull up, with an option to lock the door. Smart.

“Hey, what’s wrong?” Kayan asked and mirrored her.

“It’s… I was missing Comet and thinking about the water jawhar.”

“Yeah, that’s a lot. We need to be prepared and stay positive.” Kayan smiled at her. “Besides, this place really does look cozy.”

Nezha regarded Sapphire, who was on her way to the bathroom. "Yeah, you're right. You're our positive reinforcement."

"I can't take all the credit. We need your resolute nature. Not Thunderbolt's impulsive behavior," Kayan said and glanced at the angel.

"Hey, I heard that, you know. I'm standing right here." Thunderbolt brushed his fingers through his hair.

"Anyways, so we know that elemental is with Lexa, but not why. Maybe if we knew, we could do something about it."

"Hey, that's a smart thing to say." Kayan winked and then ducked as Thunderbolt threw a pillow at him.

Nezha had a playful smile on her face. She tossed a pillow at Thunderbolt, and it hit him in the face. She pressed a hand to her lips to keep her laughter in and spoke. "Yeah, but what about the angel's body? I want to know where it is, but I don't know where to look first."

"Grr. You guys want a fight?" Thunderbolt's eyes shone in anticipation as he picked up the pillow.

"Bring it on! I'm tired of doing nothing, anyways," Kayan said and hurled another pillow at him.

Nezha sighed. "Boys, settle down…is what Tasa would say." She tried to mimic her voice.

Thunderbolt and Kayan glanced at each other, then laughed and both threw their pillows at Nezha.

"Oh, now it's on!" Her lips curled and they started their barrage of pillows.

When Sapphire entered the room, pillows were flying over and around her. "A battle, I see. Shouldn't we be discussing the jawhar and the angel?"

"Have some fun, sis!" Thunderbolt threw one at her, and it hit her head.

Nezha's and Kayan's hands were poised in mid-air with large white and blue pillows.

Sapphire blinked and then a faint smile crossed her face. She created a pillow with her light and grabbed two others, throwing them swiftly at all three.

"That's not fair game! No using your light!"

"No one said there were rules," Sapphire said frankly.

Nezha laughed and one pillow struck her face again. She stilled and light glowed around her.

"Uh…Nezha?" Kayan asked. He'd hung over the side of the mattress but clamored back on top upon seeing Nezha's transformation.

Sapphire rushed over to the three. "The Angel of Mercy…"

Nezha stood up, her facial expression changed. Her eyes were at ease and she stood with a much straighter back. Her voice lowered into a soft tone. "Yes. You wish to know about the jawhar and my body," He spoke through her.

"Yes, we do not know where your body is," Sapphire said as she stood before Nezha.

"That should not be your concern. The Divine Will has said so."

"Then what are we supposed to do?" Thunderbolt asked.

"I am not an intercessor. I but convey what the Divine Will has decreed. You will need other elementals. Jawhars. Only then will you find answers to where my body lies."

"So…the water jawhar is one of them?" Kayan said. "Nezha and I felt a connection to her."

"Fire essence, wind essence, water essence, earth essence and soul essence. These humans are gifted by the divine. You have both fire and wind. Once you seek them, you will become partners."

"All the jawhars?" Kayan asked.

"But she's been corrupted by Lexa," Thunderbolt hummed in thought.

"I cannot speak further on this. Find them and you will be headed in the right direction."

"Thank you, Mirkhas," Sapphire said.

"By the Creator, I do as he wills." A gentle smile appeared over Nezha's glowing face.

"Mirkhas, what about Zul Sharr?" Thunderbolt asked.

"It is not your duty to save the prince. What the divine wills will happen. I do not know the fate of the prince. Do remember, have kindness and gentleness. When one lacks gentleness, they are deprived of good tidings. My lord's mercy is not lacking, so as He wills. I greet you in peace and depart in peace. May you be blessed."

The glow grew faint over Nezha's skin and she closed her eyes. When she opened them again, she looked around at the three who were standing very close to her, their faces in awe.

"Did I win?" Nezha said and smiled.

"You don't know what happened?" Kayan asked.

"I thought I heard the angel. He said something and then I fell asleep."

"Mirkhas spoke to us, Nezha," Sapphire said.

"He did? What did he say?"

“He said it’s not his body we should be looking for right now. We need to find other jawhars. Amaya is one of them.”

Nezha’s eyes widened.

Chapter 11 Breathe

With each step, the thought of the fox lingered in Amaya's mind. The bitterness of the shadows bit down on her skin in their icy maw. She felt like she'd become a puppet. She knew she was, but the shadows wouldn't let her keep herself together. *I don't want to be here, but I need to find that fox. He hurt me in the past and now I'm here... If okaasan could speak to me through my earrings, then that means they're the reason I'm here. These earrings are connected to this place*. She didn't know exactly why she was here. Was it so she could get her revenge, or was it something else?

She wanted to escape. Even though this land was alien to her, she wanted to go and seek out the fox and the woman who would help her. Another part of her didn't mind being here. There was a sense of calm. A false bliss of having a roof over her head, food plated before her and at least some kind of company. When Lexa didn't give her a command or wasn't physically close, she could feel her own desires and thoughts rise to the surface.

"Amaya, welcome back." She leaned on a wall, cloaked in shadows. She bit her lip and stepped forward. The moon lined one side of Lexa, bathing her skin in a milky glow.

“Yes, I’ve done as you said.” Amaya stood before her, her voice hushed.

“Mmm. Good job! At least they know what you look like. It’s late and I’m not a cruel woman, so get your sleep. We have so much to plan!” Lexa said in delight.

“When will I get my answers from the fox?” Amaya asked, her voice tinged in a menacing tone. The shadows crept over her chest, the chill numbing her skin. She held her head high and tilted it back at an angle.

Lexa licked her lips. “You’ve only done one part, Amaya. You don’t even understand your own powers yet. How will you face him? His kind are otherworldly.”

“Tell me where he is and after I break him, I’ll gladly aid you.”

Lexa walked to Amaya and grabbed her by the throat and squeezed. “Don’t test me, human. You’re getting on my nerves about that fox jinni.”

The shadows kissed Amaya’s skin with chills as they snaked around her neck and arms. She couldn’t breathe. Lexa let her go.

Amaya fell to her knees, gasping for air.

“Fear is a powerful weapon, Amaya. The jawhars have seen you and they know I’m behind it. They’ll be afraid of what will happen.” Lexa used a mocking tone as she spoke. “What is Lexa planning? What are we going to do? Is the jawhar on our side? We’re so scared!” She chuckled and faked trembling. “Use this fear as an advantage. You might not trust me, but you will be grateful for what I’m doing. You will get your answers. You will meet the fox, but the time isn’t right.” Lexa pushed back a few red curls from her eyes. “No more about the fox, water elemental. This was your last warning. You wouldn't want to meet the angel of death before exacting your vengeance now, would you?" Lexa sneered at her with hooded eyes.

Amaya's tongue played with her front teeth. She would have to be careful of what she said. She'd play this game. It seemed the water needed to remain frozen. Slumbering, only to awaken at the right time, alive and strong. "I will be a weapon." She slowly stood to her feet.

"That's more like it," Lexa said and faded into the walls, merging with the shadows.

The chill softened over her skin, the pressure lifting from her chest. Amaya's gaze slid to the stairs, and she headed up. *I'll be patient.*

***

Lexa's eye twitched. The water jawhar had become overbearing with her demands about the fox. Lexa just wished she could have possessed her body, but that would take too much energy. Who did she think she was, ordering a jinni as powerful as Lexa?

She lounged on a maroon cushion, playing with a bangle around her wrist. The silver was decorated in small green pear-shaped apatite gems. Her heart thundered in her chest. It had been a while since she'd sat in seclusion. There was no peace for her.

She had to send a message. With the small number of allies she had, not a day went by that she didn't think over her plans in her head. How many times had she thought about what she'd do to anyone that even thought of betraying her? Make their organs rupture? Bleed them out slowly? Perhaps torture them by shifting into a lost beloved? She scoffed. No one would dare.

She tapped on the gems around her bangle. Last time, Zul had blown a whistle to summon a jinni to send and receive messages. She still couldn't shake off the painful ringing in her ears for hours after that. She took a deep breath in, relishing the moment of quiet. She raised the bangle to her lips.

"Yusha, I have a message for you."

A swirling mass of energy appeared before her and a jinni stepped through. The dog jinni Yusha was the most reliable for her errands.

"Ah, darling. I haven't seen you in ages." She made her way to him, grinning as she saw the faint look of annoyance on his face. It was always hard to tell, but the downward turn of his lips gave it away.

"Tell me what you want." His voice was smooth as a silk dupatta. But today there was a chime to it like the beadwork on a scarf. His gold eyes gleamed. Did he feel her energy? How excitement rushed through her blood?

"So aggressive," she said with a small chuckle and brushed her fingers through a lock of his long white hair. He was dressed in a textured maroon waistcoat with a high color over his black kameez. His black pajama was wide near his thighs and tapered downward.

"Yusha darling, it's not time to pout. I need a message sent immediately." She wouldn't tolerate anyone's insolence. Well, other than Zul or Rana. If it weren't for Yusha being a dog jinni with powerful blood and magic in his veins, she would have slit his tongue in two. Besides, he had such a youthful and handsome face, it would be a shame to mar such beauty.

She crossed the small room to a table and picked up a scroll of beco crystal parchment and handed it to him. The blue crystal glowed under the moonlight. "Make sure he receives it tonight."

Yusha pressed a hand to his heart and turned. The portal of energy opened up and he disappeared through it.

Lexa sat on her cushion with a joyful sigh. Now, she felt *much* better.

***

"Yes, Rustam. We saw the water jawhar. She was alone this time," Sapphire informed the mayor as they sat in his office.

"If anything comes up, let me know. I want to protect my city."

"We will. Don't you worry," Thunderbolt said, as they all stood up. They left his office and walked out into the street. It was afternoon and time for lunch.

"Hey, we didn't get to really celebrate Nezha returning. How about we have lunch, milkshakes and just chat," Kayan suggested as he walked beside Nezha.

Nezha blushed as all eyes focused on her. "That sounds great, but we don't know a place here. Although, I don't want to be pushy."

"I've got that covered! I looked for a great place in Veer City last night." Kayan grinned as Nezha's eyes widened.

"Did you stay up all night?"

"Nope. I went to bed, eventually."

"So, that's why there was light shining near my bed," Thunderbolt said, shooting Kayan a look.

"I thought angel unicorns didn't sleep. Just napped."

"What if I decide to sleep longer, huh?" Thunderbolt said.

Nezha chuckled. "Come on, you two. So, Kayan. What's the place?"

"We can walk there. It's just another two streets down."

"Just two streets? All right, let's see if it's worth it." Thunderbolt put an arm around Kayan's shoulders. They started conversing as Sapphire and Nezha walked together.

"Are you concerned about me?" Sapphire asked.

Nezha's head whipped to Sapphire, who's gaze was sad. It had taken her off guard since Sapphire had been so quiet.

"Yeah, but I won't push you to talk about it." Nezha smiled at her.

"When the time is right, I'll want to talk. Thank you." Sapphire smiled back.

They arrived at the shop. A sign stood outside in orange: Delightful. Handmade and local foods and treats.

"Nezha, don't get mad, because there's a lot of sweets here," Kayan said and held the door for her as she stepped in.

"Why'd I be mad? Obviously, it'll have treats. You all know me and my sweet tooth…"

As they entered, they noticed a small fridge to their left filled with small tubs of ice cream and drinks. In the middle was a cash register with a white marbled counter and a large glass display of sandwiches, bowls of meals and chocolates in an array of fillings, muffins and ice cream in all sorts of flavours. Ice cream such as vanilla with flecks of gold and caramel, meringue with rainbow sprinkles, black sesame with a dark chocolate ripple and chili with milk chocolate and strawberry sauce.

Nezha saw the confections and her mouth gaped. "Sweet tooth, meet your heaven…treat heaven, sweet tooth."

The walls were painted white, their brightness accentuated by the ample lighting. Paintings hung at intervals on the walls. One depicted the skyline of Veer City at night. Another was of a tree bearing oranges, a lake with a river and a dock with two boats.

"Wow, it's so bright in here," Nezha said as they walked up to the marbled counter. A woman with red glasses and dark brown hair tied up in a bun was busy making a milkshake in a large blender. A young man and another woman were taking orders from customers. This large parlor was busy with people, children giggling, one baby crying and others focused on their conversations. The air was fragranced with a sweet chill reminding them of ice cream.

"So, you guys up for milkshakes?" Kayan asked, excitement in his voice as they examined the menu on the wall.

"I'm actually looking forward to having dessert," Sapphire said as her eyes scanned the wall.

"Yeah, I'll pay. My treat," Thunderbolt said.

Nezha grinned. "Sweet!"

"You're both crazy for sweets," Kayan said.

"Sir sour, what are you getting?" Nezha turned to Kayan, her smile widening.

"At least I don't act sour?" Kayan shrugged and his face colored when Nezha laughed.

They'd all decided what they wanted and sat at the tables. After a meal filled with vegetables and a tangy dressing, the barista with her hair in a bun walked to their table and placed their shakes in front of them. "Here are your drinks. If you need anything, let us know. Enjoy." She smiled as they thanked her and then turned back to her other duties.

"Mmm. We're all going to be on a sugar rush," Nezha said as she slid her milkshake closer. Her drink was filled with cookies and cream ice cream, chocolate syrup and a salted and spiced caramel sauce, topped with whipped cream.

"I'm always on a high. You know, being a wind elemental and all," Kayan quipped, and took a sip of his drink. His had vanilla ice cream with whipped cream on top. It was drizzled in caramel with lemon meringue pieces tucked in.

Sapphire quietly sipped her coconut milkshake with fresh strawberry puree. She didn't have any whipped cream.

"The barista's smile looked so genuine; it made me feel guilty." Thunderbolt slipped the straw out of the whipped cream and with it came away some mint ice cream and mocha syrup that he licked off.

"Guilty about what?" Nezha asked.

"They must be exhausted, but they're forced t' smile. I feel a bit bad."

Their conversations started to pick up as they enjoyed their drinks.

Kayan held the straw and sipped. It was sweet and spiced.

Not his drink.

As his gaze went from the drink to Nezha and back to the straw, his lips parted and his teeth released the straw. Heat balmed his mind, tingled over his lips, pressing a gentle sweetness. The wind around his face teased him and he imagined it relished his embarrassment. He breathed heavily and his heart drummed. *Did I just…she drank from this! An indirect…* he dragged the back of his finger over his lips. The feeling let go of him in a slow deliberate release as if peeling away.

If anyone had taken notice of him, they'd see how red his face was as he nudged the drink to Nezha's side. She was too busy laughing and teasing Thunderbolt and was none the wiser.

He opened his mouth to speak, and then Nezha glanced at her drink and sipped from it. She offered him a quick smile and then spoke to Sapphire.

Kayan's eyes widened. He gulped and took his drink. *This doesn't taste as good as hers…* Kayan forced a smile over his lips, despite shyness gripping him.

When they were all done, Kayan stood and they walked out of the parlor.

"That was great!" Nezha said.

"Yes, it was nice to have some leisure time," Sapphire said.

"Hey, Kayan, you had fun, my zaan?" Thunderbolt asked as they walked on the sidewalk and he clapped Kayan on the back of his shoulder.

"Yeah, it was fun!" He grinned. *Sweeter than I expected.*

***

He rollerbladed on the side of the road, weaving through two cars, with a hockey stick in one hand.

"Hey, over here!" a boy called, thumping his stick on the pavement.

The boy's rich brown hair spiraled over his head as he doubled his speed and passed the puck to his friend with a smirk.

The boy was soon by his friend's side again. His friend passed the puck back to him and he coiled his stick and scored in the net.

"Yeah! Nice one, Asad!"

Asad circled him. "You're the champion, my man!"

"No, you are!"

"You're right. I am," Asad said and heard his mother call him.

"Asad! It's time to go for hockey lessons!"

"Okay!" Asad called back and then clicked his tongue. "Catch you later!" They shoved each other around and Asad laughed with his friend and his younger brother.

Asad clicked his tongue for a few minutes until he found it. He wasn't too sure what it was. Perhaps a bird. He lowered to the ground to get a better look. It was a bird. Lifeless.

"Asad!" his mother called.

"In a sec, Mummi!" He reached out. He could feel it. There was no pulse, no energy to sense.

"Okay, I'm coming!" Asad ran off and where the bird used to be, it was now swooping above a tree and gliding over their roof.

Asad and his younger brother walked into their house. They dressed up and Asad took his white cane and collapsed it.

Asad had been blind since the age of five. He'd click with his tongue, using echolocation, a self-taught technique to find his way around. When it came to going outside the house, to unfamiliar places, he reluctantly took his cane with him. Now that he was seventeen, he'd been trying his best to be more independent. He'd never considered himself to be blind. His mother always told him, if he could imagine it, he should put his mind to it and do it. Whatever made him more free, happy, safe and caring for others.

"Don't forget your bags, you two," their mother said as their father opened the front door of the van and stepped in.

"Come on boys!" their father called out.

"Bye, Mummi!" Asad kissed his mother on the forehead.

"Allah hafiz!" she said back to him.

He grabbed his bag and joined his brother. His cane with him smacked against the seat as he climbed into the van.

Chapter 12 Security

Zul Sharr awoke with a burning in his chest. A hunger he hadn't felt in so long. Along with it he felt a pang of regret, but it soon faded. The jinni aura coursed through him and was as fervent as it used to be. A battle of blood and heart poisoned by wants. Eid had passed and today he had no reason, no more excuses to try to persuade Lexa or the other jinn to stay away from him. The bitterness of longing embraced his heart. He wanted to keep the angel from awakening. He had failed at hiding its soul, so all he could do now was keep Nezha and the others from finding its body.

Zul missed the delight of the power coursing through his veins. A control he could orchestrate without even lifting a finger. Possessor of evil indeed.

As the day passed and afternoon approached, he returned to his room and turned to the birds. They had been fed, their bellies full of seeds and worms. "Hey, you two. You must be feeling better now, huh? I can't really afford to have anyone else under my care anymore…" Zul Sharr's voice was laced with disappointment. He liked when they cooed and expressed their love for each other. His thoughts bowed to the memories of Sanari. How kindly she acted and how exuberant she was when others laughed and enjoyed her company. He believed animals had souls. They felt pain and joy and were full of life. He remembered well when he had tucked the injured dove in his tunic. Its eyes were wide and it stilled. It knew he was trying to save it. Zul Sharr had enjoyed their stay and knew he couldn't keep them.

He opened the cage. The two birds cocked their heads and ruffled their feathers. With a slow and gentle hand, he lifted them both together in his embrace. He was shocked to see they didn't scurry from him or peck at him.

"Shh."

They cooed, and the one who had been injured looked him right in the eyes. "You're both well, so it's time you go back home." Zul hadn't been idle. He had made a wooden bird house for them both and hung it in the very tree he had found them in.

He brought them outside and walked to the tree. The air was light with the cold and he had made sure to give them a warm home with insulation. Mostly feathers, wool and fabric. He tucked both in his tunic and raised his hands forming a ladder with the iron. When he reached the top, he raised them to the opening of the tree house. "Do you like it?" he asked, smiling. Being around them had given him almost a sense of innocence. He pushed them gently to the house. They both settled on the perch before the bird house. They rested for a few moments and then took to the air. They made laps around the tree, and then flying and cooing loudly, circling around each other, and again perching on the tree. Freedom. The sweetness of movement. After a minute, they had both taken a liking to the home Zul had made for them. "I'm glad you like it." He wouldn't have anyone in his care now. He couldn't risk it. Everything he cared about was eventually taken from him. He didn't want more of that pain.

He returned to the mansion, but there was no sign of Lexa or Amaya. Obsidian was the only one, standing at the doorway to the main room in his angel form.

"Hey, Sire. Are you ready?" Obsidian said as he turned to look at Zul Sharr.

"Ready for what?"

"Didn't Lexa tell you?"

"Do you mean about using more magic for breaking the iron casing on…you know."

"Yes, that's what I'm talking about." Obsidian rose an eyebrow. "Are you up for it?"

"Yeah. Why wouldn't I be?"

"Just checking." Obsidian trailed after Zul Sharr up the stairs and to the bedroom where they found Sanari and her parents.

Zul Sharr was quiet as he stood before them and held his hand up.

"Here's the first…one." said Obsidian. His hand was trembling. The pulse of Noorenia dimmed in him, but it was there, constantly doing its best to push back the jinni magic that had fused with the red collar around his neck. Every time his mind would regain consciousness and remind him who he really was, the shadows would pulsate and grip him in bitter coldness. They would leave his mind fragmented. The memory of someone still lingered there. He knew who it was. He was plagued by images of him smiling with others, standing at a mountain where molten rock had cooled. A name would form in his thoughts. Someone with a calm demeanor which was a perfect partner to his own determined personality. Even that had been consumed by the malicious energies that aimed to subdue him.

Zul Sharr nodded as purple and black shadow wrapped like ribbons around his fist and the glow poured over Sanari.

Nothing.

Zul made a face. “Hmm…another one.”

This time an oozing blue slime wrapped around the iron-encased Sanari. Zul Sharr grimaced while he watched it consume the iron.

Once again, nothing happened and the slime faded.

Zul Sharr sighed. “Give me more.”

“There’s no more, Sire,” Obsidian conceded and stretched his arms over his head.

Zul Sharr ran his fingers though his hair and paced.

“Well, what about Lexa? She hasn’t reported anything to me.”

“No. I think she’s still on her diabolical plan,” Obsidian said with a grunt.

“At least I tried.”

“What about blood manipulation?” Obsidian asked.

“I’ve tried. Never mind. Thanks for being here, Obsidian…. Now, let’s go.” They left the room, sped down the stairs, grabbed their coats and walked out into the chilled evening air. “I know part two of her plan.”

***

“I’ve drawn a blank about that water jawhar.” Nezha gazed through the window at the buildings beside their hotel. “I don’t know why…but I feel like something’s missing.”

“I know what you mean. She’s somehow connected with us. I feel like this is a good thing.” Kayan sat on the small couch.

"What's good about it? We don't even know how other jawhars are meant t' help us find the angel's body," said Thunderbolt.

Sapphire remained silent as she drank a glass of water. Her gaze was fixed to the liquid.

"That's it, though. We don't know how. I don't know where to look. Right now, it would be a matter of us stumbling on it." Nezha laughed hesitantly.

"We need to try. Don't we all have the elements inside us? Water, oxygen, our skin, bones and spirit. Somehow, they'll all work together." Kayan offered, a gleam of hope in his eyes.

Nezha's lips parted. "Yes. That's what I need! This energy of optimism. I really missed that!" Nezha said and beamed at him.

Kayan grinned back. "So, you missed me, huh?"

Nezha raised a brow. "I missed all of you. We can't just sit around. Anything could be a clue. We need to ask questions."

"Precisely." Sapphire finally spoke. "Why did the jawhar choose Veer City? Why was she covered in blood and the scent of Lexa? If we seek, we'll receive our answers one way or another."

"It was an honour to hear you, wise Sheikh," Thunderbolt said, smiling at his sister.

"I listen, think and then speak."

"Didn't the mayor say it was a full moon?" Kayan asked. When no one replied, he added, "If you think about it, the moon controls the tides. They said their swamp flooded."

"The swamp," Sapphire said with realization.

"We need her on our side." Nezha adjusted her hijab. "That's our main objective. The angel said we should have all the elementals. We have fire—me. Wind—Kayan. Now the water jawhar shows up. We still need earth and soul. I keep getting this feeling calling out to me."

"What do you mean?" Kayan asked. "Because if we're both feeling the same thing…then I do too. Somewhere in this city." He reddened.

"It's like when Kayan and I met the elemental." Nezha pressed a hand to her chest. "I was meaning to tell you all, but I wasn't sure. I didn't feel it until we were in Veer City."

"Maybe your souls are reaching out to each other," Sapphire said.

"We've never waited around, so we need to get out there and find out what it is!" Thunderbolt leapt from his seat.

Nezha nodded and they all headed out into the street.

***

"Nezha, I can feel it over there." Kayan pointed as he walked beside her.

"Me too." She turned a corner. They passed other people and then walked through a construction site. There were no workers. Simply half a building with long bands of stone and material stacked up into piles on either side of them.

"It's getting stronger…" Nezha said as she continued to walk.

Kayan kept a hand on Ali, his sword. "Whatever it is, I'm prepared to fight if you are."

"If it comes to that, we must," Sapphire said. "Although, it would be nice to get through this without a skirmish."

"You know it doesn't work like that, sis." Thunderbolt rolled his head. Electricity fizzed around his hands. He had gone still and opened his mouth to speak when a black spear sped through the air.

Kayan stumbled back. His heart raced as he realized the spear had torn a part of his hair. "Wha—"

"Kayan. Are you okay?" Nezha gasped as flames erupted around her arms.

"Yeah. I just got a hair cut…" He sucked in air and laughed hesitantly, his heart still pounding.

They turned their attention to the direction the weapon had come from.

Cherry-red hair and the gait of a leopard, Lexa stalked toward them. "Ever heard of a false sense of security?" With a lopsided grin, she formed five knives out of shadows between her fingers and flung them.

Both Nezha and Kayan had no time to react. As fast as Kayan was, he couldn't dodge one of the knives. The blade was created from shadows. A chill webbed across his chest as it dissolved on impact.

Nezha glanced at him with concern and then sent a swath of flames toward Lexa.

Kayan's heart was thundering, goosebumps forming on his arms. Fear held him hostage and he could not move.

As flames and shadows danced, one knife struck Nezha. She, too, froze where she was and stumbled.

"Nezha!" Sapphire was by her side as electricity crackled from Thunderbolt's palm and surged to Lexa. The jinni jumped back in a graceful spin as they locked into combat.

"Nezha…what happened to you both?" Sapphire said as she lay a warm hand over her, the light bathing Nezha's chest.

"I'm scared…she's done this before. I feel scared…and I don't want to do anything." Nezha eyes widened.

"You can fight this." Sapphire encouraged, just as two knives flew past her head and struck the ground.

"Everyone will taste fear…" Lexa said as she spun toward Sapphire. Balls of light formed from Sapphire's hands and they burst as they collided with Lexa's blades. The shadows snaked around them. They coiled back as Sapphire's light beamed over them. They ran toward the building. Sapphire entered it. Lexa appeared from a corner and sent Sapphire crashing into a pile of bricks.

Lexa stalked toward her. "I don't expect you to falter, angel unicorn."

Sapphire pushed the bricks off her, revealing smooth, purple crystalline skin.

"The purple Sapphire." Lexa's eyes hooded and her tongue traced her bottom lip as if she were licking blood from her red lips.

Sapphire jumped up and collided with Lexa. The shadows dripped around her, attempting to strangle Sapphire. She was too quick as she bolted through the building.

Nezha soon appeared, the fear leaving her panting. Fire scorched the bricks and crackled as it spun and enveloped Lexa.

Kayan's sword Ali burst through the wall, sending forth broken stone and dirt. Then it transformed into a ribbon, nearly slicing Lexa's arms as she changed from her shadow to human form. The jinni melted against the walls as Sapphire ascended a staircase and hopped through a window onto a jagged roof.

The angel fell through, and Kayan formed a net of wind, helping her with her fall as she landed on one knee.

"You're cornered, Lexa," Sapphire said, just as Thunderbolt appeared behind his sister on the other side, electricity skipping around his feet and up his legs.

"Not nice seeing you here, redhead." He grimaced at her.

A few crows began to roost on the crooked building, their cawing like murmurs.

Chains of light shot out and coiled around Lexa's body, squeezing her. She groaned and screamed as they tightened and bit into her skin. Thunderbolt's lightning popped and snaked up her legs, jolting her.

"Noorenia will belong to the jinn. I will defy the Divine and damn all the humans to Hell! Damn you all!"

"Tch. Thunderbolt rolled his eyes. What a despicable jinni."

The chains around Lexa tightened, but she flexed her arms and stretched them out. The chains crumbled and she was free. "So close. You actually scared me." The cuts around her arms and torso were bleeding. "They're waiting for leftovers." Lexa panted and gestured toward the crows.

"Damn it!" Thunderbolt shared a glance with Sapphire.

"There's a presence…" Sapphire said as she stood.

Lexa raised her arms, with her remaining energy, her shadow-knives fanned out, each marking all of them with fear.

Seeing her opportunity, Rana swooped from among the crows and morphed into her human appearance. Lexa backed away, taking this time to heal.

Sapphire's eyes widened as Rana drew near to them.

"Your energy is mine."

Nezha gasped as Rana tilted her head up with a feather. She couldn't move at all.

Rana pressed her hand to Nezha's forehead. Her lips nearly grazing her cheek as she whispered. "Scream and I will break your bones. Stay silent and I'll be gentle."

"D-damn it." Kayan gritted his teeth.

Nezha's eyes widened, and Rana began pressing her hand harder against Nezha's head. Her shoulders sagged, her eyes became heavier as Rana sucked the energy from her.

"N...no." Nezha's hand twitched and then a light shone around her, rippling out in every direction. It was enough for both Sapphire and Thunderbolt to attack.

Rana jumped back to Lexa's side. The blinding light must have burned her as Nezha heard her gasp.

"We're not a free meal!" Thunderbolt said as Sapphire formed her boomerang and flung it, and electricity fanned toward both Lexa and Rana.

A sphere of rolling blackness rushed out from the two jinn and Nezha and Kayan began coughing. The darkness encased Rana and Lexa and as the burst of energy faded from the collision, Sapphire saw a crow and mist fade into the air.

Kayan and Nezha fell to the ground.

"That wretch really got you with her knives." Thunderbolt grimaced.

Sapphire bent down and placed a hand on Nezha's shoulder. "Nezha? What did Rana do to you?"

"I think…she took my energy."

"Nezha, are you able t' get up?" Thunderbolt walked up to her.

"Yeah, just out of breath."

"I felt cold. It's like I was scared." Kayan blew out a breath.

"That's what it was." Nezha agreed. "Lexa's done this to me before, the time I was in the ruins. Her knives hold fear in them somehow."

"At least it's over…" Thunderbolt said. "Come on, kid. You need a hand?"

"Nah, I'm good." Nezha smiled at him.

"Kayan, are you okay?" Nezha said as they left the site.

"Yeah, I'm good. Really. Thanks, Nezha."

She sighed. "Good."

When they reached the other side of the street, a large poster caught their attention.

Sapphire read aloud, "Dance at the magical Plume of Paradise Masquerade and meet our elemental entertainers."

Chapter 13 Two of a Kind

"We need lettuce, potatoes and celery," The boy said as he scanned the produce section in the grocery store. He had just dropped a bag of lettuce into his cart, when his phone dinged, notifying him of a text. He pulled it out from his pocket and checked the screen.

Hey bro. I heard someone say my name outside the window. I'm in my room.

Dante rolled his brown eyes as he continued to push his cart and text.

Maybe it's the wind. He replied.

In reply, his brother sent: *Bro, this isn't funny!*

Dante: *Do you see anyone out there?*

Bro: *Why would u do that?!*

Dante: *Do WHAT*

Bro: *I see u! Why are u just standing at the tree?! I'm at the window. How are u texting me? I don't see your phone.*

Dante: *Don't be stupid! You're freaking me out! I'm at the store getting groceries.*

Bro: *I see your face!*

Dante: *That's not me! Get back from the window. What's this guy doing? Just standing there?*

Bro: *Yeah. Looks just like u. You better not be messing with me!! I'm getting scared.*

Dante: *Seriously, why would I scare you? I don't prank you! I'm at the store. I'm going to checkout.*

Dante: *Where's dad?!*

Bro: *In the backyard shed. He's using tools.*

Dante: *Just forget it. He'll probably leave.*

Bro is typing...

Bro: *HES CLIMBING!!*

Dante: *What?!*

Bro: *THE TREE! HES CLIMBINGG!!*

Dante: *Just keep the window closed.*

Bro: *OH MY GOD! HES SMILING AT ME ITS SOOO CREEPY*

Bro: *HE'S COMING!*

Dante: *Bro, call the cops!!*

Dante: *Call the cops! Call Dad in!!*

Dante: *Bro!!!*

Dante: *I'm coming home!*

Bro: *I cant txt. He broke into house. I have a knife.*

I'm hiding

Dante: *IM HOME*

***

Dante slammed the door open. His heart pounded, his nerves on edge. He climbed the stairs. His look-alike appeared at the top of the stairs in front of the bathroom door.

Dante's eyes widened and he nearly tripped on the stairs.

"Hello, Earth Jawhar."

"How did you—Whoever you are, I've called the cops." Dante smirked at him proudly.

"Humans… So ignorant. If the rest of your kind are as emaciated as you, they can't harm me. No human can."

"You break in, scare my brother and you talk smack about me? That's it!" Dante lifted his hands and the carpet surged out from under his look-alike's feet, sending him tumbling. "Bro, wherever you are, do not come out!"

His copy slinked back up like a snake and launched itself at him.

"Why are you even here?" Dante shouted as he jumped the stairs and ran into his room. There, they tussled as fists flew.

"I am from Noorenia."

"Noorenia?" Dante spat out as he bent his body sideways and spun around to the side. He knew what that was. His mother had gone to visit relatives just a week ago. And then she'd disappeared. He figured she was taking her time, but she never called them. While James thought she'd abandoned them, he didn't believe it. She might have been a bit negative, but she was his mother. He had a feeling she was in trouble. "This isn't about my…" Dante didn't want to finish his sentence.

The being sneered at him. "Your mother? Did you think she abandoned you? You won't find out once I kill you."

"Won't happen! That's all ya got, freak?" Dante flexed his upper arm, and his corded muscles rose on his dark skin. He rose an eyebrow at him. A gesture to bring it on.

"You will regret fighting back," his other spoke.

"You'll regret it being *me*."

The other person shoved him and Dante's arm hit the sound system, turning music on.

Dante stood up and they both momentarily paused, glancing at the iPod now blaring out hip hop music with an electro remix. Then Dante flashed his teeth at him. "Let's dance!"

Dante was a street performer in downtown New York. His father had told him to earn his own money and this was what he chose. Why not do what you love? He had two other friends join him and together they'd become quite a success.

Dante shrugged his shoulders to the beat, and then jumped into the air, doing a triple twirl and sending his look-alike crashing into a wall.

"Dance battle? DJ Dope's up to represent. Be warned." He snarled at Dante.

"Man, shut your mouth!"

They started to move, their arms in waves. Their legs shook as they dodged each other's kicks and their feet moved rhythmically to the beat.

Dante's eyebrows shot up. "Not bad," he said, raising his lower lip.

His look-alike smirked and launched himself forward, spinning and then swinging his legs in an arc, nearly missing Dante's head.

"Damn!" Dante drawled. "You are not upstaging me in my own house! It's on!"

They both interlocked their legs, hopping, and then Dante spun backward, bent his leg sideways and kicked him. The jinni stumbled and Dante ran toward the window, but before he could open it, the jinni grabbed him from behind. Dante dropped to his hands and locked his legs around the dumbfounded Jinni's waist. He pushed himself up, bending backward and over the jinni's head. releasing his twined legs, he shoved the jinni's head and launched himself into a flip behind him. Before his opponent could react, he punched him in the side.

"Freestyle!" Dante shouted.

The jinni grunted and Dante twisted his hands, causing the windows to fly open. He made chirping sounds, some whistles, growls, and snarls. He smirked back at the jinni as shadows started to pool around the sinister being. The jinni growled. Dante did a backflip out of the way, as the jinni charged.

In a heartbeat, sparrows, pigeons and seagulls swooped in through the window and began pecking at the jinni.

"What—"

As the jinni waved his arms above his head, Dante whispered to the tree. "I need your assistance. Let me guide your vines."

The tree creaked as vines flew through the window and entwined around the jinni's body.

"Damn you…" The jinni hissed. Its wide eyes were dripping with blood as the vines constricted it, the thorns digging into its skin.

"Ugh. Stop looking like me!" Dante growled in disgust and tore apart the stone from his outer wall and built them up around the jinni. The vines still writhed like snakes. Dante closed his eyes, not wanting to see himself—or at least someone who looked like him—being crushed. "Bye." He slammed his hands together and the stones crushed the creature.

The vines recoiled, returning to the tree, slowly slipping over the window. After the stone crumbled, Dante dared to move toward it. "What is that? String…wait. No… it looks like my hair." The feather and curly hair both disintegrated into plumes of smoke.

"He wasn't a bad dancer, I can say that much." He blew out a sigh, replaced the wall before anyone noticed and shut off the music.

Descending the stairs, he called out, "Bro! James, you can come out now!"

The bathroom door creaked open. "Are you sure? Is he gone?"

"Yeah. Yeah, he's gone," Dante said. "You missed the most epic dance battle, though!"

"I thought he—that thing… was going to kill me!" His brother said, still clutching the knife.

"Nah, but its moves were killer." Dante grinned as James shoved him.

"Whatever… I'm just glad we're okay. You *are* okay?"

"Yeah. Not a scratch on me." Dante messed up James's hair.

The brothers went downstairs and into the kitchen. There, James drank a glass of water and sat at the small dining table.

"Dad won't get a whiff of this, okay?"

"Yeah, Okay. I won't tell him. Are you sure you have to go?" James asked, as he sat opposite of him.

"Yeah, I am. It might be the only way." He had dreams about three people. A girl with brown skin—almost gold— who could juggle fire and form it. A gentle smile over her lips. A boy with a smile on his face who could move swiftly and beckon the wind, make it dance for him. Then there was another boy around his age with brown skin who could bring the dead to life. He was blind, but he held another kind of sight. Intuition. The first few nights it spooked Dante so much. He thought he'd known them from somewhere. He wasn't too sure, but he could sense them, smell them. As he thought about the dreams, it was as if a piece of the puzzle had fallen into place. Noorenia and those other elementals were clues.

Dante's father met him in the living room as James watched T.V.

"Son, is it true what you've been dreaming about?"

"Yeah. I mean, they're dreams, but there's something about them. I keep having them over and over. They keep saying… 'we need you here.'"

His father inhaled through his nose and then approached a desk where he kept his suitcase. He unlocked it and took out two deep-green gloves.

"You can have these."

"Dad? Did mom leave us?" Dante asked, a lump forming in his throat.

His father was silent. He gave the gloves to Dante and closed his hands over them. He held his son's hands and looked into his eyes. "Your mother loves you, Dante. We had our tough times, but she'd never willingly leave you or James. When you were younger, you lived in Noorenia for a year. You had relatives there. One day, your grandfather died and there was no reason for you to stay, so we moved back to earth. Dante. Whatever it is, go. Maybe you'll find her, and if not, you'll find yourself."

Dante looked down at the gloves. "Myself? Dad, I'm already myself." Dante took the gloves and slipped them on. "Thanks," he mumbled. "Really."

Dante stood and went to the door. "Uh, how do I get there?"

“The tree in the backyard. The Tree of Worlds. Touch it and then say where you want to go. It’s connected to Noorenia.”

Dante regarded his father and then embraced him. His father patted his back and then pushed him gently toward the door.

James gave him a thumbs up.

“What about Sarah and the others?”

“Go, son, before I change my mind.”

Dante turned. He’d already said his goodbyes to both. Now all he had to do was reconcile with himself.

He stood at the tree with a backpack of food and a change of clothes. “Oh man.” He pressed his fingers into the trunk and felt the energy. The tree’s pulse as if the sugar it formed was coursing through it like blood. “I want to go to Veer City in Noorenia. Since we used to live there.” He could feel the tree reply to him. Whenever he connected to the earth, or to the animals, he couldn’t really hear them speak, but it was like he could hear their thoughts. Like when he thought of something in his own head. Words which had no sound, but held power, because thoughts had the potential to become ideas and those ideas could become actions. The tree welcomed him. *Greetings, human. Peace and glad tidings. I am the tree whose roots run through two worlds. I feel your intention, I hear its integrity. Have a safe journey.*

The trunk melted around his fingers like butter over a hot pan. Dante’s hand disappeared into the void. His heart pounded, his skin prickled. He knew he had to do it. Everything inside his heart, his mind and even the tree was urging him to move onward. He took in a breath and stepped forward, disappearing into the tree.

When he emerged, Dante stepped outside a park by the street. He'd done it. He looked around at the people walking by. He turned and felt a sense of déjà vu as he stared at a building.

"What the heck? I've seen that somewhere..." He began walking. "In my dreams... Yeah..." he mumbled and continued toward it.

***

After his hockey practice, Asad had returned to his room. He typed out on his brail writer. He'd had a good poem stuck in his head the last few minutes as he had walked into the house.

Then he heard it. A faint voice.

Asad, it's time.

His fingers froze over his keyboard and he sat up, pushing his writer aside. "Hain?" What? he said out loud and clicked his tongue as he walked to his door. *I might be imagining it.*

He'd noticed this happening for a week now. It was more prominent when he was busy with something. He figured when his subconscious mind was more active. He'd hear his name, or someone say to go somewhere. He wasn't sure where.

There had been dead animals a lot lately, and every time, he was able to successfully revive them. That never happened. It was always a game of luck, or rather, fate, for them. He'd rarely come across an animal who had passed. This time, he'd revived birds and even a fox as he happened to walk by the forest. He knew he was a soul elemental when he'd once cried over a dead pet budgie and revived it when he held it. His parents had known he had something strange or rather special about him.

He remembered that day well when his parents told him how they had met. Both knew each other's families. Although now, he lived in Canada. Most of his relatives lived here, so they'd moved. He never knew entirely why. They said they thought he'd be in more danger in Noorenia, since there were people who became suspicious of him. Especially his aunt and uncle. As he grew up, his parents loved him dearly, but then his uncle and aunt started to become jealous of his family. They would say horrible things to his parents and even to him. One time, he was at their aunt and uncle's house overnight and they tried to hurt him by making it look like an accident. Taking advantage of his blindness. From then on, he learned some people who could harm him and he became more distrustful of people and more careful around them.

Asad hadn't been born blind, but a disease had taken his sight at the age of five. His mother was his confidante. The first time he told her he couldn't see anything anymore, she told he still had hands to hug with, a nose to smell sweet things with, ears to hear her voice, and he could see in other ways. She was like his best friend. She'd been there for him for everything and he knew he could tell her anything. She never betrayed his trust. He loved his mother dearly. She was never a crutch to him. She was a force to be reckoned with and he would learn to be one too.

Asad opened the door and went downstairs.

"Oh, there you are, beta. It's your turn to vacuum," his mother called from the dining table.

"Acha… I'll get to that, mummi," Asad said absentmindedly, his mind still trying to focus on the voice. He couldn't hear it, but his intuition was urging him toward the forest a few blocks away from his home.

"Is something wrong?" his mother said and stood up.

"Something's been going on, ma."

"Like what?" They walked to the sofa and sat down.

"I keep hearing a voice call me. And, I've been having dreams about a group of people. Some have wings, some are horses with horns like unicorns and some are wielders of wind, fire and earth."

His mother brushed aside his brown hair as she listened to him. "I'd always thought about your being a soul elemental. There had to be a reason. A calling. Maybe that's what this is. Trust your intuition. You've told me it's always helped you and never did you any wrong. Trust it and do what's right."

"Mummi… I can't leave you and my brother…" Asad said, his voice wavering. Realization kissed his heart, and thundered inside his rib cage. His intuition worked in mysterious ways. Whenever he would become worried, it was a good sign. It would all work out. If he was nervous, it would be a real cause for concern. When he became scared, he'd fight through the fear, knowing he'd be victorious. He'd been testing it out as he grew up. He was only seventeen, but it was just the beginning of his understanding. Right now, his stomach and chest were tightening with worry. He knew it would work out. A speck of hope was shining within him.

"Sadke javaan. Don't worry about us, beta. I'm… I just want you to be safe, but if this is what you need to do, I know you'll continue to do great. My blessings are with you." His mother kissed the top of his head.

Asad heard the inflection in her voice.

"You're crying." He said it like a statement. "I don't need to see it to know." He reached out and wiped away one of the tears from her jaw.

His mother held his hand and kissed it. "Asad. A mother always wishes the best for her child. Take care of yourself."

"You know I can." He smiled. "Take care of yourself, mummi and Harun and baba. Is it right for me to leave when he's at work?"

"You do what you need to, beta."

Chapter 14 The Calling

Asad picked up his white cane from his closet. He folded it and tightened his fingers around it. *This cane shows others I can't see like them… I can't walk anywhere I want like them. Because I was never like them. I don't need it. But I'm going to an unfamiliar place. I guess the white lie has to go with me.* Asad had nicknamed his cane White Lie. It was something he had to show others. That he needed it, as if it was an extended limb. He didn't need it. He knew he was capable, but he wasn't a fool. A new place that he hadn't mapped out in his head urged him to use the cane. Asad stuck it in his belt loop. His mother had sewn a pocket for it with a button to keep it secured.

Asad opened the door. He'd be eighteen in another month and he'd be going off to university. He wasn't sure what he'd do. He wanted to keep learning. It was funny because he knew he could learn anything, anywhere and knowledge never stopped. He taught himself how to echolocate, a feat that to a person who had good vision sounded impossible. He knew it was improbable but that never stopped him.

Asad crossed their parking lot, clicking his tongue, the echoes telling him where he was. He could picture the outline of the garbage can, and the neighbour's cat. He strapped his rollerblades on and turned to the left. Worry kept gnawing on his insides. He narrowed his eyes, those two which sacrificed themselves so he could adapt. He continued to click as if he were a car signaling he'd turn any second. He picked up speed and concentrated on his hearing.

Asad. The forest. Soul elemental.

He knew where the small forest was. That's where his intuition guided him. He was getting there, closer and closer. To his left, as he passed other homes, was the busy street below the hill and a river. He probably wouldn't get a chance to see the river glisten again, but he could hear the burbling of water and smell the last of the flowers—the stubborn and determined ones like him who held on. He thought of a verse. *Even the leaves that fall, He knows.* He kept his faith alive. His faith had been his guide, his hope on days he thought he couldn't live. Seeing didn't have to be believing. By Allah, hearing and intuition would be his eyes.

Asad slowed as his worry increased. He clicked and rollerbladed toward the forest. His clicks picked up the branches, the outlines of leaves in his mind. He pulled at his coat and continued forward.

The voice was louder this time.

Noorenia calls you.

When he stood at the mouth of the forest, he realized the nature of the words. They didn't have their own voice. It was his own, like a loud whisper. There was a pulse. A strong one. He stood still. *I should go into the forest.* He asked his intuition and the energy in his throat moved. That meant a strong yes. That's how his intuition worked. If he asked himself a question he'd concentrate on his throat. If he felt no energy, it meant a no. If the energy surged, it was a yes.

It was intuition alone that led him there and continued to. A warmth bloomed across his chest and a swirling mass of energy formed before him. He had ties to Noorenia, so when he'd felt that, he'd known it was fate. He gulped and took his rollerblades off before taking a step forward. He waved his arms in a circle, breathing slowly, his pulse thumping in his palms. He took another step and water droplets splashed against his palms. The energy hummed louder. He had opened up the barrier there. His own door. He took another step and joy filled him where worry had once settled. *I want to go to Noorenia. To wherever those people in my dreams are.*

He slipped through.

Asad swam to the surface, thanking God that he had learned how to. He pulled himself up from a small pool. He didn't smell flowers, but smoke, and the sounds of cars driving past the park where he emerged. He stepped shakily onto land and clicked his tongue. *A lamp post, or maybe a tree? It's a tree. Where am I?* He listened. Children were laughing. His lips scrunched and he snapped White Lie open and began walking. He grumbled as he reached the edge of the street. "Stupid White Lie. Stupid new place..."

There was another smell, like construction of some sort. He walked along the sidewalk and his intuition was quiet. Not much for him to go on.

The chatter of the birds quieted. Instead, two girls were chatting beside him. He overheard their conversation as he walked past and then stopped.

"I've got my tickets too!" the first girl was saying.

"Great! I want to see the water dancers. I heard they'll be using bubbles and ice," the second one said.

The first girl gasped. "Did you pick your mask yet? Mine is white with silver swirls."

"Yeah, mine is a pretty red and gold."

They must be talking about elementals. Asad asked his intuition and he felt the calm energy lower. *I need to go there.* "Excuse me, do you know where the masquerade party is?" Asad asked.

The second one turned to him. "You mean the Plume of Paradise? It's across this street at the main Joziba Circle. *Glamour Circle.* Uh, sorry. Would you like an escort there? I wouldn't mind." She must have taken notice of his cane.

"Yeah, it's further to walk and we're going there too," the first girl said.

Asad grinned. "I see… sure."

The second one chuckled and the other girl hooked an arm around his. "So cute…" she whispered to the other girl.

"Thank you, kind miss. Now, shall we?" He asked and the girls led him. *This is easy... But the difficult part will be getting in to that masquerade. I'll find a way.*

Asad and the girls stood in front of the building. He put his hand to the building and the smooth marble sent a shiver down his spine.

"It's made of marble and glass. It has a balcony too," the second girl explained as she tapped his shoulder.

"Oh, well it sounds pretty nice," Asad said.

The other one chuckled. “So, hope you have fun in there. Are you waiting for anyone?”

Asad smiled. “I’m one of the performers.” He had to get in some way and he had mixed feelings about it. Nonetheless, he had to fit in.

“No way! Well, looking forward to your performance,” the second girl said.

Asad saluted them. “Have a lovely night, ladies.” He turned away, sensing his pulse and leaving the two girls giggling and high in their conversation as they walked in.

Come on, I need some kind of energy for me to work with. Asad kept clicking his tongue, echoes reverberating off things. As a soul elemental, he could see more detail in the images that would form in his mind. A door and a sign. He turned around and felt no one there. He clicked and pushed the doors open.

A furor of people milled about. As he stepped forward, he bumped against what seemed to be coat hangers. His hands became sweaty. Worry again entered his chest. One woman happened by him and reversed her steps to him.

“Woah! Wait young man. What’s your business here?”

“I’m a soul elemental,” Asad declared and stood taller.

“Hmm.” The woman had hair down to her shoulders and wore a blouse. “Soul elementals can alter emotions. Make anyone feel anything. Can you change mine?” the woman said and he didn’t need to see her expression. He could hear the challenge in her voice and feel the way her pulse heightened.

“No problem.” Asad could see her outline as if she were a silhouette. He hovered his hand over her chest and concentrated.

He heard the woman gasp, her heart hammering and her skin heating up. She breathed heavily. Judging by her silhouette and some details, he could tell she was fidgeting with her blouse.

"Oh Divine..." Her voice came out in a purr.

"So, are you convinced yet? Or do you want me to go deeper... into your heart?"

She gasped. "Please... I can't." Her legs were shaking.

"My pleasure...rather, yours." Asad grinned, relishing her embarrassment, and waved his hand over her chest again. He could never force anyone to do what they didn't want to. Whenever he did invoke anyone's energies and heighten their senses, it was only with consent.

She leaned on the coat rack and then cleared her throat. "We're... not starting yet, but here's your mask and official clothing with the Plume Paradise emblem." She handed him the clothes. "A white undershirt and a black coat on top. I gave you a black lace mask."

Asad tucked in White Lie and smiled at her. "Thank you, ma'am."

"I know you have a cane, young man. Here's the dressing room. She guided him by the elbow to the men's side.

"Kind of you," he said.

"Get dressed. You'll hear the announcement twice before the show starts. Don't have too much fun now!"

Asad nodded.

He donned his clothes, which were a bit loose on him, but he didn't mind. He slipped the lace mask over his eyes. It was made of cloth and was transparent over his eyes. The lace trim ran across his nose and above his cheek bones.

He began clicking as he walked out and captured some people turning their heads to him. He walked slow and steady as he found the stairs and almost stumbled. He held on, and his cheeks heated.

Asad had made it to the dance hall. The room was starting to fill with people. He continued clicking and realized it was a very large place. Challo phir… *I guess it's best I stay close to the stage. I'll have a better chance at finding the elementals and those people with wings. I know I'll sense them. My intuition will help me.*

***

The posters for the Plume Paradise Masquerade were plastered on various buildings and walls. *Some party, huh? My calling.* Dante smirked as he walked toward one poster and read the details. "What?" He read the price for tickets. Fifty riatas/deolos? He was surprised there was English. There were at least three other languages on the poster. *Whatever that is, it sounds expensive as hell! I'll just have to get in my own way. If they want elemental entertainers, I'll give 'em one."*

When Dante arrived, he stood before the building in the centre of the large, busy circle. There was a mall and countless other shops and cafes. The roofs were in teal and most doors were patterned in the same colour. He gave a long whistle and sized up the building. In silver writing it read 'Joziba Circle.' A row of people formed a line as the crowd was kept at bay with long yellow ropes zipping with electricity.

He walked to the side where his eyes caught two men with blue masks who were letting in the elemental dancers. The water elementals all donned white filigree masks with water beading the sides and were tipped in frost. The fire dancers' masks were dripping with red jewels, golden waves, and tendrils of flames on the left side. The earth elementals had dark green masks detailed in gold stems with leaves. Each was topped with a green jewel over a wreath, glimmering from the light flashing from the door. Small black flowers dotted about it. They hadn't worn any official clothing other than the masks, so it gave Dante an idea.

He snuck up behind one of them as the line paused. "I think i'm cursed." Dante pulled at the dirt and piled small sleek black stones together, fashioning a hat. As the elemental in front of him turned to seek the source of the noise, he added, "the burden's heavy, just like this rock hat."

"Too bad, zaan. You lost your mask?" the man asked him.

He fell for it. He knows I'm an elemental too. Dante inwardly smiled and it took all his willpower not for it to show over his lips. "Yeah," he breathed in defeat.

"Don't worry, they'll probably have spares. I'll vouch for you." The man nudged him and smiled.

"Really?" Dante collapsed the stone hat and returned the black stones back to the side of the walkway.

"Thanks. We're going to rock the party tonight!"

"Oh yeah," the man agreed and they chuckled as the line began to move.

Cheers roared as Dante and the performers walked in. A woman greeted them. Her brown hair was down to her shoulders and she was wearing a white blouse. Her pink lips turned into a polite smile. "Welcome dancers! The show won't begin until an hour from now." Dante stared. he didn't mean to, but damn she was beautiful. She had east Asian features. Her green eyes pierced his soul. He just hoped she wasn't some soul elemental or she'd kick him out. She pointed to a coat rack. "First, you will receive your official costumes. You have time to freshen up, rehearse and join the ball room floor. Enjoy."

Dante was eventually given a costume and, just as the man had said, he'd convinced the woman to give him a mask. Dante drew the mask to his face and looked out into the crowd. *Now, to find the elementals as I mingle.*

***

"For a city that doesn't want elementals on the streets, they sure do commoditize them." Thunderbolt wrinkled his nose.

"I don't like it either," Nezha said.

Kayan looked up the party's location. "That building is right behind us. Just a block away from here."

Thunderbolt grunted. "Yeah, and it looks like it starts tonight."

"We need masks," Sapphire said, as they walked along the sidewalk.

"I'll find a shop!" Kayan took out his Tome. Nezha looked over his shoulder as they stood huddled beside a tree. A sudden feeling caused her to lift her head. A familiar presence of some sort. She turned, witnessing two girls across the street, their arms linked with a younger boy. For a moment Nezha thought a red-blue glow made a halo around his head, illuminating his brown skin tone. Nezha noticed his white cane. She turned back to Kayan before she could think anything of it.

“There’s a shop selling masks just another block from here,” Kayan said.

“The masquerade’s starting soon, we need to hurry.” Thunderbolt warned, tapping his foot on the concrete.

The group walked into the costume shop. Nezha’s fingers slipped over the silken cloth of dresses that lined one corner.

After ten minutes of wandering the rows of clothing, a man approached them.

“See anything you like?” A tall gentleman with black hair and a coy smile tilted his head at Nezha and Sapphire, his gaze shifting between them. He spoke in a smooth and low voice.

“We’re here too, you know,” Thunderbolt muttered as he gestured to himself and Kayan who now stood beside him.

Nezha blinked at the gentleman. “Ah, yes. This silver dress.”

She smiled nervously, not meeting his gaze. He had looked at her too intently. Kayan positioned himself between her and the shopkeeper.

Sapphire was still looking through the clothing.

“Oh good.” He smiled at Nezha. “When you’re ready, I’ll be at the register.” He glanced at Sapphire, nodded once and then stalked off.

Kayan narrowed his eyes at the man until he was out of sight. “So, Nezha, how’s this look? he asked in a cheery tone as he turned to her, holding up a blue leather mask. Inward golden curls framed the edges. On either side, small white wings—like clouds against a backdrop of blue sky—fanned.

“It suits you,” Nezha said with a grin.

A mischievous smile grew over Kayan’s face. “Yeah?”

"I found mine." Thunderbolt turned, displaying a hawk mask in bronze with a yellow beak.

"You just like being golden." Nezha laughed.

"There's nothing wrong with that." Thunderbolt tilted his head back and grinned at one of the mirrors.

"Vanity is his second nature," Sapphire joked as she held up a delicate mask adorned with snow-white feathers. A small crystal swan decorated the side.

"Finally found one!" Nezha waved a glittering blue mask in the air. A golden jeweled peacock sat atop peacock feathers poking out from one side.

Thunderbolt was dressed in a maroon tunic fashioned from a thicker fabric Nezha had never heard of before, but it was silken when she pressed it between her fingers.

Sapphire chose a vibrant indigo dress in a pattern of bold orange flowers. It fanned out near her legs. Gold lace dripped over the collar and down the sides.

Nezha wore a smoky blue and gold kaftan dress. It was glimmering gold from the waist down. Above her waist, it was dotted with golden buttons over her chest and a long stripe down each arm.

Kayan stepped out of the dressing room with a hand over his gold sleeve cuff. He was wearing a bright royal blue sherwani.

Nezha averted her gaze as he looked up at her, noticing her staring at his clothing.

"Did you intentionally match me?" she said.

"Yup." Kayan grinned as they paid the shopkeepers.

As they left the shop, they donned their masks.

“Don’t forget what we look like,” Thunderbolt joked.

Nezha gave Kayan a sidelong glance. “I don’t think Kayan will.”

He smiled at her lazily. “So, have you already given me a once-over then?”

Nezha’s cheeks heated. “I didn’t—”

Kayan chuckled as he walked beside Thunderbolt.

“I think we need to remember why we are here. It’s not for entertainment. We need to find the elementals,” Sapphire said, worry lacing her voice.

Nezha gulped. That was right. She and Kayan could sense them. As they approached the building, her skin prickled. “Yeah, we need to find earth and soul.”

“They’re definitely in that building somewhere. Hey, look over there! I think those are the elemental dancers.” Kayan motioned his head toward a line of people in masks.

Nezha noticed one of them making a hat out of stone he had lifted from the ground. She couldn’t help but stare. A long stare as the dark-skinned boy grinned and spoke to the man in front of him.

Chapter 15 Dancers

"Nezha," Sapphire said, ripping her attention from the line that shrunk and the interesting boy who was out of her view.

Kayan and Nezha shared a look.

They had no chance to speak. At the entrance was a man who asked for tickets. Kayan approached the man and showed him his Tome. The man scanned it with a device and nodded to him. "Thank you. Enjoy the masquerade and a have a magical evening."

"Wait, how'd he let you in?" Thunderbolt pushed Kayan's shoulder.

"I bought tickets on the way. You can get them over the Tome." Kayan grinned and showed the screen, revealing he had bought tickets for all of them.

"You really thought ahead. That's good. I was worried Thunderbolt would be a jerk and try to knock him out otherwise." Nezha glanced at Thunderbolt.

"Hey, I wouldn't do that.... Okay, I might have tried."

Nezha tisked him. "That would be messed up."

"We have entered the correct way, so let us move onward," Sapphire cut in.

"Woah," Nezha and Thunderbolt spoke in unison as everyone walked through the door to the wide ballroom.

They'd made it on time. The doors closed behind them after a few minutes as Nezha continued to stare at the empty stage.

"I'm so anxious to meet them," Kayan breathed as he followed Nezha's gaze to the stage. His fingers tapped against his thigh.

People began to pour over the ballroom floor in clusters. Woman laughed and some men had their hands over their partners' waists. She overheard a couple speaking.

"Do you like my choice?" The man said, his lips curved into a smile.

"Yes. You couldn't have chosen a better place to visit."

It seemed Veer was a tourist hotspot. No wonder Nezha had seen all sorts of people in the crowds.

Nezha backed up and nearly bumped into Kayan. *I can't bear being in a place like this. But... We need to find them or we can't give the Angel of Mercy, Mirkhas his soul, or find his body. I won't let Noorenia die.*

"It's a little boring right now," Kayan began, but when he noticed her expression, he added, "Something wrong, Nezha?"

"Be careful of what you think around here... I don't know what it is, but I keep smelling something sharp and tangy, but also cold. There's this vanilla scent too."

Kayan averted his gaze. He placed a hand to his mouth and then lowered it gently. "I've been smelling that, too and it's filling my head."

Sapphire moved to Nezha's side. "It's jinni magic. It smells like blood. They're masking it with vanilla, as you noticed."

Nezha gave Sapphire a look. An energy hummed under her skin.

"We can't help it, though. As much as I hate it here too," Thunderbolt said.

"It's different. It's not our normal. But we shouldn't let fear be the reason we quit. We need to find a way." Sapphire wore a determined expression.

"Then how about we try to get backstage? Maybe the jawhars we're looking for are among the dancers?" Kayan suggested. All eyes were focused on the stage.

"That's a good idea, but how?" asked Nezha.

Music echoed through the hall. It was upbeat, melodic and heavy with bass.

"Welcome!" A man's voice announced from the stage. His voice rang out in enthusiasm as the music dropped to a hush. "Welcome all to the Plume Paradise Masquerade! Join us tonight for our wondrous elemental dancers. They will enthrall you with their magical performance. They will be performing in half an hour. Remember to enjoy the night and let yourself flow with the magic." The man brushed back the red curtains and vanished. The music became loud again, but it was enough for others to hold conversations.

Nezha's eyebrows knitted as her breath became shallow. "The magic is making me uneasy."

Thunderbolt squeezed her shoulder. "I know. We'll have t' find them before we get swept away by it."

Kayan held a glass of sparkling lime water in one hand. He took a sip and his gaze slid to Nezha and Thunderbolt.

"We need to join the dancers somehow," Kayan announced with a grin.

Nezha noticed the shine in his eyes and returned the grin. "You're thinking of something." She was still scared, but she knew they had to do something before the magic influenced them.

***

The stage lit up with revolving lights as Zul Sharr and Obsidian entered the Plume Paradise Masquerade.

Obsidian's iron dragon mask reflected the light display. His steely gaze fell on Sapphire as they walked toward the middle of the floor. His heart started to boom and it jolted him. He'd never seen her before, but as he continued to look at her, it was as if everyone else had become slow and out of focus.

"Stay vigilant, Glass Dragon," Zul whispered to him and tilted his head. His silver filigree mask glinted as it caught the light. He was wearing a black tunic with a tinge of purple to it. The cuffs were gold.

Obsidian hadn't heard that name in a long time. Glass Dragon. He'd been called that only by Lexa. A long time ago, he had suffered a blow to the head. The first person he'd seen as he'd regained consciousness was her. She had offered him refuge and a job. He wasn't sure where he had been before. If he had left family or friends behind from his past identity. He turned to Zul Sharr. "Right. I'll be around," he said and sauntered off.

Zul waited for Lexa. She'd told him she'd be near the entrance.

He hated the warm vanilla notes that spilled over the magic. There was a part of him where the jinni aura coursed through his veins that delighted in the icy, sanguine scent of magic. The tang had filled his head and he scowled and crossed his arms. "Where is she?" he hissed.

"You missed me, Sire?" Lexa walked in. Her hair was jet black instead of its former curls of flame.

"Lexa?" Zul narrowed his eyes as she approached.

"Yup! Like the cat mask?" She flicked the ear. It was an Egyptian cat mask. All black with gold details on the nose, inner ear and eyes. The forehead had an upside-down crescent moon and the eyes had golden curves painted under them. She purred. "Meow."

"Yeah, looks good on you, actually."

Lexa cleared her throat.

"So, Amaya didn't join us?" Zul asked, glancing over her shoulder.

"She's here," Lexa said, her eyes gleaming.

Behind her, Amaya appeared from out of the shadows. Her auburn hair seemed darker. "I felt drawn to this place. The jawhars are here."

"Oh, hey, Amaya." Zul Sharr blinked. It was as if he were speaking to a shadow. For some reason, she was refusing to walk out into the ballroom. He surveyed the floor, as people continued to eat, drink and dance. "So, are we going to stalk them?"

Lexa's lips curved into a devilish smile. "You'll see. I have something I need to do. Sire, they'll be intoxicated by the magic. They may even destroy themselves."

"What? I told you we're not killing them," Zul Sharr spat, as Lexa started to sway to the music. The jinni aura had been kept at bay when he had been celebrating the day before, but now he could feel it boil inside him. The jinni energy crept up into his blood and it was taking him over again. The hunger for chaos beckoned him.

"Hmm? Sire, I'll be crushing their spirits. My knives, let's say…stabbed them with magic. Destroying who they are is so much more pleasurable than seeing their souls taken from them. If they die in the process, that's not my fault. Magic can be like that."

Zul Sharr shrugged her off when Lexa touched his arm. "As long as they're alive. Other than that, have fun, Lexa."

Lexa laughed. "Oh, I will, Sire." She laughed and leaned against the wall as Zul Sharr slipped away into the crowd.

***

"You should taste the lime sparkler. It's really good." Kayan smiled broadly at Nezha and handed her a glass.

"Thanks, Kayan." Nezha carefully accepted the drink and sipped it.

The song had changed into another beat best suited for dancing with a partner. She downed the rest and gave the glass to one of the waiters who passed by.

Kayan turned to look at her and his eyes were intense, brimming with something she couldn't understand. Nezha's eyes widened as she tried to pinpoint just what it was that had shifted his demeanor. A sudden burst of wind whisked her against the wall.

Kayan sauntered toward her, the wind the only barrier between them. Its touch was warm as it danced over her skin. Really warm, almost hot. He placed a hand to the wall, his arm nearly brushing her waist. He was too close. Her eyes roamed his face, trying to figure out what he was doing. "Kayan… what are you—"

Kayan's lips parted and then turned into a roguish smile. The heat of fear rushed through her chest. Air spun over his finger, and it pushed her chin up so he could meet her gaze. His eyes scanned hers and he looked from her lips to her eyes again. "Don't be scared, Nezha. We should have some fun." His voice had a sultry edge.

This couldn't be him. It had to be the magic. Nezha wriggled and the wind loosened its grasp. She slipped to the side.

"What? It's…" She could hardly think and bit her lip. She tilted her head down and looked up at him. Her hands trembled. Kayan's eyes were still on her. Watching, waiting. It was her move. Nezha stepped toward him.

His hand rose slowly, his forefinger brushing the cloth of her shawl. He captured it between his fingers and pressed his lips to it.

Nezha couldn't move.

Everyone, everything around Nezha seemed to melt away. It was simply him and her. His eyes were green and blue and seemed to coax her closer. So pretty.

Kayan tilted his head and smiled, his eyes shifting to the side and then back to her. He began walking. It was an invitation to follow. Nezha started after him as he weaved through the crowd. Her heart was pounding. Something latched onto her mind and refused to let go.

She followed him, or more like cornered him on the stairs which led to a balcony.

"Where are you running to?" Nezha said, her smile curling in pauses up her reluctant lips.

Kayan's nostrils flared and then he ran up the remaining stairs. Nezha blinked and exhaled. A part of her tried to remain conscious, but it was swept away by the vicious magic. It was beginning to excite her.

Flames escaped her palms and slipped around Kayan's body as if they were capturing his every move, the soft curl of his silken hair, the warmth of skin. Everything unreachable to Nezha. She stepped closer and stopped as he turned to face her.

Kayan tilted his head and his eyes rippled with hunger. The wind danced around her waist, toyed with the cloth around her shoulders, slinking up, brushing her cheeks. She gasped and pressed her palm to her mouth. Sparks blossomed up her spine. He leaned closer to her, but there was no touch. Only elemental.

"Nezha," he growled. Then his voice softened. "I'm…" He winced as if he was battling the magic's grasp on him. As soon as his real self emerged, it vanished again, drowning.

"Kayan," she said. Her voice came out in a rasp. Nezha shook her head and her arm fell to her side. "I don't know…what's happening."

A surge of water rushed by Kayan, shoving him aside and knocking Nezha down and the breath from her lungs.

A woman appeared near the edge of the roof. Dressed all in black, waves of shadows rippling around her legs. She wore a white fox mask with red details under its eyes, a line down its long nose and a circle at its forehead.

"It's…Amaya." Nezha sat up onto her knees.

Kayan stood and lunged toward Amaya, the wind swelling up to knock her down, but Amaya moved aside with a fluid grace.

Kayan turned back and rushed to Nezha. Nezha glanced at the glass door on the other side of the balcony which led to the main floor. In a panic, she shot up to open the door and stood on the other side, Kayan entering right after her.

They watched Amaya approach. Nezha kept a hand on the knob. Her heart was fluttering inside her chest so loudly that it was the only thing she could hear. All she could smell was the tang of blood.

Kayan's eyes remained intently on her.

Amaya rose a hand and pressed her palm to the glass. Where her skin met the surface, crystals formed and spread out, layering ice over the door.

Kayan's lips parted and he inched closer to Nezha.

Amaya inhaled sharply. She had stepped back. She pressed her palm again to the glass. Nezha backed from the glass, huffing. Cracking sounded from where Amaya's fingers pressed against the glass. The cracks formed like veins, rippling across it, and it shattered. The blast sent Nezha and Kayan back against the wall. Amaya stood motionless for a few moments and then slipped away toward the stairs and disappeared.

Nezha didn't know how long it had been when a man passed her and approached the shape she thought was Kayan. Her sight was rimmed with stars and unfocused. She tried to keep her eyes on Kayan, but the room spun. The next moment the same man was beside her. She could see his dark purple tunic, a sleeve with gold trim and his lips reciting something. There was no light, no scent of magic; just relief that began to pour over her heart as the fire of excitement was doused. She blinked, closed her eyes and he was gone.

And then, Kayan was beside her. "Nezha! Hey, are you okay?"

"Kayan?" She turned her head to the side and then back to him. "Yeah. My arm feels bruised, though. Are *you* okay?" Nezha's gaze didn't leave his as he used a gentle wind to lift her to her feet.

"Yeah… just a small cut on my arm." Kayan breathed out.

There was silence between them as they stood before each other.

"There was someone here who…helped us," Nezha began slowly.

"I thought I saw someone too. He put a hand to my heart and was saying something. A supplication? I don't know what it was, but I don't feel…" Kayan's eyes softened as he looked at Nezha.

She wasn't sure when it began, but Nezha liked him. All this time she thought it was kindness since he was a companion. She'd only been thinking of her duty. To avenge her aunt, to find the angel's soul orbs. To protect Noorenia. Kayan had been there to support her. He'd never tried to change who she was. He wanted to be her confidante, not a crutch or a barrier. She liked the moments he was playful, the moments he'd smile bright, the moments their gazes met for a little longer than normal… Maybe she *did* care about him. *I… Do I like Kayan?*

Kayan's face was back to normal. That expression as if he were about to smile. That kindness and boyish charm. Now, though, there was something much more serious about him.

"Nezha… I—"

"Nezha, Kayan!" Thunderbolt had run up the stairs. "I heard glass shatter. I was trying t' keep an eye on you two but lost you in the crowd. Are you two okay?"

Nezha turned to him. "Yeah."

As the companions started back the way they'd come, Nezha walked in front of Kayan. She didn't meet his gaze. "We need to talk about this later," she whispered. "I don't know, but I can't look at you right now. All that happened was awkward."

***

"Oh yeah, we definitely need to." A hesitant laugh escaped Kayan's lips. "It was the magic. It made us feel these intense emotions." He was thankful to the stranger who had helped them. He wasn't sure how he knew. Maybe Lexa had something to do with it, or the magic itself in this whole place. And there was also Amaya. Appearing like a wraith behind him. *That made things awkward for us. Nezha's not looking my way. I remember what I said...What I did. I can't believe I did that. I didn't have control, but...*

***

"I know. Now's not the time. We need to find the jawhars."

"Right," Kayan agreed, his lips quirking.

"Where's Sapphire?" Nezha asked, as the three approached the stage.

Thunderbolt looked across the floor. "She said she wanted time to herself."

"Thunderbolt, the magic made me and Kayan lose control…" Nezha said, looking toward the stage as she spoke.

Thunderbolt stepped closer and held her arm. Small pricks of electricity tingled over her heart. "Whatever it was, I don't sense it in you anymore. I did keep sensing Lexa around you two. It might have been her."

"And…we saw Amaya."

"What? What happened? Did she hurt you two?"

"She froze the glass door, but we're good." Nezha played with her hijab, trying to focus on the familiarity of the elementals she'd felt earlier. "I hope they're both here. The jawhars."

Kayan sighed. Then he put on a grin. "I have an idea."

"I'm listening," Thunderbolt said.

Chapter 16 Showtime

Sapphire heard the music slow. When she turned, a man stood before her. He wore the mask of a dragon. The silver shone as a fraction of light hit it. He simply bowed his head and extended his arm to her. An invitation. Sapphire stepped closer and placed her hand into his. As they moved through the sea of dancing couples, the stranger faced her and placed a gentle hand onto her back. Sapphire straightened as he moved with grace. He led her as they moved and she pressed her right hand to his chest. The way he moved reminded her of Obsidian. If it weren't for that feeling, she wouldn't have touched him.

She met eyes with him in a glance and his were deep green. She wasn't sure if they were as dark as they seemed right now, as the lighting had dimmed. Something in her pulled her toward him. A feeling that she knew this person. That he was Obsidian. Strange. There was something different about this man, though. There was a sadness that reflected in his eyes. A spark was dimmed. Obsidian was more of a leader. An inspiration to his friends and family. The only characteristics this man had in common with him were his determined and purposeful steps.

She couldn't take her eyes off his face. Her mind was trying to figure out just who he was. She never relied on her emotions. She was a logical person. Even though her heart kept shouting to her about Obsidian, she didn't believe it. She ignored its pounding. As they moved, his heartbeat was getting louder and it had synced with her own. The thrum loud against her hand. Two beings in movement so fluid. Even as they glided around other dancers, it felt so natural. A part of her wished it was him.

A memory of him popped into her mind. When she had been upset and unable to tell anyone. She found Obsidian beside her.

"What's wrong?" he said, a small smile on his face as if he was amused she was hiding it from him of all people.

"Nothing, I'm fine," she'd told him.

"That is the fakest 'I'm fine' I've ever heard."

She'd laughed, despite the ache in her heart. The one she'd felt when she hadn't seen him in weeks. When the war had torn them apart. Obsidian had been on missions and left her heart in pieces with his absence. She couldn't put into words how his gentleness, his presence always made her feel. As if she wasn't simply a guardian, but a being who needed protection too, whose wants meant something when her own darkness became her enemy.

"I... just had a tough time while you were gone."

Obsidian had stared into her eyes then. When she couldn't meet his gaze, he grabbed her hand and leaned in to her. "You took too long to say I missed you."

The music had regained its tempo, and her mind fell back into reality.

"I'm..." No other words could slip out. His hand fell from her back and he led her to the stairs and toward the balcony.

He didn't speak. More painful memories resurfaced. *I can still remember his voice…but only a faint memory.* She studied the way he stood and looked up at the moon. She followed his gaze and stood beside him. For a moment she saw Obsidian on a moonlit night, blood on his face, a gentle smile as he carried her to a patch of grass. Obsidian shielding her. Her sword of light killing a rebellious jinni. Obsidian looking up at the sky and then pressing a kiss to her temple.

"It is far away, but we see it so clearly," she said, taking a deep breath.

The man turned to her. He nodded. In his eyes she thought she could sense recognition. As if she had just said something that belonged to his own thoughts.

Sapphire thought about Nezha, Kayan and her brother. They had to find the other jawhars. She couldn't stand here and ponder the identity of this man.

"Thank you for your time. It was a delight." Sapphire dipped her head politely, smiling faintly at the stranger.

The man nodded in return, his lips curling into a solemn smile.

He began walking away before she took another step. Her gaze followed him and her heart continued pounding. A small voice was telling her to stop him, to ask him who he was. She didn't listen.

He stopped before the door and looked over his shoulder. "The pleasure was mine. The moon borrows light and makes it brighter, easier for our eyes to see its beauty. You are as the glowing moon. Giving life to rock as if it were molten lava." He turned away again and disappeared out of view.

Sapphire stood there, frozen. His words had struck a chord somewhere in her mind. She could picture Obsidian shoving Thunderbolt and smiling broadly. Obsidian standing over a mountain and leading her over the rocks. Obsidian at the front of a group of fighters charging toward violent jinn, his eyes determined and his courage unbreakable. Tears welled up in her eyes, but she brushed them aside.

Her feet regained their use and she fled from the balcony. She wanted to run after him, but as she returned to the crowd, there was no dragon-masked man to be seen. Her eyes fell upon Nezha and the others and she walked toward them, her strides much slower.

***

"Light and earth elementals, you are up first." The woman in charge of the entertainment held a tablet.

All the elemental dancers were behind stage. Unbeknownst to each other, Dante and Asad waited for their turns and to find the other elementals they'd both had dreams about.

"Go give them a show they won't forget!" She shooed them toward the stage. As light elementals walked past, Dante caught a whiff of a spring breeze. "I can't pass up a chance to dance."

The crowd roared as the dancers began their show.

***

Thunderbolt watched Sapphire approach. "Oh, hey sis. Did you enjoy yourself here? Even though there's sickening jinn magic and its smell wafting with vanilla."

"Yes," Sapphire replied simply.

"We're going to have a dance off," Kayan declared with a grin. "Once I distract them, you need to get onstage. Sapphire? Can you distort light?"

"Yes," she said, seeming reluctant to pull her gaze from the crowd as she turned to him. "What are you planning?"

"When you and Nezha go toward the stage, I want you to distort the light so the others can't see them."

"I can do that," Sapphire said.

"Smart zaan," said Thunderbolt. "I'm impressed."

Kayan lifted his hands submissively. "Hey, I just have the ideas. I need our teamwork to get it done. Nothing is impossible."

"Your can-do energy is so contagious." Nezha didn't meet his gaze for long. Her eyes simply flickered to his face as she watched the elementals on stage.

Kayan smiled. "Why, thank you. While I distract them, you two can get to the back, change into their uniforms. After that, we'll find the jawhars. I can sense them around here."

"And how are we going to do that?" Thunderbolt said.

Kayan grinned. "You'll see."

***

On stage, an earth elemental stood with his arm out. He held a palm full of earth. Before the audience's eyes, he waved his hand and an orange and white cat appeared. Another wave of his hand and it became a red macaw, glistening feathers as red as rubies. He waved his hands in different ways, various animals appeared and finally a bouquet of flowers poked out from his ears, then out of his nose, then seemed to simply appear in and out of his hands. He threw a vibrant blue flower at a woman who giggled and screamed in glee. He stroked the head of a monkey and placed it into a cage with white silk over it.

A light elemental worked with him, shining lights that would twinkle or shimmer like the surface of the ocean. A water elemental joined and the earth elemental freed a palm-sized fish into the water, moving it through the air, keeping the fish within. The light elemental let light fall as if it were rain lancing down the people. Gasps and cheers sounded from the audience as the lights changed colours. The fish glowed as it swam through the stream of water in the air. The earth elemental and light elementals bowed their heads and took their leave.

Unknown to the crowd, soul elementals would tweak the emotions of the people whose eyes they could see. The soul elementals walked out behind the crowd. They waited until one of the air elementals began to sing.

He stood to the side of the stage. His voice carried the echoes and melodies of music. Air elementals could sing exceptionally well. It was like nothing Nezha had ever heard. It reminded her of the rhythmic way the one who said the call to prayer, the muezzin, would recite it. His voice was so beautiful and full of emotion.

"So, Kayan, what's your idea?" Thunderbolt asked.

Kayan spun the wind around his body and hopped onto the stage. His hair swayed with grace and his eyes carried mischief as he took hold of the mic and said, "Dance battle!"

The air elemental continued to sing and the soul elemental dancers looked at each other and started nodding and grinning.

"Hey!" the manager of the performance said, but before she could say any more or move, a boy spoke.

"Hey, I like his idea. Why not?"

"Yeah, dance battles sound amazing!" an air elemental chimed in.

She looked at her dancers all grinning and chatting.

The audience was cheering loudly as the air elemental started beat boxing. His voice became many instruments at once. Nezha kept trying to see if there really were instruments being played.

"Oh yeah!" one soul elemental drawled loudly into the mic as Kayan handed it to him. The latter stood in the middle as two soul elementals and three fire elementals surrounded him.

"Here we go!"

That was their cue. Nezha and Thunderbolt ascended onto the stage with Sapphire right behind them. She had distorted the light as they walked behind a water elemental who was dancing and forming bubbles and ice crystals around herself. No one could see them since the person they walked in front of didn't react.

People in the crowd were whistling and hollering as Kayan and two other elementals began dancing.

One elemental backed up and did a flip. They stood with their companions as Dante joined them in the circle.

Asad clicked his tongue and made out the forms. There was something strange. His mind picked up colorful energies. Around Kayan was a colourful aura which was predominantly green. Asad left the side of the stage and walked toward the group. As he passed Nezha, he saw her outline and her aura was in colour also. A bright yellow aura. Asad continued to click and moved his head. Then he saw Dante's outline in his head. A red aura. He knew something about the energy of humans' souls. He knew red meant the root chakra and its element was earth. It all clicked, literally. *They're the elementals I needed to find. They have to be. Why else are they the only ones whose energies I can see stronger?* He walked toward Nezha.

Kayan didn't want all the attention to himself. He backed out and some air elementals congratulated him.

"Nice moves," one boy said.

"Yeah, that was slick as the wind," a girl said and smiled at him.

"Thank you." Kayan's eyes were looking for Nezha and the siblings. He could feel the energies of the other elementals around him. The wind picked up as he walked towards Nezha, Thunderbolt and Sapphire. An unfamiliar boy was standing a few paces away from them. When the boy suddenly turned toward her, Nezha froze. Kayan held his breath. Despite the friends still being cloaked by Sapphire's light distortion, the boy appeared to be focusing on Nezha.

"Hey," Kayan heard Thunderbolt hiss as he approached the three. "What's wrong?"

Nezha discreetly jutted her chin towards the boy. "He's looking at us."

“That cannot be,” said Sapphire, standing motionless. “I have you veiled with light.”

The boy began toward them and stopped just inches from Nezha. Her eyes widened and flames began pouring around her palms. They swirled like ribbons, encircling her arms as she looked into the boy's eyes.

Sapphire stopped distorting the light around them, their bodies visible more clearly again.

Kayan widened his eyes as he watched the flames swirl around Nezha. He closed the remaining distance between them.

Asad was starting to emit a sound. A sweet hum rumbled through him. He was reacting to them.

“You’re… Are you the elemental we need?” Nezha asked. “I can hear it. That sound.”

Asad tilted his head. “You’re a fire elemental, aren’t you?” he said. “I can see a yellow aura from you in my mind.”

Kayan also heard the humming. “What’s going on? Is he making that sound?” The wind continued to move, sifting through Asad’s hair.

Nezha nodded. “Yeah.”

Asad turned his head slightly when he heard Kayan speak. “You’re a wind elemental… I’m a soul elemental.” The sound continued. It was low but a sweet and airy tune.

***

Dante was still dancing, but soon he let someone else have a turn and his skin prickled. He looked around and his eyes fell on Nezha, Kayan and Asad. *There's that weird energy again. Oh yeah, those element wielders. I need to find them. I was havin' too much fun.* The energy pulled at him and he pushed through the crowd toward them.

"It really is you two… We're missing earth," Asad pointed out.

Catching movement out of the corner of her eye, Nezha turned and so did Kayan.

Kayan looked at Dante. "Well, there's someone coming this way."

Dante soon stood before them and cocked his head. "Yo." Flowers began popping up between his fingers and the stems from his mask were twining around his head.

Thunderbolt snorted, placing a hand on his hip. "I guess that means he's the earth elemental."

"Wait, hold up. Are y'all elementals?" Dante asked.

"Yup. And from our reaction, I guess you're all the elementals we need," Nezha said.

Asad smiled. That was what she had said in his dream. *The elementals we need.*

"I'm Asad. Nice to meet you." He smiled gently.

"The name's Dante." Dante held a hand out as he turned to Asad.

Asad turned and shook the other elemental's hand.

Kayan and Nezha introduced themselves.

"You have a different form of sight," Sapphire observed as she stood before Asad.

Asad's eyes widened and his skin heated in embarrassment. "What…"

“I already knew that he’s blind.” boasted Dante folding his arms.

“What?” Nezha’s brows rose.

“Yeah, yeah. I am blind. But I can see in other ways.” Asad clicked his tongue and pointed to the curtains. “There’s a light up there. And there’s a tall person standing beside me to the far right.

“Wait…how?” Kayan asked.

“I echolocate…” Asad explained in monotone, seeming a bit irritated about explaining it.

Sapphire absentmindedly stroked the small crystal swan on her mask “That explains the high clicks I heard from you.”

“Well… that’s something,” Thunderbolt said, unsuccessfully trying to conceal his amazement.

“Anyways… someone’s goin’ to notice us here if we keep showing off,” Dante said, eyeing the woman who was staring at their group.

“Yeah…” Nezha agreed as they all began walking toward the stairs.

The elemental dancers had finished the dance.

Dante looked over his shoulder and saw the boss approaching them. The same woman who had given him his mask. “Uh, we’re going to be busted if we don’t move faster.”

Asad turned and clicked. He could feel her energy and see her silhouette. “That irritated woman again. Yeah, she’s the coordinator for the performance.”

The water elemental dancers were casting bubbles and icy designs in the air.

Everything went dark and the audience gasped and screamed.

Chapter 17 Connection

Asad's heart drummed loudly as he heard people screaming.

"Hey, I can get us out of here."

"What? How?" Thunderbolt asked. They hadn't moved from the stage, but people shoved and bumped into them.

"I can echolocate. A bat can navigate its way in the night, and I can too."

Sapphire flicked a light from her palm, but then it winked out of existence. The notes of vanilla and a honied-tang became stronger, the magic permeating the whole room.

"I can't form a light. It seems the magic has become stronger."

"We have to stick together." Kayan considered for a moment. "I'm going to make a current that'll act like a vacuum. Just put your hand around it and it'll be like holding onto a rope."

Everyone searched the air until they could feel it.

"Whoa!" Dante's hand had probably met the funnel of wind.

"Everyone got it?" Kayan asked.

They all voiced their assent.

"Asad, lead the way," Nezha said.

Asad clicked his tongue. "We're at the stairs. Try not to trip."

They heard loud banging, screaming and shouting. Someone called out, "We're trapped!"

"The magic's getting worse. All I can smell is that tang," Kayan said.

"Why do you need us anyways?" Dante yelled.

Nezha kept a tight hold on the rope of wind as they slowly descended the stairs. "Didn't you get a sign? We were told by the Angel of Mercy. We could sense you both here. And you reacted to us. Isn't that enough of a reason?" She was gritting her teeth, irritated by the magic.

"Some monster attacked our home," Dante said.

"A jinni…" Nezha breathed.

"Genie? Nah, he only wanted to grant a death wish." Dante chuckled. "And I knew about Noorenia before anyways."

"Well… My intuition led me here. And I used to live here a long time ago," Asad informed them as he guided them safely down the stairs and to the ballroom floor.

"We're all connected because of our ties to Noorenia," Kayan observed.

"What happened when you defeated the jinni?" Sapphire asked, panic lacing her voice.

"It disappeared," Dante said and swerved as someone bumped into him.

An announcement blared, echoing across the building. *"Please head to the exits to the right and left of the stage. We're sorry for the inconvenience. Please head to the exits to the right and left of the stage..."*

"Inconvenience…" Asad mumbled in annoyance.

"How?" Sapphire asked. "How did it disappear?" She pressed on.

"There was a feather and some smoke. I dunno. It was freaky. The genie or whatever looked exactly like me."

"Rana had once made doppelgangers of us all," Sapphire said.

"Yeah, it does sound like what happened to us." Kayan agreed.

"A trap..." Nezha said.

"I sense Lexa…that damn red-head," Thunderbolt snarled.

Asad continued clicking. "There's someone on our left." He clicked more. "We need to speed up! Everyone's gone!"

They headed toward the doors.

"Welcome to the show!" purred a sultry female voice.

"Lexa…" Nezha struggled to catch a glimpse of—or sense—the jinni and her companions.

"Hello, humans and angels!" Lexa had a wicked smile over her face as the lights slowly brightened again.

Thunderbolt threw his hand forward, but no electricity formed. "What the hell?"

"Oh, the heart of Noorenia won't let you use its energy here. Its all magic. Beautiful jinni magic is all around you!"

Dante gritted his teeth. "Who the hell is she?"

"She's a jinni and the one who sent that monster after you," Kayan said. "The angels can't use their powers…but we can." He leaned toward Nezha.

"Something's wrong." Nezha stood closer to the group. There was nowhere to go. Magic had suffocated them.

Lexa walked off the stage, her footfalls over the stairs menacing. She spoke as she made her way down. "You thought this would be a fun reunion. You're wrong. You know I have something you want."

"Where is she?" Thunderbolt demanded.

"That's right…there's a water elemental too," Asad said.

"Yeah, an East Asian girl…" Dante said, recalling his dream.

Lexa stood in front of the stage. She was still far from them.

"You poor souls. Jawhars thinking they'd united." Lexa tisked and shook her head.

"Shut the hell up!" Dante said.

The lights were now bright.

"Amaya, would you like to join us?" Lexa glanced to the side.

Amaya walked into view from the shadows near the stairs. Her dress lapped at her legs.

"The water jawhar…" Nezha said as everyone stumbled backward and faced the stage.

There was a silence as Amaya drew closer. She stopped before them. Her eyes were dull. Her burgundy hair was over both her shoulders. She held her head low and then raised it higher. Her arm lifted and she opened her hand. Water poured out.

Nezha's heart slammed into her chest. Kayan leapt into action and waved most of the water away with the wind. droplets splashed them.

Lexa's eyes widened and the shadows around her thickened. They unraveled around her body and lashed out at them.

Nezha's flames, Kayan's wind and even Dante's vines didn't stop them. The shadows glued their feet to the floor and began wrapping around their bodies.

Lexa bit her lower lip and tilted her head, as if she found delight at their struggle.

Thunderbolt formed a fist and as much as he tried, he couldn't summon the electricity. "Damn you and your magic!"

"Hey, I can't move! What she do to us?" Dante squirmed.

"The shadows…they're trying to do something…to us." Asad could hear the pulse inside the shadows. It was beating low and loud. At a time like this, he was thankful he couldn't see it engulf him.

Amaya's hands were shaking as she walked toward them. In her hand was one of Lexa's shadow daggers.

Lexa was breathing faster. "Do it."

Asad could hear her approach them with slow deliberate steps. He clicked with his tongue again and saw the colour of Amaya's aura. An orange that was dimmed and not as vibrant as the others. *She's one of…one of us.* Asad still couldn't understand exactly why he was here. But he trusted his instincts. He did know he was meant to be here.

"Just you wait! You stab me with that and I'll get you back, you son of a—" Dante said just as Amaya stabbed him with the dagger. His body froze.

Asad thought desperately about what to do. He clicked more and from where he heard Lexa, he could see her silhouette. And around her, wisps of smoky energy. It was all darkness. There was a pulse. Similar to the shadows around him. He breathed in sharply and lowered his head when he heard Nezha speak.

"No…we need them…"

Amaya sent the dagger through Nezha.

"Nezha! You monster…you're not going to win! We will!" Kayan spoke. Asad could hear his voice shake. He sounded as if he spoke through gritted teeth. Amaya approached and he, too, was hit with the dagger's icy fear.

"You waste your breath humans. Now you'll break your souls and it'll all be over." Lexa laughed.

Amaya was advancing closer to Asad. *Come on... I can't be scared. I need to keep trusting my intuition. Please Most High... Help me... Help me understand.*

Asad shut away his fearful thoughts and concentrated on the energy from his throat and the aura around Amaya. When the dagger was about to pierce him, he finally reached her thoughts.

Her hand stilled. *Do you hear me? Amaya? Are you afraid? Don't be. I'm not here to save you, but you can save yourself. You need to believe. You need to trust your heart. Trust the Creator. This can't be what you're meant to be!*

Amaya's aura grew stronger. The jinni magic was dissipating, slowly at first and then more and more quickly. And then it winked out entirely.

Asad's body began to hum and energy formed around him, pulsing loudly.

"What—" The energy surged toward Lexa and she was sent crashing into the wall.

Everyone regained the use of their bodies.

***

"Asad! You did it!" Kayan exclaimed, smiling widely as he shrugged off the dark clinging to him.

"Whoa. That was actually awesome!" Dante said and walked toward him.

Sapphire and Thunderbolt turned to Lexa.

"Ugh, I still feel sick and weak." Thunderbolt groaned. "Sorry I couldn't do anything."

"Don't worry." Nezha reassured him.

"We need to leave. Before the magic in here regains its energy," Sapphire said.

"What about Amaya?" Nezha turned to look at the girl.

Amaya's eyes were wide and she was staring at Asad.

"We can't leave her!" Nezha pleaded, meeting the siblings' gazes.

"We can't do anything right now. We need t' leave." Thunderbolt insisted, grabbing her arm.

"She has the advantage here, since they've filled this place with jinni magic. We'll be killed if we stay longer." Sapphire's eyes were full of remorse as she glanced at Amaya. "We'll help her, Nezha. But right now, we need to save the two people we found."

Nezha turned to their new companions. Dante was playfully nudging Asad. "Yeah. We'll see her safe one day though. I won't rest until she's out of Lexa's clutches," Nezha conceded and they all walked out.

"That's the Nezha we know!" Kayan said, grinning at her.

Nezha didn't meet his gaze, but she smiled.

When they made it outside, there was a small crowd of people. No one had been injured, but they still looked shaken by the ordeal.

“We were nearly killed in there!” Dante said in exasperation. “Look, I’m not here to just join your group. I know there’s somethin’ going on between us all, but I can’t find her if I’m not alive.”

“You act like you’re breaking up with us,” Asad said flatly.

“You’ll get killed if you leave. Lexa’s after all of us,” Thunderbolt said. His irritation hadn’t left even when they couldn’t smell the magic anymore.

“We need to stick together. The Angel of Mercy, Mirkhas, said that we need the jawhars to help him find his body. Or at least it’s something to do with his body,” Nezha informed them.

“Let me do my thing and I’ll get back to y’all.” Dante started walking.

“You’re being a fool!” Thunderbolt snarled.

“You’re making a mistake. We need to find the angel’s body before it’s too late!” Nezha started after him.

“Let him go.” Kayan raised his arm in front of Nezha. “We need him to trust us. If we force him, we’ll risk losing him like we have the water elemental.”

Nezha’s shoulders slumped. “Yeah, but…”

Sapphire had been observing as everything went on. “He will return to us, Nezha. If the divine wills it, he will. You are all connected. I don’t have any doubt.”

Nezha sighed heavily. “Just know that I’m really upset about this. We finally had us all together…”

“I get you, kid. I’m not exactly thrilled, either,” Thunderbolt said.

"It sounded like he has someone he's trying to find," Kayan remembered as he stared after the lone jawhar. "You know that too well, I'm sure."

"He did say a *her*." Nezha realized why he was so adamant about finding that person. Lamis was like a sister to her and she would have done the same. "I understand now. It's someone close to him. Let's go." Her voice was soft as she made her way to the sidewalk. They headed back to the hotel.

Chapter 18 A Choice

Back in the hotel, Mayor Rustam had kindly given them another room. Asad and Kayan shared it with Thunderbolt. They were currently sitting in the room with Sapphire and Nezha.

"So, let me get this straight, there's an angel without its soul?" Asad asked.

"Yes," Sapphire said.

"Okay. So, Zul Sharr's pretty much a puppet of the jinni we saw. Lexa, right?"

"A puppet, huh?" Thunderbolt said and folded his arms across his chest. "You could say that."

"We needed you and Dante, since the angel said we needed you both," Kayan said. He leaned on the mattress and shifted his sitting position.

"I thought we were finally getting somewhere… But because Dante has something he needs to do, we'll have to find a way to get Amaya on our side." Nezha looked out the window to leaves twirling in the wind.

"Hmm. Do you think she was brainwashed by Lexa?" Asad asked. He placed a hand to White Lie, snug in his belt loop. Just thinking about someone's mind being filled with lies and half-truths, it made him feel like he could understand. It reminded him of White Lie. Having to rely on the way it knocked into things as he moved the rod around. Before he could echolocate, he was never sure what he might run into.

"I think that's highly likely," Sapphire replied. "She does have the scent of that jinni around her."

"Ugh, falling victim to *her*. I can imagine she must be scared," Nezha's voice softened.

"Yeah, that monster. She gives me the creeps when she licks her lips." Kayan mock shivered.

"So, what are we going t' do right now?" Thunderbolt leaned toward the others. He sat on the couch with Sapphire. "Dante left on his own mission, and we still have that girl, Amaya. We're out of options and I'm going t' get real mad if I just sit around."

Kayan sighed. "Come on, zaan, we can't just charge in without thinking about it. We'll find a way to do it."

Sapphire remained quiet. She stared at the painting of a black stone. Around it were feathers and a white light.

Asad tilted his head. "Hmm. You know, both have things they need to work through. You said the angel wanted you to gather the… jawhars together. Maybe he wants us to help each other too. Or at least when we feel more peace in our souls, we can be helpful."

Kayan's face lit up with an open-mouthed smile. "I think you're on to something."

"Yeah. Dante wants to find someone, and we don't really know what Amaya might be going through, except of course being brainwashed by Lexa," Nezha said. "Right now, we need to sleep. We'll discuss it in the morning."

***

Amaya sat in her room. She could still hear the boy's voice in her heart. It almost sounded like it wasn't his. In a strange way, it was as if it were another part of her that he was voicing.

Her gaze lifted to the door. Downstairs, Lexa and Obsidian were busy discussing things. She could hear shuffling and their muffled voices. She wasn't sure what Zul Sharr was up to. She pushed back a lock of hair, shifted from her bed and crossed the room to the window.

It had begun to snow tonight. The plump snowflakes shook away from the sky as they descended. She shivered, more from the cold inside her, than winter's chill. She'd never tried to fight Lexa's hold on her. The bitter shadows had latched onto and enveloped her heart. They refused to let go. Icy hands. She raised her head. She wanted the feeling to go away. She missed Okaasan's kindness, Rin's laughter, Tamaki's support and her father's love. They were all muddled in her mind. How had father died? Was it the fox? Did the fox demon even exist? She knew she'd seen him and he'd chased her. But he was just a fox. All this confusion was too much. *If papa was here, he would have told me to do what's right. But here I am, just going along with it... Papa, I miss you.*

***

"You're leaving?" Rustam asked. The mayor stood up from his seat and it nearly toppled over as he lay a hand on it.

“We understand, but you will be safe. If we continue to stay, we’ll only endanger the city,” Sapphire said. Her gaze passed over Nezha and the others.

“If you’re in danger, I can keep you all safe.”

Nezha shook her head and smiled. “Rustam, you don’t need to endanger yourself for our sake. We’re supposed to protect others.”

“Mm-hmm.” Asad nodded.

“Yeah, don’t worry.” Thunderbolt wrapped a hand over the mayor’s and kept a hand on his heart. “My sis and I are guardians, remember? We know what we’re doing.”

The mayor exhaled through his nose. “Yes. You’re right. I just… Please, if you do need anything, I’m a call away.”

“We’ll keep that in mind,” Sapphire said.

The companions made their way to the bus stop, raising their voices to be heard over the bustle of midday traffic.

“So, we really are leaving,” Asad said.

Thunderbolt spoke. It was as if he wanted to keep reminding himself why, even though he didn’t agree with it. “That zaan Dante’s somewhere, Amaya’s somewhere and this city’s in danger if we stay,” he grumbled.

Nezha patted Thunderbolt’s arm. “Yeah. We can use this time to, well… do some soul-searching of our own.”

“But we already found the angel’s soul,” Kayan said and grinned when Thunderbolt raised a brow at him.

“I know what you meant… Just thought I’d remind Asad.”

“I’m blind, not an amnesiac.” Asad huffed.

Kayan pouted and folded his arms. "I was just trying to be helpful."

Nezha chuckled. "Sapphire, are we going back to Tasa's? I miss Comet."

"We might as well," Sapphire said just as their bus arrived and they hopped on board.

"I can't wait to see her!" Nezha was practically jumping from her seat.

Kayan raised his brows and his cheeks reddened as he saw her smile and converse with Sapphire, who sat beside her.

That awkwardness hadn't left. With all that happened at the Masquerade, it was looming over him like Lexa's shadows. When would they get a chance to talk again? Would Nezha ever look at him again? He could still remember all the details. The way his wind has pushed her against the wall. The way her scent had explored his mind. That feeling of… He wasn't exactly fond of reliving it. But that didn't stop him either. It made his cheeks burn and his breath catch. He thought of the moment he had pushed her chin up to meet his gaze, and that stupid grin that had spread across his face. Kayan felt a shiver go down his back. He didn't want Nezha to ignore him, let alone hate him. He wasn't sure what she'd do. A million scenarios were running through his mind. Maybe she'd distance herself? Kayan shook his head.

He touched the back of his neck and gazed out the window, watching the trees zip by. The world was spinning and inside, he was a storm. A storm? Be a storm to their silence. That's what his mother used to say to him. Although she'd meant he should help others. All he'd ever wanted was to be free and to love others. His life had involved joining his mother in raids to help the weak, taking care of his sister and father after she'd died. He'd given them his all. Until he'd given too much of himself away. It always seemed to end up like that. Being chained to responsibility. Smiling even though he wanted to tell someone how he really felt. Laughing even when he wanted to cry. But, somehow, when he was with the angels and Nezha, things changed. He wanted things for himself too. Sometimes, he thought it was selfish. To want to relax, take time to simply do things that made him happy, to laugh and have fun. Kayan smiled. He had to learn to love others, without losing the freedom to love himself.

***

They arrived at Tasa's doorstep. Nezha was the one who rang the doorbell.

"Welcome back! Blessings be upon you," Tasa said, her face glowing with happiness. She turned to Asad. "Oh, who's this young man?"

"I'm Asad. As Salaamu alaykum, nice to meet you, ma'am."

"Oh! Wa alaykum as Salaam! I'm Tasa. There's no ma'am stuff around here! He's so polite," she whispered to Nezha.

"You could call her mom," Thunderbolt mumbled and grinned at Tasa.

"Tasa. Bless your amazing self!" Nezha smiled wide and her eyes darted around behind her. "Uh…yeah, he's a soul jawhar."

“Looking for Comet?” Tasa said. “She’s snoozing by the loveseat in the living room.”

Nezha nodded. She squeezed Tasa’s shoulder and then walked past her.

“Glad tidings, Tasa,” Sapphire greeted as she embraced her.

“Thank you. You too.”

“What’s Sketchin’… Mom.” Thunderbolt grinned.

“Not much…son.” Tasa burst into laughter and Thunderbolt joined her.

Kayan nodded at her. “Hope you’ve been doing well.”

“Oh, I have. It’s great to see you all.” Tasa joined them in the living room, where Nezha and Comet reunited. They were currently sitting in the loveseat together. “So, how was Veer City?”

“Oh, it was very productive…” Sapphire said.

“Yes, very.” Nezha passed her fingers through Comet’s fur. Her purrs rumbled against Nezha’s hand.

“Oh, good,” Tasa said. “So, Asad, how do you like everyone?”

Asad smiled. “They’re good.”

“Great! Are you from here, Asad?”

Asad turned in his seat on the couch. “I’m from another dimension. I live in Canada, but my parents are from Pakistan.

“Ooh!” Tasa smiled at him.

“I’m Pakistani too!” Nezha said.

“Time to get to know you,” Kayan declared, leaning forward in his seat.

“Yeah.” Asad chuckled. “I’ve been able to bring animals back to life…and recently there’d been many of them around my home. I started hearing a voice inside me. Well, I'm intuitive, and I trust my instincts. I had dreams of you all too. Unicorns with wings...people who controlled fire, wind, water and earth. The voice—intuition—told me to go to a forest. That's where I was able to pass through a portal to Noorenia." Asad tilted his head and the muscles around his eyes softened.

"Wow. I'm glad you found them. By the way, have you seen Nezha's feather bracelet? It can become something really interesting."

Asad's back straightened. "I'm blind."

Thunderbolt nearly choked. "How does he just say it like that?"

Tasa remained silent. "I see...oh, wait. No. I..." She pressed a hand to her mouth.

"Don't sweat it." Asad laughed. "You don't need to treat me any different. By the way, check this out." Asad stood up. He walked up to her and started clicking his tongue. He pointed to various things and named them. "There's your shoulder. Nezha is sitting with Comet over there. You have a bag on the ground over there, and you..." Asad leaned in. "You have lovely long hair." He spoke to her ear.

Tasa's skin pinked. "Uh...wait...how did you know?"

He straightened. Asad clicked his tongue again. "Hear that clicking I do? I can echolocate. And, since I'm a soul jawhar, I can see silhouettes and energies too, when I click." He leaned in to her and whispered, "Can't see, but don't need to when I know it's lovely."

"Oh. That's amazing!" Tasa said and gulped as he drew away.

As Asad passed Kayan on the way back to his seat, Kayan hissed, "I heard what you said. You're smooth." Kayan raised a brow at him. "She's way older than you, though."

Asad turned his head to him, grinned and winked, then continued walking.

Tasa glanced at Kayan and then at Nezha. Everyone else was conversing, but she noticed they didn't meet each other's gaze.

Tasa leaned toward Kayan. "Lover's quarrel?" She whispered leaning over her arm rest to reach him.

"W-what?" Kayan said, his eyes widening.

"Trust me, women know these things. I can feel the tension between you like Nezha's flames, and I'm not even a jawhar."

Kayan brushed his fingers through his hair and glanced at Nezha.

"You definitely care about her. Am I right?" Tasa asked.

"Y-yeah." Kayan conceded. "No use hiding it."

"Hiding? I knew it would happen. You're kind and lively. Nezha's got a temper. You're made for each other."

"Well, I wouldn't say she has a temper. More like she's headstrong," Kayan said defensively.

Tasa smiled at him. By the look on her face, he knew just why she said it. "You said that on purpose…"

"Yup! I knew you'd defend her. It's so sweet! You have my blessings."

"Aw, zaan." He sighed, but his childish grin gave everything away.

"I think the girls and I should have some me time!" Tasa blurted out as she stood up.

"Huh?" Nezha said. "You know, that sounds good, but we need to be prepared to find Amaya…"

"Nezha, you all need the rest." Tasa linked her arms with Sapphire and Nezha. "Come on, it'll be great bonding time too! And, since I'm an herbalist, we can have a spa!"

"Well…" Sapphire began, but Tasa had begun pulling them.

"You boys can have your time to yourself. Zaan to zaan." She spun on her heels with Sapphire and Nezha.

"Finally, some time away from the girls." Thunderbolt swung his arms back and tucked his hands behind his head.

"Uh…" Kayan coyly looked at Nezha before she was out of sight. "So, Asad. Seems like you're good with the…ladies." He grinned.

"Yeah, what if I am?" Asad rubbed his nose with the back of his finger.

"Well, there's this girl… I don't know how exactly I feel about her."

"It's the fire jawhar, Nezha, right?" Asad said.

"How did…"

Asad pointed to his throat and then his heart.

"Intuition."

"Even *I* knew that. Wait…it is her, isn't it?" Thunderbolt asked.

"Y-yeah, it is." Kayan sighed.

Chapter 19 The Heart Knows

"I think I like her."

"Finally, you're going t' tell her!" Thunderbolt said.

"I don't know. For some reason, the water jawhar gave me a feeling of familiarity too," Kayan said.

"So? Look at the differences between them. How do they make you feel? Both Nezha and Amaya," Asad asked him.

"Nezha makes me really happy, but also kind of anxious. Amaya makes me feel like I know her."

Asad rested his elbows on his knees and steepled his fingers together. "Who makes you feel you'll go crazy not knowing what it means?"

"Nezha…"

"Does the water jawhar make you blush? Do you like, like her?" Asad inquired. "Really want to be with her?" He winked.

"No, I don't know her!"

"There's your answer." Asad leaned back. "We have the answers. It just takes others to see them in us for us to understand."

"You're really wise," Thunderbolt said, "for a kid."

"Yeah…thanks, Asad."

"Are you going t' tell her?" Thunderbolt asked with a grin. "She seems to like you back, from what I can tell."

"I…guess I'll need to."

"Don't guess. Do it!" Asad urged him. "You'll regret it if you don't."

"He's right. Listen t' him," Thunderbolt added.

"All right!" Kayan stood up, poising a fist in the air. "I'll tell her how I feel…after they have their spa thing, though." Kayan rubbed the back of his neck and sat back down. He glanced at the window. It had gotten dark already.

"So, guy time?" Asad said. "By the way, what does zaan mean?"

Thunderbolt chuckled.

***

That bunny wouldn't leave him alone. He'd been walking for the past hour. Dante side-eyed the animal and sat down under a tree. The snow had begun falling from the sky, but that rabbit didn't want to leave his side. He'd hardly noticed it when he'd first set off. Its white fur did well to camouflage it.

"You alone too?" Dante said as it approached him and placed a paw on his leg. Its pink nose wiggled at him.

He was a mess and he knew it. First his mother was missing, then he had to join up with others like him to find an angel's body. Now, he was all alone. Tired, hungry and cold. Damn.

The rabbit climbed into his lap and started snuggling against his stomach.

A small smile tugged at his lips. “Okay, I get it. You’re cute. Listen bun, I need food, so I’ll be on the move again.”

The afternoon was colder than Dante thought it would get. With Bun by his side—that’s what he’d decided to call him—he kept walking. He knew their relatives’ addresses. Specifically, his grandma’s. She’d told him countless times that he’d memorized it. Without the local currency though, he couldn’t eat anything, and he was quickly getting exhausted.

Dante crouched down to his rabbit friend. “Hey, Bun, you know where I could get a bite to eat?” He placed a finger on the bunny’s head. The critter looked up at him and Dante could hear him in his head. That same thought. A voice without a sound.

Glad tidings, human. I can feel your intention. There’s a bush nearby with fruit which will not harm animal or human. I shall lead you there. And, thank you, I am cute.

Dante stood up and smiled. “Thanks a ton, Bun. What you waiting for? Let’s go and eat!”

***

Tasa applied a gray clay mask on Sapphire’s skin. Nezha’s green mask was starting to dry up.

“You looked extra happy today,” Nezha said. She was lying on her stomach.

“Yes. There was a certain glow over you.” Sapphire met eyes with Tasa.

“Oh. Well, yeah.”

“Do you wanna talk about it?” Nezha said and held her face in her hands, smiling at the older woman.

Tasa smiled back. “I was getting married… But, to a guy I didn’t really care for. I mean, he was a nice person and all, but, he didn’t seem like a person I could get along with at all.” Tasa stood up over the bowl of water and washed her hands. “My dad wanted me to agree, but after a long time, I finally told him I couldn’t. Then I found someone. We’ve had chaperoned dinners and meetings. He’s really sweet and kind and his goals meet with mine. I’ll be getting married in three months.” Tasa smiled.

“Go, girl! I’m so happy for you!” Nezha hugged her.

Sapphire smiled up at her and sat on the bed. “That’s good you were true to yourself. Also, you didn’t want to hurt the other person. It shows valiance.”

“I needed to be brave. I realised I had a choice. I had a choice all along. When you are the eldest daughter, you are brought up as the one who must carry others’ needs as her own. You find worth in being in service, and obeying your parents’ every word. We are told to not hurt our parents, and listen to them, but many of us forget we don’t need to listen if we will become cold-hearted replicas of their whims.” Tasa’s eyes softened a touch as Nezha squeezed her hand.

“You stood up for yourself. I wish most women knew they can.”

Tasa smiled warmly back. “Now, come on, cousin, we need to decorate your hair!”

“But I cover it up!” Nezha said, her hands flying to her head. Right now, her brown hair was in waves down her back.

“So? There’s no guy here. Besides, it’s not for them, it’s for us.”

"You're right. I guess I'm just used to not taking it off around here, since Kayan is with us."

"Ooh, that nice smiling boy? He seems so sweet." Tasa winked at her.

"Uh, yeah. He's nice."

"Nice? Girl! I know you like him."

"What? Who said I did?" Nezha said it as if she were threatening them.

"You proved it to me just now."

"Hmm?" Sapphire turned to Nezha. "You like the wind jawhar?"

"Woah, wait, girls… Don't get carried away. This is girl time! I mean I—

"She's so cute when she gets all mad and embarrassed! Don't deny it. You're a match. Both of you fighting to save the world together… You're not a damsel and knight. You're like a…" Tasa pressed her finger on her lips in thought.

"A pair of bodyguards?" Sapphire suggested.

"What? Not you too, Sapphire." Nezha tilted her head and sighed.

"She's not denying it," Tasa sang. "Yes, yes! They got each other's backs and they help others. Like heroes!

"Ah, yes. That scenario works out," Sapphire said.

"Hello? Is anyone even listening to me?" Nezha waved a hand in front of Tasa's face.

"It's just so adorable and epic! I'm sorry, zwina…you do really like him, though?" Tasa raised her eyebrows at her.

"Well…he's not a bad guy, and he's smart, kind and selfless. He's got a really cute smile."

"Good. So you do," Sapphire stated and brushed back Nezha's hair as it had gotten in her face.

Nezha raised her shoulders, embarrassment taking over her. She nodded.

***

Bun had led Dante to the bush with fruit. It looked like it had been sprinkled with powdered sugar. "Ah, food! Alhamdulillah!" Dante rushed over to the bush and started popping berries into his mouth. After a few, he looked down at Bun.

"Oh, you want some?" Dante held three berries in his hand and crouched to Bun's level.

Bun twitched his nose and nibbled on one of the berries. He looked up at Dante and ate the rest.

"We've eaten like Kings!" Dante laughed. Even he thought the joke was lame, but it felt so good to have a full stomach again. "Let's go to Grandma's. Heck, I feel like Little Red Riding Hood."

They stood outside a community of large houses. Gravel lined the outsides of the homes and the winding street met a small park.

"Looks like here's where we part ways." Dante turned to his rabbit friend.

Bun looked up at him when Dante patted his head and kept his hand there.

You have reached your destination, human? We share the same ground, but our paths differ. I enjoyed our moments. May you be blessed.

May you be successful in reawakening Noorenia's Heartbeat once more. Farewell.

Dante stood up and Bun hopped toward a field. At one point, Bun turned and stood up on his hind legs. Dante waved and watched as the rabbit turned and disappeared into the bushes.

"Smart bunny. He knew who I was." Dante turned to the homes. "Grandma… Momma should be there."

He couldn't help but look back again. Bun—well, the rabbit—was really gone. It made him think of the time he discovered he was an earth jawhar.

One night his parents had been arguing. His father was telling his mom to lower her voice, but she was yelling at him. His parents had slowly been growing farther and farther apart. When they used to go to the park, they'd both take him there, but then it was one of them who did. Eventually, it was only his dad who took him. When it was time to eat out, it was his mom who took the initiative.

The next night, he overheard his mother saying she wanted to separate. It crushed his tiny seven-year-old heart. He ran into the backyard and began crying. A cat, a few birds and a squirrel gathered around him. He remembered hearing their voices inside his head. At first, he thought it was just his own. Then he brushed his fingers on the grass and the blades elongated and he learned to wrap the tree roots around to form a tent around him when it began to rain. "You'll never leave me, right?" he had asked. That was the day he had found his abilities as an earth jawhar.

Dante took in a deep breath and began walking to the home. To grandma's house it was.

He rapped on the door and held his hands to his stomach. He wanted Momma to be there. She had to be there. Her disappearing was the worst of his problems in his mind. If she wasn't, he couldn't imagine what he'd do.

The door creaked open and there stood his grandma. Brown curls over her head and she didn't look a day older than fifty. Black mommas were forever young.

"Ooh, Dante?" His grandma chuckled and pulled him in.

"Mamma G, lookin' good!"

"Don't try to butter me up. You've never tried to contact me. How long has it been?" She lightly tapped his shoulder.

Dante shook his head and simply smiled. She was like a firecracker, in voice and personality.

"Come in and sit down. I have cookies and a load of hugs."

Dante walked into the living room. It always smelled like sugar cookies. He wasn't sure if she'd expected him or if she had visitors.

"Expecting me, G?"

She smiled at him and patted the space beside her on the sofa.

"Dante baby, I didn't expect you'd be here this early."

"So…you were expecting." Dante sat beside her. Her arms wrapped around him. The thought of his momma was nagging in his head, like when he'd get an itchy throat. He'd have to use his tongue to ease it and he needed to ease the itch now.

"Is…Momma here?"

"See for yourself, Dante," his grandma said. Her gaze turned to the back door.

Dante stood up. Upon seeing her turn into view through the door, his blood boiled. All those emotions he thought he had hidden came to the surface. Why didn't she tell him? First his parents lived separately and then she had to start keeping things from him.

"Why? Why didn't you tell us…why didn't you say you were staying here?" Dante's voice was quiet.

"Dante…" His momma closed the door behind her and rubbed her elbow. "You can't trust anyone… I had to be careful. Besides, your father probably didn't care."

"Nina!" Dante's grandma reprimanded.

"Mom… He needs to know! The world is a cruel place. People are innately greedy. All they want is for themselves!"

"You can't—"

"Momma, stay out of this." Nina walked toward Dante and held his arms. "Son, you shouldn't go back. Stay here. You won't have to suffer anymore."

Dante stared at her. She was right. People were greedy. He thought of the other jawhars. They only wanted him for their own needs. They said they needed him. He was wrong for wanting to trust them, wasn't he? He wasn't sure what to believe. He knew he was an earth elemental and Noorenia needed help. The Most High had given him this gift. He couldn't forsake the earth itself. He felt its pain when he came here. It felt sad. It felt empty. It mourned for the heartbeat it used to have. It was numb.

"You should have told me, momma!" Dante groaned and turned away from her.

"Listen, Dante! You don't understand. I had my differences with your father…but we can have a good life here too."

"I have my dance team and James. You'd really just leave him too?"

"No, I'd visit him."

"You can't," Dante said, his voice catching.

"What?" His momma let go of him.

"It's harder to leave Noorenia than it is to come in. Something happened to the barrier, Momma. I'm not sure if we can get back easily. Besides, I'm a jawhar. Maybe this world needs me. I don't know yet, but I need to do somethin' if you ever want to get back."

"I didn't know." His momma walked over to the couch and sat down. She sighed.

"When I came here, the earth was sad. I can feel it. It's mourning. Its heartbeat is slowing down and it feels numb. Maybe it needs me. Are you gonna tell me the earth is greedy now?"

"Don't talk to me like that, Dante. I'm your mother!"

"That's why I'm sayin' it. You have to understand. Forget about people. The earth needs me. Noorenia might need me."

Dante's grandma sat beside him and placed her plate of cookies on the coffee table.

"Come on, Nina, let the boy go. He's not your small child anymore. He's a man now."

"A man…" Nina said and looked off into the distance. "Be careful, Dante."

Dante reached for a cookie, and held it in his hands.

"I'll be careful. I'll see you later." He stood up. "Mamma G, I'll take these to go."

“Now I’m a fast-food joint? Ya know my homecooked food is love and quality.” His grandma stood and kissed his head.

“You got nothin’ on them, G.” Dante smiled faintly. He needed to do this, if not for anyone else, for himself and his family.

“It’s late, Dante baby. You should stay the night,” His grandma suggested.

Dante looked through the window. The snow had stopped falling. He yawned. “Yeah, okay. But, first thing in the morning, I’m off.”

“After pancakes though, right?” his momma teased.

Dante chuckled. “Yeah. Pancakes first.”

Chapter 20 Confessions

That night had been strange for Zul Sharr. Being at a masquerade party had felt freeing. No one knowing who he was. Even though the general public didn't know what the Iron Prince looked like anyway. He felt like he could be himself. Not the hate-fueled monster he felt like he'd become.

What really shocked him was when he'd heard the glass shatter on the roof. When he'd gone to inspect it, he'd seen Nezha on the ground. She'd reminded him of Sanari. Her body across the ground, encased in Iron. Zul wasn't sure what had gotten into him. He had the inclination to help them. That's when he remembered his dream. The shattered glass, the two people on the ground. Had his dream been a premonition? It was the first time, but he couldn't help but think that if another of his dreams were to come true…that it was a sign from the Divine.

Jinni aura coursed through his veins, so how was he able to supplicate and use his iron to get rid of the magic's hold on them? Maybe the times he prayed on EID had cleansed a part of his heart. A true sign of the Divine's…mercy? But…his iron was cursed. It ran rampant and had encased the Fire Kingdom family and the unicorns in the Valley. Was he cursed with misfortune too? A shard of hope still lit inside him. Maybe one day it would become better. That's why he'd let Lexa give him jinni magic.

Zul looked down at his hands. He could feel his veins coursing with the jinni magic. That strange pulse when he concentrated on the feeling of want inside him. Feeling a cool wind across his face, he turned to his window and stood before it.

The darkness outside still induced fear in him with the uncertainty it held. It could clothe the monsters. He'd be none the wiser.

Something about the wind comforted him. Maybe it was the movement. He'd craved the freedom he couldn't have as Prince of the Iron Kingdom. His mother had always been controlling him. Telling him what to feel or stealing his thoughts for her own. He'd been a prisoner yearning for the chains to break.

Now that he had his own mansion, there wasn't anyone to mess with his mind. No one to constantly lie to him or smother him. It was also terrifying. He didn't want to make mistakes, but he'd gone this far. This far only so he didn't have to be so weak. He had jinni power and a way to save Sanari from the iron.

Power. It was power that he needed, didn't he? Yes. That's what was important. If he had that, he could fix everything.

His eyes burned orange in his reflection on the window. He also hated this magic squirming through his veins like a worm. He hated it. He also hated how much he'd come to rely on it. He hated…how much he wanted to abandon it.

He wanted to know why Lexa had saved him the last time he had confronted Nezha and the angels. *Lexa. Where are you?*

***

Lexa appeared in a cloud of smoke and leaned on the wall beside him. “You called, Sire?” She wore a lopsided grin.

Zul Sharr jumped and blew out a sigh. “Lexa! Don’t scare me like that!”

“What’s on your mind?” Lexa followed him when he sat on his bed.

“Why did you protect me?” Zul glanced aside.

Lexa’s eyes widened. She twirled a curl of her red hair around a finger. “You have jinni aura in your veins. Sire, you’re someone who relies on that power. Why wouldn’t I?”

Zul turned to meet eyes with her. “That’s not all.” His lips formed a tight line.

Lexa pursed her lips and sat beside him. “I’ve marked you. Zul Sharr, we have a bond.”

“Darkness and a soul. You veil me from the things I don’t want to see.” Zul Sharr sighed.

“Oh, Sire. You’re not losing your trust in me, are you?” Lexa leaned in and swiped his hair from his eyes.

“I just… Why am I still able to do things like pray? Aren’t I full of hatred? Darkness in my heart? A monster?”

Lexa searched his eyes. “You’re a powerful prince. You are no monster. You can’t take my place as Queen of Shadows.” Lexa grinned.

“I’m serious, Lexa.”

“I mean what I said. You can do all that because the jinni aura doesn’t change your heart. You know, your hair’s really silky. What shampoo do you use?” Lexa inquired and smiled.

Zul’s lips parted. “Uh…it’s the olive oil. And, I’ve never seen you smile like that before.”

Lexa’s hand fell to the bedsheet, and she leaned back. How could she tell him why she smiled? There was an innocence he held. Since she had him marked, she could hear his thoughts. She knew how he felt. She felt his love for others. How he only wanted peace. She knew his childhood from his memories. That childlike purity was hidden under the hurt. His love had been betrayed by his mother. His element betrayed him and encased his beloved. And so, she knew he betrayed himself. It hurt Lexa to even think of feeling sympathy for him. But she couldn’t ignore it. When the darkness held a star, the light was bound to change its shade. A part of his hope touched her heart. She saw her younger hopeful self in him. But the magic would also cast doubt on his heart. That was something she relied on. To what end? She wasn’t sure. “Sire, don’t you have pressing matters to attend to?

Zul grabbed her arm and pulled her closer. Curiosity was flickering in his eyes. “Why are you doing all this? What’s your reason? Tell me, Lexa.”

Lexa’s eyes widened. “The same reason as you. You want power and to break the curse on Sanari? Well, I want power too. I want to break the shackles put on my people.”

Zul’s grip loosened on her arm and his fingers slipped away. He listened as she spoke.

"Before the war of Jahalia, my people, the jinn, lived peacefully in our city. Then some humans started summoning us. The more corrupt jinn among us lured the humans with our magic, and the unlimited power it possessed. They were called the shaitan. Devils. They thought they were tricking the humans by damning them to hell. But they were wrong. We were all in danger. Our magic, our power. Then the war happened. I was there that day." Lexa stared into the distance, her gaze sad and piercing.

"Then…what happened?" Zul's voice was but a whisper.

"I fought in the battle." She grazed a finger on a long scar over her shoulder. "The Angel of Mercy shot me with his light that day." Lexa gritted her teeth.

"I'm…sorry."

Lexa looked up at him. That mischief and glee returned to her eyes. "The angel paid thanks to you, my prince. And the humans will too. Those who used us like toys."

"You know, a part of me loves my mom…for the good memories. Although they're clouded by the pain. The times she'd take care of me in the middle of the night if I had a fever. Make dinner for me when I returned from school. Thunderbolt made a whole feast and he was happy." Zul chuckled. "But then… I hate the way she treated me. The pain when she punched me. The anger when she blamed me for her problems. Degrading me. Treating me like a toy. Telling me she loved me one second and then…and then an hour later she'd tell me I was dead to her. She'd say it so many times, I'd tell her, 'Again? I've lost count.'" Zul chuckled.

"You tried to joke around to cope," Lexa whispered.

"Yeah. I'd try to laugh things off. Make jokes to diffuse the tension. It didn't work, but it wouldn't hurt as much." He sighed.

"Sire…"

"Yeah?" Zul looked up at her and smiled. He'd *smiled.* "I want justice. So no one will be thrown away like a broken toy. We'll achieve it one day," he assured her.

"Well." Lexa began to depart, her walk much softer and slower. "I'll leave you to sleep, unless you want company." She winked.

"Uh, goodnight, Lexa." Zul Sharr drew his blanket over himself and lied down.

"Goodnight." Lexa breathed out and melted into the shadows.

The moon peeked through the clouds, illuminating Lexa's face as she sat atop the hill. Bathed in the moonlight on a quiet night like this was comforting. A silence she preferred with no company. Tonight, Lexa had brought her carefully crafted walls down, revealing a part of her heart. She'd never tell Zul Sharr about the way she used to hope for good. That maybe there was a way to act peacefully to help her people. She'd been wrong.

As a teen, she'd felt powerless. Other jinn ranked above her. Physically, she was undermined. "You're too thin and weak," they'd say. Her femininity was undermined. "You're only good as a pretty little face." Her mind was undermined. "Stay home and be a good girl."

Some of the jinn would whisper to the humans and lead them astray. Lexa obeyed and kept obeying. Her childhood was about obeying and staying low. She'd never imagined she'd leave the gates of Ahjnam. The gates that kept the jinn in their own city.

One day she did.

When the shaitan—the wicked beings— had tried teaching humans magic and some humans blamed the jinn for the darkness and chaos and for the human trafficking that burst through the world of Noorenia. Jinn started blaming themselves. Those who had done nothing wrong, the ones who had their own lives, their own families, their own hearts. Most kept to themselves. Like Lexa. But this slander had been too much.

The jinn had decided to attack when some humans summoned countless jinn and sealed them away. The jinn had had enough and attacked the Fire kingdom, wanting to topple the government before they destroyed the surrounding cities. This was the War of Jahalia.

Lexa drove herself into the battlefield when the streets of her city were lined with jinn soldiers. She couldn't stay out of the way anymore. Not when the humans had decided they wouldn't either. She'd crept past the army, undetected. Outside the safety of the city, she'd been surrounded by her slaughtered people, her family among them. Bleeding, torn.

Rage made a home in her veins. Tearing up human soldiers and manipulating others to attack their own. Shackles gone, teeth bared, claws out, her heart pounding for once in her life. Gone was the jinni girl who stayed silent and quiet. How much longer did they think they could shackle her as if she were a zoo animal? Expecting her to dance to their whims? Something had snapped in her that day. She'd realized that as her kind were being coerced, the humans, too, were attempting to take her freedom to choose. It existed and she'd choose. She'd choose to fight. No one would own her mind, her body, her soul. It was hers. It belonged to her.

The Shadow Jinni king was impressed by her show of courage and prowess. From then on, she grew in rank and not only did the shadow jinn, but all jinn came to know her as Lady Lexa, or Empress of Shadows.

She was a master of manipulation. Her undeniable beauty and sensual voice drew them in and bent them to her will. She could use these things against those wretched humans.

This is what she was. A jinni who was free and wanted to free her people. To stop the humans from summoning them. She'd do it by exacting her vengeance upon the humans and the angels who'd betrayed her people's trust. She'd take their power and use it against them. She would rule. She'd make her mark and have no mercy.

A soft tickle began on her arm and she glanced down. A white moth sat upon her grey-hued skin. Its wings were dusted in silver as if it were a gem. "You, too, follow the light?" The image of Zul Sharr's smile peeked into her mind. "Get too close and you shall burn." She raised her arm and the moth fluttered its wings and then took to the night sky, its path toward the moon.

***

Zul dreamed. He was walking beside someone. He wasn't sure who. The images were going by too fast. Everything was drenched in colour so vivid it was as if he were awake. The scents of roses, jasmine, vanilla and barely noticeable musk wafted in the air.

A soft masculine voice began speaking. "You are not a monster."

Zul Sharr's eyes widened. Tears began springing from his eyes. "What?"

“Did you believe your mother’s cruel words so much that you began to become them?”

“I…I thought I’d lost my mind. Nothing ever made sense.” He held his head steady. “I thought it was all my fault.”

“It wasn’t.” The soft masculine voice was a warm squeeze.

“There was all this pain. She’d constantly tell me it was my fault for everything that would happen to her. She’d make fun of me, hit me…and sometimes she’d seem kind.”

“You may be surrounded by darkness, but your hope is a light. Hold onto it.” The young man advised him. “Make amends. You still have time.”

“The hardest part isn't that you’re surrounded by darkness... it's when you don't see your own light. Thinking it's been swallowed whole by the shadows, so in turn you turn in on yourself,” Zul whispered.

“Why do you think the iron *betrayed* you? It encased Sanari? Why it bled out to imprison the unicorns in a slumber? Yet, it is not why, but what.”

“Who are you?” Zul squinted, searching desperately for the source of the disembodied voice.

“Consider me your future. We will meet once the beast storms your heart.” A bright light shot around his face.

Then another scene played out. Beside him was Nezha, a smile across her face. On his other side was Thunderbolt, whose arm draped over his shoulder. They were both dressed in colourful clothing.

In the distance, he saw a woman with curly brown hair. He couldn’t make out anything but the crown of flowers atop her head. It was Sanari.

Zul's eyes opened. He inhaled and sat up in bed. "Make amends? Divine… Oh hearer of hearts… Can I really fix this?" He turned to see the time. It was five a.m. He lied back down, slumber soon taking him.

***

Asad listened to Thunderbolt and Kayan chatting and nodded a few times. How did all this even happen? He'd known he could revive animals and even change people's emotions if he was physically close enough to them, but what he'd done when they were at that masquerade…it was beyond strange. That water jawhar had been attacking them and he'd somehow spoken to her soul. Or maybe he'd somehow coaxed her soul into awakening that moment. Telling her the truth of what she wanted and needed. Her desires had become coherent.

Asad still wasn't sure about these people. He did feel energetically comfortable around them, but something inside his mind didn't. This kind of thing always happened. New people made him second-guess himself. All he did know, was that dream was real. A reality he was now living. Away from his home, his parents and brother, and here with other jawhars like him. Essences of elements he'd have laughed about if he hadn't, well, felt it himself. He couldn't see, after all. He still believed it. A part of him was scared being with strangers, and also sad being away from his family.

"What do you think, Asad?" Kayan asked.

Asad blinked and then smiled faintly. "I think…I need to rest."

"I don't blame you. It's a lot t' get used to, huh?" Thunderbolt said.

Kayan yawned. “Yeah, we should probably go to sleep soon.”

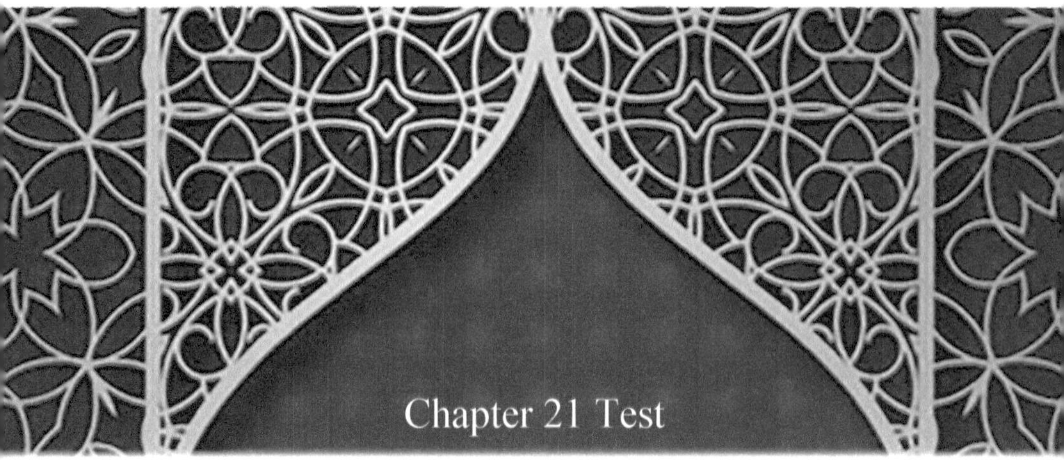

Chapter 21 Test

"Nezha…" Kayan stood behind her, his voice soft and low.

The moment she heard his voice, it was as if he was a key to her smile. It opened up on her lips. She turned, momentarily meeting his eyes, but shifted her gaze. "Hey, Kayan."

"We should talk." He stepped toward her, closing the gap between them.

Nezha nodded. "Yeah, I think it's time." She turned and Kayan fell in step beside her.

"I thought maybe we could spend time in the garden." Kayan stopped before a bed of yellow and red flowers. Three feet away, Tasa was planting more. Beside her, Sapphire, Thunderbolt and Asad sat chatting.

"Oh."

"Just oh?" Kayan tried to search her eyes.

Nezha turned to the patio seat and sat down. Kayan took a seat in front of her. "I'm just not sure what to say about what happened at the masquerade. I… My flames were alive. Too alive."

Kayan leaned in, his elbows resting on the table. "What if you're getting in the way."

"What do you mean?" Nezha looked down at her hands, eyebrows furrowed and heart pounding.

"Your fire isn't wild. It's like it follows your movement, your emotions."

Nezha sighed. "I know. My emotions are valid. I need them for the fire. But that was different. Back at the party, your wind and my fire were doing more than just moving around." Her cheeks heated and she was more aware of his gaze on her.

"I know. I felt everything, Nezha."

"How are you always so open?" she began, irritation causing her voice to waver. "Aren't you—"

"Aren't I what? Why won't you look at me?" Kayan was leaning closer.

"I can't." Nezha gulped.

"Are you scared?"

Nezha nodded. "If I look at you, I'll just remember the way you make me feel! It'll remind me that if I get too close to someone, I can lose them and it hurts more."

Kayan paused. "I once told you about Ali. My sword. This sword was given to me by my mom. This is all I have left of her."

"I remember you telling me that. I'm sorry."

"It's okay." Kayan smiled sadly. "She gave me this sword six years ago. We used to fight the rebellious jinn. Back then, before the war of Jahalia, tension grew. My city was known for its jinni slayers. Our group was called Azatuthun. *Freedom*. My mom told me to fight for those I loved, for those who were smothered by cruelty, to be a storm to their silence. I've seen so much bloodshed, Nezha. I've seen humans and jinn die. Some of them by our hand. Even now I struggle to breathe when I smell blood. Sometimes, I fight back the nausea when we're in battle and a jinni is slain. Even through all that, it was love that she wanted me to carry on." His voice caught. "It's strange talking about her. It's almost nice, though. Like it's normal."

"There's a lot of pain and love too… I understand, Kayan." Nezha looked up at him, meeting his gaze for mere seconds, and then looking away. "I have something my aunt gave me too. A pin for my hair. Back home, I had to hide my fire abilities. I was scared of how wild they were. That I'd hurt my family. Once, I nearly burned our house down as a kid. That's when I started pushing it away. I'd hold my breath so the fire would die. My aunt Lamis could control flames too. She believed in me. She was there for me. We joked together, shared our secrets, ate sweets together. She was more like a sister to me than an aunt." Nezha looked up, fighting her emotions. "You miss your mom too, don't you?"

"Mm-hmm. Every day." There was a silence as Kayan then tapped his fingers on the table and turned to look at the trees, the sun peering behind them. "I haven't heard you be so open about your past or aunt before." He looked into her eyes.

"It's been months. It still hurts." Nezha's gaze slipped to the tree. It didn't get easy. She didn't think it ever would be easy. Only more days that she didn't cry. Only more days where Lamis would come to mind only if something or someone reminded her of her aunt.

"Tsavt tanem," Kayan breathed, and met her gaze again.

"What does that mean?"

"Let me take your pain." He pressed his hand to his heart. No smile on his face. Just a gentle recognition of their quiet strengths.

For a moment that felt like hours, their gazes lingered. It was peaceful. *Peaceful*. He really did take away her pain. Every time he was around her. "Kayan… It's easy being honest with you."

She adored that he was honest and caring. That he didn't become quiet or withdrawn. He made an attempt to understand and relate to her. Not put words into her mouth, or speak on her behalf.

Nezha seemed to reach a surprising understanding. "I'm not only Moroccan, I'm not only Pakistani. I am both. I don't have my own place. But, Noorenia brought these two sides together. In Noorenia, the angels, and you, I found home. I found a place. I can use my fire freely here. I can belong here. This is the place I've made my own. I don't want Noorenia to die. I can be more here."

"Then, be more honest, be more you. Be more with me."

His eyes were greener. She couldn't look away now. Not when Kayan's eyes were pulsing with emotion. Not when his scent of flowers and grass on the wind was growing over her, blooming in her heart. Not when the softness in his voice matched the raw beating pulse in her neck, her heart echoing it as he leaned in closer.

"Kayan, I…like you." An awkward smile appeared over her face. "You make me feel comfortable. But I also feel like I can be so much more. The way you carry joy and warmth with you wherever you go. Even though you've had to see so much suffering. Even when you had to take care of others and neglect yourself. When you speak to me so gently, it's like it's only us, a secret between us." She looked away, shame heating her cheeks. "Okay, let's go."

"Hey, wait…" His lips were tugging upward. Nezha couldn't get over the warmth glowing over his face and the shine in his eyes. They were caught in a long moment of silence. Just what was he thinking? She'd probably said too much. In a way, she thought she'd never say enough. How could she tell him he was the spring breeze that swept her windows open. She used to hold her breath. Not anymore.

"Don't I get to say it too?" Kayan's voice was soft again. Nezha chuckled.

"I really like you." Kayan tilted his head. "When you have that playful tone in your voice. You fight for what's right and you have this determination that keeps going. Kind of like fire. You're bright and unstoppable." Kayan's lips parted and he smiled.

She wasn't sure what to say to his heartwarming admission. "Well, that's a lot of liking." Nezha's cheeks reddened. She stood up and Kayan followed suit. Again she was caught looking into his eyes. They were smiling at each other. He faced her fully. His shoulders relaxed, a tilt to his head. This moment, she'd felt the closest with Kayan. Sharing their experiences, their sad pasts, and their hopes.

"Well, Nezha jan, all those small things you do are a lot to me."

They walked a few paces and then Kayan turned and stopped in front of her, his whole body facing her. From the pack on his side, he reached into it and pulled out two books and a small canvas with paint. "I thought maybe we could spend time just reading, or you could paint beside me. Just being together." His face flushed and he ran his fingers through his hair.

Nezha reached out to take the canvas and paints from him. Oh God, when he played with his hair, she just felt her cheeks heat up more. He was already attractive to her, but when he did that, it was so much more. She'd noticed something about him. He was considerate. The way he'd want her by his side. She thought of what he'd told her. How much suffering he'd seen. How he'd been fighting at such a young age. Wanting her beside him doing their own thing? He'd been taking care of his father so long. She couldn't blame him for just wanting to be beside the ones he cared for, no matter what they were doing. He valued their company and happiness.

Comet appeared, pressing her arching back against Nezha's legs. Then with a bounce in her step, she walked over to Kayan, and brushed her head against his legs and meowed up at him.

"That sounds wonderful." Nezha's lips parted and it was a warm, gentle smile. A full smile that glowed over her face.

Out under the sun's touch of warmth, Nezha didn't realize how long they'd been there. When he said he liked her, she wasn't sure if it meant more than that. He'd said it all so easily. Was he finally getting comfortable around her? She had deeper feelings for him. But, did he? She knew how amicable Kayan was with others. He was love personified. But, if he didn't like her in a romantic way, she wasn't sure if it was worth the risk of losing their friendship.

She glanced at Kayan as he flipped a page in his book. For just a fleeting moment, she wondered how his thumb would feel brushing over her lips. Nezha looked away and stared at her painting of the grass, Tasa's garden and the tall tree. *Kayan, damn your romantic notions. Oh God, forgive me.*

Thinking of books, she remembered something. "I almost forgot! I'm going to fail!" She stood up.

“W-what?” Kayan looked up at her and turned his book in his hands.

“I have an exam today. I need to go back home.”

“Oh, is that all?” Thunderbolt appeared behind her.

Nezha jumped and turned to him with a glare.

“What are you, a ghoul? You scared the hell out of me!”

“Damn, Nezha, how could you call me one of the jinn? I’m offended.” Thunderbolt feigned hurt and stepped aside as Nezha began picking up her brushes and tucked the canvas under her arm.

Sapphire and Asad walked over.

“I hear a commotion. Probably not good, unless this is normal for you all and I’m missing something because I can’t see,” Asad joked with a small grin.

“Well, my brother and Nezha tend to show their affections by way of loud accusations,” explained Sapphire.

“I just need to go back home for an exam and I forgot it was today. I am in so much trouble if I don’t get there. I even studied for three nights straight for it!” Nezha turned to Sapphire.

“What’s the other way to earth’s dimension?” Asad asked.

“I’ve been using the pond outside Tasa’s home.” Nezha walked toward the door, the others following behind her.

Inside, Nezha packed up her books and stood at the front door, slipping her shoes on.

***

Asad stood beside Kayan, his head tilted toward the door. He knew he'd entered Noorenia through the forest, somehow creating a portal there. Sapphire had told him about the water in Noorenia— how the rivers, the ponds were doorways to the other dimension.

"I'll try to be back soon. I only have one exam today, so I shouldn't take that long." Nezha stepped onto the grass. The noon sun shone brightly over them.

"It must be strange passing between worlds. For me, I was in a forest back home. It felt like I'd pushed through plastic film. And the energy was like my heart was going to burst through my chest, my skin sweeping with small sparks. Really strange," Asad said.

"Yeah, it can be… I've never really felt it that strongly."

"Well, have a safe trip. Good luck on your exam! I hope you ace it In Sha Allah!"

"Yes, In Sha Allah I hope I at least pass," Nezha said.

"Yeah, be careful, Nezha." Kayan's smile glowed over his face. She felt a strange feeling wash over her. Not to leave Noorenia. To stay with the others, especially with Kayan. Maybe their tender moment had brought it up. *No, I need to go. If I don't pass this exam, It'll be the end of my dreams to be a botanist.* Nezha turned to the others as they stood a few feet away from her. Comet was in Sapphire's arms. She didn't want Comet coming with her this time. It was better for her to stay behind.

As Nezha approached the pond, she took one last glance over her shoulder at her friends. Then she whispered her intention to return to Morocco and disappeared into its depth.

***

Amaya exhaled. She stood before the large window pane, watching the snow drifting across, snowflakes melting and sliding down the glass.

There were times she thought of the past. Warm, smiling moments with Tamaki, holding his hand when she was sick and he had wrapped a blanket around her when she'd been shivering. Even the cold times of arguing with each other. When she'd curl up in her bedroom and soon find Tamaki by her side, turning to her, apologizing and urging her to tell him how he could fix it and that he'd said too much. How she'd not said enough and had lost her temper. In the end, he'd make her favourite food and buy her the latest manga she wanted. She'd watch his favourite movie with him and then give him alone time. And then they would sit together, listening to a nasheed. The summer days where he took her, okaasan and Rin to the ice cream shop they liked. Chatting as they ate sweet strawberry parfaits. One such day, he had proposed to her. She still remembered trailing her fingers over the simple orange moonstone set into a golden ring.

Maybe it was the coldness now that brought those memories back. Those sensations tucking into her mind, creating memories like small crystals of ice. She missed the warmth of touch. His touch across her arm, through her hair. Mama's gentle touch on her head and cheek, Rin's arms holding her in an embrace, poking her side when Rin wanted her attention. All of it was a memory like the grip of winter after summer's caress.

"I can't stay here." Amaya turned to find herself alone. In the distance, she could hear Lexa's voice in conversation. "I will not…stay," Amaya repeated, trying to push the darkness away. The dress tightened around her chest. A cold touch. She breathed in deeply and smiled.

It was too late.

Pressure built up inside her abdomen, hardening inside her. Ice crawled over the glass and spread out across the walls. As she walked through the white hall, ice trailed behind her, coating the floor. As she moved onward, the slippery cold devoured the beaded pillows, the wooden tables. As she moved into the living room, the walls ran slick with glistening ice.

***

"Amaya. You've graced us with your presence," Zul Sharr greeted, wrapping his arms around his torso. "Who turned on the air conditioner?" he added with a smirk.

"Hmm. Lexa, is she supposed to be doing that?" Rana rounded a corner, raising a brow at the ice that nearly nipped her feet as it finished coating the floor.

Obsidian's gaze followed the glittering ice and then rested upon Amaya, who stood with her head tilted upward and a small smile over her lips. In her eyes, he recognized an emotion he could hardly feel himself. Comfort. A knowing gaze.

"Oh, Amaya, dear. I was waiting for you," Lexa said with a close-lipped smile.

Amaya took a step closer to Lexa just as the others circled around her. Most of their gazes were curious, although Obsidian's was pointed, as if he was waiting for something.

Amaya's gaze fastened to Lexa's as the former took another step toward her. Ice trailed behind her, crackling as it began reaching Lexa's feet, nearly blanketing the floor beneath her.

Lexa sighed in joy. "The forest."

Amaya's eyebrows rose. "What," she said flatly.

"You'll find the fox in the forest. The fox you so desperately want to kill," Lexa explained.

"So, you're finally telling her," Zul Sharr said.

Rana glanced at Lexa and then pulled his sleeve.

"Sire, I think we have other business to attend to."

"Oh, right." Zul Sharr cast one more glance toward Amaya, then Lexa and Obsidian. "I'll take my leave, everyone."

Amaya turned, her back to the retreating Rana and Zul Sharr.

"Obsidian knows where it is. He shall lead you there." Lexa motioned to Obsidian who was still staring at Amaya.

She walked with grace, the dress fanning out behind her. She reminded him of a thief. He wasn't sure how he remembered. Back straight, head held high. Her lips stained a red so deep, it was blood-soaked. Her face was paler, as white as the freshly fallen snow. Paired with eyes devoid of guilt, only smug pleasure.

He met her gaze. Her breath puffed out, whispering out to Obsidian's face. When Amaya reached the door, the ice had stopped forming around her. She pushed it open, stepping outside. The door slammed behind her.

"Obsidian…"

After he had taken a step, he stilled, his face toward Lexa. She raised her eyes to him.

“If she kills the fox, kill her.”

Obsidian nodded briefly, his muscles wanting to disobey, and followed Amaya.

Chapter 22 Distant Melancholy

Nezha had just submerged into the water, bubbles dancing around her.

She couldn't breathe.

She gulped in water, her lungs constricting, her throat burning. This hadn't happened before. Panic shot through her. Noorenia's barrier was weakening again? No sooner had she swum up, the water pulsed and pulled her down. As if hands had gripped her legs. Nezha jerked her body forward. She couldn't breathe. It was pulling her *hard.*

If she couldn't, she'd drown.

Her fingertips touched the surface, the air cooling against her skin. She kicked and wanted to scream as she attempted to pull her body from the water's strong pull. Her fingers finally curled on the bank of the pond at her home. The skin of the pond shimmered as her eyesight blurred. *What's happening? It's trying to pull me under.* Nezha kicked her legs frantically, until the water's pressure disappeared and she pulled herself up and onto land. She gasped and coughed loudly, trying to clear the water. She spit up the liquid that had entered her lungs. She was glad she'd left Comet behind. Really glad.

Nezha lay there for a few minutes, gasping for air and staring at the pond. Small snowflakes began scattering down around her. December's snow had arrived. *Looks like we're running out of time. If we don't get Amaya or Dante on our side...I don't even want to imagine what'll happen.*

She stood up and walked over to her back door. If she didn't hurry, she'd be late for her exam.

As Nezha was greeted by her parents, their warm embraces, and the warm food at the table, she thought of her present and future. On one hand, she had her dreams of becoming a botanist, working at their flower shop. And then there was the other world. She had to restore the Angel of Mercy, Mirkhas, so that world and hers wouldn't be taken over by the jinn. To work with other jawhars, to fight for a future where the land would get its pulse back. It was life on either side. Just different definitions for both. And then, there was Kayan. How his smiling, kind self snuck into her heart. She cared about him so much. But, another part of her worried about what would happen. Could they be together? Would her parents accept him? But she couldn't think too far ahead. Right now, she had an exam to pass. What she once thought was her biggest problem now was the least of them.

Nezha stood at her door, her school bag weighing her down. She wore a deep-brown hooded jacket and a long teal tunic with a mauve shawl, the part near her forehead pleated. Her straight-leg pants were a sandy brown. She waved to her parents. Her two silver rings—one on her forefinger with a blue gem and the other on her pinky with three small white triangles—glinted as the sun peeked from behind the tumbling clouds.

***

Dante stuck his fork into a pancake glistening with bright maple syrup and a mound of whipped cream. By his side sat his mama. The morning light swept through the room. When he shoved his fork full of food, he glanced at her. The light illuminated the curls of her short black hair. The weirdest thing that came to his mind was cigarette smoke. When his dad used to smoke, the blacks would twirl out grey. He remembered Mama annoying the hell out of him every day about it. He eventually quit, but took it up again when they separated.

"Dante…" his gramma leaned over the table, plopping another pancake onto his plate.

"I don't need more, Mama G. I need to slip soon."

"Nonsense. Boy, you need to grow more," she said with a playful tone and a smile.

Dante exhaled through his nose. Only a fool would argue with their gramma. They all seemed to care too much. It was like when God knew someone was to be a gramma, he made sure he made her heart big, golden and stuffed with extra love. Like these pancakes. Dante smiled wide. "Thanks."

"Where are you goin' to go?" His mama didn't look at him as she spoke. She still had half of a pancake left.

Dante turned his head to her and then back toward the table. Momma G was removing her apron and walking over to the table to sit with them.

"Since I found you, I need to help Noorenia's pulse, Momma. I'm not sure where I'd go."

"You're gonna do without thinkin' again?" His momma shook her head and he could see a faint smile on her lips.

"Nah…I just…Yeah," Dante conceded. "I'll ask the earth what's hurting it."

Momma G took her seat. "Ask it? Dante baby, you've matured. Even some grown men don't want to know what's hurtin' someone and just yell at 'em."

His momma sighed and made a strange grumbling noise. "Let's not start…this early in the morning. Tch."

Dante still had one more pancake left with a smudge of whipped cream. "The pulse's weak and I dunno if we have enough time. But if I'm supposed to be here, then I'm helpin'. One way or another."

Momma G smiled at him.

Ten minutes passed and his gramma stood up.

"Don't worry about the dishes or anything, either. I'll clean up."

Dante stood, picking up his dishes and then Momma's. He'd do whatever he could here. Who knew how much time they had? If Noorenia was dying, he had to go. Maybe this part of him was selfish, but he knew his powers could disappear along with it. Without his earth powers, how could he feel like *him*? Who the hell was he? He wasn't Dante without them. He still remembered the day he learned more about the Most High. How much made sense to his soul. How much his powers made sense. The Most High gave him this power, and he sure as hell wanted to keep it. He wasn't safe without them. He faced his gramma. "I'm helpin', G." Maybe he was a fool after all. A nervous, scared for their lives fool.

***

Dante slipped his arms into his hoodie.

"Dante…" His momma walked up beside him and wrapped her arms around his shoulders.

He'd found her after so long. She'd missed him, hadn't she? The way she held him now. Her grip tight. The smell of cocoa and vanilla rewinded time. The weekends spent at their favorite café. His parents smiling at each other, hand in hand at the table while he and his brother ate their food, dipped their fries and pretended to fly airplanes with 'em. Damn. Fridays when they all went to the mosque. Dad's cologne wrapping around him, his prayer beads clinking beside him as they prayed next to each other. All those good times. Weekdays where momma pulled his hair back in his cap, kissed his cheek and told him to keep his head up. Highschool nights when he was out too long and she'd sit at the door when he snuck in, telling him he needed to be two steps ahead of everyone. To always think of being safe, not sorry. She was always careful back then. Always lost in her own mind before she disappeared.

"I need to go, but…tell me where you'll be." Dante looked down.

She paused. She bit her lower lip as if she was trying to hold back her words and not let them loose. As if they'd bite. "Here. I'll be here, Dante." Then, her jaw relaxed, her lips parted and her brows furrowed. Damn, she wasn't going to hold back anymore. "Baby, don't think even for a moment that I didn't care about you or your brother." She held his arm when he turned. "I might not trust no one, but my love for you'll never break."

Dante searched her wet eyes. He was an idiot for being mad at her. A *big* idiot. She was his momma. She loved him. She showed it all his damn life. It wasn't him she ran away from. He pulled her into a hug and stood there in her arms as Momma G kissed his momma's head.

He'd been afraid. Afraid of her abandoning him. Afraid of losing her and his powers. Afraid of losing what made him who he was. "I'll be back. Y'all can bet."

"How many cookies should I bet?" Momma G said with a grin.

Dante chuckled. "Make it a cake and we got a deal, Mamma G."

"Mmm, you hustler." Mama G laughed and to his surprise even his momma cracked a smile.

"Go, Dante." She gave him a small pat on his shoulder.

"Take this, Dante." Momma G handed him a backpack. "There's food, money and a jacket."

Dante nodded. "Thanks." He kissed them both on the head and then opened the door and stepped onto the white blanketed ground.

Now that I've found her, there's Noorenia to take care of. Dante looked down at his hands, breathed in the cold air and went to his knees. His gloved hands sunk into the snow. *Talk to me. Tell me what you need. I want to help. Come on.*

Then he heard the voice. The thought of the land.

I am the body of Noorenia. The pulse is fading. Winter is a slumber, but for me I may never wake again. Before Winter's end, we must have the Angel of Mercy. Earth Jawhar, you must find his body. Then the voice faded.

Dante gasped and almost fell backward from the shock. Damn it. He cursed under his breath. "Tch. Before winter's gone?"

He continued to walk. For a few minutes, all he could do was make his way to downtown Veer City. Back to where he'd met the other elementals. Jawhars. That's what he was called too, huh? Now he knew they weren't joking when they said they needed him. It didn't matter. Still, he had to look for the body. Was he the only one who could find it? Because he could speak to the land.

Only he could find the body.

As he approached downtown, he put his jacket on. The wind had picked up. He sunk his hands into the snow, reaching for the ground again. This time he didn't have much to go on.

I am the ground, the body of Noorenia. The Angel of Mercy must be found.

Dante blew out a breath. "Oh man, where do I start, though?" *I guess I need to find those jawhars or whatever again.* Why'd he hafta be with them, huh? They were strangers. But he didn't have any other choice. Noorenia said it needed the Angel and if the earth needed him, he couldn't turn his back on it. Even if he was afraid.

Never.

The thing is, when they told him they needed him, he'd been shocked. No one ever said they needed him. And it scared him. At least no one ever needed him to save the world. That just sounded like lines out of a freaking super hero movie. He had his dance group who needed him, sure. They were a team, surviving together in a world that he knew would reject him for his powers. A world that still didn't tell him he belonged anywhere. Even as a convert Muslim. He worked himself twice as hard to show he damn well did belong.

***

Nezha walked up to her high school doors and entered the building. The white walls, white marble floors and wide hallways always made her feel small. As she passed by one set, she looked at the calendar. December fourteen two thousand and eighteen. It had been that long since she had set foot on campus grounds. She missed being here. Even though she'd worked hard online and made sure she'd done extra credit assignments, she knew she'd missed so much more than the work. She used to be in the Japanese and Korean Club and she remembered starting to enjoy the gardening club. All those trips she'd probably never know about when she'd been swept away to Noorenia. Noorenia still clung to the back of her mind.

She needed to get to her exam hall, but before that, she needed to refresh her mind. The exam wouldn't be for another half hour. And she still had two other exams this week. Fortunately, school wouldn't start again until January fourteenth. She had time to go back to Noorenia.

Nezha sat in the library, motivational posters on the walls, countless books she wished she was reading instead of her thick science textbook. The memory of Kayan reading, his gentle smile snuck into her mind. She closed her book and blew out a sigh, before reading it again. She had to focus.

Nezha took in a deep breath and opened the door to the exam room. She walked past students in their chairs. There were a few familiar faces who smiled back at her. She took her seat and waited for the teachers to tell them when to start. When her exam papers dropped to her table, Nezha breathed in again. She had to do well on this. To be a botanist. For her future.

“You may begin your exam.”

Nezha turned her papers over and picked up her pencil.

***

Comet pawed at one cup as she pushed it dangerously to the edge.

“Comet. Come on, you can’t keep knocking things over,” Tasa scolded. When she reached for the cat, Comet mewed and jumped onto the tall fridge.

“Naughty kitty.” Asad walked toward the fridge and clicked his tongue at Comet, who tilted her head at him.

“Oh.” Tasa flinched. She’d hardly heard him.

“Nezha wasn’t kidding when she said she has a ton of energy. I gave her toys and she sat in my boxes, and then knocked over a pot.”

Comet leaped down to the table next to the fridge, allowing Asad to scratch her chin. “I’ve been getting this weird feeling, lately.” He then picked Comet up. She purred and rubbed her head against his.

“Uh… What do you mean?” Tasa stared at Comet. She’d never seen the cat so cuddly, at least not with anyone other then Nezha.

“A buzzing. A hum whenever we go outside. I can feel it. It’s Noorenia’s heartbeat. It’s pulsing slower and slower.” Asad turned to Tasa and smirked. “Oh, Comet seems to like me,” he drawled.

“She’s never been like that except with Nezha.”

Asad stood closer to Tasa. “I’m a soul jawhar, remember? I can affect people’s and animals’ emotions. But, not for too long.” Comet squirmed in his arms and he let her go. She stalked away, tail in the air.

“Asad…” Tasa started and tucked a lock of her hair behind her ear.

"Hmm?"

"I was thinking about you all. Being jawhars. How does it feel?" She'd always wondered how it was. Being a part of a family of fire jawhars, she hadn't inherited the elemental power. In some ways she'd had to compensate for it. When someone was hurt, she always wished she could just gently touch their wounds and heal them. When she started reading up on herbs, her passion for medicine gave her that power. That strength. She could be useful.

Asad turned his head. "You'll think I'm weird if I describe it my way."

Tasa shook her head. Her fingers passed through her hair. She'd almost forgot he couldn't see her shake her head. "No, no, I won't. Nothing is weird in Noorenia."

"For me it's an energy, almost like a pressure. Hmm, no, like a sensation like when we touch something with our hands. When I use my intuition powers, I feel a sensation going up or down my throat. A rhythm."

"Wow." Tasa exhaled. "As an herbalist, all I feel is my heart pound in joy and relief when I can make someone feel better, or if I can cure someone of their illness."

Asad smiled. He wasn't facing her and opened his mouth, about to say something.

"Hey, you two!" Thunderbolt appeared at the kitchen door. A paper in his hand, his hair more ruffled than usual.

Asad turned around at Thunderbolt's voice, his eyes widening.

"What's wrong?" Tasa instinctively reached a hand out to Thunderbolt. "You look like—"

"It's Veer City. There's about t' be an attack."

***

"Wait, Nezha's not here." Kayan observed as they sat in a cruiser—the fastest way to reach downtown Veer City.

"I know…" Thunderbolt said, gritting his teeth. "We had t' go. Besides, Tasa's there. She can tell Nezha where we are."

Sapphire remained quiet. She stared out the window at the tall buildings like teeth and the forest, rapidly-approaching like a widening maw.

"Sis, you feel it, don't you?" Thunderbolt said. He was sitting beside her, while Kayan and Asad sat in the seat behind them. The cushioned blue seats were soft, made of a gel-like material.

Sapphire met his gaze and nodded. "There's strong jinni presence around Veer."

Asad stiffened beside Kayan. His hands were shaking. "Hey, Asad, are you okay?"

"I'm not sure, but probably. I can just sense something bad is going to happen." He inhaled. "I'm nervous."

Under Asad's feet, a paw swiped at his shoelace.

"Did you bring Comet with you?" Kayan bent over and Comet revealed her face and meowed up at him.

"Huh. How'd she get here?" A lopsided grin appeared over Asad's face.

"You smuggled her in, huh?" Kayan shook his head and smiled.

“She’s comforting, okay.” Asad dangled his hand over his seat, where Comet licked his palm.

“It should be okay if we all work together.”

“No…you don’t get it. Whenever I’m nervous, something bad happens.” Asad tilted his head. “I trust my intuition. I just wish it wasn’t true.”

Kayan sighed. “I’m not sure what to say now…”

“We need to protect the city,” Sapphire said, turning her head to Kayan. “That is what we need to *do*.”

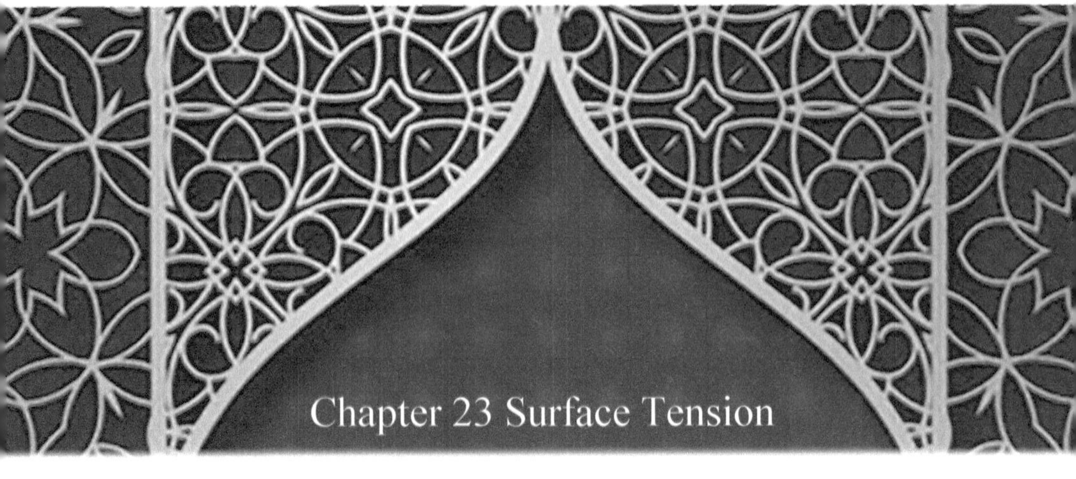

Chapter 23 Surface Tension

After her exam, Nezha had travelled back to Noorenia. She met Tasa before she set out to Veer city. She'd made her way to the mayor's office and had been standing at the door when her friends had arrived.

A pen rolled across the oak table. Mayor Rustam sat at the head with Nezha and Kayan on either side of him. Sapphire and Thunderbolt sat at the end with Asad.

"Another threat?" Thunderbolt clenched his hand into a fist, placing it on his lap.

Rustam nodded. "It was a jinni this time. Although we keep our gates fortified with energy from beco crystals, he gave us a scare." Rustam's eyes narrowed.

"So, he did not breach the barrier, I assume," said Sapphire.

"No. Security notified me as soon as they spotted him. I believe this was a warning. When I arrived at the scene…the jinni stood there. He simply stared and then disintegrated. As if he were dust."

"He? What did he look like?" Nezha asked, raising her head.

"Tall with blond hair. Or perhaps it was black. Skin as pale as snow. On his arms he had something green. Bracelets, perhaps. And his eyes were red."

Nezha's eyes widened, goosebumps crawling over her skin. Green bracelets, red glowing eyes. Could it be Savan? "Did he look like a young man with a pointed face?"

"Y-yes. Princess… Have you seen him before?"

Nezha stiffened and glanced away.

"We had an encounter with him before…" Kayan explained.

"A jinni that looks like the one you described is responsible for killing my aunt." Nezha met Rustam's gaze.

"I'm sorry for your loss. If my people are in danger, then I need your help to protect my city." Rustam sat taller in his seat.

"You don't even need t' ask," Thunderbolt said, his voice quieter.

"We will," Nezha promised.

"There's one thing bothering me. Why are the jinn attacking Veer City? I mean, we weren't here. There are no orbs anymore, either. Why this city?" Kayan asked.

Asad hummed. "Good question."

Rustam turned to the picture on his wall.

"Yeah, I'd like to know that too," Nezha added, brushing her fingers against Comet's back.

Rustam clasped his hands behind his back. "It must be the past. Once, Veer City was a part of the Earth Kingdom. We had Earth Kingdom royalty. They had…been a part of the ruling common nations of the Fire Kingdom."

Nezha raised her brows. "How long ago?"

"About twenty years ago. At the time, jinn had just begun their hostility toward humans. And Veer had just begun adopting more technology and magic."

“Magic…you mean they used the jinn?”

Rustam nodded. “Veer City became known for magic and that was a betrayal to Noorenia and so the Fire Kingdom cut their ties with them. It wasn’t long after when the jinn were fed up with Veer’s use of them. They rebelled and attacked our city. Hundreds of humans and jinn died. That was when the Iron Kingdom was able to appease the jinn with a peace treaty. They told Veer to stop using the jinn and imported their technology to us. We built upon it and this city lost its greed for magic. Although now, I am afraid they have not abandoned the practice all together.”

Kayan sighed. “So the jinn are filled with vengeance.”

Sapphire tilted her head. “The Iron Kingdom found the jinn were still a threat when humans were summoning them near the city of Wadi Alma. They then sealed away those jinn who were summoned. Thus began the War of Jahalia.” Sapphire’s gaze was glazed. As if she still remembered what had transpired long ago.

“It’s still fresh,” Thunderbolt said.

Nezha was glad they spoke about it. Not that there was war, but the reasons and the history. Thunderbolt was right. It had been ten years ago. The scars of the past were still visible. And with the Angel of Mercy Mirkhas still missing, his soul inside her, and the heartbeat of Noorenia fading, the jinn had all the fuel they needed to exact their vengeance. Still, a part of Nezha ached for the other jinn. The ones who did not interact with humans. Those who lived in their own homes, in their own country.

“I want to protect this city from the events of the past. You would not know, but I have done everything in my power to keep my people from using magic. I know they may find a way, but that was why we’ve kept a good relationship with the Fire and Iron Kingdoms. They gave us their technological support." Rustam's voice broke. "I have a daughter and a wife. They are my only family."

Thunderbolt stepped up to Rustam and placed a hand to his heart. Sapphire followed, and then Kayan, Asad and Nezha.

"My sister and I are guardians. We might be from Wadi Alma, but we serve all living beings. We'll help you; you can be sure of it." Thunderbolt smiled gently.

"Yes. We shall help protect your people," Sapphire promised.

Kayan's eyes were glossy. "We're here to help. As long as it takes."

"I might be new, but I trust my intuition, so I'll help," Asad offered.

Rustam brushed tears from his eyes. "Thank you. Be careful, there is an eclipse tonight. A super blood wolf moon eclipse."

Asad frowned. "Wow. That sounds super scary–"

"They might be using that as cover!" Kayan cut in.

"We need t' hurry!" Thunderbolt said.

The group rushed out of the Mayor's office and headed to the main gate.

Above them, the skyline began to blush in shades of orange and pink.

Nezha tilted her head up. It would be getting darker soon. Of course it had to be an eclipse tonight. Of all things. Darkness would consume the city, and the blood moon would seep its red into the sky. There was silence within the group. Even Thunderbolt—who would usually grin and say something sarcastic—didn't speak. Nezha always thought he'd been using humor to deal with pain, but this time he'd been restraining himself. Duty before desire. That was what she'd heard the siblings say so many times. They were guardians and all that weighing on their shoulders must be heavy with responsibility.

"Nezha…we're going to do this together," said Kayan. She turned to him, feeling his gaze on her before she'd looked at him. Maybe he had noticed her expression.

Nezha nodded. "Yes." She inhaled. "We need to protect this city and find Amaya."

"Do you sense her at all?" Kayan asked.

Nezha shook her head and bit her lower lip. "No. I thought we might, but…I don't."

"Well, hopefully we'll have her by our side soon," Asad said, a small smile on his lips.

"Yes, soon," Nezha agreed.

Kayan smiled—that smile that touched his eyes but never shined in them. "We got this."

Nezha's lips curved up. "Yeah."

They were nearly there. The gate was not too far from their reach when Nezha looked down for Comet. She wasn't by her side.

"Comet?" Nezha turned around, her eyes scanning the ground, the trees nearby. Her breathing hitched.

"She…Comet!"

The others turned around.

"Hey, what's wrong?" Thunderbolt's eyebrows furrowed.

"I can't see Comet. She's…she's gone." Nezha breathed harder and walked toward the path they'd come when Thunderbolt caught her arm.

"Hey, you can't go alone, Nezha. We'll—"

"B-but, we have to protect the gate too. Ugh! I need to find her. I can't lose…" Nezha's voice cracked, her body shaking. A lump formed in her throat and tears pooled up in the rims of her eyes.

"*We* means Sapphy and I. Not you, Asad, or Kayan. The two of us will continue t' the gate while you three look for Comet." Thunderbolt let go of her arm and placed a hand on her head.

Nezha's lips trembled. "Thunderbolt. I… But the city needs us!"

"It is our duty," said Sapphire as she brushed a hand across Nezha's cheek.

"We'll find her, Nezha." Kayan assured her. "I'm going with you."

"And I'll stay with the angels," Asad chimed in. "Someone needs to have their backs."

"It is not necessary," Sapphire said.

"I want to help. I'm new and I'll need to catch up with how it works around here," Asad added. He tilted his head toward Nezha. "You'll find Comet, don't worry."

Nezha gulped. Thunderbolt's hair tickled her ear as he pressed a soft kiss on her head. "Go. Go find her."

Kayan began walking back down the path they'd come. He turned and walked backwards, facing Nezha.

"We'll retrace our steps."

Nezha grabbed the siblings' hands. She wasn't sure what to say to them. She didn't want to let go. She didn't want to lose them. But even the silence spoke volumes between the three. Their sad smiles, Thunderbolt's tilted head and a nod. Thoughts of loss, of sadness and grief shot through her mind, making her fingers curl tighter around their hands. Hope burst into her dark thoughts, embracing it as its sun. Even if it was for a moment. Maybe then... she could make herself believe what she was doing was right. Nezha's fingers slipped from theirs and she turned, catching up with Kayan. She couldn't lose someone else. First it was Lamis, then she almost lost the siblings. It couldn't be Comet now. No. She needed to find her. Sapphire and Thunderbolt were guardians. This was their duty. But, even though, even though she knew that they were powerful angels, resilient, together…still, she worried for them. She didn't want to lose the family she'd formed here.

"Comet!" Nezha formed a flame in her hand, using it as a flashlight. The warm orange glow illuminated crevices in the streets and climbed up the trees. "Comet?" She looked underneath the brush, around the trees, only her desperate voice echoing back at her.

"We'll find her," Kayan held a ball of flame entwined in the wind between his fingers. He moved onto the grass, bending over a bush.

"Ugh! I can't believe this happened! I can't lose someone else again…"

Kayan followed Nezha as they continued searching.

Tears brimmed in Nezha's eyes. "Comet…where are you!" Her voice cracked and she pressed her hand to a tree and started sobbing. "Oh Comet…where are…"

Kayan stood beside her, his hand close to her cheek, but he pulled it back. "Nezha… Don't give up. We'll find her."

A lump formed in her throat and Nezha wiped her tears. "I know…We'll find her. Whoever did this will pay! Ugh, I hate them for hurting me…for making us have to leave Sapphire and Thunderbolt behind…for taking Comet!" The flames in Nezha's hand flickered and grew in size. Her face warmed. "Let's look over there." She continued walking, retracing their steps.

Kayan continued to flash the flames in different directions.

Then, there was a distant meow, a pleading meow.

Nezha met Kayan's gaze. "A meow! Where…which direction?"

Kayan pointed one way. "I think it was that way!"

They both ran, firelight dancing across the ground and the walls of buildings.

Nezha breathed in and sighed loudly. "It stopped!"

"Divine's sake…"

Another five minutes passed, Nezha and Kayan kept thinking they heard meows, but still, there was no sign of Comet.

"What's that?" Kayan crouched to inspect something on the ground. Nezha ran to catch up.

He held something round and blue. When Nezha got closer, she knew what it was.

"Comet's collar."

Kayan handed the collar to her.

"She…she was around here." Nezha's grip tightened around it.

"Maybe we should check that area again," Kayan suggested. His eyebrows furrowed when they met her gaze, but then a small smile curved up his lips.

“We’ve checked this whole area at least three times already!” Nezha turned and then stood still. “We…we should head back.” flames licked her arms. Even though she was able to control the flames now, she didn’t mind the fire winding around her body. She let it. She was its guide. She showed it its path.

“What?”

“We had to leave Sapphire and Thunderbolt behind. The city still needs us. I have the angel’s soul inside me, and they might need that power.” Her heart was pounding inside her chest, the sides of her eyes burning. It was stupid. She shouldn’t have left them behind. Still, she just couldn’t forget Comet.

The wind played with Nezha’s hijab; there was a small pulse and a feeling of warmth. She turned to Kayan, his hand outstretched, a warm look in his eyes as firelight caressed his skin. He was a glowing beacon of love.

“Responsibility binds us, I know that. Nezha, all I know is to trust your heart. Whatever you think is right. Comet will find her way, I know it.

“This feeling…”

That’s right. Kayan was manipulating the wind again, the feelings were a strong embrace over her heart. Their connection as jawhars was palpitating. Just like when she had found him poisoned and the wind had guided her, her flames had turned into a bright light… it had happened again the night of that masquerade. Nezha’s cheeks heated and she redirected the fire to the ground, not wanting Kayan to see her flushing. But, did it matter? He could probably hear her heart beating.

Nezha didn't want to go back. She wanted to keep looking for Comet, no matter how long it took. Even if she spent the whole night. Then, there was the need. She needed to protect Veer City, aid the siblings and find the other two jawhars. Guilt gnawed at her heart.

"I had Comet when she was a kitten. Lamis gave her to me as a gift. I remember the litter of kittens and Comet. How small, how cute she was." A sad smile appeared over Nezha's lips. It was Comet—that tiny kitten—who sat in my lap. She meowed at me and I fell in love." The memory was still vivid in her mind. The plush fur of the mostly-white kitten lying on her lap, then reaching out, pawing at her cheek.

"Let's ask people as we head back," Kayan suggested.

"Kayan, thank you for being out here with me."

"I'd do it again. Whether it was in pitch dark or a path of thorns… Flowers may wither…"

Nezha smiled. "Roots will be the anchor."

***

Teeth scraped against metal.

"Quiet, you!" A short man in a navy tunic banged a cane at a cage. The ping echoed in the small storage house. A green light cast shadows against the damp, gray walls.

Comet hissed, her back arched, hair on end. The tips of her fur brushed against the bars; the box holding her could hardly contain her whole body.

"A spunky creature, are we? Well…" The man's face closed in on her cage, making her shrink back and mew in a quiet voice. He held a belt in his left hand. "We can fix that." His crooked smile grew deep.

"Hey, are we ready?" Another man crept up behind the man with the cane.

"Yeah… Everything's all planned accordingly."

Beside comet's cage, a fox sat in the corner of another, its eyes bright against its orange-and-white fur. It paced, locking eyes with the man for mere seconds. With a flick of an ear, it turned on its heel and continued its pacing.

***

The sun hung low in the sky, fingers of light combing through the grass. Savan's shadow was long and stretched, standing at the edge of Veer City. His lips tautened. How long had it been since he'd seen his lady? It had been too long. Too long since his fingers laced through her hair, braiding it into a crown. Too long since he'd had her company. She deserved a crown. She deserved peace. They both did. They all did.

Too long. That's all he could think of as he stared at his shadow. The breeze played through his golden blond hair. He was a shadow jinni. One of the few left after the War of Jahalia.

"Soon… We will reunite soon, my lady."

His green cuffs flickered in the sunlight, the sky mirroring the buttery glow igniting the clouds. It reminded him of Nezha. The fire jawhar who had spared his life. He remembered her anger, her hatred as bright as the setting sun. His honour, his promise would crush him over and over. Every time he turned his back to the light, he'd be wary of her. The girl with vengeance in her eyes, with a fire that consumed equal to the shadows.

He welcomed the darkening sky with a song.

"*Oh darkness my dear friend*
Tell me this night will never end
Hide my sins, hide my doubt in your embrace
Tell me, tell me you won't disgrace

Oh
Oh,
Tell me I won't lose my chance
Moon's going to light my way
Night's going to sing my name
The shadows are my dance
Give me fears, lend me a chance"

His body sped down toward the city gates. The metal winked back at him. The light was fading, the darkness yawning. Beckoning him. The thrum of magic in his veins the only reminder that he was alive. That they were the only hope for the other imprisoned jinn.

Savan's nails elongated, and he pierced the barrier the humans of Veer city used to keep the jinn out. He sometimes envied their assured minds. That arrogance. That what they made with their very own hands could not fail them. That they could do no wrong. How naïve. Savan brought his claws down over the barrier of energy, the beco crystals which held the city's electricity. The crystals hummed with Noorenia's energy. Its depleting life force, its heartbeat.

He would end its life and give it another.

Give it another pulse. A pulse of magic.

The darkness will set us free.

Savan's nails tore through the film of energy, sparks dancing like fireflies around his pale skin as white as the moon's face. A gaping hole expanded. He made his way through the gate, alarms echoing out into the night.

He watched the sky turn black. Night swallowing the day. By his side, shadows took the shape of wolves—elongated snouts, pointed ears, powerful legs. Their teeth drinking in the large round moon's light, slowly melting into red, bleeding into the dark. They sped off into the city, teeth bathed in red like blood.

Chapter 24 Hunted

He gripped the belt tightly and then whipped it at the cage. The bars shook and the cage edged closer to the corner of the wooden table. Comet shrank back and hissed; her teeth bared.

"There's not a beast I couldn't calm," the man said and raised his hand again. "This time I'll get you."

A loud bang on the door took him aback. Another bang and the door swung open. In a flurry of black feathers and crow wings appeared Rana. She strolled in, passing the other man.

One look from Rana and the man with the belt dropped his hand. "Here to inspect us?"

Rana did not give him another glance. Her gaze was steady on Comet. Rana sighed. "Inspect them, please." A grimace tugged at her lips.

At once, the crows which were by her side flew in. Their wings flapped madly over the men, whose screams became gurgling whimpers as the crows pecked and tore them apart.

"I do not meet the needs of men. Akh, we're not used to killing our prey, you know. Oh well, it had to be done." Rana looked down at Comet, who stared at her with two wide blue eyes.

"Did you think I did it for you? I just can't stand animal abusers." Rana slashed the bars with her sharp nails, freeing Comet. The bars sliced apart and fell to the ground with loud pings. "I'm done here." She turned, the feathers on her long kameez fluttered with the movement, and she left the facility, closing the door behind her.

Comet shook her head and jumped down, her paws hitting the smooth floor scattered with small pebbles and blood.

The crows left the bones of the men behind. Picked clean.

***

Shadow wolves draped in reds from the blood moon's light, swept through the grass.

Sapphire, Thunderbolt and Asad approached the gate of Veer City only to see it torn open. Sparks flew, spurting into the air.

"Seven hells…" Thunderbolt hissed under his breath as the wolves of shadow made their way to the city.

Sapphire's eyes widened. "Brother…they…"

Thunderbolt simply gave Sapphire a quick nod and ran toward the wolves. "No…" This was a nightmare. The moon dripping in red. An attack on Veer city.

This time would be different. No one told him to run this time. He and his companions might not know who was in Veer city personally, but he'd protect them. There were children, elderly, people who loved and had loved ones. He'd protect them all. No running away this time.

"Na. Na. Not too close, angel." Savan appeared before Thunderbolt in wisps of smoke, curling around the jinni's body like snakes.

Thunderbolt raised his head, his hair flowing wildly over his forehead as the wind picked up. His arms popped and his body moved in quick bursts as lightning struck the ground before Savan's feet.

"Get out of my way!" Thunderbolt raised both hands, lightning wildly sparking around his body, then it shot outward, raining over Savan. Savan's body moved like liquid, missing all the sparks.

The jinni shook his head. "You can't stop what's already done."

Thunderbolt didn't even spare Savan a look. He drove through the shadows climbing over his body. Lightning kicks and thundering claps echoed into the night. He simply grinned and moved forward. From the side, he saw Sapphire, lights shimmering from her hands, and wolves of shadow falling at her sides. "You're right. I'm unstoppable." Thunderbolt's hands shot out again, landing a full force of energy as thunder clapped and struck Savan to the ground.

Savan's head turned to Thunderbolt's retreating back.

Sapphire raised her hand and felled one of the snarling shadow wolves. "Brother…" In the distance, Thunderbolt's form moved with shadows wrapping around him, but bursting into the air as his lightning shocked them.

She'd seen him fight before. Tonight, he was an indomitable force. Sapphire stepped to the side and landed a kick. A stream of light from her foot sliced through two wolves that were in mid-leap.

Behind Sapphire, Asad's body hummed. Any wolf that touched it perished into a cloud of black particles.

"Sapphire, you're holding up well." Asad grinned.

Sapphire's lips curled into a small smile. "Do the wolves hold an energy?" Another wolf ran to her side, but with a snap of her finger, a light popped and disintegrated the demonic wolf. In another move, Sapphire formed her boomerang from a beco crystal. The weapon spun around in an arc and cut through three other wolves.

"Yeah, but I thought you'd say, well, 'You cannot see,'" Asad replied with a small chuckle. He raised a hand and ran as Sapphire sprinted forward.

"Well, I do not need to say such a thing." Sapphire glanced again at Thunderbolt who was still outside of Veer city, yet so close. If she did not reach him, how could they protect the city? For most of their lives, they'd been together. She didn't doubt Thunderbolt's power. Her brother was both stubborn and strong. She knew he'd make it. Another part of her weighed their potential. She could keep the wolves off her, yet the wolves managed to throw themselves on top of him.

"Asad, I want to aid my brother."

"Okay, go. I got this." He waited for her response. "Are you worried about me? Don't be."

"Ah, but it is my duty to protect you."

"I'm not going to be a burden. I can protect myself." Asad ground his teeth. The sound around him grew louder, the hum a higher pitch. This time, the five wolves surrounding him turned to clouds of grey.

Sapphire gulped. "I didn't mean to offend you. You are not a burden."

"Just focus on the city! Go! I'll stay here to keep the wolves back." Asad's jaw clenched.

Sapphire turned and ran toward the city.

Thunderbolt gasped as Savan gained on him. Shadows and a strong demonic miasma engulfed him. It burned in his lungs. He'd never felt anything as painful as this. One spear-shaped shadow tugged at his legs and Thunderbolt hit the ground. If only he wasn't tied to the rules of having a mortal form. A unicorn. An angel. He was both, not one alone.

"Too soon?" Savan grinned, exhibiting his fangs. His face appeared through patches of black and grey. It only took a moment, like the slip of a scimitar across skin. A gap of shadows opened up, revealing the city of Veer with wolves running through streets. They'd been too late. More wolves shot out from Savan's side and ran past him. Thunderbolt's body numbed. He met eyes with one of the wolves, the moon's red light dripping over its fangs. From behind him, he heard his sister call out his name. Sirens, then screams, tore out from the city of Veer.

"Didn't I tell you, you can't stop what was already done?" Savan tilted Thunderbolt's head with a dagger-shaped shadow. "Na, angel. You have lost."

Thunderbolt's gaze went to the city. To the people running. To the vehicles swerving, shots of energy being fired out from officers, yet the wolves lunging for them and the officers collapsing. His gaze shifted to the large red moon, then Sapphire, her blue hair seeming purple, the light shining from her as if it were her horn. The sound of whinnies, the sound of hooves echoed into his mind from the past. Thunderbolt's fingers shook as he crawled toward the direction of the city. His fingers dug into the ground. "Stop." Before him, Savan vanished, along with the wolves around him and inside the city. Movement returned to his body. He stood up, his wings drooping to his sides as he looked out at the city before him.

The blood had been shed, the moon still drenched in copper. Its large roundness yet another drop of blood tonight.

***

Kayan and Nezha had asked countless people about Comet. Showing them her collar, a picture of her that she had in her own phone. No one had seen her or heard of her.

"Damn it…" Nezha turned her head to the sky. It was just moments away from sunset. "I can't stop looking…"

Around the bend they saw a person. "Hey, we should ask him," Kayan said.

"Sir… Have you seen this cat anywhere?" Nezha showed him Comet's picture.

The older man tilted his head, his green eyes gleaming back at them. "I haven't seen her, but there has been a pair smuggling animals. Rumors have it that they're by the storage house abandoned months ago." The man gave them directions.

"Thank you," she said and walked speedily past him.

"Wait, Nezha!"

"I know he said they're rumors, but it's all I've got." Nezha's voice wavered.

"I know…Just be on the alert, Nezha." Kayan's hand spun with wind.

Nezha turned to him, a small smile and a palm full of flames. "Don't worry."

They'd made it to the door of the storage house. Nezha stepped on a feather. "There's feathers everywhere."

Kayan stopped and the wind tugged at Nezha's arm. "I smell blood."

Nezha's eyes widened. She didn't hesitate to bang on the door. "Damn it…"

"Nezha…" Kayan went over to the door and pulled it hard. The door swung back and hit the building wall with a loud thud.

Nezha gasped. Her heart was ready to burst out of her chest. "Comet… Comet!" She walked in.

Kayan was right by her side. He stepped in front of her swiftly, his boots crunching over a bone. "Divine have mercy…"

The sight of the blood and bones over the floor sent shivers down his back.

Nezha didn't realize any of the carnage. She rushed past him. Loud mews echoed through the building.

"Comet! Where are you?"

A small form ran up to her. Comet meowed loudly and pawed fervently at Nezha's leg.

"We found her…" Kayan said with a smile of relief.

"Comet… Com Com. Oh, my sweet angel…" Nezha scooped her up and cried, tears rolling over her cheeks and a big smile on her face. She laughed. Laughed from all that pain, and from all the relief and worry washing, pulsing, through her heart and veins.

Kayan closed his eyes and raised the wind, making it dance and gently play with Nezha's clothes, run through Comet's fur.

Nezha blinked a few times, feeling her tears wipe away and that soft warmth hush around her. Calming, sweet, caring feelings, Kayan's emotions caught on the wind and passed on to them. She held Comet closer to her. "Kayan…"

Kayan smiled and turned toward the entrance. "Let's complete the group and get back to the angels and Asad. Hopefully they beat up whatever jinni was trying to threaten Veer City."

"Yeah."

In the corner of one cage, the fox who had been Comet's next door cell mate whimpered.

"What was that?" Kayan turned around and walked toward a pile of cages, the bars sliced apart. One was still intact. A white-and-orange fox looked up at him. "We can't leave him here."

"Definitely not," Nezha said.

On the tip of Kayan's finger, wind formed a thin spiral. He stuck it into the cage's lock and it snapped open.

"You're free…" Kayan's voice cracked. His heart ached looking at the creature in such a small space. Freedom. Freedom was one thing Kayan hoped he'd never be barred from ever again.

Kayan pulled the cage door open. The fox jumped out and stared at them for a moment before darting to the door. Its paws dragged against the wood, leaving tiny scratches.

"Let's go." Nezha opened the door, and as soon as she did, the fox looked back at them one last time and darted through it, disappearing into the city.

Sirens and screams wrought through the darkened sky.

“What’s—” the words were torn from Kayan’s throat when a black wolf stalked toward him and leaped right at him.

A sharp tune cut through the air and the wolf fell. It shook its head and whined.

Nezha stepped forward. She’d blown on the feather, the song ringing through it.

Kayan unraveled his sword, Ali from his belt, and kept one hand in front of him.

“The city’s under attack,” he stated somberly.

Comet meowed loudly in Nezha’s grasp. She didn’t want to let go of her, but she needed to protect herself and the city. She placed Comet down.

“Nezha?” Kayan looked back at her. In the distance, the screams tore through the night again.

Nezha grabbed the feather from her cuff and formed it into a sword. The blue flames licked the air. Heat radiated through her body. She ran, with Kayan by her side, Comet behind her.

Wolves blurred from all sides of them, their fangs bared at Kayan, but Ali cut down all of them, reducing them to tufts of smoke rising into the dark sky.

Above their heads, the moon was swollen and red. Blood Moon. Nezha turned toward the city, every part of her heart wanting to save all the people from this horror. One man on the road before her had a bloodied leg. A wolf held him down by one arm. Nezha’s arm arced and the blue flames cut through the wolf, disintegrating the beast.

Kayan fought off the wolves, which took turns snapping at his legs. He was swift just like the wind he commanded. He'd saved other people on his way. But not all of them had the same fate.

Nezha and Kayan reached the road heading toward the city gates.

"Bastards!" Kayan roared into the night as he cut down multiple jinni wolves with his blade. Nezha saw tears glistening over his face. That was no surprise to her. Kayan's heart was filled with love and compassion. It must have been a wound itself, seeing the loss of innocent lives. Seeing the bodies, the blood scattered around them.

The thought of Lamis intruded her mind. Ashes on her aunt's fingertips. She had fought for her life before she lost it. A lump formed in Nezha's throat and tears gathered in her eyes. Nezha would not stop. No. She had to keep going. She gulped. Even if Lamis's smiling face flashed in her mind. Even if she knew no matter how much she cried, it wouldn't bring Lamis back. She groaned when one wolf smacked into her body and she stumbled but did not fall. She simply threw her sword at it. The flames hissed as it sunk into its back, turning the creature into an exhaled mist in the cold night.

Nezha's breath caught in her throat. The screams around her tore at her heart. Through the city, officers and vehicles patrolled the streets. People were being directed into buildings, or told to remain indoors. The alarms blared and the weapons being shot into the cold darkness made her ears ring.

Then, the wolves around her stilled. They looked up toward the sky and howled. Nezha grabbed her sword and followed Kayan.

One by one, all the wolves burst into smoke, melting into the night air as if they'd been an exhale in the dead of winter.

From afar, thunder bellowed and the faint dance of lightning cut through the sky.

"Could that be Thunderbolt?" Nezha asked and met eyes with Kayan.

They both ran toward the lightning.

The closer they got, the more Nezha could make out Thunderbolt from the distance. He was on his knees. Sapphire was sitting beside him, her arms wrapped around his shoulders.

She'd expected to be greeted by him grinning at her, saying something along the lines of it not being that hard to fight when she was gone. But when Nezha finally made it to him, his wings were limply by his sides, his head held low. Tears streaked his cheeks. The breath was squeezed out from Nezha's lungs. Gone was that usually cheeky smile on his face. He'd fallen apart. She fell to her knees beside him and threw her arms around him. The sparks surrounding them fizzled out. Beside her, she felt Kayan's arm press hers and Comet squeeze her body between her and Thunderbolt's legs.

They held each other, the city behind them drenched in sorrow, gripped by the panic of the attack. All she could do was be close to them. In this gasping night of distant sirens and people's cries.

What had Thunderbolt seen? What had happened while she had gone to find Comet? Guilt crept into her heart. If she hadn't gone, maybe she could have stopped the wolves from entering the city in the first place. Maybe she could have stopped it, but...then, the small voice in her head said, 'It's not your fault.' Even then, it didn't stop her from feeling that aching guilt. She couldn't speak, only tighten her hold. Her head pressed against his chest and his heart fluttered, a panicked bird... An angel whose heart was restless, aching, hurting. Then, a voice rent through the silence. It was Asad's voice. He was...singing? No, he was reciting.

"The Creator does not burden a soul beyond what it can bear!" The inflection in his voice echoed in her heart and the warmth of calm folded over her chest.

"Thunderbolt... You are greater than all this pain..." Kayan rasped.

Nezha raised her head. Kayan's eyes were wet with tears. She couldn't find her voice, but she knew they had to move on. Even one small step. It hurt, it did, but they wouldn't let it become a heaviness that would drown them.

"You have us and the Most Merciful by your side. Pray with us..." Kayan's voice softened.

That's right. Supplicating could soothe their souls. Even if a little.

Nezha wrapped one hand around Thunderbolt's and the other around Sapphire's. "Let's make dua and leave the rest to the Most Merciful." She breathed out.

Thunderbolt lifted his head. "Oh Creator..." He sighed.

"All good is for its own benefit. All evil is its own loss," Asad continued to recite.

"You're not the only guardian," Nezha said.

"... forgive us, have mercy on us. You are our only guardian." Asad said his final line.

Thunderbolt raised his head and opened his palms, his fingers trembling.

Nezha raised her own hands and smiled faintly at him as he met her gaze.

"Oh Creator, grant us victory," Thunderbolt said.

"Ameen," Nezha, and the others said in unison.

Kayan smiled. "May the Divine smile upon us."

"Flowers may wither." Sapphire pressed her cheek to Thunderbolt's shoulder.

Thunderbolt blew out a breath. "Roots...will be the anchor."

Nezha's heart was overwhelmed with hope, with warmth at Asad's recitation. They needed that reminder. She stood and walked ahead of them before the city. "Oh Creator...please...help Veer City." She lifted her hands up. Light poured out, shining bright and reaching far, the light cupping over the streets like a gentle hand. "You are light, you are the most loving." Nezha praised. She lifted her head to the sky. "Oh Creator, please...please help them. Please help us..." The light grew brighter, washing through the city. The cries of the people were louder at first, and then Nezha heard it. A faint sound. The prayers of the people. The prayers for mercy, the prayers for healing, the prayers for comfort. Then the thought.

"By His will, this light is a mercy. By His will, I join you in your dua. May He accept your prayers. Ameen."

The Angel of Mercy spoke and then fell silent again.

"Ameen."

At Nezha's wrist, she felt Comet's soft fur and wet nose. The feather cuff was being pulled at. Soon, the cuff slipped off her wrist as she jerked her hand back. It wasn't Comet. It was a fox, and it seemed like the same fox she and Kayan had freed when they had found Comet. It held her cuff in its teeth and sped off. The swelling shock didn't let her register the gravity of what had happened until the fox was already too far away.

It had stolen the feather.

Chapter 25 After Despair

Ice trailed after Amaya as she made her way through the field. The darkness made her heart feel safe. But her mind was rife with dark thoughts. Kill the fox: fight him, make her blood run, make his run faster. Amaya's breath feathered into the sky as she exhaled shakily. It was all wrong. These thoughts, these feelings, they felt so good. That strange freedom to move, to use the water, made her smile. A strange smile that made her just a little guilty for liking it. It was a strange comfort that she'd realized she longed for. Somehow to feel at ease. As if for once, the water was a comfortable fit around her body.

She'd been stagnant for far too long. Now she had a chance to find her father's killer, to find the one who tried to kill *her*.

It was... I that should have...died that day.

Amaya's body kept moving through the field, the black dress flowing behind her, but her mind was lost in the past. She was supposed to die that night, wasn't she? The way the fox's teeth slipped past her neck and instead her father had been killed.

She couldn't forgive herself. A part of her wanted to be merciful, but for such a thing? Even if it was an accident, she wasn't sure if the mercy she felt would be stronger. No, she could have forgiven anything else, even if it was against herself, but to her dear papa? No. This guilt swelled inside her. That she was at fault. She couldn't even forgive herself. If only she could have stopped it. If only she'd done something—anything— that night.

Amaya's feet carried her faster. She wanted to run away from these thoughts. From this darkness that had awakened inside her. She had to keep going. She needed to follow the fox. The ice and water droplets lulled back and forth as she tailed him, following his red and white body, his tail like shimmering snow bathed in moonlight.

The fox traversed this path, jumping beyond the field, and then, Amaya had come to a stop.

A long patch of mud gurgled before her.

And that's when she felt it. A hum. A small pulse in short bursts. *What?* What was this she was feeling? Again, the small pulse echoed through her ears, up her legs. It was Noorenia's heartbeat, wasn't it? Its lifeforce. Lexa had mentioned the heartbeat before. How it was faltering. As soon as she'd felt it, it ebbed and the dark thoughts of pursuit engulfed her mind once more.

She wouldn't let some mud stop her. She stepped into it and trudged through. The sticky glop weighed her feet, but she would continue onward. The past wouldn't change, no matter what she did, she knew that, but she couldn't help remembering it. She'd change her future. She would be the justice her father needed. Even if it involved the blood of that fox. She'd hold onto this strange comfort. She'd been stretching herself out for far too long. This feeling of slipping into something just felt right.

***

The fire cut through the grass, trembling around Nezha's body. That fox had stolen her feather. The only weapon that couldn't hurt a human, but could kill evil jinn—the shaitan. There were too many thoughts cutting through her mind. To help Veer City recover, to protect Noorenia from the jinn, to get the feather back and find the angel's body. She had to move. She had to do *something*.

"Did that fox just..." Kayan met Nezha's gaze and wiped his eyes.

"You have t' go. We'll stay back," Thunderbolt said, still on his knees.

"I won't leave you again!" Nezha turned to face Thunderbolt.

Sapphire stood and urged, "You need to,"

"No. I will not split up from you two. What happened last time, huh?" Nezha wouldn't let them take that burden again. So what if they were guardians? She couldn't lose them. She wouldn't let anyone take anyone from her again. She'd had enough of this. "We will go together, or stay here. I will do what I can and prioritize. The rest, I leave to the Creator." Nezha turned her head and inhaled sharply. She wouldn't let her emotions be trampled over or smothered like she used to. She learned she needed to feel, even if it was to feel fiercely. In return, the fire obeyed her emotions and her brightened will. It flared and sparked by her chest and spun to a small flare over her head.

Thunderbolt chuckled. "Nezha, I can't win with you—" Then, his head spun back, as if he'd heard something or maybe felt another energy. He was looking at the field behind them.

The others followed his gaze and in the distance this human-like form walked toward them, dressed in a soft pink thobe, and cream shalwar. As he got closer, Nezha realized this was someone familiar.

“Ansam?” Thunderbolt pushed himself up, sucking a breath through his teeth, and stood.

Ansam, the angel of hope. It was he who stood before them with his gentle smile, his warm eyes. “As Salaam alaykum. I’m here as a part of Veer’s hope. Please, don’t despair of the mercy you have waited for.”

“Ansam...” Thunderbolt placed a grin on his face. “Of course, you’re here. Why wouldn’t you be.”

Ansam walked up to Thunderbolt and embraced him. Sapphire too, hugged the angel. It was as if both siblings fell apart in his arms as they squeezed him tightly and softly cried again.

“Lady Sapphire, Thunderbolt, I am happy to see you again.” As the siblings stood back and smiled at him in return, there was no sadness in his eyes, only warmth, only joy upon seeing his companions. Nezha wondered. As hope, did he ever feel any sadness? Did he ever experience any kind of negative emotions? Maybe he didn’t. At least, it never looked like it. She’d never once seen him frown.

“Ansam, what about Mayor Rustam? Will he be okay?” Kayan said.

“He’s not alone,” Nezha added.

“You’re right, lady Nezha. I’m here,” Ansam declared with a gentle reassurance. “There’s no need to worry. I’m here to help the city recover.”

“Will *you* be okay?” Kayan placed a hand on Ansam’s shoulder.

Ansam seemed confused. “Yes, my zaan. Of course. Why wouldn’t I be?”

“People have been killed, and all this negative energy could attract other jinn...” Kayan’s eyes were wet again.

Ansam placed a hand on Kayan's head. "I am hope. I am a promise. An angel who has no will but his Creator's. Where there is hope, there is a light, and no evil jinn can fight that."

Nezha saw that soft look in Kayan's eyes. That sparkle. His shoulders softened. It was as if Ansam's bright energy had embraced him and soothed his spirit. "Okay. May the Divine smile upon you."

Ansam smiled brightly and his cheeks coloured. That soft pink. Ansam always seemed to be embarrassed, despite that softness in his eyes. "And to you, Kayan!"

Ansam turned to Asad. "A new friend, I see."

Asad tilted his head. "Yeah, very new."

The two introduced themselves.

"Your soul's really bright and your energy makes me feel like I know where I'm going," Asad said in a soft voice.

"That is hope. A compass leading you toward the straight path." Ansam pressed a hand to his chest.

***

Crow feathers drifted out into the dark sky. The open window invited the cool breeze in to play with Rana's hair as she sat by the windowsill. A thought passed Zul's mind. When he'd first met Rana, it had been at the windowsill. He couldn't clearly remember it, even though it wasn't that long ago. Maybe his mind was trying to protect him, or maybe all the gaslighting by his mother had mangled his memories into jagged pieces, too sharp to put together.

"Rana, do you think Amaya's going to be okay?"

Rana didn't look at him as she answered, "Perhaps. Do you think I know?"

"I was just wondering. Since she's going after that fox and all." Zul's pulse quickened. He wasn't sure what it was, but he had this nagging feeling. It wasn't even a thought; it was just that— a feeling, a sensation that something was wrong. He knew whenever Lexa and the others were up to something, it would lead to terrible situations.

Rana's long black hair wound around her shoulders. She'd been looking out the window, up at the red moon. The deep red moon, a drop of blood over the darkness. "If it quells your curiosity, Zul, she is safe."

Zul gave Rana a long stare. He'd never expected Rana to answer him in such a way. As if she was certain about it.

Without him even asking, she said, "The crows told me." She turned to him and he saw this strange softness in her dark eyes, and then it was gone.

"I'm glad. Rana, Lexa hasn't told me what her plans are, except for them involving the moon."

"What you must do is be patient."

"I know, but..." Zul wasn't going to remain sitting, but what else could he do? Lexa had kept the details hushed. Amaya was out there in the darkness with Obsidian. Both caught by the whispers of darkness.

Sanari was still in her coma. He should be thinking of a way to wake her.

He stood and walked to the stairwell. Rana had said nothing, but she followed him in silence. Her long grey firaq reached her ankles where she wore a silver anklet. It chimed with each step.

A laugh echoed in his mind. The jinni energy, whatever darkness inside him, laughed at him. His veins pulsed with that energy again. Zul wouldn't yield. He closed his eyes and thought of Sanari's smile. He thought of her presence. Her strength, her compassion, her fierce determination. And then a small hope that maybe he could fix what his iron had done, that maybe he would find happiness one day.

Curse you, it whispered and that cold ache in his chest melted away.

He had to do it. He wasn't sure how many times he'd done this before. Zul raced up the stairs and stumbled into the room where Sanari and her parents lay. Red moonlight stretched over the silver-encased Sanari, draping over her face and falling over her shoulders. She was lying in a bed with purple sheets and a thick blue and white blanket made of sheep's hair.

"As Salaamu alaykum," Zul Sharr murmured as he sat on his knees before her. "I hope you've been okay, Sanari. Have you dreamed of anything? I hope it was sweet if you have." He was never sure if she could hear him. If she could sense someone was beside her. He'd hoped to the Creator that maybe she knew she wasn't alone. That he'd been there. "Oh Creator," Zul said, cupping his hands, palms facing upward. He was going to supplicate. To beg the Creator to wake her. It felt like he'd done this thousands of times. "Please, please wake Sanari and her parents up. Please, wake her up..." Zul Sharr's voice cracked, his eyes wet.

He could sense Rana behind him. Her anklets clinking with a few steps and then falling silent. She wasn't stopping him. Maybe she felt for him. Whatever reason it was, he was thankful to her.

"You are the one that loves the most...so you understand my love for her. Please, wake her up, oh Creator. I can't live without her! I need her... I need to see her smile again. I want her to be okay. Even if... even if she doesn't care about me. Please..."

His tears fell, his skin prickled, but, nothing. He wasn't expecting her to suddenly open her eyes. He never did before. Even so, he stared at her. His gaze shifting to her hands, to her eyes, waiting for any movement, any sound. Then, he saw it.

Her finger twitched.

He released a breath he didn't realize he was holding.

Her hand twitched.

Zul shot up. "Oh Creator..." He breathed out. "Sanari... Sanari, wake up. You can hear me, can't you? Wake up, Sanari. Please, wake up. You're safe. Please wake..."

Then, nothing. But he hoped. A smile stretched over his lips, and even Rana was beside him.

"She moved."

"Yes. She moved." Zul bit his lower lip in anticipation and wiped his tears. Would she move again? He hoped she would slowly become conscious. This was a sign. It was still a sign for him to not lose hope.

Several minutes passed, but nothing happened again.

"It's a good sign. I just...thank you." Zul pressed his palms to his chest, feeling his heart beating loudly. He hadn't felt this alive in a while. "Oh Creator...help anyone who was cursed by the iron. Wake them, please." Zul Sharr stood. "Sanari, you'll wake up. You will. And when you do, we'll be together and we'll beat this darkness. We'll be together again."

***

“What now? Won’t more jinn be attracted to the city because of the negative energy?” Kayan asked.

“No. I feel large amounts of good energy. Was it one of you?” Ansam said.

Nezha walked up to Ansam. “The Angel of Mercy shone a light through me. That energy you feel must be mercy.”

“That supplication we did must have helped too. Asad was reciting and it made us feel more hopeful.” Kayan gestured to the soul jawhar.

“Yeah, the city must have felt it too. I tried my best to make the energy reach as far as it could,” Asad explained.

Ansam held Sapphire’s and Thunderbolt’s hands. Maybe he’d noticed how they’d been looking at him. “Do not worry. Mercy, hope, this will begin the healing for Veer city, Creator willing.”

“I wanted t’ stay...” Thunderbolt said. “We have t’ protect them.”

Ansam smiled. “You must find the feather and the water jawhar. I might not understand your pain, but I do understand that hope is about justice, about a good heart. Believe in yourself and act for justice. Leave the rest to the Most Merciful.”

Thunderbolt’s head seemed to raise higher, as if he was trying his best to be brave. He turned to the others.

“Come on, we can’t stand around. Let’s go.”

Kayan and even Asad patted him on the back.

“Have a safe journey. May the Divine smile upon you.” Ansam called out to them and waved as they departed.

***

Comet dozed, curled up in a bubble Sapphire had formed and which floated by her hip as they walked. The grass pricked and stabbed their legs; it had been scorched by the forked lightning that had battled with the shadow jinni Savan. Even as they walked, Thunderbolt and Sapphire seemed to stare ahead, their gazes never lowering.

The energy of Noorenia, despite it being low, hummed in skips. Nezha could still feel the angel Mirkhas's energy inside her heart. "I feel some kind of energy, like Mirkhas." She pressed her hand to her heart. "I think it's the feather's energy. The angel's letting me feel it, but I don't know exactly where to go."

"*I* know."

Nezha was caught off guard by Asad's voice.

"Shno?" What?

"I can feel it. It's almost like it's calling out. Like a bird's song echoing into the cold dawn."

"You sound like a poet," Thunderbolt said, nudging him.

Kayan laughed. "He's a soul jawhar. Doesn't surprise me."

"Oh? Don't do anything stupid or embarrassing or I'll immortalize it." Asad winked.

"Was that a threat?" Thunderbolt raised a brow.

"Lead us," Sapphire said, falling back as she matched Nezha's and Thunderbolt's pace.

***

The scents of smoke and charred soil were faint as they walked through the field. Asad's heart pounded in his chest. He'd never imagined he'd be in this kind of place, with people he'd hardly known. He didn't mind not being able to see, but the feeling inside his heart was much more terrifying. The way a steady pulse beat at his throat and how he couldn't feel anything other than that call from the feather and Amaya's energy. He wasn't sure how long they'd been walking. He'd wondered why Kayan didn't use his wind to carry them off. Maybe it was what both him and Nezha had been through. All they'd seen in the city. All that blood and agony. For once in his life, he was glad he couldn't see it.

Asad sensed the others around him. And faintly in his mind he could see the colours of their lataif; the swirling energy points in their bodies and the strongest ones shining brighter. Nezha and Kayan's head lataif was dull. The one responsible for their energy. He turned his head and beside him were the two jawhars with Sapphire to his right, her brother lagging behind her.

He clicked his tongue and raised one hand, trying to grasp something when he almost stumbled. But his fingers only met the air. The skin at his fingertips prickled. Right. White Lie was neatly tucked away into the pocket by his belt. Of course he didn't need that stick. Still, his instincts demanded it. He didn't have to follow every one. Only the two energies, the calls that beckoned him.

***

The distant ground appeared like thick soil, the type that could swallow them under. Nezha wasn't sure what they were heading into. Finding the feather and Amaya were her priorities. No matter where they steered them. She'd always found herself pulled in a direction. Pulled, not by her own will, but by the needs and wants of another. If they didn't head this way to these strange lands, then she couldn't find the angel's body and that would mean Noorenia would die.

Asad walked ahead of her, his tongue clicking. Occasionally, she noticed his hand lift, as if he were grasping at a wall that wasn't there. A wall to brace himself. He couldn't see the world like she could, but she couldn't imagine how it was feeling those energies all the time, having a touch on the pulse of life. Her lips parted in awe. The powers they held could be beautiful, but also overwhelming. And that, she knew they could all understand about each other. He would lead them to the feather and Amaya, the energies still calling to her as if she was only hearing a phone call, while Asad could hear a voice and knew which direction it was coming from. He came to a sudden stop. Then, Nezha saw her.

Amaya.

She was struggling through the mud. That's what the strange thick ground was. The wind whispered, carrying the freshly-falling snow past her face.

Chapter 26 Sapphire's Heart

Struggling as your heart shivered from the pain in your chest, as if the overwhelming emotions were the icy maw of winter. That was something Nezha knew she and Amaya shared. Whatever reason Amaya was out here for, shoulder-deep in the mud, Nezha couldn't help but think the reason was the fox. Maybe they both shared the same enemy.

Nezha blinked back repeatedly, the snow surrounding her, dancing around them, dusting the mud.

***

"Amaya, right?" Kayan stepped forward. "We're here to help. You probably feel alone, but you're not. We're jawhars like you. I command the wind, and the others, they, too, have an element that abides them by the Most High's will." He knew how it was, to feel so alone. To have no friends by your side when you needed someone. When he had met Nezha and the others, he didn't feel as lonely. They were there to make him smile. A true smile. People to share joys with, people to speak with and have by his side when sadness pulled him under its dark sky.

"He's right. You're not alone!" Nezha said next.

Asad kept quiet.

Amaya's fingers wrapped into a fist. The mud crystalized into gleaming icicles around her knuckles. The ice was sharp like shards of glass and Kayan thought she'd cut herself. Then, the ice scattered around her into small needles. They spread outward, raining over them.

Kayan swiped his arm over his head. The wind spun over them, whisking away the needles of ice before they could peck their skin.

The mud coated her body, frozen and crackling. Amaya rose, as if she was a dark creature who had just emerged from the depths of a lake. The ice shattered around her. It seemed like nothing was going to stop her. She shot forward as water surged from her hands. Her ice-coated shoes allowed her to skate over the ground unencumbered.

He knew he could easily seize her with the wind, but he didn't want to. To force her was against who he was. Imprisoning her in the wind's grasp would be hypocrisy. Freedom without responsibility was selfish. Both on his part and on the wind's. Both wanted freedom, the ease to be themselves. So, as they sped after her, neither Nezha, nor the siblings, nor Asad used their elements against her.

At least this ice had made it easier to get through the mud. In one blink, Sapphire and Thunderbolt turned into their unicorn selves, their wide wings stretching above their heads. Outside the city of Veer, the restrictions on their elemental powers didn't apply. Kayan felt the soft touch of Thunderbolt's muzzle on his hand.

"Come on, Kayan." Asad reached a hand out to him.

Kayan nodded and climbed onto Thunderbolt's back. Beside them, he saw Nezha riding Sapphire. She glanced at him, a small reassuring smile on her face. But, at this moment, the wind dancing around her, Kayan couldn't look away. His eyes widened; nostrils flared. He didn't think about what was happening—all he could feel was awe. He wanted to be by Nezha, always. As close as he could be. For a few moments, the fox, Amaya—it all vanished. Only Nezha's warm smile and beautiful brown eyes remained. That gaze, sparkling like the fire she could ignite. For a moment, Nezha held his stare. Then he turned away and ran his fingers through his hair. No, he couldn't let anything distract him. He was supposed to help them get Amaya on their side. To uphold that duty he'd promised his mother long ago, to be a fighter for those who couldn't. To not let their voices drown.

***

They were following her. Amaya didn't spare them a glance. She needed to find the fox. In the distance she saw him again. She couldn't lose sight of him. The cold in her veins was dissipating. The whispering shadows wrapping themselves around her were quiet, not deafening like before. She didn't care. All she wanted was ease again. Who was responsible for this turmoil in her mind?

The boy said she wasn't alone? Even if there *were* others like her, she couldn't do anything about it, not right now. Not when she was getting closer to the fox. Not when she needed to fulfill the urge to get her answers. She needed to know what exactly had happened the night her father had died.

The fox slipped into a quiet forest, his legs elongating, his fur seeming to melt into a brush of soft colours, like paint mixing with water.

With her arms fluid as water itself, Amaya spun around as soon as her feet landed on the fresh snow. She exhaled, her breath snow and tiny flakes of ice, spreading out into the air. The shadows around her arms shot up into the air, piercing the sky. Clouds rumbled above her, then thunder clapped and snowflakes surged down, plunging them into a storm.

***

The siblings' hooves touched the ground, but before they could transform back into their angel forms, the ice and wind struck them, sending them flying back. With a sharp gasp, Nezha was knocked off of Sapphire's back, tumbling into the snow. Her hijab clung to her face, her long tunic was soaked, and the cold nipped at her skin. She held tightly onto Comet who was still in Sapphire's bubble as she rolled through the snow.

Nezha's head whipped back to them. She couldn't see where they'd gone. Flames burst from her palms, water now at her fingertips and grass emerging, drinking up the melted snow. Then she held her breath. What if the fire hurt Amaya? She knew Kayan was never injured by her, but she couldn't risk it on Amaya. She wanted to melt it, warm the air around them, but she couldn't. She knew the consequences of an unruly flame. The magic that shot out from Amaya must have created this strange storm.

Comet meowed loudly, piercing her ears. She butted her head and pawed at the ball. "Shh. It's okay, Com Com. We'll be okay, Mithi."

Amaya fled. All Nezha saw was a glimpse of her black dress slipping away like a shadow. Snow bit Nezha's skin, snowflakes clinging to her lashes as she struggled to her knees. She gasped for air, her chest rising and falling. She couldn't see anything now, only keep blinking.

Then she heard the howl of wind and Asad's hum. She stood and followed the sounds until she stepped on a shoe.

"Agh. Who's there?" It was Asad's voice.

"Nezha... Are you okay?"

Asad shrugged. "Maybe. Let's pray I can keep my foot." He grinned.

He sounded like he was okay, for sure. Nezha turned, seeing Kayan through gaps in the storm, his arms arced, the wind wrangling the flakes and ice.

***

Cold clasped her in its teeth. She trudged knee-deep in the snow. Sapphire's wings were flecked in the snowflakes as she made her way to the black shape in the distance. She'd turned herself back into her angel form. Her horn around her neck shone, lighting her way. She wasn't certain how far she'd fallen. Her legs were heavy, her heart pounding loudly, its pulse louder in her throat. She hated to admit it, but her gut instinct was right. It was Obsidian who stood there, in his unicorn form. His black wings folded by his sides like a curtain.

Sapphire's throat stung as the cold air rushed into her lungs. She made her way to him, her arms reaching out, until she finally made it to the field where the snow was like a thick sheet across the yellowed grass underneath.

Her breath turned to smoke as she stood before him.

"Ob—"

He turned to her, his ears swivelling back. Their eyes met as she cautiously walked toward him and stopped when she was but an arm's length from him. The snow dotted along his face, down to his nostrils and over his lips. He turned his body to fully face her. His black mane was tousled. Some wisps of hair curling up toward his ears. And, in his eyes she saw emotion, a wanting, an inclination she could tell he was resisting. It was that familiar look. How had she not seen it before?

"Sapphire." Plumes of his breath soared up through his nostrils. His voice was soft and tender.

"Obsidian. You are really… you're here." Sapphire wanted to embrace him. He was still her husband, no matter if he was on the other side. He still was her mate, wasn't he?

"Why are you here?"

His words were an icicle plunged into her heart.

"I waited, Obsidian…. I waited for you. Don't you know why? I never gave up hope."

Obsidian stepped closer to her. Sapphire's head was bowed, tears stinging her eyes. Her skin was afire and her bones were cold. She didn't want to stand here, and yet... she wanted to pull him into her arms and return to the others. And yet, she couldn't move. Her legs were light, and they betrayed her with their weakness.

His head brushed hers. "Time was always against us, Sapphire. I, too, didn't give up on seeing you… I still don't know what you are to me. But you know what I am, don't you? So long as this curse courses through my blood. I am your enemy. And, time can only tell."

Sapphire enveloped his neck with her arms. “No… You are not my enemy. We’re each other’s partner. You are my mate, my love. We’ll set you free.” Sapphire held his face in her hands.

“You remembered me.” She pressed a kiss to his face. Her mind shouted at her to let him go. That he needed cleansing and it would take long for him to be purified of the jinni magic in his body. But, Creator, she didn’t *want* to let him go. It scared her.

Obsidian nestled his face to her neck, his breath warm against her cold skin, and then turned from her. The cold rushed in to fill the gap. Her eyes widened as he slipped away from her and then glanced back. “Don’t forget. The spirit never does.” And with that, Obsidian galloped off into the snow. A shadow drifting farther and farther away from the light that was Sapphire and her love.

Chapter 27 Siblings

A loud whine filled his ears, and then Thunderbolt drifted into consciousness. It was all snow around him and under his fingertips. Just all cold. His breath disturbed the freshly-fallen snow at his lips. He struggled to his feet, shaking the snow off of his wings.

He wasn't sure how long he'd been knocked out. The memory of what happened slowly came back to him. They'd seen Amaya, then the snow blowing over him and... right, he and his sister were thrown back. He had to find her.

"Sapphire!"

She was smart, so smart, that he knew she'd be okay, but...still, he knew her better than anyone. She was always thinking, always calculating how to go about things logically. But, not everything was about logic.

"Sapph... Where are you?"

The wind whistled past him. Snow circled around him, the flakes a swarm flying into his eyes as he blinked them away.

His eyes dimmed, then he shook his head. That fall must have been hard. Only now did he realize the small pulse at his head. He could feel her energy, a loud hum around his head. Why hadn't he tried to sense her before? He had to find her. A small sensation at his heart led him, pulling him, and he followed it.

"Come on, Sapphire! You better be okay! If...if you don't show up soon, then I'll get sarcastic! I know how much you hate—that." His voice quieted. She'd been his only family until they'd found Nezha. At the time, he'd considered her to be a weak girl who would just get in their way, or be loud and obnoxious. But, her humor, perseverance, compassion—They all snuck into his heart. Now, he considered Nezha a sister too. Someone to protect, adore and pick fights with. A smile tugged at his lips.

"You're both annoying..." A tear rolled down his cheek.

Five minutes, an hour—he wasn't sure when, but it was Sapphire in the snow, her footfalls slow as if she were gliding through.

"Sapphire!"

Thunderbolt ran to her and grabbed her shoulders.

"Hey, are you okay?"

Sapphire kept silent but nodded.

"Nah, something happened, didn't it?"

"I saw him..."

"Him? Who?"

She swallowed. "Obsidian..."

"He's alive?" Thunderbolt held her shoulders harder and then loosened his grip. "Wow...so, he's alive. Oh, zaan...alhamdulillah, he's alive. What did he say? Where is he?" He looked around.

"He left. I saw him at that party too."

"What? Did you talk t' him?"

"No, it wasn't plausible. He was a stranger to me after all."

"Sapph, why do you make things so complicated for yourself?" Emotions— they were something she rarely showed easily. Tightening her hands, silent tears...but always holding back. He'd tried talking to her about it before. Every time, she'd smile and say not to worry, that she was okay.

"We had our duty to uphold. We needed to find the jawhars. I could not let my heart control me." She lifted her eyes to him.

Thunderbolt shook his head. "When have you ever let it? You're always using your head."

Sapphire pressed her lips into a thin line. "I need to be logical. What the best option—"

"Sometimes, you need t' think with your heart. Especially when you love someone, sometimes you need t' let your heart feel."

"I do care. I have emotions."

"Well, you can't just close yourself off. Damn it, Sapphire!"

Sapphire flinched. "Why would you feel the pain on my behalf?"

"Because you're always selfless. You're always thinking of others and being this…wise woman. When you care about someone, then you feel their pain, their happiness, their sadness. So… I'm hurtin' for the both of us."

Her eyes were welling up with tears. "Thariq..."

"Shut up ad cry. Don't you dare lock up those tears. You're going t' keep hurting in the silence. I just know it. Let it happen, sis." His voice softened and he folded her into his arms.

Sapphire's shoulders trembled and then she pressed her head to his shoulder and her cries tore from her lips. Years of pain tore from her lips. Years of the weight, the responsibility, poured, screamed from her body. Emotions, all of them that were desperate to be carried off by the cold wind.

Sapphire lifted her head.

"Better?"

"Somewhat..." Sapphire's eyes were puffy, her nose red.

"A good start, sheikh. What did we learn?"

Sapphire smiled back and smacked his shoulder. "That no matter your experience, your age, knowledge is boundless."

Thunderbolt sighed. "That was rhetorical, you nerd."

They both chuckled.

Chapter 28 Revealed

"Kayan!" Nezha stumbled, and then pulled Kayan's sleeve. The wind circled them, dissolving the snow and revealing the dark sky. She could only tell because of the stars winking back at her and the moon that was shedding its copper. "Kayan..."

"Nezha... Asad." He breathed out, his cheeks bright red from the cold. Small crystals decorated his hair.

He'd stepped closer to her. Nezha tucked the bubble Comet was in under her arm, despite the protesting meows from her. Nezha held on to Kayan's sleeve even tighter. A burning bloomed around her arm. She hadn't noticed she was bruised until now. For some reason, she didn't want to let go. *Just a little longer.*

"Hey, you two okay?" Asad asked.

"Yeah." She gulped, her breathing deep. She'd lost Sapphire and Thunderbolt in the snow...and she'd nearly lost Comet before. No more. She wouldn't lose anyone again if she could help it.

The moonlight glowed behind him, so strongly that she was blinded. When she opened one eye to glance at him, she saw Kayan's gaze was so warm, his smile soft. Even as cold clung to her, biting her, frigid air danced over her skin, Kayan's warmth flooded her heart. Kissed her heart. As their gazes locked, she couldn't sense anyone else around her, but him, not that she wanted to. He seemed to lean in to her, his lips parted. She wanted to simply be embraced in the warm and sweet peace that blanketed her body. As he moved in closer, the moonlight feathered over his shoulders. She knew she wanted to be with him. Anywhere Kayan was with her, she knew it was normal. It had become natural to have him by her side.

"I... I saw Amaya run far into this meadow." Nezha's fingers slipped from his sleeve and her arms wrapped around Comet, her gaze still on Kayan.

Kayan nodded. "Okay..." He seemed breathless. In a way, she hoped it wasn't just because of him protecting everyone from the snowstorm.

"And I still hear the feather calling out. It's out there somewhere." Asad pointed.

"But Sapphire and Thunderbolt are still out there," Kayan protested.

"We need to stay here. If we go anywhere, we'll miss them," Nezha said.

"So we'll just freeze here. Cool." Asad blew out a sigh.

"Who said anything about freezing?" Nezha lifted her palms, fire hissing to life.

"Oh good, a personal heater!" Asad said, lifting his hands.

"Huh, I can charge, ya know."

"Thanks, Nezha jan." Kayan smiled, that soft smile.

"Of course." Nezha returned the smile. They had to wait here. Wherever the siblings were, Nezha hoped they were safe and together.

The wind had long stilled, no more snow flying through the sky. But, there was something her fire and the starlight made visible in the sky. Large wings, the black silhouette of a bird. Its long neck seemingly featherless.

"Vultures," Nezha breathed.

Kayan looked up with a gasp. "Divine's sake..."

"Do they know we're still alive?" Asad asked, unamused.

"I hope so," Kayan replied.

The crunching of snow made them all turn to the sound. It was Sapphire and Thunderbolt heading their way. They both flapped their wings and took to the air, gliding before the three. Their powerful wings created a downdraft, spraying them with snow.

As soon as he landed, Thunderbolt had a smile on his face, along with Sapphire. Kayan and Nezha both ran to them. Kayan grabbed Thunderbolt into a hug and Nezha hooked her arms with both siblings. They were back. They were back and they were okay. Nezha's heart was about to beat out of her chest.

After several minutes, Asad spoke. "Hey, welcome back. Hate to say it, but we have company above us."

"Vultures." Sapphire stared at them. "They follow death." She bent down to Comet who was still in the bubble. "You will have to stay in there, sweet hurairah."

"Yeah..." Nezha wouldn't risk Comet being taken again. She'd be safe and warm inside the bubble.

"And at night like this?" Asad asked.

"Something's not right." Thunderbolt tilted his head.

Someone stepped out from between two skinny trees. Sapphire glimpsed him first. Tall and dark. His brown skin was as rich as moist soil, glinting in the moonlight. Shades of orange over his cheeks like molten rock spilling down a volcano. Two black wings draped over his shoulders.

Obsidian silently stared at her, eyes wide, lips parted. His gaze soon shifted to Thunderbolt and stayed there for several seconds until he spoke.

"Sapphire, you are with them?"

"Obsidian..." Thunderbolt gaped at him.

Before anyone could take a step or say another word, Obsidian shifted before them. His black muzzle, his pointed ears and long black mane growing before them. His black horn caught the starlight. Then he raised his head and a loud neigh swept over them.

From ahead of them, loud stomps into the crisp snow echoed out into the night and then the beasts appeared. Their hooves were black, their legs thickened with dried blood. Their deep red eyes stared back at the angels and jawhars, their teeth bared, heads nodding. Their sharp knife-point horns flickered in the light.

Jinni unicorns.

Chapter 29 Plight of the Jawhars

Dante sat up in bed with a start, gasping for breath. The dream about those jawhars had woken him up. They were in danger and needed him. Dante didn't remember much. When did he ever remember a whole dream anyway? But what did stick with him was the images of animals, their faces long, horns sharp and bloody.

He rubbed his eyes. Dante had made a fire in the woods, the flames crackling. He'd made himself a makeshift tent with the roots of a nearby tree, its leaves and the rocks scattered through one path in the forest.

A wolf's bark echoed in the night. Dante removed the blanket made of sheep's hair and sat up. He made his way to the entrance of the tent, clasped his hands around the stone, making it shift to open like a door. He stepped outside.

"What's wrong, girl?"

The wolf's tongue lolled when it saw him, making it look like it was smiling. This wolf had been his guard tonight. Not that difficult to convince her, either, since he'd been able to feed her the meat from the chicken spring rolls he had. For himself, he still had a big ole container of spaghetti and meatballs; two bags of marshmallows; graham crackers and chocolate; snack bars; fruit salad; and his favourite BBQ crispy chicken burgers. Mama G knew how to spoil a man.

He yawned and stretched his arms above his head. "Damn, who the hell would mess with me so late at night?"

Anyways, he didn't care. No one was here. He might as well just talk to her. He pressed a finger to her forehead.

Thank you for the delicious meat! Earth jawhar, I sense danger not too far. My pack needs me. I shall leave you to your journey. May the Divine smile upon you.

Dante's lips turned up in a small smile. "Yeah, get outta here. Thanks."

The wolf wagged its tail and sped off, its paw prints in the dusted snow being swept by the breeze.

***

"I can't just sit around anymore. I feel useless." Zul Sharr stood. Seeing Sanari move renewed his hope. "I can't wait for Lexa anymore. Rana, you're close to her, aren't you?"

Rana averted her gaze. "Yes."

His gaze fixed on Sanari for several seconds before he turned to the stairs. "I'm going. And I won't ask you to come with me. I understand if you won't go along."

"Where are you going, Sire?" The way she called out behind him, following him as he descended the stairs, made his back shiver. Was that fear spilling in her voice?

"To Veer City. I can't take the silence anymore."

"I cannot allow it." Rana barged past and then spun to face him, her long black hair nearly whipping him in the face.

"What?" He had to go. "What do you mean?"

"Lexa said for you to stay here. She will tell you your next move."

"I have this terrible feeling in my gut. I need to go. I'm sorry, but I won't stay."

With one swipe of her hand, Rana gripped his arm and shoved him against the wall.

"Don't make me hurt you."

"Please, this isn't for me." Tears sprang to his eyes.

Rana searched his eyes. "I know."

"Then, you should understand. I'm supposed to be a prince, but I feel like it's just in name! I want to be with Sanari... I want peace and love around me. If anything terrible happened to Veer and I could have prevented it..." His voice shook. "Oh Creator, I'd never forgive myself."

Rana loosened her hold.

"Do you have someone you love?"

He saw the way her eyes softened at his sudden question. Emotions were a motivation more powerful than any material need. Fear, joy, hate, jealously, love… they could end lives or change people for the greater. For several seconds he saw her expression shift. Her lips parted and surprise in her gaze. She let him go.

"Thank—"

"Go, before I change my mind." She turned her back to him.

Zul stole one last glance at her and then left.

***

Obsidian huffed, his breath feathering out into the darkness. They were surrounded by the jinni unicorns. Sapphire stood before the others, tall and elegant as she usually was. In her eyes, Kayan could see a look of longing he'd never witnessed before. A deep, sad look. Kayan glanced behind him at Nezha, the fire swathing her fingers and flickering, reaching out to her shoulders. Bathed in light, lightning crackled around Thunderbolt.

Kayan breathed in deeply. He would end this. He was a jinni slayer, after all. One whip of his sword Ali and the blade would tear the beasts apart. They didn't need to waste time. The feather was being carried away by that fox and who knew where it would end up and how quickly. He stood apart from the others, his fingers pulling at Ali. The blade unraveled from his belt and obeyed the sharp wind.

Then again, it would be chaos. And long ago he had told himself he'd never be a jinni slayer again. Until he met Nezha and the others. Until Noorenia itself was wounded and he had to protect it.

The scent of blood used to bring bile to his throat. The memories haunted him. The nights they would hunt down rebellious demonic creatures. His heart thudding violently in his chest as the creatures were felled by his sword. As the wind carried the scent of blood and malice. As the wind screamed with terror and unbridled emotions. The painful feeling would lance through his mind. If the creatures were many, he'd be driven mad by their terror and blood-lust. Some days, it took hours of his teammates and his mother to console him, or he'd even hunger for the taste of chaos.

Streams of wind flitted around him in circles. Nausea swam in his belly. He would risk it for the ones he cared about. "I'll take care of this."

Nezha turned to him, her mouth opening, but her voice was drowned out by the loud nickering of the jinni unicorns.

"Go..." Kayan ordered, his eyes turning a gleaming shade of green.

"No. We're staying with you." Nezha replied, her eyes now sharper than usual.

"It's okay, I can handle it." He felled a unicorn, as it crumpled away into a sigh of smoke.

"That doesn't matter! Stop trying to do this by yourself." Then her voice softened. "We're here for you. I'm here for you."

Kayan's lips parted. When he was alone with Father and his younger sister, he'd always been pushing himself to be the one to take care of them. Going out to work hard and earn them money, getting supplies, giving his family hope. When he found himself alone with his thoughts, they were loud and incessant in worry and fears. He was the protector. He was the one to fight. He had to shine brighter in the darkness.

Then, seeing Nezha and the angels by his side right now, he could feel he wasn't alone. He wasn't alone, right? He wasn't the only one who had to protect them, right? They were a light, brighter than the darkness of his own thoughts. And he found that these beautiful beings were quieting his doubts. His sword Ali seemed to agree. The wind murmured until it quieted, and Ali's blade which was quivering had stilled.

"Ali…"

Nezha gave him a small smile as his gaze shifted from the angels back to her again.

Why did Nezha have to care so much? Why did she have to make his heart pound so loud? It was tough reminding himself he didn't have to give all of himself away. That there were others by his side, ready to help *him. I guess… I can ask for help…* Nezha was there. She made him want to be by her side, and for her to never leave his. His Nezha jan…

"Then prepare yourself, Nayzak."

"Oh? New name. I love it." Nezha's lips curled into a crooked grin.

Chapter 30 Blood-soaked

Why was he running? Zul Sharr's heart was loud, thunderous. His breath, his heart—they were all he could hear through the forest. He had to reach Veer. He couldn't bear knowing that something terrible could be going on in that city. He wouldn't...he couldn't just sit around and do nothing.

A dark coating caked the bottom of the trees. He'd remembered what Lexa had been telling him. That Amaya had gone to scare the city. Blood... Was it Amaya's? He gritted his teeth. Why did it always have to be about sacrifice and loss? This had been too much. He still couldn't understand what Lexa was up to. Why did she need Amaya? Why was she attacking Veer?

Branches and the blood-soaked ground squelched under his footfalls as he passed more trees. The scent of copper and pine coated the back of his throat and entered his head in waves. His muscles were burning now, aching, screaming for him to stop. He stood for a minute, taking deep breaths. He couldn't afford to stop for too long. He didn't think he deserved any rest, not when people's lives were in danger. He would be at fault too.

Energy, sharp and blooming, surrounded his head, his veins pulsing. The demonic energy coursed through him.

What are you doing? The jinn energy challenged.

"None of your business."

It laughed, the voice like shattering glass, nicking his peace of mind. *I know; you want to save them? How pitiful. You are just a lowly human.*

Zul stretched his arms, bent his legs and was off again.

"Maybe... But my faith is increasing. I can do something! And because I can, I won't let you stop me!"

The jinni energy vibrated with what he interpreted as fear. *You can't get rid of me.*

Zul took a shaky breath. He wouldn't let it take him over again. Not anymore. No more! That sharp energy melted away, the energy quiet now. He kept going. That's all he could do. Run. That's all he could think of doing. To get there and do something good for the city. The fear that something awful had already happened crushed his chest. Still, he needed to be there.

From afar, a gap opened. No trees. He was nearly out of this forest.

Every time, he just sensed what others were going through somehow. Not exactly, but their emotions. The undertones in the way they struggled, or smiled, or hurt. The sharp and aching energy in how they carried themselves. It always tugged at his heart. Zul wasn't sure why he let others hurt him so much. It hurt, whenever others hurt. That's how it was for him. It had always been like that. He planted his hand against a rock, fingers shaking, breath unsteady.

He walked, his body no longer able to rush, to move as fast as he'd wanted. It didn't mean he would stop. Covered in dirt, leaves braided between his hair, he kept going.

Oh Creator. Tears welled in his eyes. The gate of Veer city, made of beco crystals, was torn apart. Pain gutted him, dull and aching in his chest. Had he been too late?

Chapter 31 Fight

The gate was torn, blues and purples of the jagged crystals reflecting the moonlight. Zul stared. His gaze shifted to the moon, now engorged and white. No longer a bleeding spot in the dark sky. A shiver snaked down his sides. As he passed through the gate, the scene opening before him struck his chest, fear and shock taking the breath from him.

The streets were lined with streaks and pools of blood. There was one vehicle, lights flashing on its hood. Two people pushed a cart with a white sheet covering a body. They were still taking bodies away. An arm swung free, blood and bite marks on the person's palm. He still couldn't wrap his mind around the fact that there were bodies that had left all this blood.

Zul pressed a hand to his mouth, quieting his scream, now coming out as a muffled whine. He turned away, falling, his knees striking the concrete. No. No. No. He'd been too late. Why? Why? *Creator!*

Tears overflowed from his eyes. He blinked, freeing them to run down his face. He pressed his hands to his eyes, teeth clenching as he sobbed. Pain, all that pain clawed at his mind. All these people... These innocent lives. They'd done nothing wrong. Oh Creator, the children! Zul covered his face, his scream turning into a sob, piercing his heart. No, he couldn't take knowing all those people were gone. His throat ached and his fingers shook as he hugged his body.

He needed to help them. He stumbled to his feet and sped toward the city, tears blurring his vision.

"Sire," Lexa's voice whispered before him and he came to an abrupt stop.

He shoved her, but her shadows snaked around his arms, down his legs.

His whole body was shaking, skin cold and prickling. "Let go of me!" He pulled at the darkness, writhing and stretching around his arms, but the shadows were sinking into him, a cold blooming over his skin, a cold worse than winter. "Stop, Lexa!"

Lexa pressed a hand to his chest.

"I have to do something." Zul screamed, but his body was pinned. "I have to help them!"

"It's time to be free."

"I don't want to fight anymore! I need to right what wrongs I did." He gasped. His breath caught like a nimcha prodding his throat. "I'll give the Iron ring back and learn another way to break the iron's curse."

"What other way?" Lexa asked.

"Supplications and my hope. I know how powerful they are… They can heal. I want to use faith, not magic."

Lexa pressed her hand harder against his chest, and the scorpion tattoo rippled.

Zul gasped. "What…wait—"

Lexa shook her head. "You need this, Zul Sharr. You can't just pray it away. You need to do something. Fight them. I need this too. If we can weaken that fire jawhar, my plan will work. I'll be powerful. I'll be closer to freeing my people and you will free your Sanari. We can free everyone. No one else will die."

"People *have* died." Zul Sharr's hands shook, his chest buzzing with the jinni aura. "Not this way. Please, Lexa. You have another way, don't you? I…can't."

"The shadow wolves only killed men. I harmed no women or children."

"You think that makes it okay?" Zul was incredulous. People had lost their lives. "Those men were people with their own dreams, wants and families!"

But Lexa closed her eyes. The dark lines grew over his neck, as if the scorpion had started to extend. More intricate lines of shadow crawled over his jawline, inking his skin, flowing up to his cheek and then tracing around his eye, over his eyebrow, alongside his nose and chin. Half of his face was now tattooed with the living shadow. That's when he heard the demonic voice. The jinni energy flowing freely through his blood.

the demonic aura whispered in his mind. *They're dead. They died a useless death.*

"No. They didn't need to die!"

It's your fault. If you had stopped those jawhars, this wouldn't have happened.

"No. You're lying!" Zul Sharr's voice sounded like a lion's roar.

Then stop them. You'll never break Sanari's curse if you're allowing others to take your voice. Get angry. Use it or else you're weak.

"I don't want to be."

Yes. If you fight them.

"I can't fight them. They didn't do anything wrong! The angel didn't wrong me! Thunderbolt and the others are only trying to protect—"

Protect? The demonic voice snickered. *They're in your way. The angel did not help you the day your iron encased your beloved. They didn't show you mercy. Why should you be merciful to them?*

"Mercy... Mercy..." Zul Sharr felt as if he was drowning in the darkness, his own mind becoming a dark forest, and he was walking deeper inside. Hushed away by the tall trees.

The voice roared with laughter. *No one showed you mercy. Don't show them. These lives lost are a waste.*

The part of him that was Eisen sunk deeper into his mind. Memories of him crying, memories of him smiling with his friends, memories of the times he showed kindness, where he blamed himself for the pain others put him through. He was tired. The gentle part of him lingered. Eisen didn't give up. But right now, Eisen was angry. He had had enough.

Zul raised his hand.

The blood rushed to his hand, the droplets lifting from the ground, looping around until they formed a rotating circle of red. The nails from his other hand dragged against the cement and then he stood. He gritted his teeth. His body buzzed with wanting and ached from the loss around him. He wouldn't let this be a waste. He wouldn't let more people die. His love and desperation were his fuel.

"Zul Sharr," Lexa coaxed. "Remember what you want."

"No one will suff— Justice. I want justice!"

"Justice is begged for. Justice is made by those who were treated as collateral damage for simply living. So remember why you need this. You almost said it."

"So no one else dies or is enslaved ever again!"

"Good. You'll have to fight. Fight, Zul Sharr. Keep fighting, even when they try to kill you. We need to make sacrifices and I won't hesitate." Lexa gave him a small smile. "I almost envy your empathy. You won't let the darkness completely take you. It's been too long since i've encountered a human on the precipice of despair but choosing love." Lexa pressed a dagger to his chin, tilting his head up. "You always fight for love and that love is worth the fight."

"I will fight on… These people didn't die for nothing." Zul Sharr formed a kilij—a Moroccan sabre—with the blood. A strange hum sang across his palm where he held the sword.

"Lexa, go ahead with your plan and I will tire them. After all…" Zul Sharr grinned. 'We're doing this for the ones we love."

I will break the iron's curse. I'll be with Sanari again. Now, no one will die.

Chapter 32 The Following Mourning

The earth's small pulse echoed through Dante's heart. Falling, yearning, Noorenia's energy—its life was slipping. Dante stumbled to his knees, hitting a patch of shining, cracked ice. He reached his hand out, pressing his fingers to the ground. "Tell me..." The chill of winter swathed him, his body and mind. He had to keep his powers, he had to help Noorenia. It made him what he was. This is why he was doing all this. He wanted to bring Momma back home. But the border between Earth and Noorenia was closing. He'd try to reason with Momma to return home.

A sudden thought broke into his own.

My heartbeat... It is failing. Help me.

"Tell me where the others are."

Which others?

Dante gulped. He was out here to find them. The other elementals. Aw man, what were they called again? Jaw-something. Jaw? Jawhars. Right.

"Please tell me where the jawhars are. The ones with the angels."

Unite The Angel of Mercy's soul with his body. Give the angel back.

Goosebumps pebbled Dante's arms. His heart thudded in his chest and tears welled in his eyes. This feeling wasn't his. It was a rush of sudden mourning, of haplessness. He pressed his face to the ground, his tears rolling down his cheek, sliding over the blades of frozen grass.

"I'll help you. Where are they?"

To the west. You will find them in the forest where the vultures circle. Help me, Jawhar. Find the angel's body.

Then, that soft, shaky voice quieted.

Dante sighed, got to his feet and brushed the snow from his knees. To the west. Looked like he needed to get directions. With no compass, he'd just have to keep talking to the animals. As usual.

***

The whole expanse was just snow. It was all Dante could see in the darkness. Snow sweeping off the few trees around him, carried by the breeze. The mountains jutting out from the distance, cutting through the sky like shards of glass.

A tiny mouse sat on his palm.

"So little guy, you said this way, right?"

Yes, but I warn you, there are many with sharp teeth who live there.

"Cute. You're scared for me?" Dante said with a lopsided smile. He wasn't scared of any animal. It was the opposite. They should be careful of him. He was human and not all humans were kind to animals. He knew that much.

The mouse made a small peep.

Bye bye, jawhar. Be quick.

Dante placed him down and he shot like an arrow, disappearing into the brush.

He blew out a sigh. Damn. He got why the mouse was scared; it was small and vulnerable. But still. He had to get going. It didn't matter what thing with sharp teeth was in this place.

Where the vultures circle. That's what Noorenia had said. But how the hell would he be able to see that? And at night, too? Dante raised his head to the dark sky. So many stars. His lips parted. "Wow." Glimmering, all gathered together, the starlight was as bright as the street lights back in New York. For a few moments, he was caught up in the sight. His thoughts melting away. But it didn't last long.

A howl pierced the night.

Wolves. Was it wolves that the mouse was warning him about? Dante took a deep breath. He'd had one as a guard tonight. No way in hell would he be scared of some wolf.

Deeper into the snow, farther and farther away from any city, Dante found himself among spindly trees.

The howling got louder and this time, a growl made him snap his head around.

It snarled at him, teeth bared, taking one small step.

Dante swallowed. Being out here for so long, his throat was coated in the biting cold. He drew a breath.

"I'm only passing by. Lemme talk to you." He bent down, slow, calculated, never leaving the wolf's gaze. Maybe they could both communicate, since the wolf was touching the same ground. His gloved hand pressed onto the ice.

Get out! The wolf's snarling thoughts, its disembodied voice rang in Dante's mind.

"Oh, so it's your turf, huh? I'm—"

You are not welcome here. Humans destroy our lands. This is the only place we can call ours.

"You feel safe here, right?" He could relate. With his powers, he always felt safe. With Momma and dad together, he had felt safe. Bein' able to expect someone would be there, and he... didn't have to be scared they'd leave him. When he wasn't trying to survive out in the cold in a place he didn't know. He felt for the wolf.

The wolf eyed him again, not snarling anymore, but there was that hard look in its gaze. *Safety. This is our safe place. Now that you have seen it, we cannot let you go.*

"Whoa, wait—" Dante slid back, his hand still on the ground as the wolf and three others surrounded him.

Two leaped into the air, their mouths open, teeth bared.

Dante stomped his feet and gestured up with both hands and spun his arms. The ground rose up, rumbling to life under the wolves and capturing their bodies. The stone and dirt like fingers wrapped around their fur.

Then all he saw was feathers. A crow cawed and fluttered its wings before him. In a blink, that same crow became a woman. She seemed like her crow self, as if she had puffed her chest up in pride. Her chin tilted a bit higher.

Rana. One wolf bowed its head, the others following as they turned to her. So this woman was Rana. Dante wasn't sure who she was. But, if she'd been a crow, she was no human.

“What are you doing?” Rana spoke in a clear voice with a deeper edge.

He has invaded our territory.

Rana turned to Dante, her gaze steady on him, then flickering to the rocks.

“Earth Jawhar,” She said, as if she couldn’t be bothered to say more to him. She waved an arm. “Let him pass.”

Are you sure? He is a trespasser.

“Pass.” This time she directed her attention to him. Simply turning her head to the side, her back to him.

Dante gulped. Why the hell was she letting him go? Whatever. He’d take it. Even if her eyes were so cold. There was something weird about her calm. She was a little *too* calm. As if she could snap at any given moment under the surface, the way the ice did under pressure.

“Right.” Dante rushed past the wolves, farther away into the field, snow drifting down around him again. Waves of fear, of determination kept him from looking back. He had to get to those jawhars and fast.

Chapter 33 Jinni Unicorns

She was swift as a spear, bright as a shooting star, just like the name Kayan had given her. Nayzak. Nezha couldn't stop repeating it in her mind, imagining him saying it to her again. His Nayzak.

His lips curled into a smile.

Nezha's skin heated.

The wind whistled past her, one of the jinni unicorns making a stabbing motion with its horn. Blood and spittle flew into the air, nearly falling on her. Disgusting. She didn't want to hold herself back anymore. Amaya wasn't anywhere to be seen. She was surrounded by jinni unicorns thirsting for their blood. She raised her arm over her head, flames flaring around her.

Then, one of the jinni unicorns snorted and backed away.

"I do not want to fight." It spoke in a sharp tone with a softer huff.

Nezha lowered her arm and parted her lips. What did it just say? Even though she knew some jinn were good, it still took her off guard.

Beside her, Thunderbolt and Sapphire had transformed into their unicorn forms. Thunderbolt's horn was locked with one of the beasts, its teeth bared at him. Lightning flashed and struck the ground around its hooves.

"It's unicorn against unicorn!"

Kayan met Nezha's gaze. She saw the look in his eyes, that soft and contemplative look.

Kayan moved with grace past one unicorn stomping toward him, the cut of his blade, Ali, zig zagging through its neck. Blood and its dark miasma bloomed into the air. Then, Kayan was sliding on his knees, back arching as another leapt over him, its spindly legs stretching over his head. He spun and approached the jinni unicorn who had spoken to them.

"Please...have mercy."

"Go. You are free," Kayan said to it, his eyes glittering with tears.

Nezha watched as the unicorn's head tilted and what looked like a smile appeared over its muzzle. It nodded, turned on its hoof and galloped away into the night, fading into the distance without the slightest huff.

Nezha tightened her lips. How could she fight anyone who had pleaded for mercy? That would go against her code. Against her faith. It didn't matter if it was a jinni. It didn't want to fight them. If it no longer held malice, then she wouldn't needlessly fight it.

She couldn't gaze at Kayan too long, as Sapphire's wings raised before her, soft feathers brushing over her cheek. One of the other bloodied unicorns whinnied and huffed. Its hooves raised before her. Comet remained in the bubble of light Sapphire had placed her in. It slipped past Nezha's legs. Comet looked up at her and meowed. Before Nezha could move, Sapphire impaled the jinni unicorn with her horn. Dark blood slipped down her horn and the beast's body disintegrated. Its whinnies faded out, its body blurring away into plumes of smoke, it became one with the dark sky.

That blood, the coppery scent made the jinni unicorns' nostrils flare. Soon they were all charging at them from all directions.

She couldn't think. All Nezha could do was move. Move by instinct. Her arms flew up, flames gushing from her palms, arcing into blades made of the very fire that obeyed her. She breathed in and blew out, flames fanning out from her lips and felling three of the beasts. One horn came close to her face, nearly piercing her neck. Its horn blackened and then layers flitted off of it, melting into the darkness in a sigh of gray.

Her head snapped to the side and she made a punching motion, flames shooting out and blazing over three other beasts, consuming them. She saw Thunderbolt beside her, still in his unicorn form. His horn was entangled with another's, lightning in a viscous dance around him. One of the horns grazed Nezha's cheek, sharp pain cutting across her face. Warmth bloomed over her skin and then blood drew a line down her chin.

"Nezha!" Kayan called out to her, but the snapping wind swallowed the rest of his voice as he came to stand before her. Light from Sapphire's horn whined. Nezha didn't fall back. Beside her, a loud hum emanated from Asad. Energy formed in his palms, pulsing and circling around his fingers. One blast flew at the dark unicorn, causing snow and ice to rain down on her.

She was firm on her feet. She simply kicked in an arc, the flames rushing out, eating away at her boots as they spun out. She shoved Sapphire aside as one jinni unicorn snapped its teeth where Sapphire's head had been. Its red eyes peered into hers. The heavy weight of malice surrounded Nezha. It was pure evil she was looking into. And she wouldn't be afraid.

"Fall," It rasped at her.

Nezha tilted her head at it, a lopsided smile growing over her lips. "I fall for no one but to my Lord in prayer." Flames twisted from her palms. Her arms fell in one sharp motion, slicing the cold air. The flames engulfed the skeletal creature. As the fire rose, it snapped and crackled, the beast tumbling into ashes.

***

Every sense of his heightened. The copper of blood sharp in his nose, the touch of the cold air glass across his skin, the snow groaning under his boots. Asad raised his hands, palms facing outward, energy shooting out to the jinni unicorns before him. One charged for him, but he made an upward motion with his hand, making it fly into a group of its kind, knocking them down. With a fluid motion, a whirring energy struck them, and they disintegrated, joining the other plumes of mist into the sky.

All their amassed energy weighed on his body. The thick malice of the jinni unicorns, Nezha's determination and will burning like the sun, Thunderbolt's stubbornness, solid as stone, Sapphire's calm demeanor, a sharper tumble of emotions on the surface. And, still inside her bubble, Comet's soft pulse of energy— almost unnoticeable. But there was still that tremble of fear, and an energy he could only explain as her hunting instinct and love for Nezha. Wherever he felt Nezha's energy, Comet's was there too. Then there was Kayan. The love, that warmth, but also his anger burning, a piercing light. It all took over Asad's mind. He gritted his teeth.

This was one reason he hardly wanted to trust anyone, because then, they wanted to trust him in return. Sometimes that was a trust given to him without consent. And that trust became holding onto a part of that person, whether he wanted to or not. For him it was far worse. As a soul jawhar, his own spirit was like a sponge, every emotion and energy holding onto him, begging for him to be aware of it. Then, he thought of the world as it was. That's how it was. Few were willing to get to the root of anything. Even when it was emotions that needed to be realized. Because it's buried. And to dig that up took work. It took patience. Everyone wanted quick fixes. Not healing... He had to do something about all this, or he'd lose his mind.

Lose... Maybe that's what he had to do.

Asad breathed in deeply and asked his intuition. Should he do it? Should he take their energy away? Then he asked if he shouldn't take the energy away. The energy pushed up his throat. An answer that he shouldn't. But, even though he trusted his intuition, he wasn't sure why it didn't want him to do it. Maybe he wasn't focusing? And, how could he? There was too much commotion. Okay, then he'd try containing the strong rivulets of darkness attempting to drown his mind.

The pools of glowing colours concentrated into one pulsing form. Snaking off of the jinni unicorns and congregating into a large ball, as if it were a river held in one drop. His own energy hummed over his skin, the sound becoming louder. The other jawhars must have noticed, since one by one their energies were jumbled, filled with a mix of confusion and relief as they withdrew from the jinn.

Heat and pressure pinched his skin, mostly around his head. He needed to separate the jinn's dark aura so they could handle them better. He didn't know if the other jawhars had dealt with so many at once, but he'd have to try to make it easier on them.

“Kayan, Nezha...use your pow—” But then, sharpness cut through the back of his mind, his hands trembling as he held the evil aura around his fingertips. Warmth pooled at his eyes and fell over his cheeks.

“Asad!” Kayan called out to him. “Stop!” The wind shoved him, knocking him down.

“What the hell? I can handle it!”

“You’re hurting yourself,” Kayan warned him, just as Asad felt Sapphire’s calm presence drawing closer to him.

Asad clenched his teeth. “I know how to do things myself,”

“Zaan.” This time Kayan’s voice was a combination of concern and surprise. “Your eyes are *bleeding*.”

Asad wiped at his eyes and pulled away something sticky. The copper tang wrapped over his tongue. Blood was at his fingertips. “What?”

He couldn’t hold onto the sinister energy any longer. Its cold bit down at him, the prickling energy trying to seep into his heart. Panting, his arms fell to his sides. And that was a big mistake.

***

Thunderbolt stood before the others, his body marred by cuts and blood smeared over his muzzle, making his hair stick to his neck.

Nezha hadn’t realized how much everyone had been injured. Asad had taken up all the negative aura of the jinni unicorns. So much pain, so many wounds stained her companions’ hearts. She groaned. Prickling energy washed through her head down to her gut. Her eyes stung, and she thought she was crying. She wiped at her eyes, but what stained her fingers wasn't what normal tears looked like. It was red. She and the others were crying tears of blood.

"No..." Nezha pressed her fingers to her temples. The others were all showing their pain, doubling over, holding their heads. Their eyes glistened with the blood dripping from their faces. She wasn't sure how long into the night they'd run after the fox who stole the feather and now, they were running out of time.

"Don't move!" a voice shouted into the night. Nezha spun around, her sight blurring. Someone was here and his energy seemed like a bandage across her pain.

The earth rumbled to life under the beasts, their skeletal mouths widening. A guttural scream rang in her ears. Fingers of stone and frozen earth took hold of the beasts, binding them to the spot.

"Earth...jawhar," Asad rasped.

Nezha blinked back her blood-tears and then she saw the person. The very ground underneath him moved like waves in the sea, rolling under him as he rode the large ripple. It brought him before her.

"Found you." He raised a brow at her and motioned toward the ground, raising her to her feet.

Chapter 34 Wounds Run Deep

It was Dante. Nezha wasn't sure how he'd found them, but she was glad he did. "Dante?"

"Yeah." Dante just glanced at her and then turned his attention to Asad. He walked up to him and poked his shoulder. "Hey, we'll have to team up."

"With you? Where were you when we needed you?" Asad tilted his head.

"I had somethin' to do. Come on."

Asad sighed. "Yeah, okay."

"Y'all gotta stop bleeding everywhere; it's scary as hell," Dante said with a grin, and judging from Asad's exasperated expression, the soul jawhar didn't seem to mind too much. He simply focused on listening to Dante.

Dante stomped at the ground, making sure the earth that jutted out from the ground still kept the jinni unicorns in their grasp.

Asad raised his hands again, that hum pulsating through the air around him. The dark aura of the jinn had unraveled, but with shaking hands he held it again. "If I keep their aura away from them I might bleed again."

"I'll help too," Kayan came to stand beside him.

"The kid's right. It'll be a team effort." Thunderbolt nudged Asad's shoulder with his snout. Despite his condition, with cuts still marring his legs and a wounded shoulder, he held himself up.

Nezha joined them. "Yeah, we got you."

***

The wind sang through the air and Kayan's eyes, still bleeding from the dark energy, began glowing green.

"I'll bring calm to you, Asad. Feel it through the wind. Dante, you do your thing."

"Uh-huh." Dante pressed his hands to the ground, focusing on the jinni unicorns who were kicking and neighing.

When he got here, he wasn't sure how he'd meet the others and in what condition. He was expecting them to be angry at him. That he'd be too late, or maybe that they didn't need him anyway. But, seeing them all bleeding from their eyes, and the pain written on their faces, he was just glad he got here. That he was here and that he was needed. They hadn't turned him away.

Together, with Asad keeping their energy at bay, Thunderbolt's lightning flashed and popped. The beasts screeched, their horns wildly flailing, stabbing and prodding at the others beside them, and teeth chomping down, blood spraying into the air. The electricity numbed the creatures, their limbs trembling and then frozen in place as if they were statues.

Then it was Dante who delivered the final blow. With a wide stance, his heels dug into the snow. He slowly brought his hands together, fingers curled. The closer they were, the more the icy ground cut around the jinni unicorns and grew around them, until they were completely covered in ice and rock. He made a twisting motion with his wrists, his fingers turning. The stone crunched and crushed the demonic creatures.

Nezha raised her hands, palms up, whispering something as the flames from her burned bright and a white light glowed around her, feathering out toward the round spinning darkness that was left of the jinni unicorns. It wrapped around it, consuming the heavy energy, until it became nothing—only light. That light dimmed and hushed away. Had she just cleansed the dark energy with a verse?

The jawhars were bleary-eyed, exhaustion making their shoulders slump. Dante wondered if they'd been out in the night for hours. Last he checked, it had been a few hours to midnight when he'd left the wolves.

"Nice one, Asad," said Dante.

"Yeah, you did great," Kayan chimed in.

"Oh, zaan..." Thunderbolt transformed into his angel form, exhaled and fell to his knees.

Dante then noticed one other person. He had wings too, but he didn't seem to be a part of their group. He'd never seen him before.

Sapphire's gaze met that man's. And they both stared at each other in open concern. "Obsidian."

But the man simply turned, and before Dante's eyes, his form shifted into that of a black unicorn with dark wings. He did not look back as he turned and his wings flapped, taking him into the night sky.

Nezha held Sapphire's shoulders and the angel wrapped her arms around her and stayed like that for several minutes.

Damn, they were all broken. What the hell had happened here? And who was that guy?

"Dante," Nezha said. "Thank you for helping us." Comet was still in her bubble, but Nezha picked her up, pressing a hand to the thin layer, with Comet meowing and rubbing her head back.

"We really needed it," Kayan agreed.

"I guess you were pretty cool," Asad said next.

"Yeah, no problem." Dante rubbed the back of his neck. It seemed he was stuck with these people. Jawhars like him.

***

Thunderbolt was bruised. His arms bleeding, scratches over his legs. He'd been injured the most during their battle.

The lazy smile absent from his face, smudges of dirt on his cheeks, his shoulders slumped, a strange softness in his eyes. He'd been so good at hiding his worries, but upon his body being wounded, the wounds inside appeared too.

"I'll be okay soon enough. Let's go get that fox. He needs t' learn not t' steal from us." Thunderbolt shifted to his side and winced.

"No, you're badly hurt!" Nezha sat on her knees beside him, Sapphire and Kayan on either side of her. Asad stood beside Dante.

This time, Thunderbolt had no sarcastic reply.

"Brother…we need to get you help." Sapphire was in her angel form, and touched his shoulder.

Thunderbolt managed to stand and then fell to his knees. "I can't just sit around!"

"You have to. For once, stop trying to push yourself too hard. You're only hurting yourself." Nezha moved closer to him.

Thunderbolt tipped his head forward. "It hurts t' do nothing. Because then I'll just think of them. My parents and Eisen."

"I know it's hard to stay still when there's so much going on. But, what's the point if you stay hurt? You need to rest, Thunderbolt."

His eyebrows furrowed. "I don't want to be a burden," he murmured.

Sapphire shook her head, disbelief blossoming over her face. "This is how you felt?"

"You're not," Kayan spoke and met Thunderbolt's eyes. "You matter. Where's the tough guy? Where's the guy who was so brave? You know what makes you so brave? You're scared, but you don't give up. Zaan, resting and healing is not giving up. You're a champion."

Thunderbolt relaxed against an icy rock, one of his legs bent, and looked between all of them. He smiled at them. Such a warm, gentle look on his face. Something Nezha had hardly ever seen.

"With you all by my side, how could I give up, anyways? I'll never do that. I just didn't want t' be a problem for you all."

Nezha grabbed the collar of his tunic, tears in her eyes. "You are not a problem! You never are and never will be, you got that, pretty boy?"

Thunderbolt's eyes widened. She loosened her fingers around his collar and buried her face into his chest and breathed out loudly. He pushed her head back to wipe the tears from her eyes. A lopsided grin stretched over his lips.

"I'm old enough t' be your dad. A handsome one too, which I'm glad you admit."

Nezha shook her head and embraced him, with Sapphire and Kayan also wrapping their arms around him. They stayed there for what felt like hours.

***

Asad sat beside Dante as the others gathered around Thunderbolt. A loud and calming vibration echoed in his body. Where was it coming from? Asad listened intently, until he went to his knees and stretched his hand out before him. The smooth bubble that Comet was in touched his fingers.

He could make out her silhouette and the swirls of energy: her lataif inside her body. She was curled up beside Nezha and purring. That's what that sound was.

The sharp pain around his forehead melted, until the pressure lifted. The purr sang across his skin, melting every burning sensation and every stiff muscle. Asad sighed out from the relief. He couldn't understand it. The purr was still going, rumbling around him everywhere, inside and out. Was she healing them?

"Comet's purr…" Asad said.

"What about it? Is she okay?" Nezha said.

Asad nodded. His head felt like it was being massaged, he could hardly speak. "Mmhmm. She's healing us."

"Healing?" Sapphire said.

Asad's lips parted. He felt Dante beside him and they both sat together with the others. "Pop the bubble she's in," he breathed out.

Upon Asad's skin was a soothing, soft feeling. A mother's gentle hand rubbing her child's back, kind of feeling. And for a moment he felt his throat tighten, tears push at his eyes at the memory of his own mother.

Sapphire must have understood why he wanted the bubble gone, and popped it. The energy burst into the air and as soon as the bubble disappeared, the frequency of Comet's purr became louder. His mind exploded with colour. A bright green, red, yellow and blue with several other colours radiating around her. A galaxy. Waves of pure bliss poured over him.

He heard the others gasp in response. Comet was winding her body between them all, her head butting at Thunderbolt's shoulder until she settled in the centre of them all, her purr continuing.

Asad's shoulders sagged. The snow begged him to succumb to its icy touch, but Comet's purr was much more persuasive. Without him knowing when, he'd sat closer to the others, basking in the warmth, the healing of this cat.

He could never actually allow himself to relax. What was relaxation? No one had ever let him relax. Most people would tell him it must have been so hard not being able to see. Always telling him what he was missing out on. As if they knew anything! He'd wanted to tell them if it was so hard, maybe they were making it tougher by annoying him. Being a soul jawhar, everyone's feelings always seemed to mean they were his, but, here there was no emotion to worry about. No one to tell him what was supposed to be hard for him. It was a submission of their souls to a moment of bliss. *It's like my soul's getting a massage.* He didn't want it to end.

***

"Mithi," *Sweety.* Nezha stroked Comet's head, her silky fur, her purr blurring away any stress in her mind. She'd never heard Comet purr so loudly before. Comet would curl up beside her whenever she wasn't feeling well, purring away, or pressing her head into Nezha's hands as she lay in bed. It wasn't strange, but the way it felt now was different. The sound was silkier against her skin, begging her to fall asleep and submit herself to dream.

Maybe it was because of Noorenia and its heartbeat. Whatever it was, all she needed was rest. Her mind was going blank. She inhaled and her lungs seemed to open up more. The tension in her muscles melted, despite the snow's cold touch.

Thunderbolt rolled his shoulder. "I can move it," he said, surprised. He flexed his fingers and sat up.

"Damn, my neck was killing me. Thanks, Comet," Dante said and stretched.

Kayan inhaled deeply and was scratching Comet's chin. "You're such a good girl. Look at you making everyone feel better."

Nezha's lips turned up in a soft smile. It felt so sweet. They deserved this tender moment.

***

"We need to go this way." Asad pointed again. It was toward a forest.

“Right. That forest is where that fox must be,” Nezha said.

Sapphire had told them it was called Dying Forest. It didn’t sound like an inviting place—that was for sure. Regardless, they had to find the feather. Even if sleep tugged at her eyes. Without that part of the angel, she didn’t feel right. She could feel the ghost of the cuff around her wrist. Another thing missing from her.

Chapter 35 Campsite

“Listen, y’all can’t keep going like this,” Dante spoke and the others stopped walking. Like hell they could. Nezha could barely keep her eyes open, Asad was stumbling, his head nodding countless times. He wasn’t even sure if the angels were all there, especially the one with blue hair, Sapphire. She had a distant look in her eyes, that he was sure was because of that other black unicorn.

But then she turned to him, eyes lidded, and faced the others. “We need rest. We have been through emotional turmoil.”

“But we need to keep going. We need to find Amaya and that fox has the feather.” Nezha was searching Sapphire’s eyes.

Kayan closed his hand over a yawn. “She’s right. We’ve been out here all night.”

Nezha’s shoulders scrunched up to her ears and she leaned in to Kayan. “But he took something of mine!” Her hands balled into fists.

“I get it, Nezha, but we can’t keep going. I want to, but we’ll pass out.”

“Asad can track the feather, so we will be able to find it in the morning.” Sapphire placed a hand on Nezha’s shoulder. “Please, you need sleep. Leave the rest to the Creator.”

“I just don’t feel right without it.” Nezha expelled a frustrated breath. “It’s a part of the angel, but also *me*.”

A part of her, huh? Dante could relate to that. He knew if he’d ever lost the ability to talk to the earth and animals, he wouldn’t feel right. If their voices weren’t there, his heart would be too silent, devoid of life.

“But...” Nezha bit her lip.

“I’d prefer if you weren’t a Nezha popsicle, too.” Kayan said, smiling at her.

Their gazes lingered, a little too long. Dante got a feeling that these two were more than just companions. As if they had feelings for each other.

“Yeah, Nezha, can you be our heater again?” Asad hugged himself.

“I can do better, I think. If we can have some wood to burn...”

“Sure,” said Dante. “Who.”

“Huh? I don’t know. Who wants to go into the forest to get wood?” Kayan asked, not seeming like he wanted to from the way he took a step back.

“Not a who. Who,” Dante repeated, calling out into the darkness.

“Why’s he hooting? Is his brain freezing or something? What’s up with him?” Asad inquired.

Without a sound, a large brown owl glided over Asad’s head, its wing skimming his hair, and grasped Dante’s outstretched arm with its clawed feet.

“This who.” Dante grinned.

“I felt a breeze.” Asad waved a hand over his head.

Thunderbolt blinked. “Whoa.”

“Oh, an owl, that’s who!” Kayan’s cheeks flushed.

“Clever,” said Sapphire.

“Hey, could ya please get us some pieces of wood? We need a fire.” Dante pressed his hand to the owl’s head. It hooted back once and then it flapped its wings, taking to the sky and disappearing.

“You can talk to animals?” Asad said.

Dante pulled at the ground, rock turning into a sheet under their feet and one sloping over them, as if it were a roof. “Yeah. I guess I’m connected to the earth and all, so it’s something I can do.”

“Once that owl comes back, I’ll light us a nice warm fire,” Nezha rubbed her arms.

“I hope he hurries, because my wings are starting t’ numb.” Thunderbolt’s wings shook as he sat on the rock.

Soon the owl had returned, sticks stuffed in its beak and bunched in the grasp of its feet. It let them fall before Dante, on a dirt hole he had formed.

“Hurray, we won’t freeze to death, just starve.” Asad inched closer to the bunches of sticks as Nezha touched them with her fingertips, the fire hissing and crackling to life.

“We’ll need more wood.” Kayan stood. “I’ll go out and find food somewhere too,” he offered.

“Nah, I got that covered, too,” said Dante.

“Yeah, what are you thinking, Kayan? We’re out in the middle of nowhere with snow for miles.” Nezha shook her head.

“I just thought—”

“I think the cold’s making him lose his mind.” Thunderbolt patted the spot beside him. “Sit down, zaan.”

Kayan made a face of dejection and sat. "So, what did you have in mind, Dante?"

Dante unzipped his bag. "I've got some bars, fruit salad and marshmallows for smores."

"Huh? What's that? And why do I want more of it already?" Thunderbolt said.

Nezha chuckled. "It's a treat we make back on Earth. Basically, marshmallows and chocolate sandwiched between graham crackers."

Dante brought them out and picked up a marshmallow to cook over the fire. "You do it like this."

Soon, the owl had returned with more wood.

Nezha picked up the marshmallow bag to read the ingredients. "Oh hey, there's no animal products in this."

Asad smiled. "Good, we can eat it without worries."

"Yes. I might have cried if I couldn't! I'm so hungry." Nezha pressed her hand to her stomach.

"Well… I'm Muslim too, so…" Dante said, poking the fire with a stick.

"Thanks for all this, Dante." Kayan smiled at him.

"Yeah, you really saved us back there...and here." Nezha grinned.

Sapphire placed a hand to her heart. "I am grateful."

"Zaan, you just swooped in like a true hero." Thunderbolt winked at him.

Asad chuckled. "Man, I'll admit you were pretty epic."

They all seemed so warm. Maybe the fire's glow was making them out to be much nicer, but whatever it was, for some reason, Dante really felt warm and kinda safe.

***

These people were all like him. Not the so-called normal humans. People who had powers like him. So, that's why they didn't tease him about talking to animals. But, even then, it was so strange. Damn, he wasn't the weird one for once. Thanking him, and not being angry with him? He didn't get it. Why were they being so nice? It wasn't like back then when he was a kid. When he'd been playing at the park and squirrels had been following him. He'd thrown one of the nuts at one for it to eat. Another one took it from his very hands. Two kids had come running up to him.

"He's playing with squirrels! So lame."

"Yeah, he's nuts!" The other kid shoved him and they both had laughed at him.

The stings on his elbows and arms, the burning on his back—he could still feel it in his bones.

"You're such a weirdo!" Then the kids had kicked him.

When he'd come home to his momma, he didn't want to worry her, so he'd tried to be quiet. But, of course she'd been close to the door. "I'm home, Momma."

"Oh, Dante—" She'd turned to him and then stared. "What happened? Why do you have cuts on your arms?"

"I just fell from the swing. I'm okay."

But she pulled him in. "Oh, Dante..." Her voice shook and he felt wetness on his shoulder.

"Huh? What's wrong, Mommy? I said I'm okay."

“I’m sorry, baby.” She’d tightened her grip on him and tears rolled over his cheeks as they’d both cried.

“Hey, Dante.” Kayan called out to him and Dante blinked, his mind returning to the present. “Uh, your mallow thing is burning.”

“Oh.” Dante then blew on it and returned Kayan a smile.

The others were eating their smores. The crackling fire warmed his skin, chasing away the bite of the cold. Maybe he could get used to these people. Big maybe.

Sapphire poked the bubble Comet was in and freed her. The cat first scratched the back of her ears with one leg. Then she sniffed the air and jumped into Nezha’s lap and meowed at her.

“You must be hungry, my poor Mithi. Aren’t you, Com Com?” Nezha rubbed her hands all over the cat’s back and cheeks.

“Hmm, maybe she’d like some fish?” Dante suggested.

“So, how are ya gonna do that? Dante Airways express delivery?” Asad bit into his smores.

“Well, duh.” Dante placed a finger on the owl who was sitting on his shoulder. “Hey, could you please get us some fish? If you can, I have some chicken with your name on it.” The owl’s thoughts swam into his mind.

“The lakes are frozen, but I will get it to you, earth Jawhar. I am quiet and capable.”

The owl flapped and then took off, silently swallowed by the night.

When the bag of marshmallows was empty and there were no wafers or chocolate, everyone sat back and relaxed, bathed in the warmth of the fire. Dante poked at it with a stick, the fire crackling as Nezha dipped a finger, the flames growing again.

They shared a small smile.

The owl had returned, swooping down from the velvet dark and landing with its claws full of two big silver fish.

"Hey, good job." Dante lowered his arm to the owl who stepped on to it and hooted.

"Yeah, tell it we said thank you," Kayan said.

"Hey, your feathers aren't even wet. How'd you do it?" Dante tore a piece of chicken from his sandwich and the owl plucked it from his fingers.

I had the help of a restless bear. He told me he had trouble sleeping. I promised him that a belly full of fish could help. So he complied.

Dante laughed. "Damn, you're one brave owl."

Anything for a jawhar saving our home.

"Thank you." Dante raised his arm and the owl flapped its wings.

Farewell, jawhars. It was as if it had disappeared into the sky, no trace of it, not a feather, nothing of it ever being there.

"Guess we have dinner now," said Asad. "I kinda wish we had a heavy plush blanket. You know what I'm talking about, right, Nezha?"

"Oh my God, yes! You have one too?"

Asad grinned. "You know it."

Nezha had inched closer to Kayan without even noticing it. "Mine had flowers on it and it was so warm!"

"Ours had tigers on it. It was so heavy to lift though, but I miss it right now."

Kayan picked up the fish, stuck the sticks through them and stabbed the sticks into the ground with the fish dangling over the fire. "I guess almost everyone has one somewhere, huh?"

"So, what, I'm the only one left out?" Dante said with mock disappointment.

Thunderbolt snickered.

Dante shrugged. "Let's eat."

After they had their fill of the fish, Dante rose up the stone and ice, creating a big tent for all of them. Inside, they made separations for Nezha and Sapphire and the others. He made a makeshift bed for everyone.

He was glad he didn't have to have a wolf guard him tonight, or stay up all night. Somehow, being around people like him made him feel safe. Made him feel like that was his blanket tonight.

Chapter 36 Nightmares

This dream tonight had been the worst yet for Nezha.

Lexa stared at her with her sharp green eyes and a smile, dripping in wicked delight. Nezha's shoulder brushed against a tree, the roughness making her shiver.

"Nezha, you made me have to seek you out."

Her breath quickened. Her heart was the only sound she could hear, as her back pressed harder against the trunk of the tree. The sky above her was a cluster of purples and oranges. The sun ready to take its slumber.

"Why..." She gulped.

Lexa's skin was cold, alabaster white. "Give me your soul." Her fingers sunk into Nezha's chest. The sharp weight stung Nezha as her scream echoed into the darkening sky.

Then, the scene changed. Darkness gave way to her aunt Lamis. Her warm gaze on her.

"Lamis!"

Lamis called Nezha using her pet name. "Nuzha, don't give her the c—"

A curtain of velvet smoke wrapped around Lamis's body. With a toothy snicker, Savan stood before her.

"Ah, jawhar. You can never get rid of us." His laugh grew into a high-pitched tone.

Nezha reached out, her hands slipping over the darkness, but Lamis was getting farther away.

"Nezha... Nezha."

"No! Lamis!"

Lamis continued saying her name, "Nezha. Nezha!" Each time, her voice grew more desperate.

Nezha's eyes snapped open.

"Nezha." Sapphire's face came into focus, her soft violet eyes searching hers, her brow furrowed. "Are you okay?"

Nezha's fingers shook over the blanket that Dante had the animals get for them. The soft thread brushing at her fingers, Comet's body pressed against her legs, the warmth of being away from the bitter cold—it all brought her back to reality. She took a shaky breath in.

"I..."

Sapphire sat up, helped Nezha do the same, and then wrapped her arms around her.

"Sweetheart, you're okay now."

Nezha tightened her hold in return.

Comet shifted and rested her head against Nezha's side.

These nightmares had kept coming back. After Lamis's passing, she knew she'd been trying too much to act like she was okay. Trying to move on once she'd returned to her dimension. Keeping busy at the flower shop, focusing on studies, drowning in her work. But she wasn't okay. How could she be okay, losing someone so close to her? Someone she loved so dearly? Lamis was like a sister to her. Every day, it was Lamis that would be there to make her smile and support her. Tears stung her eyes at the thoughts.

The jinn appearing in her dreams, Savan and Lexa, haunting her. Shadowing her thoughts even when they weren't there. Just like Lamis's memories. Days, weeks after Lamis left the world, Nezha thought she could hear her laugh, or thought she was waiting for her at the flower shop. Every day after that, there was always a hollow space in the air, devoid of Lamis. Her heart, her mind both murmured her name, but Lamis never showed.

"Thank you." Nezha let Sapphire go, and the angel pressed a kiss to her head.

"Nightmares plague us. They are your mind trying to protect you. Trying to teach you not to ignore the hurt your past has caused you. But, instead, to process it. Allow your mind to handle them and we will be here. I will always be here for you. To help your heart feel the support of understanding."

Nezha searched her eyes; seeing Sapphire like this was strange. She knew she was trying to help her the way she knew best. She hadn't ever had Sapphire look at her with such an engrossing melancholy. Like a glass gem. Shining, Sapphire's face pinched, Nezha thought Sapphire might crack if she uttered just one more word.

"You too. You can always talk to me about anything. I won't push you."

Sapphire nodded. The moonlight spilled through a crack from their makeshift tent, glowing over Sapphire's face, catching a glint in her teary eyes. She pressed her back to the wall and faced Nezha.

“Obsidian was my...mate.”

Nezha placed a hand on Sapphire’s shoulder.

She inhaled. “The day we had become mates, he had been with other angels at a mountainside. I still remember his determined look. That smile on his face so full of...love.” Sapphire’s voice wavered.

Nezha nodded. “I know. It must be a beautiful memory.”

Sapphire pressed a finger under one eye and looked to the side as if she was reliving the moment. “He walked with me, his soft fingers entwined in mine and it felt so warm. Joined with him, I had felt safe, so full by his side. As if it were him and me. No one else existed in that moment. I apologize if it does not make sense. It still doesn’t to me.”

Nezha shook her head and smiled. “It makes so much sense.”

She knew how it felt. She’d had the same feeling with Kayan. “You care about him and well, I know that you love each other. I know you’ll be together again, Creator willing.”

Sapphire smiled. A soft, careful turn of her lips.

“Creator willing.”

Nezha scratched Comet’s chin and hugged her knees. “Hey, before being a guardian, what was your life like? I mean, when you were a teen.”

It was hard to believe the angel siblings had ever been children. Nezha wondered what they had dreamed of doing when they grew up. What kind of outlooks did they have before realizing they were guardians over Wadi Alma and Unicorn Valley?

The angel raised a brow and then inched closer to Nezha. “I don’t think I ever felt like I was anything other than a guardian. Perhaps some moments in my life. When I was born, I was told I was born strong. Stronger than normal. That I was destined to protect others because of it.”

A sad smile turned Sapphire's lips. "When I had shifted into my angel form for the first time, I was confused and scared. I had been a unicorn and then I was like this." She gestured to her current form. "All these unicorns surrounded by me, but I was the only one that changed. Why was I so different? Then I learned the truth. My mama and Elder Halim told me I was an angel given a unicorn and a human-like form. I was to protect and defend the weak and to protect and defend the city and Unicorn Valley. Since I was the link to both, I had to *be* both."

"So, did you ever get to play with the others when you were younger?" Nezha asked. She wanted to know more about Sapphire. Not the guardian, but the Sapphire who had dreams and wants of her own.

Sapphire nodded. "Yes. It never felt like I could. I was enamored by beco crystals. Seeing the way they could be made into different forms…just like myself— I yearned to pick them apart. It was the need to heal which made me who I am today. My mama once told me that we are both capable of healing and destroying someone to transform them. They would not be themselves, but a different person. You can pull, replace and add, but once you destroy something, it will never be the same again."

"Completely different," Nezha added. "It sounds like you had a lot of responsibility placed on you since you were young. So much pressure… I think I know why you never were open with your emotions." Nezha's sight blurred with tears. "No one gave you a chance to be yourself. You always had to protect and defend others. They relied on you, so your own needs were never asked about or prioritized."

Sapphire met her gaze, tears welling in them the moment Nezha stopped talking. As if Nezha had completely understood and put into words how the angel had truly felt.

Sapphire swallowed. “I will not make the mistake of hiding my needs ever again. Sweet Nezha… the moments you showed you cared about my needs, the moment you wanted to know how I felt, it made me realize I should care too.”

Nezha smiled at her warmly. “I hope you value your needs as much as you value the life of others.”

In this moment, Nezha saw the true Sapphire, the facets of her heart full and shining bright.

***

Amaya had to will herself to move. Stepping over the dry, ashen ground, it cracked under her heels. A forest of spindly trees climbed into the sky and a thick silence weighed the air, making her lungs tighten. The fox had entered this place; she knew it. She’d seen him.

A small smile curled her lips. With a careful step, she surveyed the area. Not a sound, only the subtle scent of something sharp, as if it was vinegar stinging her nose.

Then something small and red fluttered by her head, dancing its way past her face, followed by more petals, raining down on her.

“Has the rabbit strayed too far down the hole?” a voice called out.

Amaya turned, but only the flower petals gathered around her, some spun into a circle and out of it, a form blurred into a human body, then a man stood in the middle, the flowers erased from existence.

She couldn’t speak. Her heart was in her throat and she’d felt like a rabbit caught in some predator’s teeth. A steady pulse beat at her hands. Was it the fox? Lexa had told her jinn were shapeshifters who could play tricks on people. He could be manipulating her, making her see what he wanted her to see.

Then the moonlight glinted off the bracelet around his wrist. It looked like a feather. He raised that arm and his gaze shifted from it to her.

Amaya took a step, but he glided over behind a tree and vanished.

"Who are you? Fox?"

"Mm. You are persistent. Following me like this." He peeked his head from the tree as if he were looking around for someone. No sign of his vulpine quality, except for his thicker angled brows.

In one breath, he stood before her, angling his head as if fascinated by her. His long silver hair was pulled back into a ponytail. The long wavy bangs parted to the left side of his face like ripples of water under moonlight, nearly concealing his left eye. She had a strange inclination to keep staring at him. As if his physical beauty was bait to lure her into a trap.

"Little usagi, shall we play?" His piercing yellow eyes met hers and then his face grew long and thin, his hair and clothes melted into orange fur and a tail sprouted from his back.

She would not be a rabbit to be preyed upon. Amaya pushed her hands out, water rushing out toward the fox.

He jumped, his small paws up in the air, his body elegant and lithe. The water gushed under him and he disappeared again behind a tree.

"Tell me what happened that night my father died!" Amaya waved her arms, water droplets spraying into the air.

"Ah...the night? What of it?"

Amaya scoffed. “You know what! Get out here. Tell me it was you who killed him!” she yelled into the darkness. She needed to know why it happened. How it did. The memory was still muddled by her stinging confusion. The pieces all jumbled. “Give me what I want, or I’ll...I’ll kill you!”

“Return mine and I will give you yours. Add some inarizushi and perhaps I will be much happier to oblige.”

Amaya panted, the cold air rushing into her lungs. Her body protested for rest as the nerves by her jaw trembled. He was speaking Japanese too. Did he follow her from back home? She’d been out in the cold night too long. Her eyesight was blurring. No. She couldn’t let her body give out.

Then, in a loud swoosh, a pair of black wings and a horse’s face appeared before her. It was Obsidian. His dark eyes looked into hers and then all of the darkness and cold consumed her.

Chapter 37 Out of Chaos Comes Order

Kayan was the first to be stirred awake by the cooing of a dove, its song echoing across the sky. He sat beside the fire, dawn's strands of light painting the clouds in teal and pink, with a glow reminding Kayan of the fire and of Nezha.

"Kayan?"

He turned to find Thunderbolt walking toward him.

"Done your fajr prayer?" Thunderbolt plopped down beside him and sighed.

"Shouldn't you be resting?" Kayan didn't see any other sign of Thunderbolt's injuries. He must have removed the bandages.

"Yeah, right! I'm an angel, so I can heal pretty quick."

"But you were injured really badly."

Thunderbolt gave him a glance. "Listen, Kayan, I know it's just your usual worried self comin' through, but I'm really okay. I've got you all by my side, so how would I not be great?"

Kayan saw a softer look in Thunderbolt's eyes. It seemed like the angel wouldn't be hiding his pain as much anymore. Usually, Thunderbolt would have laughed it off, but he was really trying to share his discomfort. Kayan was glad he was letting others know if he wasn't feeling well.

Then, Thunderbolt started to pull off his tunic.

"What are you doing? We're still in the cold. Are you trying to freeze?" Kayan tugged at the collar.

"I heard morning light is great for your skin, so I wanted my muscles t' get some sun, zaan."

"Come on, put it back on."

"I'm taking it off!" Thunderbolt grabbed his hand and pulled.

"Uh, good morn—"

Kayan turned.

Nezha stood at the opening of the tent and was staring at them. For several seconds, they stared at each other.

"Nezha!" Kayan dropped his hands.

Nezha's cheeks were so bright red, Kayan wasn't sure why the edges of her lips curled a bit.

"Join us." Thunderbolt winked at her and patted the spot beside him.

"That's not helping." Kayan's cheeks heated. He must have been as red and flushed as she was.

Nezha looked at the both of them and then a wide smile appeared over her face. "Pfft." She chuckled, as if that was what she'd been trying to hold back.

"Oh, if you could have seen your face, Kayan jan! That was so funny! You're red. It's so cute!" She just broke into laughter, with Thunderbolt joining her. She made her way over.

She wrapped an arm around the angel's shoulders and they looked at Kayan, joyful tears in their eyes.

"It's not that funny." Kayan smiled back as his heart thundered in his chest.

Hearing her call him jan, and even saying he was cute? He couldn't take all this sweetness from her. This beautiful, fiery girl was going to melt him. The way the sun rays showered her brown eyes, it made them this iridescent, honey glow. Her smile was so sweet and warm, he had the urge to pull her into his arms, kiss her head and hold her.

He felt his cheeks still hot, the feeling chasing away the dawn's cold. He turned away, focusing on the coloured clouds. He couldn't just let himself feel all that. These feelings were so nice, but they had to get Amaya on their side and get the feather back. Still, moments like these felt so good, easing the ache in his heart. Moments like these, where he could smile and see the others laid back for once.

***

Moonlight flashed over Mamluk, the kilij sword. Zul wasn't sure how he'd been able to manipulate the shed blood of those innocents, forming the iron in their blood into a weapon. Their deaths would not be in vain.

"It's gotten pretty late, Sire. I think we'll have to head back."

"What?" He'd thought Lexa would be jumping at the opportunity to attack the jawhars in the middle of the night.

"Nah, aren't you exhausted? You've just been given more dark jinni energy. You need time to adjust. I can't have you groaning and falling over as if you're a drunkard."

Zul searched her eyes. "You're right, that would be shameful." A small smile managed to appear over his lips.

"Exactly," Lexa said and winked. She pressed her hand to his arm.

“Okay, what is it really about?”

Lexa sighed. “Come now, Zul. It’s not the right moment to attack them.”

Zul groaned. He’d just witnessed a whole city covered in blood in the wake of a jinn attack. He couldn’t go out and attack the jawhars, especially when one part of his heart didn’t want to. His fingers trembled over the hilt of the sword. His mourning and confused thoughts were as sharp as the blade’s curved edge.

“You’re not in a position to fight. Not yet,” Lexa informed him and then spun her hand, shadows flowing from her fingertips.

Zul glanced at the sky and then back at her, his pulse surging in his neck. This energy had imprinted him with the urge to fight back and seek out the love he had with Sanari. That connection would never die. And no one else would die. That he knew.

“Okay.”

Lexa smiled. “Good. Wasn’t it easy to just give in, Sire?”

“Did you eat yet?”

“Of course not. You think I wouldn’t wait to eat together?” The shadows swelled into a shape resembling a door. “We should head back.”

His eyes burned orange.

“Please stop. Don’t despair.” His voice poured through. Eisen’s. It was quiet, but the words were heavy on Zul’s heart. Sanari’s smiling face, her warmth, the sharpness in her eyes when she heard of any jinn attacks... All of that spun his mind. He wanted to break the iron’s curse over her. Knowing that somehow his heart letting light back in was helping her, he thought maybe he could find happiness too. Maybe there was a chance he could fix all that he’d caused.

Only out of chaos will you find what you want. The jinni energy spoke in contrast to Eisen. That malignant entity did not seem to sway.

"Hope doesn't end in despair. Hope guides that despair into a future." The thought of Ansam cleared his mind. Only a moment. Then that darkness grew and the door closed before him. The demonic aura perfumed in saffron took over. He had become a captive once again.

The shadows swayed, and like a silk curtain, they enveloped them into the darkness.

***

"I don't sense Amaya anymore," Asad said, worry lacing his voice as they walked away from their campsite and toward the forest. They had to trek through all the snow again.

"Same here," Nezha added. She'd been so worried about getting the feather that she almost forgot that Amaya had gone in the direction of the forest. That hum of familiar energy that Amaya was giving off was no more. What else could Nezha do but move forward in this strange and dangerous world? No matter what, she would move on.

"So, y'all are looking for a feather? What's so important about it?" Dante stuffed his gloved hands into his pockets.

"What's important about it? Thunderbolt said, aghast. It's from the Angel of Mercy!"

"It's not only a feather. It can turn into a sword that kills evil jinn. It's been a part of me for a long time now."

Nezha stared at the approaching forest, its trees like a spider's legs, weaving through the clouded morning sky. The crunch of snow, the chill snaking down her back—all of it just made her even more eager to be out of the snow and to find what they were looking for. She wrapped her fingers around her wrist.

"Oh." Dante's lips tightened, and then he kept walking with the others. The way he said it, she could tell he seemed apologetic.

They'd made it to the edge of the forest, the snow meeting the ashen ground, an invisible barrier between them.

"O'layotgan Forest," Sapphire said as they stepped into the forest. "The Dying Forest which the Atlas does not have much information about."

"That's the first time you've spared us one of your lectures, Sheikh." Thunderbolt grinned as Sapphire gave him a funny look.

"So it's unknown too?" Kayan blew out a breath.

"Who cares! We're here to find Amaya, but since she's not here, we need the feather back. It's still calling out to me," Asad said, clicking his tongue. "There's barely anything around here."

"Except that." Dante pointed to a tree.

Hanging on the branches were strange apples with glossy transparent skin.

Kayan raised his eyebrows. "Some strange apple?"

Comet pawed at the tree, dragging her claws over it.

Nezha walked up to it. "Does the Atlas say anything about these, Sapphire?"

"Ah, yes. They are called ghul trees. The sap has toxic properties, so in the autumnal months they tend to seep out and onto the apples, wrapping them in a thin, sticky coating. As it hardens, the sap rots the fruit underneath, casting it and its seeds away. The sap is harmful to people."

"That's probably why no one lived to tell anything about this place," Asad mused.

"If I have t' listen to any more"—Thunderbolt pressed his temples— "I think my brain'll rot."

"Well, we should try to find the fox and get my feather back." Nezha's gaze passed over the trees and to the sky overhead. The vultures were back and they were circling them again. A small weight grew in her chest. She didn't have time to waste. "So Asad, which way do you hear the feather?"

"This way." Asad started walking in one direction while the others followed behind him.

A crackle sounded behind them, making Nezha whip her head back.

"Usagi left her friends behind." A voice came echoing out from behind the skinny trees. A fox's head peeked out, and it walked out in front of them. Its eyes seemed to gleam as Nezha's gaze fell to his neck. A silver cuff wrapped around it like a collar.

It was the feather.

Chapter 38 Reality is a Dream

Were the tides carrying her away? This strange darkness overtook Amaya. Maybe she'd drowned in the ocean after all. All of that must have been a dream. Her being transported to a strange world with angels. It must have been a dream where she'd been after a fox. It was all too strange and distant to be real. Then, Amaya's eyes fluttered open and her gaze focused upon black hair and something soft swooping through the wind, the cold playing through her hair. She raised her head and realized she was on someone's back flying through the air.

"Where—"

The wind stole the words from her.

"You're finally awake." It was the angel unicorn, Obsidian, that was carrying her, his wings flying them through the night sky. "Don't be afraid."

"I wasn't. But I am now." Her fingers wrapped tightly around his midsection. They were hurtling through the darkness. Why wouldn't she be afraid? But, in a way, she wasn't. She closed her eyes and instead, thought of the sound of the deafening wind as waves crashing into the shore. She thought of the ripples and splashes in the pool back at the university. The feeling of swimming. Then, Tamaki, Okaasan, Rin—they passed her thoughts.

She heard him make a strange coughing sound.

"We will be there soon."

"Where?"

"Where those jinn and Zul are." The way he said it, it was as if he was glad she'd forgotten about it.

The place where she didn't belong. At least, it was a place where she felt like maybe, if she'd met those people at a different time in their lives, she could have actually gotten along with them. She shook her head. What was she thinking? The women were two demonic beings and the man seemed like he was plagued by one too. It was the fox she'd been after. That made her remember what she'd been doing. She was so close to getting her answers, even if it meant fighting him.

"Hey, you need to bring me back!"

"You have been out here all night; you'll pass out from exhaustion again."

"No, I need to go back!" Amaya wriggled and pushed his back.

"Hey, you're going to fall!" Obsidian turned his head around toward her.

"I have to get answers from the fox. I can't afford sleep."

"You know I admire your persistence, but your body will fail you. Rest, and then tomorrow you may find him."

Amaya sighed. The struggle with him made her head ache. Her eyelids were heavy again. She blinked wearily, trying to listen to the wind to stay awake. He was right. Her body was giving out. "Hmm."

"Now, please go back to sleep, or if I drop you, it won't be my fault next time."

"Wait, have you dropped me before?" Amaya pulled his hair.

"Agh, no, I didn't. I didn't," he protested.

A slight smile tugged at her lips. At least she'd find the way to the fox again. He had told her she had something of his. Whatever that meant, she knew she'd get her answers when their paths crossed again.

***

Morning light poured through the tall open windows. Lounging on the purple cushions embroidered in gold, Lexa and Rana were chatting.

Zul pressed a hand to his chest. His heart was pounding. *Don't listen,* a soft voice would whisper to him. Always telling him to disregard the darkness, to remember the Creator, to think of Sanari's life and to never let go of hope. He didn't mention it to Lexa. She'd been giving him these strange glances ever since they'd returned last night.

"Lexa, are you busy right now?"

Rana had whispered in Lexa's ear and she'd laughed.

"What is it, Sire? Are you missing me that much?"

Zul rolled his eyes. "Oh yes, very much so," he deadpanned.

"I will be with the wolves if you need me," Rana said, slipping into a warmer grey tunic over her blue shalwar kameez.

"Say my regards to your pack," Lexa said, kissing both of Rana's cheeks before turning to Zul.

"Of course." Rana's eyes seemed wilder this morning as she licked her lips.

"Are you sure you don't want breakfast before you go, Rana?" Zul said as Lexa stood beside him.

"I prefer mine freshly caught." Rana's eyes gleamed red for several seconds until she took the form of her crow self and fluttered out the open window and into the cold morning.

"Well, did you want to say something to me?" Lexa regarded him with a softer look in her eyes. He hadn't missed how much she seemed anxious around him. "This better be good. Rana had a great story to tell me."

"I want to be informed about your plan, Lexa. You haven't disclosed much to me. I'm beginning to worry." Zul's eyes burned. They must have been glowing orange, from the way Lexa's lips turned to a smirk.

"We have to weaken the jawhars, of course, so we'll be heading out there to them."

"I know there's more than that." He tipped his head forward.

She bit her lip and played with his collar. He knew she was fidgety, but the way she'd been so touchy, it was making him think she was worried about him. Maybe a little too much. Maybe it was because of the mark of shadows that tattooed half his face now, instead of only the scorpion over his chest and neck. Or that she'd given him more cursed darkness.

"I want them to fight with the fox—the one Amaya has been searching for. Once they settle their problems with him, we will meet with them. All of us, including Amaya. But, that's all I can say."

"Are you vouching for them to kill him?" Zul watched her as she tipped her head back and laughed.

“Kill, kill, kill, is that all you think I yearn for? Oh no, he is more valuable to us alive. I just need pieces to fall into place.” She looked up at him.

“Forgive me for thinking you enjoyed it.” He smiled at her and she playfully smacked his shoulder.

“Oh I do, but there’s so much more I want to do, Sire. Don’t you understand? I will do anything to free my people. My parents, my sister, were killed in the war of Jahalia, but”—Lexa bit her lower lip again and then met his gaze— “I will free the others, even if it means it will free the shaiteen that were responsible for the war.”

He gulped. “What do you mean?”

“The shaiteen were waiting for their moment. When the Fire Kingdom’s daughter Sanari became more mature and she ensnared the people’s hearts with her love and warmth, the shaiteen began to despise her. I saw their hate gather in their eyes. Their wrath knew no bounds. They incited the more desperate of humans in Wadi Alma.” She laughed again, a more taunting laugh he’d ever heard from her. “Humans, shaiteen, both are to blame!”

He knew both sides weren’t faultless. Even then, all this needless killing ached his heart. His fingers trembled as the voice hummed into his mind. *Doesn’t matter who dies. They’ll all be damned.*

“I know, but someone has to end this killing and imprisonment.”

“I don’t care! That’s what you need to know. Those foolish shaiteen are trapped with my people and I don’t care if they are released. I will find them, but I need power, Zul. For that, we need to weaken Nezha and her friends. All I need is your trust that I am doing the right thing in the end.”

Zul didn't know what he could trust. All he could do was nurture the hope of Sanari waking, nurture this feeling of keeping any more innocents from losing their lives. It was a dream that he wanted to make a reality. He shook his head.

"I don't want to kill people in order to do that."

Lexa searched his eyes. She sighed and turned.

"The choice is always yours." She clenched her hands and left him with that on the matter. "We should both rest. Do something to put yourself at ease." There was a warmth in her eyes as she looked back at him. "Soon, there will be another chance." She slipped into the shadows.

***

She lay sprawled across a bed, relishing the warmth of the plush sheets and the weight of the blanket hugging her arms. Amaya sat up, and her gaze went to the table beside her bed. A glass of water sat beside a glossy sheet: a note. She stretched her arms.

So, she'd really been brought back here again. The thought of Obsidian flying her through the sky came back to her and the strangeness of ease grew in her mind. She didn't like how comfortable she'd become here, but, in a way, she did like it. She raised her hands and thought of water. A small drop formed at her fingertip, and soon more, until it was a round globule of water. She wished this was just a dream. A terrifying, freeing dream that wasn't her reality.

She stretched to take the note. It was written on a slick, smooth blue glassy material. "Just water. Love, Lexa and Zul," she read, and a small smile took her by surprise. Lexa wasn't letting that go, huh?

She removed the blanket and looked down. Dark spots covered her legs and were caked on her long dress. The mud. The mud from last night. So, it really hadn't been a strange dream after all. That meant the fox was still out there hiding, and she needed to find him.

***

They'd found him. Nezha played with a small flame between her fingertips. The fox tilted his head at them. "We aren't your prey, *little* fox."

"It's rude to demean someone when you don't know them yet," he spoke back.

Rude? They'd been led into the unforgiving cold, enduring the seemingly endless feeling of ice sinking into her bones. Nezha shook her head. They'd nearly been killed out here. She'd lost blood, almost lost the ones she cared for. She'd lost her fear throughout this journey. And now, she was about to lose her patience.

Flames plumed from her palms, rushing outward like petals dancing to the wind. She took a step, her tongue in her cheek.

"Because of you, I nearly lost people. Because of you, we couldn't find Amaya. Because of you! Give me the feather back." She raised her hand. Flames burst out, hissing as they struck the tree and charred it until it crumbled before them.

The fox took a step in his human form. He stretched out his arms, blue fire spiraling before him and twisting the fire Nezha had unleashed on him.

“Oh...you have fire too?” He moved his arm in one swipe, the way someone would flick blood off the blade of a scimitar.

“Why do monsters like to take human form so much?” Dante said.

Asad pursed his lips. “They’re sick like that. Tricking people and preying on their vulnerabilities.”

Morning light glinted off his wrist. It was the feather cuff.

“Time to fight?” Dante stretched his arms.

“Oh yeah,” Asad drawled. A blast of energy radiated off of him, like water rippling, and slammed into the fox. But to their surprise, the fox shifted into a large golden cat. It was just its face, teeth bared, and a loud shrieking meow.

Kayan whipped out his sword Ali, but then his fingers trembled.

Sapphire’s necklace brightened.

“Sorry, next game, if you please.” The cat head—who was actually the fox—winked and disappeared into a poof of smoke. Before Kayan or anyone could do anything next, particles blinked in and out of focus around them.

“What *is* this stuff?” Dante asked as he bumped into Asad.

“Divine’s sake, I sense something threatening.” Thunderbolt raised his arm, sparks popping around his fingers.

Sapphire pressed her hand to her hip where her holster was. “His aura has shifted.”

The particles grew around them, flying in different directions.

The top of Kayan’s head prickled. Something was dark about it for sure. He breathed in and then was taken aback by laughter.

“Jinne mera dil lutiya,” Nezha sang, patting her chest where her heart was and swayed her body.

"O ho," Asad joined in, his cheeks reddening as he swayed too.

"Jinne mainu maar sutiya!" Nezha sang next.

"O ho," both Dante and Asad sang together this time and swayed again.

"Yeah, I'mma dance all night!" Dante said as he danced with Asad. Both of them hollered and laughed.

"This one goes out to Kayan! Jaan! Oh, meri jaan!"

"What the?" Kayan stared at them. What was happening? They'd all started to act so strangely. The wind slipped past his face, carrying the scent of saffron. It was magic responsible for all this. The fox must have been playing his game with it.

Sapphire instructed, "Do not inhale the particles; it seems they are a strange magic."

"It's too late for those three," sighed Kayan.

Thunderbolt snorted. "Yeah, who knew Nezha had a good singing voice."

Dante and Asad were singing a song again and dancing. Dante rolled his shoulders and his head nodded.

Nezha continued singing.

"It does not affect us angels as much as it would a human," Sapphire said.

"She means this magic's so weak, I'm almost falling asleep," added Thunderbolt.

No matter how much Kayan tried to hold his breath, his lungs constricted and the magic coated his throat. The metallic cold taste slipped over his tongue. The ground blurred and his cheeks heated. A laugh tumbled out with his breath. Only one thought ran free through his mind.

Only one person. He just wanted to be with Nezha, seeing her smile and laugh. To hear her say his name in her beautiful singing voice.

The siblings turned to him.

"Nezha jan!" He stumbled to her as she turned to him.

"Yes, meri jaan." Nezha was smiling, but then her smile slipped from her lips and her eyes lidded.

Kayan tugged her sleeve. "Come on, Nezha, let's just dance."

"Kayan...wait." She looked into his eyes.

Kayan took a fold of her hijab in his hands and grabbed her sleeve. He leaned in to her. She was so close now. He could see the red blooming over her lips. Flower petals, the wind was eager to make dance. "We should forget all this stuff about the fox and jawhars. We don't need all that stress. Come on, my Nezha jan. Be with me."

He searched her eyes, finding her gaze warm. Her reddened cheeks, that smile slipping over her lips—all of it made him lose any other thought. *Divine's sake.* Warmth and joy sang through his chest. She was his Nayzak, his Nezha jan.

"That's enough!" Thunderbolt growled and poked Kayan, sending a small shock through his shoulder.

"Seven hells, Kayan."

Kayan blinked. His fingers slipped from her sleeve and he stared at Nezha who was searching his eyes, her fingers slowly pressing where he'd touched her hijab. He wanted to know what was going through her mind.

Sapphire opened her wings. "We can fan the particles."

"Worth a try." Thunderbolt fanned his wings along with Sapphire. The gusts swept the particles up and away from everyone.

The fox appeared out of the blurred air, the particles dancing past his face and then vanishing. He transformed into his human form for several seconds and slipped the feather cuff from his wrist.

“Here’s your prize.” He threw the cuff at Nezha.

She caught it and stared at the fox. He winked and then in a plume of smoke, he disappeared.

“Huh?”

“Ugh, I knew it! A trap,” Asad said.

“Damn, we were finessed,” said Dante.

Nezha fit the feather to her wrist. “Astaghfirullah. Creator, forgive me. I can’t believe I was singing. Astaghfirullah!”

Asad also muttered the same plea for forgiveness. “I can’t believe we were drunk.”

“It was a from of magic, but the fox used something in it that makes you lose your senses.”

“Same thing!” Asad complained, combing his fingers through his hair and blowing out a sigh.

Chapter 39 Sweet Nothings

Amaya poured water over her body so many times, she wasn't sure how long she'd spent in the bath. Bright blue tiles in different patterns and shades glimmered back at her in the tub. That smell of saffron had invaded her mind back in the forest. It was everywhere. In her breath, in her heart, under her skin.

She rubbed the jasmine and red hibiscus studded soap bar over her body. She needed the smell gone. More lather, more soap, and she rinsed, the rush of the water the perfect noise to drown out her thoughts. She sniffed. No, it was still there. She rubbed the soap again all over herself, repeating the process. Then she scrubbed her legs where the mud had been.

Being here in the water felt like home. She wanted to swim again, but this tub wasn't as large as a pool. She lay on her back, her head touching the pearl surface. Amaya sighed. She flexed her fingers, invoking small globes of water. She dropped her arms and let them float. She'd close her eyes for just a few moments. Just a few.

When she was out, she hurried to the stairs. On her way down, Obsidian met her halfway, his head rising to her gaze. He was in his angel form.

"I—" They both said in unison, but then he remained quiet.

"I want to know why you took me back."

"I needed to. You were losing consciousness." Obsidian stared at her. His eyes glossed over and Amaya wondered if she was seeing sadness or regret in them.

Amaya nodded and walked past him.

"We left breakfast for you," he called to her as she hurried down.

By the cushions, there were plates laid out on the floor. To her surprise, Zul was seated before one of them.

"Good morning." Zul smiled at her. Amaya tilted her head. She'd never seen him smile. He'd usually have a frown or a dour expression. With a smile so warm and kind, it was as if he was another person.

"Morning..." Amaya sat on her knees by the plate in front of him. Had he not eaten breakfast?

"Sorry if you're not familiar with some of these. Most of them are of Wadi Alman or Faliz origin."

She wasn't even sure what those two places were. But, by the looks of the food, they all made her salivate and her stomach grumble.

"Except for the Kheyar Mekhali," Zul said.

Amaya's eyes lit up at the pickled dish. It was one thing familiar in this strange world. "Thank you," She managed and looked up at him. She picked up the bread and dipped it into a bean mix.

"I hope you like it. There's baladi bread you can dip into the foul." He didn't meet her gaze and whispered, "Bismillah," before eating.

She whispered the same blessing. The spices, the full flavour burst into her mouth and she almost forgot how to breathe. Warm food, kind company— she'd missed all of it. She'd been so used to the cold dark, the cold of the loneliness and the grip of the unforgiving snowy emptiness. She'd been starved of the warmth of kindness.

Creator have mercy... A light she'd been yearning for. He was one of the strangest people in this mansion. Did he wait to eat with her? And if he did, why did he? He barely knew her.

"You...didn't eat?" Amaya asked hesitantly.

Zul looked at her with a small smile. "Nope. I knew you'd been unconscious when you got back and probably missed breakfast. So, I didn't want you to eat alone."

Alone. That's what she'd been all this time. She felt alone, *was* alone. The space around her was always hollow despite someone being around.

"Thank you." That was all she could manage to say. They'd nearly finished their plates when he spoke to her again.

"I might not know exactly how you feel, but... I might have chosen this cloak of darkness. And I know how alluring the darkness can be when it hides your pain."

"I didn't want to feel all the memories of the past." Amaya traced the ground with a finger. Those memories raced in her mind. All the what ifs and what could have happends.

He met her gaze and his eyes softened. "When you need to talk to someone, I'll be here to listen."

"Thank you. Zul, you know, you seem so out of place here." She didn't know what it was, but when she spoke to him, she felt like she could tell him anything. And that he wouldn't judge or hurt her.

"Probably a good thing." The light dropped over his head, revealing the lines in his brown eyes. They were like the rings inside a tree. Years of growth. How long had he been around this darkness? And what had he been through? What had he gained and lost? What had he seen all these years for him to give off such a warm yet sad aura?

He stood up and took her empty plates. He parted his lips as if he was about to say something.

"I was wondering where you two were." Lexa walked in with Rana behind her, and took a hold of Zul's arm.

Rana held onto a book and glanced at Amaya before turning to Lexa.

Wanting to kill the fox had been ingrained into her all this time. After facing him and feeling the darkness inside her ease up, that inclination wasn't as deep. It felt like warmth, the way a hot soup hugged her body. She realized she had to be patient if she wanted answers. Running into things wasn't like her and she hadn't felt like herself at all in this world. She'd had to let Lexa tell her how to be, especially if she didn't want to feel Lexa's cold grasp around her neck again.

"Are you planning anything today?" Zul asked as Lexa loosened her fingers from his arm and bit her lip with her amused smile.

"Ah, yes children, I have so many activities planned today." She laughed, her eyes glistening. Amaya tilted her head. Was it just her, or had Lexa's eyes softened from the last time she'd seen her?

"Aren't we just lucky?" Zul rolled his eyes and smiled.

"Amaya dear, was your sleep alright? I hope you're hydrated." Lexa winked at her.

Amaya nodded. She had to wait. Wait for the right moment to face the fox again.

"I believe we would do well to rest," Rana spoke, taking Amaya aback. The crow jinni still clutched a book to her chest as she looked up at Amaya. Even her eyes weren't as piercing as they'd been the first time she'd met her. There was just calm.

"Don't get all soft on them, Rana." Lexa nudged her and then sighed. "But you're right. I really do have plans for you all later, so why not." She turned to leave, but looked over her shoulder and stopped. "Zul Sharr, we have a lot to do, so tell Obsidian this for me."

Zul nodded to her and Lexa stepped into the shadows, melting away into the darkness. "She could use the door for once."

"Not as shadow-like; it would be a disgrace to her." Rana cracked a smile.

Seeing them like this made Amaya crave comfort. She missed the moments in prayer with Mama. The calm a gentle embrace to her heart. She missed the dinners with Tama and their families all together on a winter night. When Okaasan would refill his bowl with fragrant hot soup until he said he couldn't eat anymore. Okaasan wouldn't listen and give him more. The moments Tama would smile at her, his warm eyes melting all the stress of her day away. Comfort had its grip on her, slipping into her heart, holding her head and whispering its sweet nothings. And now, her whole body wanted to sink into the plush softness.

"Do you have videos here?" Amaya blurted out.

Zul and Rana looked at her for several seconds. Zul took out his Tome, the device that looked like a smartphone, from his pocket and faced the screen at her.

"You mean these?" Something played on the screen, moving.

Amaya nodded. "Yes."

Rana turned. "I will take my leave."

"See you later," Zul said to her absentmindedly, tapping on the screen.

"It's almost like phones back home." Amaya tapped across the screen, searching for cute kitten videos. They'd been watching different videos in the living room. She was seated before one of the cushions, with Zul having his back against one and his Tome propped against another.

"Phones?" Zul just gave her a blank stare.

"Yeah, we communicate with them, just like these, I'm guessing."

"Oh." He smiled and the way he looked at her, it was like he was glad they were having a nice moment.

"Cute kitten videos," he read and as one came up, she saw his eyes light up and an expression she'd never seen on his face before. One of wonder. It was so very soft, she thought it must have melted his heart.

The kitten in the video mewed in a high note with its round cheeks and oh so tiny paw waving at the air.

"It's adorable!"

"Yeah." Zul pressed his hands to his head and cooed at the video. "Aww someone snuggle the kitten. Someone snu—"

And then Lexa appeared into the living room through the wall. "Sire, what you up to?"

"Snu— Snuff it out... Oh." He frantically tapped on his Tome and pulled up a video about fire. "Just watching this video with fire, right Amaya?"

Amaya nodded. She pressed her hand to her lips, trying her best to not let a laugh escape.

Lexa just walked up to them, with Obsidian right behind her, and ordered, “Go back to the cute video.”

Amaya smiled and sat back as she and Zul made room for them. It was so warm, so full in the room. All their softer voices, their laughter—it was all like an embrace. She’d missed feeling this close to people.

The afternoon sun cast short shadows, smudges against the room’s walls.

Amaya stood before a wooden table, the smoke from the lit incense whispering past her face.

“Amaya,” Lexa called to her as Obsidian stood by her side.

Obsidian gave her a curt nod as he met her gaze.

A small chill crept up her sides. Amaya knew the time was approaching to say something about the fox, but she needed the right moment.

She walked to Lexa.

“Shall I tell you?” With a lopsided smile, Lexa gestured to the window.

“About?” Amaya’s heart started pounding. Was it the right moment? Was she going to finally find out what happened to her papa? To finally fight the fox.

“Really? I didn’t think I needed to explain.” Lexa motioned to Rana as the crow jinni walked in. “Would you do the honour and ask one of the crows about the fox?”

Amaya pressed a hand to her heart. Her breath caught in her throat. She’d just started feeling at ease around here, but now, the cold’s fingers swept across her shoulders, persuading her mind. The black dress Lexa had given her in the morning seemed to tighten around her waist.

Through the open window, a crow fluttered in and sat on Rana's outstretched wrist. Its gritty caw echoed across the room and then, after a pause, Rana spoke to it. Several moments later, the crow hopped onto the edge of the window and disappeared into the milky, grey sky.

Amaya's jaw tensed and she stared at Rana.

Rana parted her red lips. "The fox is in front of Veer City."

The breeze played through Amaya's dress, plunging her into its cold embrace.

Chapter 40 Encounter

Still dazed, the cold pricked at her face as Nezha and the others walked out of the forest. "He just handed it over." The fox really had given her the feather. She wasn't sure what was more frustrating, the fact that he handed it over after playing with their minds, or that she didn't know what was going on while it happened.

"The Divine smiles upon us," Sapphire said.

"At least you have it back now." Asad rubbed his hands together and blew into his palms.

Yeah, she did have it back. Her friends, her new companions—they were with her. Comet was still in the bubble, walking beside her. She meowed and Nezha looked down at her. She'd keep them all much closer. And yet, in all this open space, with snowy plains all she could see, she kept her head up a little higher. She knew if anyone or thing was going to attack them next, she had others by her side.

"We need to head back to Veer City," Sapphire declared. She took a hold of Nezha's arm and gently passed a warm light across her cheek.

"Don't worry about me." Nezha squeezed Sapphire's shoulder. When Sapphire had opened up about Obsidian, it made her feel so much closer to her. Knowing how Sapphire felt, how much she had kept her own sadness inside. She was glad that Sapphire chose to share it with her. She wanted to be there for her. To console her in her vulnerable moments. Just as Sapphire had been there for her.

"Nezha." Thunderbolt wrapped his hand around her shoulder. "So, you never told me you could sing." He grinned and gestured to Kayan.

He really had to mention that? She'd just refocused her mind on what they had to do. She'd really embarrassed herself in front of Kayan. Although she could hardly remember what she did, other than her singing.

Kayan scooped up Comet while she was in the bubble and held her in his arms as he conversed with Dante.

Nezha pressed her hands to the feather as they walked. The only one they were missing was Amaya.

"Hey, jawhars, do you feel Amaya's energy?" Nezha called out to the boys.

Dante shook his head. "Not really."

Asad shrugged. "Kind of. I feel like it's this way." He was pointing in the direction of Veer City.

"Probably somewhere around Veer City," Kayan said. "I think she's there, Nezha."

"Since we're not in Veer, how about you all get a ride?" Thunderbolt's face elongated and he and his sister transformed into their unicorn selves.

"I am *not* riding a unicorn." Asad huffed.

"Are you scared of heights or somethin'?" Dante said as he climbed onto Thunderbolt's back.

Asad scoffed. "No! I'd rather stay on the ground."

"You sound scared to me." Dante grinned at him.

“Come on, Asad, you can ride on the wind if you want.” Kayan offered, swiping his hand upward and riding on the rippling wind.

“That sounds worse,” Asad replied.

“This isn’t a time to be picky,” said Nezha, climbing onto Sapphire’s back.

Asad sighed. “Fine.” He climbed onto Thunderbolt and held onto Dante’s waist.

“We ready now, kids?” Thunderbolt said with a laugh.

“Just go already!” Asad said, his face reddening.

Just like that, the unicorns took to the sky, their wings beating, Nezha’s heart beating louder as they swooped over the glittering snowy plain. It was all snow as the ground zipped under her.

Nezha glanced at Kayan who was riding the wind beside her. She caught him looking back and smiling at her. The way his cheeks rounded, the glow over his skin lifted her spirit. For several seconds their gazes met, and Nezha felt her cheeks heat. She was lost in his eyes. Warmth and softness cushioned her heart. Why did Kayan always make her feel like she could just keep looking at him and the whole world would fall away? It always felt so peaceful. There was no pain between the space of his warm smile and soft eyes.

Suddenly, an energy hummed under her skin that made her gaze tear away from Kayan. It was Amaya’s energy. She glanced back to see Kayan’s head down, his fingers brushing through his hair and his lips parting. Two pigeons flew past them, cooing as Nezha took notice of the mud stream Amaya had frozen over. It had become mud again, the shards of ice gone.

Above the forest, there were no sounds or scents, until they reached outside the city. Nezha tightened her grip on Sapphire's neck. The scent of saffron, its bittersweet, earthy, honey scent. For a few moments, the trees blurred and a cold rippled up her back. She was smelling magic. And it was stronger here.

"You all smell it too?" Asad called out.

"Yeah, I know that smell anywhere," Kayan shouted back.

Sapphire sighed, her voice trembling with worry. "Magic. We are landing." She dove, with Thunderbolt following her.

Nezha kept her gaze on the unicorn's mane, her blue hair whipping around. It made her think of water and Amaya.

***

When they landed, Dante jumped off of Thunderbolt's back and pressed his hands to the ground. Sweet sweet ground. He missed being able to walk again. By the way Asad was prostrating on the ground, it looked like he was happy too.

The others really had it rough, with almost dying by those creatures and then the fox. The jinn. Made from smoke-less flame, they could be both good and bad. And many of them loved to take the form of humans like the fox did.

But, Dante had to focus on what he needed to do. To ask Noorenia where the angel's body was. Then he could get Momma and maybe even Momma G would go back home with them. Knowing Momma had been living in such a dangerous place, he couldn't understand why she had chosen to come back here.

The others stood beside him and the unicorns become their angel selves again. "I'm goin' to ask where the angel's body is." Dante breathed in, and then closed his eyes. He needed answers and then he could help Noorenia. For it, for his momma, for his family. "Noorenia, tell me where the angel's body is."

I need the angel. I need the mercy.

"I know." Dante spoke in a gentler tone. "It's okay, we're goin' to help."

Dante's heart raced as energy rippled under his skin, sharp and panicked.

Help me. Help me. Return his soul to him.

A strangled scream escaped him and tears streaked his face. He was left panting, and his head was fuzzy for several seconds.

"Dante, hey!" Kayan knelt beside him.

Sapphire and Thunderbolt both placed a hand on his shoulder. "Are you okay?" they asked in unison.

"Yeah... It's Noorenia, though. It's mourning. It won't tell me." His shoulders warmed and then he saw Sapphire's small, kind smile. She was giving him some kind of light healing. He'd seen her using it on the others before.

Asad shook his head. "We can't force it."

Kayan stood. "Yeah, we're just going to have to find another way."

Another way? No freaking way! Dante couldn't think of anything else. He was supposed to be an earth jawhar. The Creator had blessed him with this power. It was like he had failed at being who he was. His fingers curled into a fist.

Then, the wind sped up, rushing through the snow. The trees nearby bowed. Then it hit him hard. The bittersweet smell.

Kayan pinched his nose. “The magic’s getting worse.”

Nezha’s hands held twin hissing flames. “She’s nearby.”

“Amaya,” Asad breathed.

Before them, far from the gates of Veer City, stood Amaya. Her auburn hair danced in the breeze and beside her stood Zul Sharr, his lips a straight line and half his face inked in intricate lines.

Chapter 41 That Night's Prelude

He couldn't bear this night. It wasn't the cold, its fingers caressing his face. No, it was the silence. The deafening silence that made him want to fill the void. Savan sang.

"Days go by, and my heart is left in the deep forest.
I am sure, in this darkness,
As we live, we lose,
Standing frozen. We cry out,
Darkness my home, my journey is you."

"You long for me this much, jaanaana?"

It was her voice. The one he had waited in the darkness for.

She stepped out from the shadows and under the dark sky. Star-bathed, her short hair was the very darkness of the blackberries she used to sneak out to him from the humans. He had told her he enjoyed the tang. A taste not easy to find in any of their local foods.

Savan bowed his head and fell to his knees, raising his hand to her. He didn't care if the snow wet his shalwar, or if it stained his blue kameez a shade darker. His heart was beating loudly. Louder than it ever had. "Do you regret your absence?"

She placed her hand in his and he stood, pulling her into his arms. Her scent never changed. No matter how long it had been, he'd always remember the smoky and sweet notes. He pressed his face into her neck and tightened his hold on her. She didn't move, her arms wrapped around his torso. "Are you pleased with how much you tormented my heart?" he whispered into her ear.

"Yes. Are you pleased with how much my heart broke?" she breathed next to his cheek and he pressed his lips to her forehead. Her lips brushed his jaw and he laughed.

"No. I regret that."

Her laugh was broken, as broken as his. She pushed him aside, part of her body in the shadows again. But she held onto his hand. Her fingers twined in his.

"Did you make sure they are coming?"

"Yes." Savan breathed out. He bit his lip and pulled her in again.

"Behave." This time her voice wasn't just amusement. It was bitter. The same bitterness that welled in his throat and ached in his heart whenever he thought of having to leave. Whenever he thought of the family and friends he lost. The same bitterness that he held onto, knowing his people were imprisoned.

"Forgive me." He pushed her against a tree and looked into her eyes. As dark as he could remember.

"Savan..."

"Ask me to leave, but don't stop asking me, so this night can't end." He pressed his forehead to hers.

Her fingers found his necklace and caught on the black silken cloth wrapped around it. "You must go." She pressed her head to his. "They have it," She said, then pressing her lips to his cheeks.

He trailed a finger down her neck. "Yes."

"We need to do it tomorrow, Savan." She backed away and his fingers slipped from hers.

"I will be there for you, my lady."

As she walked into the shadows, the cold swept through him. He swallowed, tasting a bitterness with a tang. A taste he was yearning for. Magic had perfumed the forest.

Chapter 42 Drown

It wasn't just the cold making Nezha shiver, or the fact that she had to finally face Amaya and Zul Sharr. That hum of energy—Noorenia's heartbeat—was dying. It skipped and teetered across her heart. Nezha looked at each of her companions in turn as she held onto Kayan's sleeve. Her other hand reached out to the angels. She needed them close. Comet pressed her paws against the wall of the bubble she was still contained in and Nezha pressed her forehead to the other side in response as Sapphire held Comet in her arms. "We're going to be okay, Mithi."

Nezha's companions stood closer to her, readying themselves for the impeding conflict. Asad and Dante's energies sang in the cold air, reaching her heart.

The way Amaya stood, Nezha wasn't sure if she was hesitating or not. The girl held her fists up and simply stared at her. Zul was staring too. Nezha couldn't miss the dark lines covering half of his face. They were more threads to the web of darkness that shrouded him. He was different. A strange calmness fell over him, but on his face, Nezha saw tears in his eyes.

"Nezha..." Kayan smiled, his warmth like the afternoon sunbathing her. Her heart filled to the brim with hope.

“We’re getting Amaya on our side. We will.” Nezha’s fingers slipped from his sleeve.

“Of course,” Sapphire said.

“Damn right.” Dante chimed in.

“I’m worried, so we will,” Asad grinned.

“My Nayzak, shine bright,” Kayan whispered.

She held her palms heavenward, flames hissed to life across her skin and flared, bursting into the air over her.

“You’re in the way,” Amaya said and took a step.

“You are too,” Thunderbolt’s lightning spun by his shoulders.

Water rushed from Amaya’s hands, waves rippling out toward them. Just as Amaya leapt forward, Zul Sharr slammed his hands to the ground, metal seeping over the snow like puddles. In one swift movement, he raised his arms and with them, a wall of iron came up, crunching through the snow as it raced around them.

Dante stomped his foot, kicking up an icy rock and sending it darting toward Amaya. She curled her finger into claws, her ice snapping the shards of rock into dust.

Nezha studied the wall before looking back at Zul. He wasn’t moving. And by his hip, he had a strange weapon. A blood-red scimitar of some kind, tucked into his green waist-wrapping. He wasn’t making any motion to unsheathe it. Why wasn’t he?

Behind Nezha, there was a small opening. The wall hadn’t closed off. Maybe they weren’t trapped in here after all.

Sapphire and Thunderbolt didn’t engage with the attacks, especially when Amaya was focused on Asad and Dante.

Instead, Sapphire flapped her wings once and stretched one of them. She held Comet, who remained in the bubble. "I think we are being kept from something."

"Yeah, Sapph, I agree," said Thunderbolt, stretching his arms.

Ice crackled across the snow and one spike shot up, barely missing Nezha's leg. Cold snaked up her side.

If she could help it, Nezha didn't want to fight Amaya. She was supposed to be on their side. But, she had to let go. Like she'd learned to. Let go and trust the fire.

Trust the Most High. The will of the Creator gifted her this power. She could still recall the time the fire disobeyed her when she'd first met Kayan, or when it followed the wind. She breathed in slowly and let her breath go.

Nezha angled her arms and made a punching motion toward Amaya. A fountain of fire sprang toward Amaya but too far left to hit her— a warning fire. The water jawhar was swift, as fluid as the ocean waves. Her arm arced and fast-moving water formed a blade, rounding over Nezha's back and nearly slipping over her shoulder. She watched as the water slit a part of her hijab away, tearing a thin strand from the bottom.

Amaya slid back just as Nezha unleashed twin flames, opening up like the jaws of a beast. The flare extended over Amaya's head, hissing and popping as it drew into a smoky trail behind her.

"We don't need to fight, Amaya."

"Leave and I won't." Amaya huffed and pushed her arms forward in the same motion that a wave swelled.

Kayan spun his arm, siphoning the burst of water as it torpedoed toward Nezha. With the other hand he pushed his palm up, the wind carrying the water into a spinning ball. He blew over it, and the ball opened, droplets falling over Amaya.

"Show off," Dante said with a laugh.

"Listen." Thunderbolt raised a hand. "Water can carry a current and metal's a good conductor, so if I were you two, I don't think I'd be fighting me. Lightning is messy, but you know that, don't ya, Zul Sharr?" He winked and Nezha saw Zul's jaw tighten.

What was Thunderbolt trying to do? She wasn't sure if that was enough to stop them from fighting—at least not Amaya.

***

Amaya wasn't going to be afraid of his masked threat. She'd been told the fox was here. If it wasn't for the wall, she would have frozen them all to the spot and left. But she couldn't go against what she'd been told to do. To fight them. And if she did, the fox would appear to her.

Amaya's hands trembled. The icy anger crept over her. Taking over her mind—so much that she'd almost forgotten what she'd wanted most. It wasn't just the answers from the fox, or justice for her papa. It was that comfort. To see Rin and Mama smile, to be by Tama's side, to be a great swimmer. Her dreams had been frozen, all because of this darkness inside her. This dark, bitter anger.

"Patience, Amaya. You can do it," Zul Sharr called out to her.

That's what she was trying to hold onto. The same way it was difficult to keep honey from dripping through your fingers. "Move aside and I will let you go." Amaya raised a hand, ice crackling up her palms and sharpening into an edge.

The jawhars were exchanging looks with each other. It was that easy. Just move out of her way. Why didn't they listen? After she'd dealt with her past, she'd gladly be on their side. Or she'd at least try to figure out which side could bring her back home the most easily.

By the gap of the wall, a figure slinked into view. The fox in his human form. His orange armor sat over a black kimono. One sleeve was splattered in white with orange angled lines. He waved a hand to her and flicked a jewel at his ear. He was here. He was here, and so close.

Amaya rushed forward. Her patience had been rewarded. Water droplets froze into spikes of ice as she rained them down on the jawhars. One of them used his wind to crush them in midair, and the girl with the flames melted the ones that nearly hit her.

The boy with the strange changing energy stood before her, waves of power drumming her head. There was no pain, but a heavy tap against her skin. It was like trying to push herself through an invisible wall. Her fingers curled.

What do you want, Amaya?

That voice. It didn't sound like the boy's at all. It was her own. What *she* wanted? She wanted to be back home. She wanted this all to stop. The water by her sides grew wild, twisting, spinning into whirlpools. A darkness touched the water and painted it all black. It shot out, bursting outward, and made the boy and his companions fly back.

Amaya couldn't see anything except the fox. It was all him. She rushed forward, no one stopping her now as the fox stood tall and grinned at her in welcome.

***

Zul watched as the black liquid burst into the air. The jawhars were sent flying. They'd hit his metal wall if he didn't hurry. He raised his arms and the metal fell into pools of liquid. He twisted his wrists, catching the jawhars and Nezha's cat. He tried to catch the angels, but Thunderbolt flew in midair and had made sure Sapphire and Nezha were safely in his arms.

He breathed out a sigh. Creator, he wouldn't let anyone die. Sharp pain lashed at his chest and he doubled over. It was at the spot where Lexa had marked him. The stinger of the scorpion over his heart. Where his anger made a home. A scorpion burrowed in his heart.

He wasn't sure how long he'd been able to keep the jinni aura back. It seemed it was a fight he had to keep struggling with as the aura coursed through his veins, passing through his heart. He groaned, the heat gasping into life over his chest. "Jawhars, you will not leave!"

"Zul!" Thunderbolt left Nezha and Sapphire and went straight for him, lightning dancing through his fingertips. The angel's face hardened as he faced him. A look that he'd become acquainted with after becoming Zul Sharr. "Break that curse over Unicorn Valley!" Thunderbolt swung his arm.

It was time to use Mamluk. Zul twisted and unsheathed the kilij sword. It sang as it met the lightning. Emitting a sharp, echoing sound, the sword seemed to laugh at the sparks popping against it. As if it defied the angel's anger.

“I will. I will break whatever chains hold us, Thunderbolt.” He meant every word. The hope inside him was making an effort to light his heart. It came in waves, breaking up. His hope was a star on the precipice of shattering.

“Us? There’s no *us*, while *you’re* around!” Thunderbolt shoved him back and blinked as the copper sword brightened. He was sure Thunderbolt’s words were aimed at the jinni-aura-filled blood in his veins. At what he’d become.

He had become Zul the Iron Prince with jinni magic in his blood.

“I’m still the Iron Prince. Please, don’t forget how we were! You were like a brother to me!” Zul pleaded. The name he had been given was his. Zul. And he wanted to shed “Sharr” from it. Couldn’t he possess more than the anger or pain inside him? Couldn’t hope and love make a home in his heart?

Had Thunderbolt forgotten the times they had been comrades? The nights they would look up at the stars eating snacks together? The times Thunderbolt brought over food that he’d baked, without the Queen knowing he had made the mess in the kitchen. The times they laughed and cried together? Shared how much the title of being a prince and a guardian angel crushed their hearts with the weight of responsibility? A lonely prince who didn’t know how to lead his own life. An guardian angel who was adored, but his life lead only by duty. A bond of friendship between them.

Thunderbolt scoffed. “Yeah, don’t bring up the past! Zul Sharr, you bring shame to the name of brotherhood. Eisen was my…friend. And I’ll make sure I rid the world of you.”

A film like a sheer silk cloth grew around Zul Sharr. Was it the kilij sword's energy? Whatever it was, it was protecting him. Zul's skin heated. Thunderbolt's words struck him sharper than any blade could, but he had to ignore how his own blood churned inside his veins.

The blood of these people would not be shed in vain. They didn't deserve their cruel end. But he'd make sure justice and a lasting peace would come of all this.

He watched as the other jawhars stumbled to their feet, their movement blurring in his eyes. His ears pounded with the growling anger of the jinni aura, the deafening voices of the jawhars.

And then he saw her. Amaya's legs carrying her to the end of the melted iron. To where the gap had been. Her arms stretched out before her. A man stood there. Zul had no doubt who he was. It was the fox jinni that could shapeshift into human form.

The parts of him that were Eisen and Zul began to muddle together.

"No one will die." No, he wasn't two different people. As darkness lidded his eyes, he thought of the reason his hope was catching light.

Oh Creator, his dua had power and Sanari was waiting for him.

Chapter 43 Rapids

A hard stare and a slow vulpine smile crossed the fox's face as if he'd been waiting for her too. But this wasn't like falling into a beloved's arms. Amaya was waiting to tear the truth from his throat, if not his jugular. That darkness engulfed her in its inky bloom.

"Fox!" She reached out, her nails coated in ice, and held them to his chin. He didn't so much as flinch.

"Usagi, you've been so tough to keep away," he drawled and that same smile, that easy smile, split his face, making his eyes shimmer bright yellow. She wanted to slap him.

Amaya didn't look back, not when Zul's voice roared into the night. Not when the other jawhars fought, not even when that energy hummed under her skin, skipping over her heart as if it were panic. As if it were something crying out to her. "You killed my father, didn't you? You took him!"

The fox raised a brow. He pinched his lower lip, as if he was choosing his words. "I did no such thing. Rather, you took something of mine." He was searching her eyes, staring at the side of her head for several seconds.

He had the audacity to accuse her? He'd killed her papa. Taking a life was worse than whatever she may have taken of his. Even so, her thoughts were muddled as she tried to imagine her papa and the fox's sharp teeth sinking into his arm. Or was it his shoulder? Was it her papa's neck? Was the fox even in human form that day? It didn't matter.

She waved her arms, the water drilling into the air, just as the fox leapt back. He stood straight, blue fireballs fluttering in his hands. When the liquid balls touched his flames, they simply grew into grey clouds, sighing away into the sky. Was it a wasted breath trying to fight him? She wanted answers but the heavy, bitter darkness inside her seized her heart.

Sweat poured down her back, her cheeks heating, even though winter's chill crept down her stomach. Nothing was going to stop her. She launched herself into the air by jumping and then building a wave, its frothy water babbling under her feet. He wasn't putting up too much of a fight as he tossed fireballs up at her.

She dove down, imagining herself diving into a pool at her university. The excitement of the fall hitting her skin, making her heart pound. She flipped in the air, the water gliding over her arms, pouring down her feet and circling there as she descended to the fox, both hands encrusted with ice as if they were a cluster of moonstones. Darkness was falling again, the sun sinking in the sky and the moon's ghost looking on. And under this moon, she knew she would triumph, right the wrongs he'd committed and punish him.

She wasn't falling into a pool of water; it was the shadows. It was the fox, his arms open, welcoming the rush of water as it shoved him, his body sliding across the dead grass and mud. When his body came to a stop, Amaya only saw bubbles until his face cleared into her vision and she fell on top of him.

The wet ground scraped against her elbows, pain cutting across her arms, her icy hands wrapping around his neck. His hand rose, one finger flicking her earring.

He made a choking sound and spoke. "Your earring is my—" He gasped and her fingers loosened, still pressed against his neck.

His pulse beat over her fingertips. She wasn't cruel. She'd let him have his say. She was panting as he spoke again, and what he said next made her wish she had tried her fate swimming back into the river, before she'd ever stepped into the forest. "... my spirit."

***

"Sanari is alive!" Zul said it so loudly that even the snowy trees trembled at the weight of his confession.

Thunderbolt's hardened expression from before took a sudden change. His lips parted. "What?" He couldn't believe it. Was the part of him that was once Eisen still inside? Sanari was alive.

Zul's eyes brightened into that piercing orange. He growled and lunged for Thunderbolt with his blade. The tip skimmed past his shoulder. The blade wasn't aimed at him at all. It was who was behind him.

Sanari was alive. Thunderbolt's heart was as at ease as a soft silk cushion for lounging on. Sanari was alive. That meant—by the Creator! The unicorns of Unicorn Valley were alive. His parents had to be alive. And that meant he needed to rid the world of Zul Sharr.

Eisen was still in there. He'd seen the softness in his eyes, right before those same eyes burned with malicious intent. Before they burned in an orange only making him think of the burning that had plagued the prince's heart.

Thunderbolt hadn't forgotten Eisen. How could he forget when they confided their pain to each other one day. How always following duties and commands made his heart feel like stone.

Being Eisen's guardian had been a great opportunity for him to be more confident. At the time, Sapphire had always been the one who everyone relied on. He had been deligated to the one who was a strong warrior and made others laugh. And he had been bringing her down. He didn't want his elder sister to take care of him as if he was a pathetic child to look after.

With the Iron Kingdom Qadam and Fire Kingdom Wadi Alma's growing bonds, they needed a guardian angel. And Qadam wanted one for their prince. Thunderbolt hadn't hesitated at the chance.

He'd never expected he would be anything but a guard at the Iron Kingdom. Not until Eisen would talk to him and ask him how his day was. It was annoying at first. He didn't care what Eisen wanted to say. He would tease the prince relentlessly. That maybe *that* would shut him up. But, the boy was strange. He simply laughed it off.

Then, Eisen pried into his heart and pulled out dreams he never knew existed inside him. Wants and desires beyond the duty of being a guardian. Wants and desires to befriend someone.

A head of red appeared, and green eyes so bright, they glowed as the sun sunk deeper. The shadow jinni Lexa met his gaze and tore him from his thoughts. Her sharp nails were just an inch from Thunderbolt's face as he'd swung his head back.

“Lexa,” Zul Sharr growled and a strange grin split his lips.

Lexa chuckled. “Zul Sharr. The angels are not my priority. At least not yet.”

Thunderbolt unleashed the lightning. It forked through the air and popped as it struck Lexa before her feet.

“Peace to you too, angel,” Lexa drawled and her body blurred, taking her human form several feet away, appearing in a shroud of silky darkness.

“You have a death wish?” Thunderbolt called out to her. He didn’t want to waste his time on the likes of her. The sooner they could get Amaya on their side, the better.

Sapphire and the other jawhars ran up to him upon seeing Lexa.

“Are you okay?” Nezha’s palms were still lit by trembling flames as her gaze shifted from his to Lexa’s.

“Oh, this jinni again.” Asad cracked his knuckles.

“Damn, it’s a showdown,” declared Dante.

A part of Thunderbolt was okay. The other was more than that. Sanari was alive. There was still a chance to rid Unicorn Valley of the iron’s curse. And Zul Sharr was in his way. He needed him out. “Zul!” Thunderbolt snarled and lunged for him.

A shot of darkness erupted into the air before him. Feathers zipped through the darkening sky. “Wrong way, angel,” Lexa said, smiling at him. Her fingers were laced with her shadow magic as she crept closer. She tilted her head back and laughed.

Rana appeared beside her in a cloud of grey and the same black feathers scattered around her.

Thunderbolt was getting sick of the jinn getting in his way. It was always their sickening magic, its bitter scent, the way it defied the laws of the Creator. He'd had enough of them and their darkness. "Crow jinni." He rolled his eyes and a raucous laugh escaped his lips.

Lightning strands slithered out from his fingertips, dancing a path toward Lexa, joined by Nezha's flames. In waves of energy, Rana fluttered before him and opened her arms, feathers lilting before her face. Their attack was absorbed by the feathers as they brightened into white particles and gathered before Rana's chest. She breathed in and they melted into her skin.

"Satiating." Rana licked her lips.

His heart thudded. He had to stop them. "Stop, she's taking our power—" This was bad. This was...too late, no matter if the others could hear him or not. They'd already flown into action. Asad's energy bursts popped, Dante's rocks and ice were unearthed and Sapphire's light beams pulsed. But all of it dwindled to glowing white dots, absorbed by Rana with a deep sigh.

"Did she just suck up the power in our attacks? 'cause I feel it," Asad said, his hand tightening into a fist.

It was Kayan alone who stood afar and didn't make a move, Comet by his side in her bubble. "Yeah..." His fingers tapped the hilt of his sword Ali.

"I don't believe you're dolts, are you?" Lexa opened her arms. "You wanted Amaya. Well, she's here. You wanted Noorenia's heartbeat to be strong? Fight. Did you want all of that and expect me not to curse you?" Her lips curled. Shadows gathered around her. It was the sickening miasma reeking of magic and evil so pungent, it invaded Thunderbolt's mind, crawled over his skin.

"Don't breathe it—!" Kayan said, his fingers gripping his sword, the blade nearly curling out, but then his whole arm shook and he didn't move again. And Thunderbolt knew then, it was too late. But it wasn't. It couldn't be.

"Damn you!" Thunderbolt and Sapphire jumped into action, but his leg muscles tightened, the blood in his ears pounding over the noise of the others groaning and struggling. He couldn't move. They couldn't move. Lexa had dared to do this to them. He was as still as a statue, frozen like his family and friends in the valley. A horrific thought. He breathed heavily, his head, his whole body trembling. He had to move. He couldn't just stand here. No. Not like his friends.

He was supposed to get rid of Zul. Eisen was supposed to undo that curse. Thunderbolt and the others weren't meant to be cursed too.

The heartbeat of the land fluttered under his feet. Its thready pulse was weak. He had this mortal form. An angel, but also a unicorn. A guardian born to defend and protect both humans and unicorns. That's why Lexa could do this to them. That's why as hard as he tried to wriggle or roll his shoulders, he couldn't move. Noorenia was truly mourning. Their connection to all the energy, all the life, was being severed.

Lexa reached a hand toward Rana. The crow jinni pressed her lips to Lexa's palm. "You may have them, Jaanaana." Rana's cold, dark eyes widened, her tongue protruding.

"Thank you. I will savor their energy." Rana licked her lips. Her face was reddening as she stepped closer to him and Sapphire.

He couldn't move. He couldn't even speak now. His tongue simply pressed against his teeth. The others—Nezha, Kayan, the two new jawhars—were forced to watch. All he could do was stare as small white spots floated away from him and Sapphire and were drawn to Rana.

"Toray khaoray sha!" Lexa said with a laugh. *Become black dust!*

All Thunderbolt saw was a deep green. The green he wished was Noorenia's open plains, a brocade decorated with flowers, with life jumping and moving through it. Green sweeping in the spring rain as it formed into rolling paths. He yearned for that movement. But this green wasn't the ground. Snow was embracing it.

It was Zul Sharr's waist-wrap dancing in the breeze. His back to Thunderbolt, he turned and Thunderbolt saw his face. Tears glistened at his eyes and his outstretched hand was pointing at Rana.

Rana made a choking sound as her arm moved like that of a puppet as if dangled by strings. Her arm curled back, and then, his skin prickled.

Lexa grinned. "Congratulations, Zul Sharr, you have learned how to move blood."

Chapter 44 Play Your Part

What had he done? Zul felt the tears roll down his face as he stood there, hand reaching out, Rana's arm twisting as she stared back at him. "Please, stop, Rana."

As he lowered his arm, he closed his eyes shut for several moments. He couldn't look at what he'd done. Moving her blood as the energy pulsed at his fingertips. Why had it felt as simple as taking a step?

"I need a villain, so play your part." Lexa swiped a finger across his cheek, her touch hot over the dark lines rippling across his face. And there was that strange soft, almost sad smile across her lips.

Nightfall had consumed the sky, a body of deep blues and patches of purple. The darkness he knew was warring with his own body, as evidenced by the unseen bruises on his aching heart, and the jinni aura running through his blood.

He turned to Thunderbolt, seeing his wide eyes. Confusion, understanding, something of the sort swam in the angel's eyes and Zul just knew he would have trouble. Whatever it was, he was glad he looked at him without anger or burning hatred for once.

Sharp, pulsing energy shot through Zul's veins. He gasped out a cry and his fingers curled. No. No! He had to fight it. Sanari would awaken. He gasped for air and tore at his long thobe, loosening the button at his neck. "Stop..." he rasped out.

Hope. Hope is the light you'll burn over, foolish prince, the jinni aura's voice rumbled in his head.

I refuse. Zul had to hold on. *Creator have mercy...*

The killing you are avoiding will happen!

I'm not afraid of you, jinni!

Curse you! The aura whimpered as Zul felt it ripple in his body.

Zul Sharr refused to surrender. He'd keep fighting it off. Even if he fell to his knees. He wouldn't stop trying to get himself back. Whoever *he* was.

***

Zul stood before them, facing Lexa and Rana. One hand firmly on the hilt of his sword. Even if he wasn't making a move, he was still in between them and Amaya.

Nezha breathed deeply. Her skin warmed and movement returned to her and her companions. Her gaze shifted to Thunderbolt as his brows furrowed.

"Sanari's alive." He turned to Nezha and the others.

"What?" For a few moments, it was as if the words held no weight. Then her whole chest warmed as she realized what he'd just declared. Sanari was alive? How was Thunderbolt so sure? Had the Iron Prince truly been taking care of Sanari all this time?

"Eisen loves her. There's no way he'd be making anything up when it's about the princess." He seemed so sure, his face so serious, it aged him. Nezha had no more doubts.

"Sanari is *alive*." Zul Sharr turned to meet Nezha's gaze, the burning orange striking against the black of his kohl-rimmed eyes. "She's alive. She was my everything, when I was nothing. Such is love. Love is everything, yet nothing. It promises you nothing but becomes your everything. By the Most Merciful, I will break the curse on her."

Neither Lexa, nor Rana, nor Zul were making a move for Nezha and her companions. Kayan was standing beside her, the wind barely fluttering over her shoulders. The two jinn were simply watching as Thunderbolt held his arm close to his face. His blade was concealed along his forearm, ready to strike. "We can assure it by getting Eisen back!" Thunderbolt thrusted his arm into the air and strode toward Zul.

Zul deflected the shots of lightning with his sword's blade. They hardly affected it; rather, a warble sounded from the sword as it pulsed out an energy, blurring the air around it.

In the distance, Nezha saw Amaya clash with the fox jinni. He was in his human form, throwing balls of fire at her.

Thunderbolt launched into his attack, his curved sword clashing with Zul's as the prince raised his arm in defence.

The lightning burst like pockets of starlight in the darkness. Thunderbolt's strikes and punches weren't dealing any damage. The Iron Prince's skin was unmarked, except for the lines that ran over his skin on half of his face.

Every time Thunderbolt drove his sword into the Iron Prince, his blade didn't pierce him. There was an invisible barrier protecting Zul. And Zul would simply defend himself, the blade catching to meet Thunderbolt's blade in return.

Nezha glanced at Lexa and Rana again. They still did not move. They simply stood in pools of shadow, elevated from the ground, watching. Were they waiting for something?

Kayan's voice sprang into the night air. "Stop it, Thunderbolt!"

Thunderbolt didn't stop until Kayan raised his arm, summoning the wind and raising the angel's arm into the air.

"Don't you see it? He's not even fighting back. We can't waste our time like this."

Zul made no move. He simply kept his arms down, the loose cloth of his white turban dancing in the wind. He met Thunderbolt's gaze, his eyes soft despite the orange flickering in his eyes.

"We need to help Amaya." Kayan held Thunderbolt's arm with his wind.

Thunderbolt groaned and broke his gaze from Zul. He dropped his arm and stepped away from the prince. Nezha could see it on his face. The way his jaw was set, how difficult it was for Thunderbolt to step away from the person he wanted so badly to right the wrongs that had been done to him, his sister and the unicorns in the valley.

Nezha placed a hand on his shoulder. This was a change for him. The angel—the unicorn—who would not step down from a fight. But now he must have been thinking about someone other than his own victory. He must have been thinking about Noorenia, all of them, not the person he wanted to end. His desire to prevent Noorenia's destruction was greater than his anger.

"For Noorenia's victory," Nezha began solemnly. "Flowers may wither."

Thunderbolt met her gaze, and then whispered back, his voice catching. "Roots will be the anchor."

***

"Your spirit?" Amaya's voice caught. What was he talking about? It shouldn't have mattered, but she couldn't stop the guilt from creeping into her chest. The fox's spirit. She had taken his spirit?

"Give me my hoshi no tama and I will reward you." He turned his palm up at her.

He was speaking in Japanese. Had he followed her from back home? His blue flames spun past her and she jumped off him, stumbling back.

"I don't want anything from you."

"Don't be hasty, Usagi. You said you wanted answers, didn't you?" He grinned up at her, dodging the icicles she launched at him, skimming past his face. He knelt beside her. "Give it to me and I'll give you the answers you seek."

Maybe she would have to indulge him. "Tell me what happened that night." She knew the legends about the foxes back home. But, what was he? Was he a demon like the kitsune or something else entirely? All she knew was this world was strange, and yet, so familiar. She remembered now. If you gave one back its spirit, it would give you something. But she couldn't remember what that exactly was.

"Good. Isn't it nice to communicate?" He stood, his face was too close to hers now. His warm breath caressed her cheek.

She formed another icy blade in her palm. "Tell me what you'll give me."

"In exchange for *my spirit*, my hoshi no tama, I will grant you one wish. A promise."

A wish. She could find out what happened to Papa. She could...leave this place. But this was a dilemma. She didn't want to make a deal with a demon. By the Creator, if she did, wouldn't that harm her own soul? She exhaled. Wasn't her soul already darkened by Lexa's curse? A sharp pain pressed against her head.

She wanted this darkness gone. But she wanted to know what had happened. Had the fox really killed him? She also didn't want to be here anymore. She wanted to be with Mama and Rin and Tama. She missed them so much. She'd been pulled into this world of people like her. People that could command the elements. She didn't want to be here, but there was this strange comfort and one part of her liked it. The other part of her was homesick. She was so sick of never being able to know what to do. What was the right choice?

"What if I refuse to give it to you?" Amaya gulped.

"Why would you do that? I'd have to take it by force." His eyes sharpened and he grabbed her arm, his finger trailing down her cheek. "And I really don't want to do that."

Amaya shoved him and brought another wave of water splashing into the air. She wasn't sure what to do. In a way she felt bad that his spirit was gone. That she had it.

He must have been telling the truth. Foxes kept their hoshi no tama carried in their mouths or tails. He didn't have anything. To think, all this time her earring was his spirit. Somehow, that must have been the reason her okaasan was able to talk to her. It had power. It must have been a link, since they both owned a pair.

"Do we have a deal?"

Amaya's lips parted. She should do it, but she wasn't sure what her wish was yet. "Ah..."

Then, a blast of energy slammed into the fox, along with a gust of wind. Hands of the snowy earth erupted underneath him, and grabbed him, keeping him suspended above the ground in their grasp.

It came from three of the elementals, and they were closing in on her.

***

Nezha clasped Thunderbolt's hand as Sapphire pulled her brother's arm and met his gaze. "We must protect Amaya." The way Sapphire said it was strained. Her gaze soon shifted to the snowy field, as if she was looking for something or someone.

"Yeah, duty before desire." Thunderbolt squeezed Sapphire's arm and then turned to Lexa, her shadows trailing the ground.

“I don’t have the sabr for this right now.” Lexa pinched the bridge of her nose and waved an arm. Shadows spilled out from her hands and twisted their way to Nezha and the angels.

Nezha stood before the angels and brought her arms to her chest, flames hissing into twin blades licking the air.

As soon as her fire blazed, Zul Sharr moved into action, raising his blade to the plume of shadows. The darkness avoided the sword and a gap formed between Zul and the magic.

Zul was really protecting them. She wasn’t sure why and how. His eyes were glowing again, burning as he gritted his teeth and groaned. His fingers trembled over the hilt.

Thunderbolt grimaced and sighed. “Boys, you go and support Amaya!”

Nezha wasn’t sure when, but Kayan came to stand beside her, his fingers tapping over the hilt of his sword, Ali.

“What about you three?”

“Stop worrying about us!” Thunderbolt turned to him. “You, Asad and Dante need t’ go. She’ll need your powers.”

“We need Amaya, and I got this, Kayan.” Nezha nodded to him. She could control her fire better than she used to, and even if the night air was filled with the miasma of magic, she kept thinking of everyone and what was at stake. Noorenia needed its heartbeat restored. She needed it. She needed it to be alive again. Creator—he was on her side and she would keep her spirits high as best she could.

“Okay, Nayzak.” Kayan grinned at her and she smiled. Bright, kind, there was that familiar peace that embraced her heart and mind whenever Kayan met her gaze. It felt like there was a lifetime of understanding between them.

He renewed her hope. She stared at the jinn before her. "Do you know that hope is a small voice that says you want to be you, not who someone tells you to be? It says better days will come! And I am not afraid!"

They faced Lexa and Rana, with Zul Sharr standing between them, still refusing to budge. Shadows made a wall before them; the only way to go was behind. To where Amaya was fighting the fox.

"Sapph, go t' the boys." Thunderbolt turned to his sister. He was showing that side of him—the side where he pushed people into action.

Sapphire made fists. "I cannot leave your side."

"You're more level-headed than the boys, so you need to."

He tried to reason with her, and Nezha could see it in Sapphire's eyes. That pain she'd hardly seen Sapphire show before. She really was letting her walls down.

"I don't...want to lose you, and I want to see Obsidian again." The way Sapphire closed her eyes at her confession made Nezha's chest ache. It must have been so hard to admit it.

Thunderbolt stared at Sapphire in shock for several seconds before looking at her in a soft gaze. "Sheikh, that was a sermon I've been waiting t' hear you say. Confessions are terrible." He smiled weakly at her. "Listen, you've always trusted me in a fight. I have Nezha. I'm not alone. *We're* not alone."

Sapphire sighed. "Thariq, if you, Nezha or Comet are harmed, I will come running back to pummel the shadow jinni, *and* you, myself."

Thunderbolt grinned.

“Flowers may wither,” Sapphire said and she started walking back.

“Roots will be the anchor,” Nezha and Thunderbolt echoed.

***

Teamwork was one of Kayan’s strong suits. At least when the others liked him. He wasn’t sure if Asad and Dante would get along with him as much as he wanted to with them.

Amaya spun around to look at them.

“Don’t worry, Amaya,” Kayan said as he reached her. “We’re here to—” He was taken aback when ice crept up her fingers and she pointed the sharp points in their direction.

“Don’t interfere.” Amaya’s steely gaze passed through them.

Dante just scrunched his lips at her voice, incredulous to her attitude.

Sapphire came to stand by Kayan, her hand at her necklace, her other palm filled with a pulsing light.

Water rushed out from Amaya’s fingertips, but Kayan was prepared for her attack. He raised his arms, the wind spinning around them, and formed a ball, as if it was a dome that kept them out of Amaya’s reach.

“Now that we have some privacy, I have an idea.” Kayan turned to them. At this point, all he could do was offer what he wanted to try.

“Okay, shoot,” Dante said, raising a brow at him.

Maybe he would listen to his idea, but, Kayan was trying to fight off the thoughts in his own head. He already wanted to see Nezha again, and he was worried about what would happen to Noorenia. His mind was faster than his tongue, sometimes.

Asad gave him a small smile. "It'll probably be random."

"Hey, don't underestimate me already!" Kayan countered. Ah, Divine's sake, this was not going to be easy if they were already doubting him. Then, he told them his idea.

"You think that'll work?" Dante paused for a moment. "Man, you clever son of a—"

"It sounds fun and, well, my intuition seems to agree with you, even if I think it's kinda random," Asad said and bumped shoulders with Dante.

Kayan wasn't expecting them to react the way they did. Maybe they were relying on him, since they weren't from here. But, relying on *him*? It was so much pressure. Kayan just had to move the way he always did. He took a breath in. The moment, the feelings—that's what he had to focus on. That's what would get him through it.

Kayan grinned back at them.

***

Water bubbled in her palms. "This is between me and the fox." The water flowed through the air, rushing toward them.

Then, the wind redirected the water, gliding it through the night air. The energy from it pulsed gently, making Asad see it in his mind's eye.

Whatever Kayan intentioned from this, all Asad knew was that he'd go along. Especially when his intuition strongly agreed with the wind jawhar. And Asad always agreed with his intuition. He'd always trusted it ever since he'd noticed it. The way the energy moved in his throat. And whenever he started asking it questions and getting answers. It had been an experiment he started. When it all became a pattern and then a coincidence. By the fourth or fifth time, he'd stopped thinking it was just a coincidence and that it was something greater than he could imagine. It was all fate. It was all a part of him. A part that the Creator had gifted him with. While animals were given instinct, humans were given insight.

As Kayan kept up with Amaya's water, gliding it with the wind and as Amaya unleashed it every time, Asad focused on her energy. He breathed in and every few moments, he would imbue her spirit with joyful and calm emotions. After all, the world was all energy. Moving, refracting, spinning to form their physical world.

And so, Amaya was moving with the flow of her own water attacks; Kayan, sending them back to her to flow and dance by her side. Dante brought up small rounds of stone where Amaya would be gently pushed by the wind. She had no other choice but to step on them. One step and then she spun around, stepping onto another piece of stone, and more as if she was going up a stairwell. Her water rained down on her and the hum of Asad's energy enveloped her like a familiar song. Just as Kayan had planned with them. That they should allow her to feel her powers freely. It was a dance.

Two steps, and Asad's heart pounded. He was really enjoying this too. Three more steps and Amaya was gently airborne. The swirling energy points in her body were in the sky, the only thing Asad could see in his mind, as if she was a constellation.

The emotions, the energy in her body spun faster, and Asad's skin prickled at her echoed delight. The hum was a sweet sound caressing his mind, like a mother's gentle touch comforting her crying child.

After so long, he wasn't bombarded by someone's crippling sadness or tearful fears. It was Amaya's awe, her joy and comfort in their situation that flowed through the energy in his own body. Asad, the soul jawhar, the emotional sponge who was scared of letting anyone think he needed support. He was allowing the walls to come down. Even if this was a fleeting moment, he wanted to relish how much happiness it gave her and him. A small voice whispered: "It's okay. It's really okay."

***

What was this feeling? As if she didn't need to think of anything outside of herself. Amaya closed her eyes for just a moment, hearing that sweet hum. She'd been irritated at first, when one of the boys returned her own water back to her. When the water flowed alongside her, the sound a shush, quieting her mind and a gentleness against her heart, she couldn't stop herself from going along with it.

Lifted into the sky, she caught sight of the fox, his body in the clutches of stone and snow. Then, there was the thought of her papa. She couldn't be like this. Heaviness weighed in her chest, the black dress tightening around her waist and up her arms.

Her arms spun, the water growing into a spinning mass. She soaked the chunks of rock and soil and flung them onto the three boys, the mud becoming ice. The angel who had been with them widened her arms, light rays bursting outward, crushing the ice. The four stared at Amaya as she turned her back on them. Her heart was thudding. This wasn't about her. She needed to do this for her family.

Chapter 45 Gather 'Round

The moon was round and bright as Savan turned to the jinni beside him. "Yusha, it's time."

The dog jinni Yusha wore a calm expression. It didn't seem like anything bothered him. Not even the chill winter air. The wind danced through his long silver tresses. He spoke in a smooth voice. "Are you certain?"

Savan pressed his hand to his heart. "As certain as the darkness embracing the moon."

Yusha's ear flicked and he gave all his attention to Savan, taking a step forward. His eyes, which were once a golden amber, turned bright red. "Our Lady is waiting."

"Yes." Savan swallowed. To think, all the pieces were being placed. His lady was gathering them. Yusha, a jinni Savan only saw in passing. He'd seen the dog jinni taking messages, a loyal errand boy. Tonight, he saw something far darker in the jinni. A delight, a wanting he'd never seen, gleaming in his eyes.

Even as Savan felt the magic ebb in the air, inside Yusha's blood, he felt it stronger, smelled the sweet, dark scent.

"For our lady. To our freedom." Savan placed a hand on Yusha's chest. It was silent. There was no heartbeat. His fingers twitched and he pressed his hand to his heart. After all, Yusha was moving only thanks to the magic their lady had gifted him. He was the walking dead. That was all Savan knew of the once-devout jinni.

Savan rose his arm, shadows spilling out like a silk dupatta. "This way, Yusha Sahib."

Without another word, Yusha passed him, entering through the shadow door. His black shalwar kameez blurred into the shadows as Savan followed, both disappearing through.

***

At every turn, Zul Sharr stood before Nezha, his sword keeping Lexa's shadows from touching her and her companions. The scorpion mark on his neck blurred and reappeared as he moved. Somehow, his heart must have been waging war against the magic corrupting him.

Thunderbolt cracked his knuckles. Lexa raised a brow.

The flames draped across Nezha's arms, lining the bottom hem of her long navy kameez. For the first time in what felt like forever, Nezha felt her lungs squeeze. She'd been used to holding her breath before coming to Noorenia; she'd had to do so in order to smother her flames. But now, after so much time spent among her own kind—jawhars—she'd become complacent. And with the land itself at stake, she was more nervous than ever. She couldn't breathe.

Silence cut through the air. Zul Sharr's fingers were still clutching the strange sword, Lexa's shadows never daring to touch the blade. Thunderbolt stood beside her, electricity buzzing around him. Both jinn and jawhars were at a standstill, as if they each held a scimitar to each other's throats. One wrong move, and there would be blood.

A few feet from Lexa and Rana, a spot of darkness rippled like a mirage in the sky. It grew until a smoky form shaped like a door appeared. From it, two human-like forms walked out. She could only stare in open horror for several moments. It couldn't be. Not him.

Savan. Savan walked out through that opening. Savan, the jinni she had nearly killed so many months ago. The jinni who had been responsible for her aunt's death. A literal monster of her past. A door she never imagined would open again. And now, it slammed open in her face. Beside him was someone she'd never seen. Right away, her gaze was glued to the two pointed ears on the top of his head, then his long silvery hair and glowing red eyes. In them, she saw a glint.

***

That scent of magic enrobed Savan. The lack of it had coated his tongue in bitterness, but now, with it perfuming the air, it was sweetness. It made it sweeter when his gaze met hers. His lady. That night he'd seen her felt like it had been years past. His breath caught as they both stared at each other. She was as beautiful as she had been that night. Her prowess and grace multiplied by the magic, as if it gave the energy around her an edge, as sharp as a blade. The prickling sharp energy skimmed his skin.

Savan walked up to her, their gazes never flinching never wavering. He wrapped a hand around her waist, pulling her in, his other hand closing around her head. He pressed his lips to her forehead.

***

"My Lady," Savan breathed out.

"Oh, jaanana," Lexa tipped his head back and pressed a kiss to his cheeks.

Lexa was the jinni he was embracing. She was the jinni he held tightly as Nezha's eyes remained open in shock. Lexa was his lady, the one who was also responsible for Lamis's death. She couldn't believe it, even as she saw it unfold before her. It couldn't be true. Her throat closed up, tears pushing at her eyes as she saw Savan embracing Lexa, kissing her, holding her.

Rana was walking away from Lexa when the shadow jinni grabbed her hand and pulled her to her side.

Both Lexa and Savan clasped Rana's hands. Savan pressed his other hand to his heart and nodded to the crow jinni. Nezha didn't want to keep looking, but the more she did, the more she wanted to refuse it was really happening. As if it was a scene in a movie.

Lexa dipped her head and kissed Rana's hand. "Both of you must stay by my side."

"Lexa!" Nezha pushed her hand forward, fire spouting out, spitting and crackling its way to the jinn. She felt her tears hot against her cheeks.

Lexa and Savan both raised a hand as if they were only swatting a bothersome fly, the flames dying out into smoke.

"Nezha... We meet again, fire jawhar. Have you forgotten my promise? Our word is our honor." Savan placed a hand to his heart once again.

"We shadow jinn won't go back on our word." Lexa bit her lip and then laughed.

"You murdered a whole city!" Nezha's hands trembled, her face heating. All those innocent people gone... "You have blood on your hands!" She and the flames were one, just as they always were. The heat, the pressure and the crackling sped through her veins. Right now, she didn't care where the fire began and where she ended.

"I'd shed all the blood I want if it'd free the jinn your kind have imprisoned," Lexa sneered.

Nezha gritted her teeth. "And I'll fight you with my everything to free us all."

"Divine's sake. You shaitan!" Thunderbolt raised an arm, but the dog jinni sped to them, moving as fast as an arrow. He brought his claws to the angel's jaw. The joints in his fingers cracked.

Zul was swift, his sword pressing against the dog jinni's wrist. "Back away, Yusha. I don't want to hurt you."

Yusha was searching Zul Sharr's eyes and then, he obeyed the prince's command. He stumbled back and hissed as his arm fell to his side. For a few moments, it looked like he was in pain, his forehead creasing and his eyes lidded. Then he took his place by the other three jinn.

"Nah, don't be hasty, angel. We're not that wasteful with blood." Savan pressed his head to Lexa's and laughed with her.

"You take us as prey..." Nezha felt the heat embrace her, a beloved's warmth. A passion growing deeper in her chest, and she welcomed it.

"My vow is in place, jawhar. Don't touch my lady and I will not touch any of you." Savan's fingers entwined with Lexa's and Rana's.

Nezha shook her head and scoffed. "What, do you want me to turn around and forget what you've done? I can forgive you, but all those lives you've ended won't come back!" Flaring and hissing, the flames came to life in her upturned palms, ready to strike.

"So, you have chosen violence?" Savan asked.

He really thought she was doing wrong? Her chest tightened and she inhaled sharply. "You shed blood, you violated a pure soul, you ambushed us... I chose to protect!"

Nezha raised her arm. It was time she used the feather, now that it was with her again. The feather... That was the only physical thing they had left of the Angel of Mercy. By the Creator, Nezha wouldn't give in. Noorenia was dying, people were dying.

She blew on the feather and that piercing bird call made her soul resonate, her skin prickling at the sound. It felt so good to hear it again. She pulled the sword away from its gold cuff. The bright blue flames sputtered out and hissed to life.

She glanced at Thunderbolt, who placed a hand on her head and gently inquired, "You ready?"

Nezha took a breath in and with a curt nod she gave him a small smile. She'd never really been ready. She'd been pulled into this world and she'd let it push her. She'd been pulled by the angel's will and she'd let it push her. Now, her own love and faith pulled her in. Its gravity was far stronger than any magic the jinn threatened them with.

With Thunderbolt by her side, she brandished her flaming sword, advancing for the three jinn before her. Savan gave Lexa one more kiss on her cheek and faced Nezha, shadows spooling out behind him.

***

The water swayed at her feet, the way the trees lent their leaves to the wind, inviting the seasonal changes. Here, Amaya stood, inviting the change she yearned for. To find that calm, that happiness she'd felt. Those boys were like her. She couldn't deny that she was already missing the feelings. She glanced at the fox.

"You don't have to listen to Lexa," the boy with the brown hair was saying. The one the wind obeyed.

The angel spoke to him. "We must let her go."

"But, Sapphire—"

Sapphire closed her eyes and shook her head.

Amaya stared at them. A strange calm passed between them, but she couldn't let that distract her. She struck her arm through the air, water as sharp as blades cutting through the rock and ice that held the fox.

"Do you have your wish?" The fox jinni held a hand out and flicked his ear with a smile.

"I smell more magic. It's getting worse." The wind jawhar made a face. "We need to get back to Nezha and Thunderbolt!"

Amaya wanted to go home, but what would happen? Would he really give her that wish, or would it go wrong? She'd seen it happen in movies and shows. A powerful creature granting you three wishes, but never truly giving you what you wanted. What was she supposed to—

"Amaya dear," Lexa's voice echoed into her head. No. She didn't want her in her head again, or the cold that was slipping up her spine now. Lexa continued, "Why don't you join us?" Her voice sounded sweet—so smooth in her mind, it caressed the panic shooting through her chest.

Shadows hugged her waist, wrapping their hands up her arms. Before she could think of anything to reply with, her body moved on its own. She turned on her heel, the fox, and the crackle of ice, behind her.

Chapter 46 Enemies

The inky shadows bloomed into the air, wrapping around Nezha. She gulped, feeling the heat prick at her skin, the shadows nearly brushing against her.

She couldn't lie and say she wasn't scared. She was so scared. Her heart felt like it was going to jump out of her chest. She was scared she'd die. Scared that she would be corrupted by the magic, but…her faith in the Creator was stronger. She was stronger. She wanted to protect Noorenia and her friends. She wanted to protect a place she felt at home in. A place where she could wield her fire freely. What she wanted was stronger than her fear. And so, she raised her hand, the sword's blue flames a soft hiss. The shadows shrunk back from the blade and from her at its burning light. The warmth bathed her in its embrace. The cold of winter was hardly palpable. *Creator...* Her arms were tense, but still, she drew closer to the two shadow jinn.

Savan and Lexa faced her. The shadow jinni tilted his head back at her, but his lips were pressed into a thin line.

She returned his expression with a wry smile. "Shadow jinni…careful of the light I cast. It burns bright, and your shadows *will* retreat." For a moment, Nezha saw his eyes widen, and in them she saw it. Fear.

Savan took a step, as if he was trying to push his way closer, but Zul Sharr had been a shadow Nezha didn't mind following her.

The Iron Prince held his sword out too. Their blades were side by side. Nezha stared at him for several seconds.

The prince had never left their side. These moments, she knew he was being himself. Whatever parts of himself he held on to. She met his gaze for a moment and saw a small gentle smile. She smiled back and together they faced the jinn. The shadows blinked in and out of existence, not accepting the warmth or the positive energy the swords hummed with. Nezha liked to think it was their own faith and love too. Their own need to protect. Lexa pulled Savan back, their bodies blurring and reappearing several feet away.

There was something strange about the prince's sword. Even though the prince's veins coursed with magic and jinni aura, the glow in his eyes blinking in and out as if they were a collection of dying stars—it was protecting him. It was emitting a strange yet calming energy around her. And she was glad it was one the jinn couldn't bear to be in the presence of.

Nezha caught the way Lexa looked at Zul Sharr. And, for the first time, she didn't see her smile. It was a strange, sad look, with a sharpened gaze. She wasn't exactly sure what it meant. Soon, the shadows swept in, filling the gaps around the jinn again.

"Oh, Sire, haven't you grown tired of protecting them? It's too much of a burden if you ask me." Lexa sighed and lifted her hands. "No more, Zul Sharr. I won't have you wielding that sword." The darkness feathered out from her hands and the shadow knives formed between her fingers. She flung them at Zul, the knives piercing his skin.

Nezha knew Lexa wanted to overpower Zul with fear. The jinni had done the same to her and the others before. She was taken aback that Lexa had done such a thing to the person she'd been protecting and guiding all this time. But Nezha wasn't that surprised. After all, the prince kept defending her and Thunderbolt. He'd become a threat in Lexa's eyes.

Zul's eyes widened, the orange glow deeper, almost a blood-red as he gasped. His body seemed to stiffen as his arms pressed to his sides and the sword slipped from his fingers, dropping to the snow.

Lexa walked up to him and kicked the strange sword aside. She pressed a finger to his chest. "I'm sorry," she whispered.

Nezha saw his fingers tremble and his eyes search Lexa's when he groaned.

"I won't let even *you* get in my way." It was a soft voice she spoke in, one that hit Nezha with fear, as if one of the knives had struck her. It was a soft, yet threatening tone.

"Eisen!" Thunderbolt blurted the prince's name in such a sad tone. She rubbed his shoulder as he closed his eyes, the pain on his face pinching his expression. Even after all this time, Thunderbolt had been hiding how much guilt he felt about the prince and his pain.

At Lexa's fingertip, shadows spilled out, wrapping around his chest, the marks over half of his face inked in the gaps that had begun fading.

"Now, Sire, play your part."

Zul Sharr's lips turned up in a smile. After several seconds, he grimaced. In a husky voice he said, "I'm your villain."

Electricity popped and made a trail around them. The shadow jinn and crow jinni didn't make a move again. Not until Nezha felt a warmth in her chest and a sudden energy tapped in her heart, a familiar energy growing closer.

Lexa's and Savan's fingers entangled with one another's, sending out a blast of shadows. Nezha stood her ground, head up, the fire ready to be beckoned.

***

The hum inside Amaya's chest burned. The kind of burn when ice met her skin for too long and pressed into her bones. Not this again. She didn't want to feel that cold snaking under her skin. Mama, Rin, Tama... Their memories slipped in and out of her mind. She'd wanted to go home and be with them. The way things were. The way things used to be, before she found out she could control water, or that the earring she'd been wearing since she was a child was actually a demon's spirit.

The fox was on her heels as she answered Lexa's call. There was still the wish Amaya needed to make. She could go home, but things wouldn't be the same would they? Not when she knew she had a power. Not when she knew she wasn't just a swimmer. But she wanted to forget it all. She wanted to be with Tama and get married to him. She wanted to see Mama smile and Rin carefree. She wanted home. She wanted the same life she'd been living before all this happened.

The energy was like a wall, slamming against her heart. She breathed out, the winter cold and her breath whispering into the air, bringing her back to reality. It brought her back to Lexa and two other jinn looking her way. Several feet away, the boys and the angel made their way back here too, all of them heading toward the girl who could control fire. They were gathered here.

She should give his hoshi no tama back. She needed to give the fox back his spirit. She had to.

She came to stand by Lexa. They'd called her a jinni. She remembered it now. Another being—not human, not animal, but freely able to take the shape of either.

"Hello, Amaya dear. Now, would you like to finally get your answers from the fox?"

Amaya inhaled. She nodded. It didn't feel right. Everything in her body screamed at her. The energy under her feet did the same. A terrible whine crept up her legs and through her chest.

"Amaya, no!" Nezha called out to her.

Those boys, the two angels and Nezha, they were standing together now. The angels were holding her close, the boy holding her gaze. Amaya felt like she knew them all. In a strange way, as if it was another lifetime ago. She didn't want to know them. And yet, a part of her yearned for it. A part of her wanted to be there with them, fighting on their side, smiling with them. She... wanted to help them?

***

Darkness engulfed her, but Nezha wasn't scared of them. She wasn't scared of the darkness. It was losing someone that scared her most. Her heart pounded, drumming in her ears—a beat, a song. She lifted her arms, fire pouring out, accompanied by the wind as Kayan slid to her side. He extended his arm, Ali's blade unraveling into the air. Electricity circled them as Thunderbolt placed a firm hand on her shoulder, just as Sapphire did. The angel's light streamed outward: a starburst, illuminating the sky as if it were dawn's glorious light. For moments that felt like hours to Nezha, she really felt like it would all be okay. They were here by her side. Even as the jinni Lexa's shadows snaked around them, waiting to wrap themselves around her. Even when Savan met her gaze, his burning with malice.

Asad's energy sang through the air, no jinn able to touch him as the blasts of positive hums popped into their shadows. The darkness gave way, falling into itself like a dark well, long dried from disuse.

Amaya was here, ice trailing behind her, her gaze wavering as she looked Nezha's way. She was here, so close yet Nezha couldn't do anything about it. The water jawhar had been in Lexa's company for far too long. But Nezha couldn't lose her focus. She couldn't allow any darkness to slip in and take them under its veil. The angels' had made that sure, as their electricity and light gathered around them, a gentle whine, the light spinning around them in thin strands like rings around a planet. As if they were the planets: the jawhars they were protecting.

"No one is gonna get t' you all," Thunderbolt vowed, his fists shaking.

"Yes. We will not be consumed." Sapphire's eyes held a sharpness Nezha had seen before when she had fought with her doppelganger. Her gaze was resolute.

"They ain't seen nothing yet," Dante said. He pressed his hands to the ground, causing sharp rocks to unearth under the jinn, whose bodies blurred and reappeared in various places.

The dog jinni Yusha sped past them all, but not without difficulty. Stab wounds and slashes marred his body. Blood pooled under him and in one blink, he was close to Nezha, his sharp nails glinting from the angel's revolving light. His fingers were dipping into it and he didn't pull away. Not even as it burned his hand.

"Jawhars, yield." His nails were soaked in his own blood.

"Down, boy." Nezha grinned and gestured to Dante.

Dante made a pushing motion with his hands, his feet stomping. The ground rumbled under Yusha and roots shot up, grabbing him and slamming his body to the ground.

As light, wind and shadows mingled, Nezha walked up to him.

Dante rose his arms, and the roots mixed with the thick rock and ice layering over it. Ony Yusha's face poked out of the mound. A small smile tugged his lips. "You cannot harm me."

Nezha lifted her hands, forming a fireball. She sent it hissing through the air to strike him. He didn't make a sound. Not a scream, not a gasp. She didn't see any fear in his eyes. Didn't it hurt at all?

"My fire is pure. I'm not the one who will punish you with it, though..."

Yusha didn't even seem like he was in pain. He simply twitched when the fireball struck his cheek. She reached out a hand to him and patted his head. "Soft like fur…"

"What..." Yusha gasped out.

"Dog ears... Whatever kind of jinni you are, stay here. Don't get in the way." Nezha turned her back to him. At least one of them was out of the way. For some reason, she felt him to be one of the most dangerous. Especially the way he looked at her. There was a strange warmth under his sharp gaze. Opposite to the angry energy around him. He'd walked into every obstacle they'd put out for him. He had no concern for his own safety. As if he'd throw his life away in a heartbeat.

"Aren't you going to finish me?" He kept his gaze steady on hers, as she turned her head to glance at him.

Nezha shook her head. He couldn't even move and her fire would keep his magic at bay. He was one of the only jinn she'd encountered who didn't plead for mercy. That made it even sadder to her. Didn't he have anything worth living for?

"I'm not here to needlessly kill. I'm here to defend." She turned away again. "But, if you decide to fight me, then I *won't* hesitate."

The magic in the air strengthened. The bittersweet saffron, a sudden note of jasmine perfuming the air... Nezha wrinkled her nose, and then, her body tensed, her heart pounding faster and faster. At one moment, it seemed like it was missing beats, panic setting into her chest. She panted. "What's happening?"

The jawhars were staring at Amaya, who was still standing by Lexa. And then, the water jawhar spoke.

"Papa..." Tears gathered in her eyes. She wiped her face and turned to the fox. She was holding his gaze as she put her fingers on the earring she wore. She unpinned it from her ear and held it in her open palm. "I'm ready to make my wish."

***

Amaya's hand stretched out, the earring sitting on her skin making her palm itch. For a split second, she wanted to snatch her hand back.

This world was too much of a change. Being thrown into a place where she felt like she was beginning to see another part of herself. She thought she knew who she was. She was supposed to be Amaya the swimmer, Amaya the older sister and eldest daughter, Amaya the hardworking student with two jobs, Amaya the girl who loved Tamaki and wanted to spend her life with him. Now, she wondered why she was Amaya the water jawhar, Amaya the angry lonely girl, Amaya the girl who found a connection with other people, but also wanted to go home.

The fox jinni picked up the earring and she watched, her heart fluttering in her chest. He crushed the gem in his teeth. She couldn't believe it. She had really returned his hoshi no tama to him. The crystal cracked, light rays bursting out. A bright light cascaded over her and soon, a glowing white ball hovered in the air. Two white tails unfurled out from behind him and one of them curled around the hoshi no tama and remained tucked into his fur.

He sighed in delight. "Ah, it feels so good!" He winked at her and bowed his head. "Thank you."

Chapter 47 Amaya's Wish and Nezha's Will

"My wish..." Amaya said, gulping. Her chest was tightening. She'd thought about what she'd say. Not only what she wanted, but what her papa would have told her to consider. Nothing good came out of a selfish want. That's what he'd told her. Even now, she wanted so badly to go home. But home… Home was where she felt safe, loved, filled with happiness and ease.

She glanced over at the jawhars, all staring at her. Then, her gaze remained on them. Something inside her chest tugged her. But the moment the fox's eyes glowed and he gestured to her to speak, she thought of how they must have been feeling. Who did they lose? Who did they have to leave behind? Did they ever feel alone? Tears sprang to her eyes. She would go home, but not alone.

"Fox...whcnever you meet any human, lost or not, you will help them instead of hurting them." Amaya tilted her head up. As soon as those words left her lips, he held his hands out. She dreaded what he'd say next to her.

He searched her eyes. "Amaya, you are a strange human. How selfless." His lips curled into an amused smile.

"Now, tell me the truth about my papa." Her breath caught in her throat.

"Of course, Usagi. You did return my hoshi no tama. I did not…kill your papa."

Amaya could only stare at him. He...he didn't kill her papa? "No... Don't lie to me!" Tears swam in her eyes. She gasped, and even though the jinn were fighting with the other jawhars behind her, all she could think about was that she'd been lied to. Her heart had been toyed with.

"I speak the truth. You returned my spirit. I'm bound by the oath."

"Then..." Amaya's hands shook.

"Your family did indeed take a part of my spirit and make it into your earring. That was long ago. Your ancestor was a shrine keeper, who perhaps mistook my spirit as a jewel. And so, I tracked you down. Until I saw you with it. And...after that, well, you know the rest."

"Papa died, though. How did he—"

The fox jabbed his chin in the air toward her dress.

"The shadow the jinni Lexa gave you is blocking your memories. You should get rid of it." He winked. "And now, the second part of your wish!" He slammed his hand to the ground and the snow shrunk away. Liquid pooled under his palms, growing into a small puddle. The surface shone like a mirror. "You can go back home through this. You don't have long, as it will slowly shrink. Farewell, Amaya, my little usagi."

He spun into a fiery ball of light and shot through the sky, hovering over the fire jawhar, Nezha.

He'd left Amaya dazed, her heart thudding in her ears. Thoughts spun in her mind. She needed to go home, but she needed to lose the darkness. She needed to remember what had really happened. Who had killed Papa? How did he even die?

***

As the bright fireball that had been the fox hovered above her, Nezha watched as the shadows that pooled around her and the others slipped backward. Savan and Lexa were holding their darkness around them. It stretched and spun around their bodies.

"Ah, fox." Lexa winked at him.

Nezha's head ached, a pulse beating at the back of her neck. What was he doing now? She lifted her hand, but then, a dull weight took over her chest. She couldn't move her body. Panic shot through her and the scent of magic coated the back of her throat. All she could see was the fox's bright glowing eyes and his fingers gliding over her heart. Then, her eyes lidded and all was darkness.

***

The fox jinni held her soul, as if its fingers scraped over her heart. "Give me the spirit." With a smooth, dangerous voice, it beckoned her.

But Nezha would not yield. She wasn't sure what she was seeing, or where she was. It looked like a dark room. Maybe this was a dream state. Was she seeing the struggle of her will?

She looked down and her fingers were glowing white as if she were moonlight poured into a vase. Her hands held onto two glowing balls of light. One was her own spirit, the other, the angel's soul. Both of them had their own feel inside her mind. Hers was familiar. The angel's soul was warm and peaceful. She couldn't let go of either... but if she let it have the angel's soul, it would bring calamity. Noorenia would die. She wouldn't have her place. No one would. What would happen to Earth? What would happen to the other jawhars? She'd never see Thunderbolt, Sapphire or Kayan, or have a chance to be with Kayan.

Nezha... The angel's voice came through. A gentle hand. *Do not despair.*

What could she do? *Oh Creator...* Her fingers trembled. The fox pulled, his fingers hot against the souls, and the pressure in her chest deepened, ached. She wanted to scream, but her voice was caught in her throat. Her fingers...her fingers were slipping from the balls of energy.

"I can't let it have you."

Do not despair... The angel's voice was more desperate this time.

Nezha felt her physical body's lips open. Words poured out from her. The angel's voice spoke. "*When your will and faith lay their hands upon your love, this power is the crowning essence of your heart. So, jawhars, do not despair.*"

Nezha knew what she had to do. She wasn't letting her fear stop her. She'd had a lot of weight on her shoulders: to do what she was told. To do everything for the sake of others. To risk her life to save all of Noorenia. But... She held the angel's soul in her hands. She didn't want to lose herself, either.

She gripped one of the souls more tightly. The other ball of light in her hand pulsed. It started slipping out of her palm. Then it slipped more, until the bright sphere caught on her fingertips. She had to. She had to let it go. Her heart thundered, the pain unbearable, aching in her chest as if the fox's fingers were digging into her bones.

The angel's voice sang into her ears, its effect a string of embrace and consoling keeping her together, but the pain was too much. The string was shredding.

She let one go.

***

He watched as Nezha's eyes glowed. A light beamed into the sky as the fox's hands hovered over her chest.

"Nezha!"

Kayan's arms arced through the air, Ali's blade spiraling through the shadows. They folded over him, but all he could do was keep his gaze on her. His whole body was trembling. His heart was about to leap from his chest.

"Nezha..."

Tears pooled in his eyes when he saw her fire light up around her head. It looked like a crown. All he could think about was if she was in pain. What was happening to her? He had to get to her.

The angels were struggling as much as he was as the shadows folded around them. Thunderbolt's electricity would only make pockets of cold air where the snow would sweep in. The wind would moan as soon as the shadows filled the gaps again.

"Noor's sake!" Thunderbolt faced Savan, nearly punching him in the face, but the jinni snickered at him. As they fought, angel and jinni moved at speeds he could hardly keep track of. Flashes of lightning, blooming darkness and sparks burst into the night. It was astounding.

The smell of the magic was too much. It punched him in the stomach and Kayan felt as if it squeezed his insides. The bitterness coated his mouth, the energy seeming to climb up his body as if a sharp knife was being dragged over his skin.

It didn't matter how hard it was. He'd get to her. He'd get to his Nayzak, his Nezha jan. He'd been through moments like this before, where he was surrounded by jinn. All he could do was think of being the storm his mother had taught him to be. To keep moving in the moment. He couldn't let his heart ache too long. He wanted Nezha to be okay, but if he let himself stray too long in the depths of pain, he knew he'd collapse. He just needed to get through this shadow and then he'd reach her.

"Asad, go to them!" Dante yelled across the distance.

Dante had been sticking close to Yusha, making sure he'd stay put. Kayan knew why he'd called Asad. The shadow didn't affect him as much because he was a soul jawhar.

Sapphire's light beams collided with the darkness, but again, they would get swallowed up. "Asad, you must lead us through."

Asad panted. "Uh, yeah, I can do that." He began toward Kayan, the energy around him humming again. But Rana had been on his heels. She licked her lips and stretched an arm out. White, swirling energy started dripping away from Asad's body.

Zul Sharr wasn't here anymore to shield them from Rana or Lexa. The prince was in the snow, and Kayan watched as Zul crawled, trying to reach his sword.

Looking at Zul on the ground like that actually hurt. A part of him wanted to help the prince, but if he got too close to Rana, she would absorb his energy. How could he help fight?

Comet meowed loudly. He looked down at her. Since she was still in a bubble, he kept her fastened to his side with his waist wrap. "Don't worry, Comet. I will protect our Nezha jan."

Then, he saw Amaya. Darkness shot out of Lexa's hands and snaked around Amaya's legs. The jawhar pulled at her legs and leaned forward, her arms reaching out to a pool in front of her. They were here for Amaya. They needed to save her too. Kayan gulped. He had to focus. They had to purify the darkness around Amaya and, for that, they needed to get closer.

Sapphire and Thunderbolt opened their hands to Rana, their light and electricity winding into a swirling mass and striking her, freeing Asad from the draw of her magic. Then, someone ran past them. Dante was by their side, the ice and stone lifting under Lexa and Savan and swallowing them in its shell.

Dante gasped, "Ya better have my back!"

Kayan nodded and glanced at Nezha. Her lips parted and a voice, a familiar melodic voice poured through. The Angel of Mercy, Mirkhas.

"...jawhars, do not despair."

The light from Nezha's eyes dulled and then it was gone.

Don't despair... Kayan looked around. The moment the angel spoke through Nezha, he felt it. A wave of energy so strong, it resonated with his soul. As if his soul had sung a melody into his heart. For a few moments, he couldn't feel the magic anymore. All he could feel was a resounding inclination to move and keep going.

Asad was advancing through the shadows, groaning with the effort despite the darkness hardly touching him. The angels kept close to him and Kayan, their hands filled with their forms of light, never dimming, never stopping. Yeah, they would get through it. They were strong. United.

Kayan squeezed his hands into fists. He'd hold onto that power. That reminder of hope. It still echoed inside him. And he knew, as the others were moving into action and the jinn were trapped, they had felt it too. They had to hurry.

"Nezha!" Sapphire and Thunderbolt spoke in unison. The angels' powers grew stronger. Electricity pricked and slammed against the ground. There was a charge in the air, the smell of rain and something that Kayan could only explain as a flower's scent. But this flower's scent awakened his heart and mind with a new verve.

The wind circled him, winding, winding faster until it screamed into the cold air, drowning out Comet's cries. It lifted the snow along with it like a storm, and the shadows parted into two walls, a clear path running between them. Asad led them through it, Kayan close behind with the angels on either side of him. Dante held his hands together, keeping the jinn inside the stone and ice. It cracked, but more snow, more ice would shift to close the gaps. Kayan held onto the feeling of hope. No matter if the magic cut around his head, pricking his skin.

"Hold on, jawhars!"

He was getting closer. He saw Nezha's body slump as the fox drew his hand back, and in it a light glowed brightly. A hum sang through the air and then sighed out as if it had been screaming.

"No!"

The harsh wind spun around Nezha, the moonlight dimming. What had they done to her?

They were nearly there. He'd get to her. It would be okay. Nezha fell to her knees, her head lowered, her hijab billowing in the wind, part of it covering her face. She'd be okay. She'd be—

As soon as Kayan ran through the darkness, it faded, the sky the only gloom. A piercing whine echoed into the night. The stone-and-ice shell Dante had made around the jinn shattered, and the pieces burst into the air, raining down on them. Kayan swallowed air and blew out, moving his arms as the wind held the pieces, obliterating them into a fine dust.

The fox seemed to fly as he appeared at Lexa's side. His vulpine smile returned and he handed the glowing sphere to the shadow jinni. "I couldn't get it all, but here is a spirit for you."

Lexa licked her lips. "This'll do." She tilted her head at it and smiled, then she laughed. "Oh, so the fire jawhar gave up her own spirit?" She laughed again— louder this time— and then regarded the angels and jawhars with interest. They weren't moving, so neither did Rana or Savan.

"I didn't expect to be holding a fraction of her spirit. I guess she's not as weak as I thought."

Kayan's eyes widened. Nezha had given up her own spirit? They'd taken a part of her? "Nezha!"

"Oh, wind jawhar, don't be sad." Lexa molded the sphere in her hands, and it split into two. "I didn't really care whose soul I got. Of course, I was wanting Nezha's. You haven't lost all of her." She shrugged. One small blue gem sat in one of her palms, and in the other was a white crystal in the shape of a raindrop.

The white crystal was hovering just above her skin. Strands of gold strung the small crystal into a matha pathi, dripping with round tiger's eye, diamond sunstone, chunky honey calcite and oval coquina jasper gemstones.

The headdress spun and flew through the air. To him. Kayan opened his palms and it fell into his waiting hands. Wasn't this a part of Nezha's spirit?

"Why?" he managed to choke out.

Sapphire and Thunderbolt had already stopped a few feet away from Amaya, but Savan stood by her.

"I don't want to clean up her mess. Do you?" Lexa bit her lip. She held the blue gem and waved a hand to Rana. "Go on, jaanaana."

Rana nodded. Two immense black wings sprouted from her back and she flapped her way into the darkness.

"Dante, follow her!" Sapphire cried.

He did as he was told, but then Asad spoke out. "He'll be alone!"

"We need you here." Thunderbolt placed a hand on Asad's shoulder.

"What...did you do to her?" The dull ache in Kayan's heart returned.

"Well, it's just a drop of her spirit. Good luck with putting it on her head."

Chapter 48 Our Hearts

Nezha's veins filled with burning fire. It didn't hurt, but the thrill and pounding energy scared her. She felt like she'd be torn apart and soar up into the sky all at once. The fire was alive and meant to follow her will, by the Most High's decree.

Right before a part of her spirit was pulled from her, she felt that moment of pure freedom. A freedom that blazed with a trail of its own. Destruction. The very fears she held inside. She did not want to lose herself, and now she would. Losing her own sense of self.

What would happen to the life she wanted to live? The family she found with the angels and the feelings borne of her entrance to this other world, with Kayan? This was it. The price for freedom became her own self. But it was worth it. She could protect the angel's soul. It was worth it, wasn't it?

She blinked. Her body was feeling light and, at times, her sight would blur, her head would swim with unease. Her breath was clear, though. Unlike how she used to be. She could breathe. Her lungs seemed to widen, the air, the breath a sweetness filling her body. Then, she heard his voice. Kayan was calling out to her and so were the angels. They were close by.

Her legs wobbled and she fell to her knees, the snow melting around her. Despite the grass poking through her fingers being dead and yellow, the crunch of the blades reminded her she was awake. And now, she was even closer to Noorenia's heartbeat. The panicking pulse and slow beats shot her with sadness.

She looked up to see Lexa and Savan, their magic, their shadows looming over her friends. Looming over the people she cared about. The flames crackled and hissed as they grew around her. Nezha watched as Sapphire's and Thunderbolt's faces appeared through the waves of shadow and heat. "Sapphire! Thunderbolt!" The angels. Then it was Kayan's face she saw in the distance. "Kayan!"

The flames burst into the air as Nezha strode forward, faced with Savan. She raised her arms and the fire roared into the sky. Clouds of darkness matched the shadows that wrapped around Savan and opened up in her face like a black flower. The petals twisted out into waves of darkness. Her chest tightened again. The magic bit into her skin, the saffron scent coating her throat. Then, she had no control over her body. She inhaled deeply. Her heart sped in her chest, energy bubbled up from her stomach and she moved to survive. She waved her arms and formed fists as she punched into the air, the hissing fire moving with her. The shadows would glide with her movements one moment, and another moment they would grab her limbs and chest like fingers. She met Savan's gaze. Their faces were so close, that she could see the anger in his eyes. The shadows extended over her, the fire dancing at their edges.

Savan released a low breathy kind of laugh. "You are a wonderfully terrible thing, jawhar. Magic poisoning your blood, an angel's soul inside you..."

She blinked heavily, parts of her consciousness rising, her sight clear for just a few moments. Nezha raised her arm and then blew on the feather. "I'm only human. And humans are both terrible and wonderful."

***

Asad had said Dante would be alone? *Alone*? That's how he'd felt when Momma had left them. There was a space. Emptiness was a strange thing. It was like it still held onto something. It wasn't just nothingness she'd left behind. She'd left the memories of her smile, her nagging him to do better, her smell of cocoa and marshmallows. Momma left him with so much to hold on to, the skin around his fists cracked whenever he'd thought of her.

Dante ran through the snow, huffing as his chest felt heavy. His heart was filling with memories, his lungs trying to keep the air in. *Hold on. Hold on, damn it!* His gaze followed Rana who swooped down to where Yusha was still held down by the jinni-sized mountain he'd encased around the silver-haired being.

Damn. He had to get there faster. He raised his hands and the snow crunched under him and swelled up, carrying him forward even quicker. He landed on his knees before Rana, just in time, as crows fluttered around Yusha and plucked at the earth.

He stomped his feet and the ice and rock shook around Rana, but she slid and fluttered her large wings and missed each hit. Too quick. If he got too close, she'd suck the energy out of him and he'd be useless. Nah, he couldn't...let her. His cheeks heated, and he felt his brows crease. His hands were shaking now as he was struck by another weight. There was no time for this. His own damn fear. If she didn't take him out, his fear would deal him a K.O. instead.

Dante sucked in air. A chunk of rock would crumble and he'd move to add more. Rana didn't hit him, but she was missing each fist of rock, each whip of roots that crashed into the ground and sunk into the soil underneath.

Noorenia's heartbeat called out to him, and he touched his palm to the ground to make it quake around Rana. He flinched. It was hurting.

He should call the animals. Not the wolves, since they obeyed Rana, but he could call owls or... But then, as soon as his lips parted, Rana's hands were out, her eyes glowing red. His legs wobbled. No! "Ah, sh—"

The snow, the ground was pulled from underneath him. He couldn't move it. He could only look on as Rana licked her lips and the crows continued to peck at the rock around Yusha. Dante's fingers curled. *Damn it. Damn it!*

His hesitation cost him. Those balls and specks of energy left his body, being sucked in by Rana. He really had become useless. He couldn't talk to Noorenia... He couldn't stop this crow jinni. He just wanted Momma back. He wanted Noorenia to bring him back home. If only he could talk to it. If only he could've saved it. It would save him.

He watched as Yusha widened his arms, and the rock that bound him fell around him, crumbling to pieces. A blast of energy swept over Dante as he struggled to get to his knees, but he fell onto his back. Snow pressed into his skin, the cold pricking him as he lay there and Yusha sped past him. That was it. He'd die. He'd die here, cold and alone.

Rana's legs came into view and then he felt his muscles, and his skin warm. His arm twitched. He could move. What the hell? He could move? He raised his head to her and saw his own energy leaching from her fingers and returning to him. He sat up, and couldn't believe it. She gave him the faintest glance and then turned her back to him, her large wings growing again.

"Hey...wait."

She took to the sky before he could say anything else.

He couldn't understand why she'd helped him. Just like people, maybe not all the jinn were bad. Was she only following some kind of orders? Whatever it was, at least he could move now. He stood and breathed deeply before heading back. Noorenia needed him. He'd almost given up and he damn well deserved this guilt building in his stomach for it, but he had to move.

***

The heat built in her stomach, and Nezha's chest tightened as the feather sang its call. She pulled the sword free from its golden sheath. Savan's shadows were squeezing her neck, pushing down on her chest, but she focused on the blade made of blue liquid fire. She gasped as she struggled to breathe. Her sight was blurring again, the world a dirty paintbrush bathed in a cup of water.

She'd lost herself.

For a few moments, the blurring cleared and she saw that dog jinni Yusha, his fingers bloody. Sapphire and Thunderbolt were battling him. Her gaze went back to the sword and then to Kayan who was ahead of them, his sword carving through the jinni's skin. He did not stop, even when Dante and Asad joined.

She'd lost...

In all this, she glimpsed Lexa watching, as if the jinni relished the chaos unfolding. The feather sword sighed in Nezha's grip, the blue flames spitting at the shadows.

She'd lost—

Wind brushed past her cheek and a piercing whine shot past her. A spear had flown by, nearly missing Lexa's head, striking the tree behind her. But who had thrown it? Strands of Lexa's hair danced into the air like drops of blood.

Savan's head tilted toward Lexa, his voice dripping in panic as he babbled words Nezha couldn't make out. The feather sword was hissing louder, the fire dancing across Nezha's face. Her heart was pounding, Savan was turning, and then...

She panted, her lips parting. This was the right moment. While he was distracted, she could use the feather sword. The shadows were tighter around her neck. She jabbed the sword forward. With a loud ring, and a hiss, the flaming sword stabbed Savan in the chest. She still couldn't breathe. Her eyesight was blurring again. She sucked in air and Savan fell back into Lexa's open arms, his body slipping away from the fire.

Chapter 49 Devour

Her tongue stuck to the roof of her mouth. Nezha could only struggle to get a glimpse of what was happening between her blurred sight and the undulating shadows, as her sight would clear and then become unfocused again. Savan was lying in Lexa's arms and the shadow jinni had tears in her eyes. Savan pressed his hand to her cheek.

"Jaanaana, wear your anger, I miss seeing it," Savan coughed, his blood trailing down his lips.

"Savan..." Lexa pressed her lips to his and held his hand against her face before pulling away.

"My queen... Kill them all. Free"— he choked, his teeth dark with blood—"our people."

Nezha could only hear Lexa's raw voice and Savan's weak response before the prickling dark energy engulfed her body. It was too much. What was she supposed to be doing? He'd killed countless people...and yet it still hurt seeing him lay in Lexa's arms like that. It still hurt her all over. Death, so much death was around her. Nezha couldn't lie to herself. For too long, she'd kept choking the pain down as much as her own tears. The way she used to hold her breath to keep her fire from burning everything around her. Now, the burn was registering.

Lexa screamed, and her voice was broken as she said the jinni's name again. He was gone. Nezha saw the way his eyes remained open. She closed her own and a sob escaped her.

Savan, the jinni responsible for Veer city's massacre, the jinni working for Lexa...the one who killed Lamis...was dead. Lamis had died months ago and now the pain of it shook her body all over again. Nezha wrapped her arms around herself. "Lamis..."

She was back in the hospital again. Lamis lying in bed, no longer moving. No longer laughing, no longer calling her Nuzha.

Then, it was Lexa's broken laugh piercing the night. For several moments, the fire spun around Nezha. Then when her eyesight cleared once more, she saw Lexa wrap Savan's body in shadows and then his body disappeared in a trail of smoke.

***

As he grew closer, Kayan saw a spear fly through the sky. He looked back to see where it had come from and saw her. "Divine's sake."

A woman appeared from behind a tree, wearing a knee-length fur coat, her long purple kameez peeking through. Was he really seeing Ishya, the world-renowned warrior of Ruhaan? It did look like her, her body like a tumbled and rounded azurite gemstone. Her embroidered blue dupatta was draped loosely around her head and fell over her shoulders.

"Yusha!" the woman called out.

Kayan had heard her voice before in the many interviews she'd done. It *was* Ishya.

Rana swooped down, taking Lexa's side. The crow jinni placed a hand on the shadow jinni's shoulder.

Kayan watched as Lexa stood, a pool of shadows extending over the snow, the energy of malice radiating off her. She spun her fingers, invoking the shadows as they spun out and wrapped around the feather sword that lay beside Nezha. When the shadows whisked away into the night sky, the silver feather cuff remained as it spun in place for several seconds before settling on the ground.

With Asad's voice loud and melodic, he formed a barrier of energy, keeping Yusha away from them.

The angels made their way to Nezha and stood beside her. Sapphire scooped up the feather sword and placed it around Nezha's wrist once more. The roof of Kayan's mouth pulsed as he quickened his pace to reach them. He caught Sapphire's drooping expression and Thunderbolt's narrowed eyes as they fell to their knees before Nezha and wrapped their arms around her.

***

The first time she'd killed one of the jinn who'd attacked them, Nezha could still remember the guilt digging into her heart. But they'd always turned to dust, and she wouldn't have to see their bodies for too long. It never made it easier, but, this time, she'd seen the way Savan bled, she'd seen someone mourn him. It was different. It was...painful. Her own sorrow sunk teeth into her open wounds. Again.

The corners of Nezha's vision darkened, and she felt herself falling backward. She felt her knees hit the ground, and then it was the loud hissing of the fire that engulfed her. It was warm arms that embraced her. It was the loud burning of pain and loss that sunk into her chest. Like tendrils of her own fire, the pain—all her feelings— flared in her mind.

***

Kayan was almost there. He was almost by Nezha's side when...something pulsed around her. "Nezha! What?" A wave of something both sharp and bitter ran over his tongue and crept over his skin.

Nezha's head lifted and when she opened her eyes, they were like pools of liquid fire. She didn't look like the Nezha he'd grown fond of. The way she smiled wasn't the one where she carried warmth, or one after a joke. It was sinister, a smile that could tear a heart apart. Both angels released her.

"Nezha, are—" Thunderbolt's voice drowned out when the fire hissed to life in Nezha's palms.

Sapphire shot to her feet, placing her arms around Nezha again, but Nezha pushed her hands downward, the fire shooting out and spitting. For several moments, both of the angels held her down. Pain jabbed at Kayan's heart, seeing the way they were desperately trying to console her... Trying to keep her down. But fire couldn't be put out so easily. The moment the fire flared, it grew. Their wings wrapped around her, their light escaping through their feathers and her arms. But the energy in the air was growing sharp against his skin. Comet yowled at him and then quieted as she met his gaze. Kayan still had Nezha's spirit as a headdress. He'd tucked it under his waist wrap. He needed to get it to her.

The angels went flying and hit the ground as Nezha propelled herself into the air, sparks popping, a shower of feathers and snow raining the ground in her wake.

Asad and Dante both stood by the angels and soon, Kayan reached them. "Thunderbolt..."

"Our duty..." Sapphire said, her gaze then shifting to Amaya who was a few feet away.

Thunderbolt exhaled loudly. "Seven hells!" His fist struck the ground. "Nezha needs us more than ever. Look at her! Look what that monster did t' her!"

Sapphire shook her head. "I know... Nezha has lost a part of her spirit. I can feel it."

The angels didn't seem to notice him. They continued staring at Nezha. Their eyes widened. It seemed they couldn't recognize Nezha, either.

"Asad...go to Amaya," Sapphire was holding her head high. Before all this, her face had seemed gaunter, her lips curved downwards as she'd kept her emotions at bay. But now that she was expressing her true feelings, they weren't building up inside her. She was allowing her tears to flow like a river passing over stones.

"Yeah..." Asad simply turned.

Kayan reached a hand out and pressed it to the soul jawhar's shoulder. "You're seeing into her soul, but don't let it hurt you."

"Well, duh. I'm good." Asad grinned, but Kayan could see the apprehension plastered across his smile.

"You got this, kid!" Thunderbolt called out as Asad made his way to Amaya.

***

The screams, the dark energy pricking Amaya's skin, her heart—all of it couldn't rival the cold sinking into her soul. She stretched her arms, so wide that she thought they would break her bones. She had to reach the pool. But it was growing smaller and smaller. Her door back home was closing. No. She had to see Mama again. She needed to get back home and be with Tama.

The shadows wrapped around her legs, squeezing her. A small pulse grew in her legs and the strange hum under her feet shot through her again. Maybe she would pass out. She couldn't stay here! She couldn't be here anymore, alone. Not like this...

She looked up for a moment and saw that boy again. The one who always emitted some sort of sound, as if he was singing. And for several moments, as he grew closer, a voice rang into her mind and it sounded like herself.

Remember.

Remember what? The mystery around her papa's death. It was the only thing she wanted to remember. What had happened? She couldn't remember anything. Amaya gritted her teeth and pulled the shadows around her legs. Tears pressed against her eyes.

Remember. Remember... Understand who you are, Amaya.

***

That brat had put a barrier up in front of him. Yusha tilted his head, his shalwar soaked in his own blood.

"Yusha!"

A woman called out to him. That energy... It was so bright, it made his lips want to turn in a sweet smile. A terrible energy. He'd rather get stabbed. He spun around and met her gaze. Ishya, the warrior, stood before him. She pointed a dagger at him, her eyes filled with that same look he'd seen only once before. A look of determination so strong, it nearly killed a jinni he'd known.

"Yusha…What have you become?" Ishya searched his eyes. Hers were the same brown as the moist soil after the rain. But now, they seemed much brighter, like wood caught by the sun's rays, soon to kindle.

"Aren't you far from home, little bird? Or do you want me to call you Ishya Warrior of Ruhaan? Ishya Beloved Healer of Noorenia?" The taste in his mouth was thick and rancid, as he thought of the way her love had touched all of Noorenia. During his travels, he'd heard all the names she'd been given. The poetess who was a warrior, fighting any mischievous jinn and healing hearts through her words.

"What of you, Yusha? Your energy is quite different." Ishya pointed her shamshir at him, its point catching the peeking moonlight.

Yusha lunged for her, but she dodged, the sword dancing at her fingertips with effortless precision. Her blade struck his arm twice, but the second time, he noticed the way she pulled her arm back. Blood poured down his arm, plopping down to coat the snow.

"Why don't you finish me off, little bird?"

Ishya's eyes filled with tears and her lips turned into a smile, one filled with pity from the way her eyes softened. He hated it. He hated it as much as he hated what he'd become. He cursed the magic flowing through his veins.

That memory of her smiling in her garden snuck in. Years ago, Ishya would sit with her uncle and they would recite together. Most days, the warmth on his skin, the birds singing— it all calmed him. Yusha would sit by their fence, listening without a sound. He'd been curious. She'd once asked him to join them, but he told her he would stay at a distance, being a jinni and all. Ishya had replied with a chuckle, "Good."

What Yusha had learned was mostly from them at the garden behind their masjid. Back then, she'd been a teacher. Now...she was a memory he wanted to ignore. She'd appeared like the deceased appearing in a dream.

"You know why I'm here!" Ishya swung the sword and it nearly cut his face.

"What?" he spat and jumped back.

"Return what you stole!" Ishya's lips parted and she recited something under her breath.

Yusha's ear flicked and he spun back. The energy around her hummed. It struck him and he nearly fell. He hadn't stolen anything. Rather, if he could be convicted of anything...it was this stolen life he was playing with. He knew she'd be disappointed to learn about the magic keeping him alive.

"What are you going on about?"

"Stop playing games with me! Please..." Ishya narrowed her eyes at him.

"I'm... I didn't do anything!"

He knew why he couldn't strike her. Not when her warm eyes were stung by tears. Not when the woman who he learned from taught him how to smile again.

Ishya didn't relent in her attack as her shamshir spun and jabbed the air. She'd been his teacher...a mentor he'd looked up to. Even with the magic squirming through his blood and keeping him alive... Even if he had meant to die long ago, he couldn't kill her. She had so much to live for, while he had no one. For a long time, he thought he'd been alone. She'd become his… friend. He had to let her through.

He fell to his knees and lowered his head.

Ishya's blade was at his chin, when she stood in place, her eyes wide as she met his gaze. "What..."

"Choti bulbul boldi," *Little bird speaks.* he whispered. He hoped she remembered the song they'd grown up on. The one every mother in Ruhaan sung to their children.

Ishya's hand was trembling, the blade shaking. "Bua kolgya." *The door's open.* She panted as she searched his eyes.

"Udja bulbul, udja." *Fly, little bird, fly.*

"Yusha…" She looked at him for several seconds, tears rolling down her cheeks. She lowered her arm and then ran past him through the snow. Her soft cries carried away by the wind.

***

Flames roared into the sky, dancing into plumes of smoke. Nezha landed before Lexa. Energy shot into the air as if a wind had picked up.

Nezha's hijab billowed, and the fire spun around her body. "Your turn to pay for your crimes!"

Nezha punched into the air, striking Lexa with blow after blow of the flames. Lexa's shadows wrapped around Nezha, but the flames cracked through, shafts of light and embers escaping and blasting into the sky.

The shadows and flames struck each other and intertwined. At one moment, Lexa's hair seemed to darken into a dusky copper, her eyes deepening until they were black. Cuts formed all over her body. The jinni grabbed Nezha's neck with the shadows. Kayan couldn't get close enough to Nezha. That powerful blast of energy was still surrounding her and as much as he tried pushing through, it shoved him away.

"Nezha..." Sapphire was behind Kayan, a gentle hand on his arm as Thunderbolt appeared behind her, pushing back harder against the blast. They had snapped out of their shock. He didn't care if it was reckless... He had to be by Nezha's side. He'd told her he would be there to support her. He wouldn't leave her. The angels were honoring the same.

Thunderbolt met his gaze and nodded. The energy pounded in Kayan's ears.

"Nezha...we're coming!" Kayan shouted. The blast softened, but the energy still whined around them, moving like a wind storm.

Cracks formed all over the dark, shadowy arms Lexa unleashed on Nezha. Splintering, they fell apart into countless shards.

"You can't tame fire!" Kayan spat at Lexa. "Nayzak, consume her!" Her burning gaze consumed everyone she laid eyes on. That he was certain of. The day he'd met her, she was a force that took his breath away. Her compassion, her fierce determination, her love for her friends and family had burned into his heart.

Swept into the flames, Lexa splayed her fingers and knives formed in between them. She flung the blades of hardened shadow which struck Nezha. For a moment, Nezha paused. Then she looked up, meeting Lexa's gaze with a piercing smile.

Kayan felt his arms and neck prickle with

goosebumps. It was terrifying.

"I'm not afraid of you! Fear won't stop me!" Her fingers curled, and the flames hissed and spat as she elbowed Lexa in the face, fire coating the jinni. Despite the severity of the burns and the amount of blood dripping from Lexa, she didn't stop.

All Kayan could do now was watch helplessly as he and the angels pushed through the energy to reach her.

***

Zul breathed out as his fingers sunk into the snow and he dragged himself forward. The sword had been protecting him... He had to get it back. It lay before him, just out of reach. He groaned. The jinni energy zipped through his veins.

Give up, prince. You're better off sleeping in the snow. The jinni aura laughed in his ears.

"Shut—" He had to get to the sword. He'd realized something. Whenever he held it, Rana and Lexa would keep their distance. Their powers hardly worked. It must have been the sword. It was pulling the magic out of the air. He'd felt the way the air softened, the hum gentle across his skin, and how it was easier to breathe. It had to be the reason why Lexa kept it from him. He reached his hand out, his fingers almost grazing the tip of the hilt. Just a little closer.

A storm of pain and thoughts spun in his mind, all thanks to that stupid jinni energy. Lexa had done this to him. He wasn't that surprised. She wanted to free her people and he knew she'd do anything for it. Betrayal was a blessing that burned. A flame come to remind him that *he* must be happy in his own skin. He gave so much of that love, that trust, that honesty to the wrong people. *He* deserved that care the most.

He still held onto his hope. He wouldn't let the magic stop him. He wouldn't let it break him.

Pathetic. You can't get rid of me! I'll eat you up alive!

He'd never give up. Sanari would be saved... His iron's curse would break one day. He would make sure of it. His fingers fell onto the hilt.

***

Kayan couldn't allow his own emotions to fall like a heavy hammer against his heart. He wouldn't break down. He wanted to unleash his wind, but a part of him was scared he'd hurt someone. He had to keep faith. God is love.

He felt his cheeks heating and he breathed in. By the Most Merciful, he'd be a storm. He raised his arms, sucked in air and blew hard, the wind whirling around him, murmuring its approval as if it were trying to assure him. The speed grew until it collided with the energy around Nezha. A loud boom echoed into the night. He raised his arms in front of him and created a barrier of wind, stopping the push of released power from harming him or the angels.

The wind tugged, caressed and brushed his body all at once. He felt the love, the warmth, the small peck of anger across his skin, lacing his heart. It wouldn't hurt Nezha. He knew, by The Most High, he knew she'd be okay. Their elements never hurt each other. So, he allowed the wind to be as free as it should, unbound to move as it pleased.

As the wind swept back, he saw Nezha standing still, the fire around her alive and dancing. She was okay.

Darkness stretched out, shooting him with a cold tingle at the back of his head. Before he could react, he was lifted and then thrown down to the ground, hard. The air was knocked out of his lungs. All he could feel was the stabbing pain in his back, the bitter scent of magic filling his chest. He lifted his head. Nezha was close now. Just a foot away from him. "Nezha..." he rasped.

He saw her on her knees, with Lexa's shadows holding her down, anchoring her to the ground. Nezha was supposed to be okay... She was supposed to be okay. Fire shot out from her lips, and she writhed in the grasp of the darkness.

Chapter 50 True Nature

A warm caress, a burning all at once, the wind passed through Nezha's sleeves, pulling and pushing her. For a moment, as her flames decorated the sides of her hijab and climbed up her head, that fragrance of water, of flowers snuck in.

Kayan... It was Kayan. She'd heard the name before. Did she know who he was? He sounded familiar. When she tried to think about his name or focus on who he was, fire flashed in her eyes. His name made her think of a sweet smile. It made her think of lemon candy. It made her think of a blushing face. It made her think of someone kind and caring. Someone who despite being hurt and broken, never dared to hurt anyone in return. *Kayan.* She looked back for just a second, seeing three seemingly-familiar bodies, and the boy collapse and darkness take over.

Kayan!

Devour everything. Devour the darkness. All she could do was feed the fire. Breathe and dance across the dark. Her knees pressed against snow, but it was a burning kiss as the wetness touched her skin. The hold of shadows encased her limbs and squeezed. They detached from the ground, allowing her to move.

How dare Lexa defy the will of fire! It yearned to grow, to swallow everything in its hot embrace. Nezha yelled, the fire escaping her lips. She watched as it rose and lit the night sky, the yellow light a flower against dark wet soil. She laughed, delighting in it blooming. She delighted in seeing the fire scatter its heat like falling petals.

***

Comet hadn't stopped yowling at him. Sympathy lanced at his heart and so, Kayan freed her from his sash.

Kayan forced himself to move. He panted and sat on his knees. He reached a hand to his sash, pulling out the headdress with a drop of Nezha's spirit set among the gemstones. He had to put it on her and soon.

Beside him, feathers brushed his legs. Sapphire and Thunderbolt were up too, pulling his arms.

"Get up!" Thunderbolt coaxed. Anger sharpened his expression as Kayan allowed the angels to pull him to his feet.

By Sapphire's feet, Comet shoved the ball she was in against the angel's legs. She took Comet into her arms and nodded at Kayan.

"Nezha!" Kayan strode toward her, the fire greeting him with tendrils slipping over his arms and past his face.

She stared back at him, her eyes searching his, as if she didn't know who he was. His heart was pricked with that look. Then, he saw her eyes widen, glowing a bright orange as if they were honied gems.

"Nezha..." His voice softened as he approached her, the angels beside him. He held the headpiece tightly in his fingers, the gem gleaming in the flames.

Thunderbolt's electricity shot out at Lexa, Sapphire's light refracting off the barrage of shadow knives Lexa unleashed upon them.

Fire leapt across his arms, and the heat pressed over his cheeks. It hurt. It wasn't supposed to. But, Divine, did it hurt. The flames were really burning him. He couldn't stop. Oh Divine, he couldn't back down. A small pocket of fear stabbed his heart, a small poke of doubt hit his chest, but he wouldn't turn his back on his Nezha jan. "Nezha..."

Her lips parted and fire roared around him, but Kayan didn't stop. Nezha stood. The orange glow bathed her face and it softened the strange sneer she had on her lips. "K... Kay...go." Her eyes softened for a blink.

"I won't abandon you! Before I met you, my wind had nothing to carry. It simply moved others. It was empty. *I* was empty." Sweat poured down his back. He would never turn his back on her. Never. "When I met you, I saw the way you urged others into action with a loving hand. Your light never dulled, despite you trying to smother your emotions. I saw your power, I felt your genuine self when you painted, or… or lit up the night with fire." Tears rolled down his cheeks as he pressed forward.

"Kay…an. I lost mysel—"

"For Divine's sake! You want to be more, right? Don't hold back anymore. Don't think of what's gone! Don't give up on yourself. Nayzak, let my wind ease your pain and carry your light."

He couldn't help himself now. Flames popped around his skin, the burning pressing into his bones. He pressed his hand to her back, the headpiece dangling in his other hand. The flames bit into his arms, as if to punish him for the physical transgression. But then, slowly, the nipping heat dissipated. "Our names are forever joined, Nezha jan." He raised the gem to Nezha's head. She shoved him and he fell back, the fire spewing out of her hands and spitting past him.

“Alif...” A woman’s voice started reciting. As her lilting voice reached his ears, he felt goosebumps pass over his spine, rippling up to the back of his head. His soul was resonating with the call.

“She’s reciting surah Al Baqarah.” It was well known for making jinn flee. It was Ishya who walked toward them, continuing to recite. Her dark brown hair bounced through her dupatta as she raised her palms up.

From the corner of his eye, Kayan saw someone rush toward them. It was Zul, brandishing his sword and holding it toward Nezha. Was he trying to attack them? Kayan stood and breathed in. He was going to draw his sword, but then his hands fell when Ishya approached them.

Lexa and Rana screamed. The two jinn fell to their knees, still screaming, until Ishya stopped reciting. As soon as she did, Lexa shot to her feet and brought a dagger to Ishya’s jaw. “Warrior Ishya, you’ve honored us with your presence.” She grinned at her, despite the blood dripping down her shoulder.

Sapphire and Thunderbolt both reached a hand out to Nezha, who swooned and collapsed into their awaiting arms.

“Divine’s sake...” Thunderbolt brushed a finger against Nezha’s forehead. “She’s not burning up anymore.”

“May the Creator have mercy... My poor girl.” Sapphire kissed the top of Nezha’s head. Both angels had tears in their eyes.

Zul Sharr stood beside Ishya, the energy around him much gentler, the sharp and bitter tang of magic fading.

“Zul...” Kayan tilted his head at him.

The prince sighed. “I’m not trying to hurt her. This sword can absorb magic... I only realized it once Lexa and Rana wouldn’t get close to me.”

Kayan wasn't sure if the prince was on their side or not, but Zul still had helped them. For that, at least tonight, he was an ally.

Dante came running up to them and blew out a breath. "Damn... Is she gonna be okay?"

"Where you been?" Thunderbolt asked him.

"Where?" Dante was incredulous. "Tryin' to not get killed in all that wind! That's where I've been!"

Comet meowed loudly and head-butted the ball she was in.

Thunderbolt stood, Sapphire staying put with Nezha in her arms. "Sorry, zaan. I almost forgot you were here." He rubbed the back of his neck.

Dante just rolled his eyes.

"She will be okay soon." Kayan lifted the headdress and fitted it onto Nezha's head. Sapphire pinned it between the layers of Nezha's hijab to make sure it would stay in place. The white gem gleamed for a moment.

Sapphire popped the bubble holding Comet and the cat jumped onto Nezha's stomach, meowing and pawing at her cheek. Comet licked Nezha's cheek and rubbed her head against Nezha's face, but she wasn't waking.

Ishya rolled her eyes. "Don't make me recite again, Lexa. I don't want to hurt you, but you'll be forcing me to."

Lexa's arm dropped and she licked her lips. "I won't waste my energy on you."

Maybe the recitation had worn her out, especially since her body was marred by cuts and burns and blood soaked her long shalwar kameez.

Kayan's heart pounded and he sniffed the air. A familiar scent of musk and flowers popped into the night. He turned, and saw a figure walking toward them from between two trees. A crown of light hair, a blushing face; it was Ansam.

Thunderbolt and Sapphire both looked up. Soon all eyes were on Ansam. The angel came to stand by Zul.

"As Salaamu alaykum. I just came from Veer City." Ansam's gaze passed over them all and then it stopped on Zul.

"Sire...we should go." Lexa held Rana's hand and raised a brow to the prince.

"I'm...going with Ansam." The prince gulped and Kayan saw the look passing between him and Lexa. Something on the skin of his face rippled. Then, bit by bit, the intricate black lines on one side of his face began blurring until they faded. It seemed he felt it. Zul pulled back his thobe's neckline, revealing his chest. The scorpion mark was fading too.

"His mark!" Thunderbolt gaped at the prince.

The black calligraphy that had curved into the word ghadab—a*nger*— in the shape of a scorpion, became adab—*morals*. Now, the lines appeared to form the profile view of a bird with its head lowered and one of its clawed talons out.

"A hawk," Kayan observed.

The prince touched his chest. He couldn't see the whole change, but he must have felt the mark fading. Kayan could only imagine how it must have felt: like a weight lifting. Perhaps even as light as a bird flying away.

Lexa's jaw clenched and she lifted her head higher, the shadows pooling around her. The scent of magic was still muffled by the sword the prince was holding tightly between his fingers.

The prince lowered his arm, the sword at his thigh. “I meant every word I told you that night. I *will* help bring justice to everyone.” He held Lexa’s gaze.

The softness in that look made Kayan want to smile. Such a warmth couldn’t belong to a cold-hearted person. There was something deeper in the prince’s heart that he didn’t show. Maybe anger truly had blinded Zul.

For several seconds, Lexa didn’t move. In a blur, Yusha appeared by her side. She raised her hand and opened it to reveal the part of Nezha’s spirit she took. The blue gem winked back at them. And before anyone could make a move, she held Yusha’s hand and pressed it into his palm. A curtain of shadows lifted around her and she laughed. That was the only sound that echoed into the night as the darkness fell and the three jinn vanished.

Thunderbolt panted, his anger boiling over as electricity forked the ground around him. “They escaped?” He raised his fist, striking the air toward the prince. “Zul...you have to pay—”

Ansam wrapped his hand around Thunderbolt’s closed fist. The electricity fizzled out.

“Huh? Ansam?”

The angel of hope shook his head and smiled at Thunderbolt. “Do not let your anger cloud your thoughts, my friend.”

“He’s right. We gotta help Amaya,” Dante said.

Kayan placed a hand on Thunderbolt’s shoulder. “You have to save your energy for what’s more important.”

Thunderbolt shut his eyes for several seconds and sighed.

Then, Ishya cleared her throat. "That gem Lexa took—is it the girl's?" Her eyes were soft as her gaze wandered toward Nezha.

Kayan nodded. "It's a part of her spirit."

Thunderbolt turned on his heel. "Sapph, you coming?"

His sister looked down at Nezha, and Comet who was now curled up beside her, asleep. "I'll stay here with her. I don't think we should move her."

"Yeah... I'm staying here too." Kayan gestured to Dante. "You two go and help Asad."

"What about you?" Thunderbolt had turned his attention on Ishya.

Sapphire nodded to the warrior poetess. "Ishya... I have read your work. Beautiful and heart-wrenching."

Ishya broke into a smile with teeth. One so bright, Kayan thought he saw a glow around her, lighting the darkness. "Aw, thank you. I will stay here too. I want to make sure you're all okay."

He could see how people adored her. So much genuine warmth and kindness exuded from her. He was a big fan of her poetry. But, this was the wrong time to even think about wanting to talk to her about her work. He was still curious as to why she was here. What had brought her from her land of heat into the snow?

Thunderbolt and Dante, followed by Ansam and Zul, nodded to the others, placing a hand to their hearts. They then began trudging through the snow, heading to Amaya who was still struggling in the distance.

***

It was closing. Amaya's eyes were blurring as her tears traveled down to her chin, turning into ice. She wriggled her legs and arms. Asad held his arms out, the hum a gentle tap over her skin, but even with his power, the shadows were tight against her body, wrapping over her torso. It was as if his attempt drove them mad.

She cried out and Asad recited, praying for her, as the hum increased. When he was finished, the sound of her heart pounded in her ears.

"Amaya...it's you."

"What?" She reached out again, trying to get her fingers closer to the pool, but it was shrinking faster before her eyes. More dead grass and soil came into view as the glistening opening withdrew.

"You have to get rid of that shadow!"

"I can—I can't! I just want to go home!"

He spoke in a gentler voice. "Look inside. All I can do is make your soul speak to you. But you have to want to listen!"

Amaya cried out again and shook her head. She choked out a sob.

"Sometimes, you have to do things yourself," Asad said.

Amaya took a breath in. Papa's death. She still needed to know what happened. She had to do this. If only he'd been here.

"Okay..."

"Focus." Asad's eyes were glowing. And when she looked past him into the distance, she glimpsed people walking toward her. There were two angels, a jawhar and Zul. She wasn't alone.

She was panting, but she closed her eyes. She needed to find it. She needed to find the answer. She focused on the hum, and a small voice spoke out to her.

Remember.

In the darkness, I speak to you.

In the light, you walk.

Under the stars, will you listen?

In the rivers, will you follow?

Amaya's lips trembled.

Asad's voice was muffled, but she caught one sentence: "Trust yourself for once!"

Amaya blinked and closed her eyes, allowing the hum to fill her mind. She listened.

Her water—that she'd made herself believe wasn't hers—flowed along her fingers and brushed through her hair. The hushing, the softness sunk her into a calm.

Amaya...

"Yes..."

Will you always do nothing, Amaya? You're a victim to your own comfort.

"Papa wouldn't be proud of me… He'd tell me I did—"

You did what? You know what it is.

"No... Don't say it."

You did nothing.

She... Her soul...*it* was right.

Always thinking of the past. Mourning it. And always wondering about the future. Fearing it. Pull yourself out of that sinkhole. You are at a standstill, rotting your true self. You are the current. Make your path!

Amaya opened her eyes. "I've always been so afraid of doing something. I was scared of getting hurt. I worked hard to help Mama and Rin…" She pressed her hands to her face. "I worked hard to be a swimmer. But I didn't want to repeat the past. I wanted my future to be bright… But I only made my present full of…

Say it!

"Guilt. Guilt! I don't want guilt anymore! I am a water elemental and I will live for today and tomorrow!"

The water sped around her body and then, slowed, blobs lulling back and forth in her hands. She passed them through one hand to the other. It felt smooth to her touch, so calm, connected...almost warm. The pressure lifted from her chest and then peeled away from her, the darkness lifting, unwrapping from her body. She passed the water over her skin, the shadows disappearing. She looked up, seeing the angels and Zul standing by her, their mouths agape. Her lips curled into a small smile. Even as the small gap on the ground filled in with snow, her arms wrapped around herself, the water washing the darkness, the guilt, the pain away. Even if it wasn't all of her pain, she still felt this small warmth in her heart.

The cold was gone. The icy maw of the darkness Lexa had unleashed on her body was gone.

Her mind opened and the thought, the memory about her father was released, like water falling into an empty basin and filling it.

"Salaam…" Amaya met their eyes. "I was pulled in through the lake. The fox had attacked me, but Lexa found me and took me in..." She relayed everything to them.

"My papa died a long time ago..." She breathed in and met Zul's gaze, the memory spilling into her heart. He nodded at her, his lower lip trembling.

"I had a swimming competition, but during it, I got the news of Papa being in an accident..." Tears welled in her eyes, but she whisked them away with a finger and formed a small butterfly. "I remember doing the butterfly technique and nearly drowning with the shock. I ran out of there. He was on a stretcher, just outside, and when I went over to him, I saw he kept the small fox pin I had given him... He died from a heart attack. And I"—tears rolled over her cheeks, her voice cracking— "I blamed myself! I had told myself it was because of all the stress that I caused him. My tuition...all the work he did for us, and he not once ever complained." Amaya fell to her knees.

Finally, the truth.

Zul came to her side, and then the angels and Dante. The angels each placed a hand on her shoulder.

"Wa alaykum as salaam. Welcome, Amaya," Ansam greeted as both angels introduced themselves to her.

"Nice t' meet ya, kid." Thunderbolt smiled at her.

"Amaya..." Zul smiled at her too.

Dante nodded up at her with a polite smile.

Amaya wiped her face and got to her feet. Maybe, even though she couldn't find the words, she belonged here right now. For once, she wasn't thinking about the past. She'd find her way home again one day. For now, she'd be here. A place she'd been drawn to.

"Amaya, would it be okay if you did one thing for me?" Zul knelt before her and held the sword out.

Amaya searched his eyes. "Of course." She would always help him. He'd been kind to her since they'd met. Zul was forever a friend in her eyes.

"Please, cleanse it."

"Cleanse?"

Zul Sharr gulped. "This kilij sword was made when the jinni aura inside me was at its strongest, and the blood of the fallen innocents in Veer melded with my iron to create it. If you can wash away their blood, they can rest in peace. This sword absorbed magic and I don't want anything to do with magic again."

Amaya looked down at it and sighed. "Mm." She nodded and took the blade into her hands.

Cleansing it... Would it really be easy for her to do it? It might not be, but the angels and those jawhars reminded her of faith. She'd been missing it. The Divine was watching her and he'd been trying to protect her. When she was here, Zul was gentle with her. Even in battle, the wind jawhar made her realize what freedom could be. Asad helped her to listen to her own spirit. Whenever she stood on the ground, Noorenia's heartbeat pulsed under her. She had to bring a little more faith. She had to have some faith in herself, too.

She closed her eyes and invoked her water. Her fingers slipped across the cold blade, the water coating it. "Bismillah. Cleanse it..." she whispered, keeping all her intention on removing the blood. She wrapped her fingers around the hilt, the water spinning around the blade. Then, when she whisked her fingers away, what was revealed was a metal blade. The copper tinge was gone. She handed it over to Zul, whose eyes widened.

"Is it purified?" Zul turned to the angels.

Ansam touched his fingers to it. "Remarkable. There is not one atom's worth of magic on it."

Zul smiled in relief. "May the souls rest in peace."

"Ameen," Amaya and the others said in unison.

"Thank you." Zul stood and regarded Ansam. When he shifted his gaze back to her again, Amaya's brow crinkled. Why was he looking at her as if this was the last time?

"Zul?"

"I'm...going with Ansam. But hey, this isn't goodbye, okay?"

Amaya smiled. "So, I'll see you later."

Zul smiled back wider at her. "Yeah. We'll have to go out to eat ice cream, okay?"

Amaya nodded. "I'll pick mango this time."

Zul laughed.

She saw the way Thunderbolt looked at him, how he met the prince's gaze. His lips parted.

"May the Divine smile upon you." Zul gave a small wave to Amaya before turning to leave with Ansam.

"Come on, kid. Let's head back." Thunderbolt turned and Amaya followed him and Dante. Amaya the wayfarer, who chose to make her own path.

***

Something tickled her cheek and it was wet. Nezha opened her eyes and saw Comet's cute nose. Sapphire was holding her. The cold of winter, their voices—she could hardly register it all. Kayan's smile lit up at her waking. Thunderbolt was grinning at her. Asad and Dante bumped shoulders, with Asad purposely waving in the wrong direction with a wink. Amaya, the water jawhar, was smiling back at her too, with a small nod. Beside Sapphire, an unfamiliar woman stood. She smiled brightly at Nezha, and despite not knowing who she was, Nezha felt a warmth blossom in her heart. Her eyes closed again.

After a few moments, she opened them and wished she could express how she really felt, even if it felt like a wall was standing in her way. She'd find a way. Even if she'd been hurt before, she'd find a way, Creator willing. Thinking of Lamis caused her heart to ache and tears drip down her face. She'd faked her strength, but there were still so many things she wanted to show and share. At least her feelings went to Lamis and Kayan through her supplications. Even if a part of her was missing, she had her will to be with the ones she loved.

Noorenian Alphabet

A =
B =
C =
D =
E =
F =
G =
H =
I =
J =
K =
L =
M =
N =
O =
P =
Q =
R =
S =
T =
U =
V =
W =
X =
Y =
Z =

Green Hope:
Selfless,
Gentle,
Joyful,
Uplifting,
Honest,
True

Acknowledgements

Bismillah. Thank you to Allah SWT for everything you've done for me. For all the hope and strength.

It's been a long journey to write the second. I opened my heart to lay bear for this book. When I first began it, I was excited to continue Nezha's story and wanted to include other jawhars. People that would bring out more types of strengths and perspectives. As it went on, I truly fell in love with all the characters. The antagonists were not deprived of emotion either. I couldn't dare to ignore their wants, desires and tender moments, especially Zul! Many of the characters experience the deep pain of loss and facing their inner demons. In a way, they helped me face mine. They became a warm embrace.

Without all these people, Crowning Essence would not be what it is.

To my editors Rachel Wollaston and Kristen Wilson. You believed in me and gave me that needed resolve to find strength in myself and my story. Thank you, Kristen, for being there each step. You are an amazing friend!

To my beta readers: Eshana Ranasinghe. Thank you for always being there and continuing to love and shower me with your support. Thank you for caring about the Villain Squad. I appreciate and adore you so much! To Naley Gonzalez for believing so fiercely in me and my story!